Barbara

Enjoy!

With Best Wishes

Geo[illegible]

D1714686

THE TRIESTE INTRIGUE

A Novel

George McNulty

© 2013 George McNulty
All Rights Reserved.

No part of this publication may be reproduced, stored in a retrieval system, or transmitted, in any form or by any means, electronic, mechanical, photocopying, recording, or otherwise, without the written permission of the author.

First published by Dog Ear Publishing
4010 W. 86th Street, Ste H
Indianapolis, IN 46268
www.dogearpublishing.net

ISBN: 978-1-4575-2418-9

This book is printed on acid-free paper.

This is a work of fiction. References to real people, events, establishments, organizations, or locales are used fictitiously. All other characters, and all incidents and dialogue are drawn from the author's imagination and are not to be construed as real.

Printed in the United States of America

For Peggy and Devin

...Always by my side

THE TRIESTE INTRIGUE

Wednesday, May 6. 1981
Piazza San Pietro, Vatican City

1

It was only ten o'clock in the morning, and the sun was already blazing down on Piazza San Pietro, Vatican City's welcoming Saint Peter's Square. The hundred and forty stone saints' statues crowning the two colonnades that edged the magnificent square stood bleached by the piercing sun. The ancient square overflowed with tourists from all corners of the world; most mingling in its center. Others, alone or in large groups, trailing flag carrying guides, mounted the steps into or descended out of Saint Peter's Basilica.

Andrei Petcov, a short, thin, balding man in a dark suit stood near the Maderno Fountain on the north side of the square surveying the crowd. The only enjoyment of his vigil was the opportunity to observe the young girls. Most walked past awestruck at the grandeur of St. Peter's Basilica and its imposing colonnades. Only one or two even glanced in his direction. Finally, he took off his coat and eased through the milling crowd to a position near the row of cement bollards strategically spaced along the square's entrance to prevent vehicles from entering.

Shortly after eleven o'clock three taxis pulled up to the line of bollards and a group of men in dress shirts and women in smart dresses emerged. From their attire Petcov concluded they were European and not American. Eyeing the swaying hips of a young blond in tight shorts, he almost missed his mark stepping out of another arriving taxi.

It was him. Petcov was sure of it. He was tall, athletic with shoulder length curly brown hair, tweed coat, white dress shirt, conservative tie, khaki trousers and brown loafers; very American, very academic.

The American paid his fare, turned and walked into the ancient square.

Petcov watched his target merge into the crowd and then approached the taxi. "Where did you pick up the American?" he asked in Italian, handing a roll of lira to the driver.

After placing the money under his seat the driver answered, "The Airport Marriott Hotel at Fiumicino."

Petcov started to follow the American, then quickly turned back, "Was he staying at the hotel?"

The driver, a middle aged man with a pencil mustache, looked straight ahead and put the taxi in gear.

Petcov shoved another roll of bills through the window.

"He got out of an Alfa Romeo Alfetta parked in the hotel parking lot and walked to my taxi when I pulled up."

"What color?" Petcov asked, gripping the door.

"Green," the driver yelled and pulled away.

Colin McHugh, a forty five year old American international business manager and seasoned world traveler did not arrive at the square as a tourist, or even on business. Standing near the Egyptian Obelisk in the center of the square, he was dressed in the tweed coat, shirt and tie he had selected the week before for the role he was about to play. Even though sweat drenched his shirt, and he cursed his decision to wear the heavy coat, he decided to stay the course and not remove it.

At six feet four inches, he could easily see over those around him. And although the heat was uncomfortable and he was apprehensive of this first-time role, those weren't the reasons the thumb on his left hand began to twitch. He had the feeling he was being watched.

Slipping on his sunglasses, he decided to study the crowd. Initially he focused on those gathered along the Piazza's south colonnade. They all appeared to be tourists; summer shirts, blouses, shorts and sandals for the most part. Just as he was about to turn in another direction a thickset man of about forty, wearing a rust colored long sleeve shirt and sagging dark jeans, stepped away from the gathering and stared at him.

Who are you? McHugh wondered, - *Your waistline and clothes certainly don't mark you as a professional.*

As if answering the question, the man broke eye contact and turned toward a throng of newcomers surging into the piazza.

Determined to see if he was really being shadowed, McHugh moved a few feet to the left to see if the thickset observer would turn again and confirm his interest.

Mindful that he couldn't do anything if the guy was a shadow, McHugh readied the German Leica camera he had been given during his preparations for the assignment. *At least I'll have a record of what this character looks like.* To his chagrin, the man waved both hands above his head and moved toward the crowd entering the square. A smiling woman holding the hand of a young girl returned the waves and walked toward him.

God, I feel paranoid? McHugh muttered. However, still edgy, he held the camera down along his side while continuing to survey the crowd; no one seemed to be aware he even existed.

He recalled President Reagan's note, given to him by Admiral Dan Stringer, Deputy Director of the president's national security staff:

I remember my first role. It was a walk-on like yours. Break a leg, RR.

It helped McHugh focus on the reason he was here.

The night before, McHugh had flown into Rome from Toronto on Alitalia Airlines to play the part of a nonexistent professor on a mission from the president. He wasn't trained in role playing or intrigue, precisely the two reasons Stringer, McHugh's Naval Academy classmate, had explained why he was selected. "You're a *civilian*, and not on anyone's watch list; our spooks don't even know you exist."

For a few more moments McHugh inhaled the mixture of the languages swirling around him and observed the people pouring in and out of Saint Peter's Basilica. Then he checked his watch: eleven-thirty. Without hesitating longer, he removed his sunglasses, took out his invitation to the Swiss Guard Initiation Ceremony and casually followed an elderly couple at the end of the queue moving toward the Bronze Doors.

After stepping away from the taxi, Andrei Petcov, the slim senior Bulgarian State Security agent followed the American into the square. In his official role as an Assistant Press Secretary at the Bulgarian Embassy, Petcov had received a courtesy invitation to the initiation ceremony weeks earlier. He initially intended to discard it, but let it sit on the corner of his desk and forgot about it. It turned out to be a decision he now regretted.

A week before, Nicolai Zhelov, a senior member of the Bulgarian State Security's dreaded 7th Department had arrived in Rome from a secret meeting in Trieste, the northern Italian seaport city tucked inside the gulf of Venice bordering Yugoslavia.

As in numerous multi- tiered organizations within communist East Bloc countries, the 7th Department of the Committee for Bulgaria Sate Security was sequestered as the last department within the Political Police Directorate. And although its innocuous operating dictum was *information analysis*, its real mandate was to destroy *enemy émigrés*, (political defectors) and carry out *wet jobs* (assassinations).

Petcov and the other agents were informed that Zhelov's assignment superceded all others. They were also directed to immediately carry out all orders he gave to them. Zhelov had taken the invitation from Petcov's desk, declaring, "I need this," and walked out.

Like all the other embassy officials, Petcov was acutely aware that Zhelov's rise into the Sofia hierarchy coincided with the assassination of Georgi Markov, the dissident Bulgarian writer who had immigrated to London.

Markov, the winner of the 1962 annual award of the Bulgarian Writers' Society, initiated a series of radio programs on Radio Free Europe openly critical of then Bulgarian Communist Party Leader Zhikov and was immediately tagged for elimination by Bulgarian State Security. Markov died in London four days after someone fired a poison-containing pellet into his leg from an umbrella while he waited at a bus stop.

Two stories flourished throughout the Bulgarian security agency regarding the incident. One asserted that Zhelov was the assassin, whereas the other claimed that he had only planned the assassination with the *Stazi*, - East German State Security. However, the overwhelming consensus was that Zhelov was a man not to be crossed.

Yesterday the invitation had been returned to Petcov with a note from Zhelov ordering him to be at the entrance to St. Peter's Square by ten o'clock that morning.

Petcov had never been an actual field agent, having served his entire agency career in administrative positions.

A cold chill passed through the Bulgarian administrator as he recalled the follow-up phone conversation. "It's Zhelov. Be in the Vatican Piazza tomorrow morning by ten. Find that American impostor and follow him. Call me as soon as you pick the bastard out of the crowd. If you don't find him or if you lose him, your time here is finished."

After a brief moment Petcov had replied, "I've a meeting at the Italian press office at noon."

"Cancel it! Don't cancel it! I don't give a shit. Now to be sure, I want you in that Piazza by nine, so you do not have any chance of missing that fuckin' impostor."

Then after a momentary pause, Zhelov had continued on in a more conciliatory tone. "At least you know the difference between a damn college professor dressed for a formal ceremony and an American tourist walking through Rome. Most of the shit agents here can't tell the difference between ravioli and cannoli. Be there, and be on time. Call me as soon as you pick out the bastard."

Petcov watched McHugh join the queue in front of the Bronze Doors and reached for his radio. When Zhelov answered, he described the American and explained about the pick-up in the hotel parking lot and the green Alfetta.

"Professor shit; he's CIA. Follow bastard and don't lose him." Agin the threatening tone.

While visualizing Zhelov poisoning an old man and relishing it, Petcov slipped on his suit coat and joined those in front of the Bronze Doors.

A member of Vatican security, dressed in a blue suit, white shirt and blue tie, stood in the center of the open Bronze Doors. When the guard acknowledged McHugh; he stepped forward and presented his invitation and passport.

The guard examined the passport, scrutinized McHugh, and then just glanced at the white cotton invitation embossed with the colorful flags of the Vatican and the Swiss Guard Regiment.

Colonel Frantz Pfyffer,
Commandant, Vatican Swiss Guard Regiment
Cordially invites
Professor John Michael Allen,
Associate Professor of Military History
To attend
The four hundred seventy-fifth anniversary ceremony,
Initiation of Swiss Guard Candidates,
San Damaso Courtyard, Vatican City
12:00 pm, 6 May, 1981

The guard looked up. "Welcome, Professor Allen. Colonel Pfyffer extends his best wishes. He asked that I advise you that he will be able to meet with you for a few moments at the conclusion of the ceremony."

Relieved to have passed this first obstacle, McHugh looked confidently into the man's eyes as his passport was returned.

"Thank you." He turned toward the entryway.

The guard put one hand on McHugh's arm and extended the other. "May I ask what you are carrying?"

McHugh stopped short, startled at first, then recovered and handed the plastic encased book to the man.

"It's a gift for Commandant Pfyffer from the Corps of Cadets at the United States Military Academy where I teach."

The guard turned the book, sealed in clear plastic, over in his hand a couple of times, and read the title, The Long Gray Line. He returned the book to McHugh and handed his invitation to a young usher standing behind him.

"Please escort Professor Allen to his assigned seat in the courtyard.

For the past two years, in addition to traversing the world on behalf of the Williston Pump Company, an Ohio manufacturer of industrial and agricultural water pumps, McHugh had occasionally carried out courier assignments for Admiral Stringer. When needed, he would extend his business trip by a day or two and place a letter in a designated hotel room or letter box. The need for water pumps worldwide allowed McHugh the convenience of arranging his travel schedule to include an assignment when Stringer asked. He never knew the contents of the letters or met the recipients. His only contact with the president's security staff was Admiral Stringer.

Today was different. This assignment was directly approved by President Reagan and McHugh had been thoroughly briefed on the reason for the meeting and the contents of the intelligence information in the package. The information was so vital Stringer had convinced his Naval Academy classmate that his professor role and brief face-to-face meeting with the Swiss Guard commandant would be as easy as his previous courier assignments.

Confident he could fulfill the mission, McHugh was nonetheless apprehensive about assuming the persona of a non-existent professor.

San Damaso Courtyard, Vatican City

2

McHugh followed the usher into San Damaso Courtyard. The cobblestone yard about the size of two side-by-side basketball courts was enclosed by high sandstone buildings with rows of upper-level windows. A portico stood in the center of each. The guard led McHugh to his seat in the third row of the section reserved for special guests. Guards' families, friends and other invitees were seated or stood behind roped off areas around the edge of the courtyard.

From his briefing, McHugh believed he was seated directly opposite the portal below the Apostolic Palace. Curtains in two of the upper windows were drawn. A shadow passing behind the curtained window on the left caught his eye and he wondered if it might have been the Holy Father.

Although it had been a number of years since McHugh considered himself a practicing Roman Catholic, he had enormous respect for this new captivating Polish Pope.

McHugh also knew that a number of senior Washington insiders considered Pope John Paul II to be a figurehead with only nominal authority within the Vatican administration. They believed that his election two years before, following the suspicious death of Pope John Paul I after only thirty three days in office, allowed control of the Vatican to remain in the hands of the very cardinals that the deceased pope had decided to dismiss for being members of a Masonic group, or involved in irregularities in the Vatican bank. The Washington insiders had inferred that the extensive international travel scheduled by the new Polish pope gave credence to their position.

McHugh preferred President Reagan's analysis: *John Paul II is a good man and the world needs him now.*

A single file of Cardinals in black cassocks, scarlet sashes and scarlet scull caps, entering into the piazza from the portal to his left, captured McHugh's attention. A few of the cardinals smiled and waved gingerly to guests they recognized, while the others focused on their seats as they filed into the two rows in front of McHugh.

On an unannounced signal, six Swiss Guard drummers beating a slow cadence marched through the portico that faced McHugh. A lieutenant colonel followed, leading the long column of guardsmen two abreast, marching with measured step to the slow cadence. With a long saber at his side, Commandant Pfyffer wearing a dark red uniform and a conquistador style steel helmet topped with a white ostrich plume stood next to the guard chaplain observing the entry parade.

The guardsmen wore breastplates over Medici style, tri-color red, blue, and yellow striped uniforms with starched white honeycomb collars and similarly colored shoe covers. On their heads they also wore conquistador style steel helmets, topped with red plumes. With the exception of the drummers and musicians, the other guardsmen carried raised ceremonial halberds: axe blades mounted on seven foot wooden shafts. All the guardsmen wore white gloves.

Again, McHugh's finger began to twitch. Knowing the ceremony sequence from the videotapes he had studied during his preparations, he decided to people-watch and slipped on his sunglasses. Everyone appeared to be concentrating on the ceremony. The families of the young recruits were easily recognizable by their proud faces. A few of the clergy seemed bored.

The flag bearer hoisted the Swiss Guard Banner with its white cross and colorful four quadrants and marched to the front of the formation escorted by two guardsmen carrying long battle swords.

Slipping out of his seat, McHugh eased his way behind the standing crowd to a position near the guards' entry portico. As he watched Pfyffer take the salute from the regimental adjutant, McHugh was reminded that the Guard Regiment wasn't just all show and ceremony. It had an arsenal of modern weapons and combat equipment, and had received extensive weapons training and defensive bodyguard tactics to insure the safety of the Pontiff.

McHugh glanced toward his empty seat behind the cardinals and noticed a slim, balding man with a dark mustache wearing a black suit, staring directly at him. The observer was seated two rows directly behind McHugh's empty seat. When McHugh focused on the observer, the man immediately turned away. He wondered if the guy was a follower or just curious because he had left his seat to stand against the wall.

With his left hand, the last guard recruit grasped the center of the Swiss Guard Banner, lowered to the horizontal position by the flag bearer. And as a symbol of the Holy Trinity, the young recruit raised his gloved right hand, with thumb, index finger and middle finger pointed skyward, and remained poised in position.

At the beginning of the ceremony, the Regimental Chaplain had read the Guardsman's Oath in Italian, French and German, the native languages of the recruits.

Now the new guardsman shouted proudly in German that he would abide by his pledge to faithfully, loyally and honorably serve Pope John Paul II. He then did an about-face and marched smartly back to his position in the guard formation.

The ceremony ended and Colonel Pfyffer led the parading guard regiment past McHugh through the portico. The retaining ropes were dropped and guests mingled together. A few of the cardinals remained and joined the milling guests.

McHugh approached Colonel Pfyffer when he returned to the courtyard.

"Colonel, John Allen. Congratulations. It was an impressive ceremony."

"Professor Allen, thank you. I'm glad you're here."

"Colonel, would you have a moment? I have a gift for the guard regiment from the West Point Corps of Cadets."

"Only for a few minutes; I must greet the families and guests of our recruits." The colonel took McHugh by the elbow and led him through the portico to his office adjacent to the guard officer's barracks.

Colonel Franz Pfyffer von Altishofen, shorter than McHugh, seemed in athletic trim for his sixty- three years. He had a square face, wide nose and a welcoming smile. His hair was gray and thinning. Behind round silver framed glasses were clear intense eyes that gave McHugh the impression of a straight forward, determined man. Previously a successful lawyer in Lucerne, the Commandant was the eleventh member of his family to command the guard.

"Join me in a glass of wine," the Colonel said, lifting a crystal decanter of red wine from the credenza behind his large polished oak desk.

McHugh surveyed the small unpretentious room. The desk, credenza and two wooden chairs were the only furniture. The floor was stone and the walls were beige stucco. A framed proclamation from Pope John Paul II commending the colonel for his years of service, and a group picture of the guard regiment along with framed portraits of previous commandants were the only wall decorations. A gold framed photograph of Pfyffer in casual clothes standing on the shore of a lake with his arm around a pleasant smiling woman stood beneath a tall ceramic lamp on the credenza. McHugh assumed the woman to be the commandant's wife.

"Sir, it's an honor to meet you," McHugh said, taking the offered glass. "I know your time is short, so with your permission, I'll get right to the point."

By the look of surprise on the colonel's face McHugh knew his formal tone now held Pfyffer's full attention. "I have been instructed by President Reagan to inform you that it is the belief of our government that there may be an assassination attempt on Pope John Paul's life. We do not know when it will happen. However, recent increases in the communications that we have been monitoring lead us to believe the attempt will be in the near future."

Shocked, Pfyffer stumbled against his desk, spilling some of his wine. Then recovering a measure of composure, he gently placed the glass on the desk.

"How do you know this?" The colonel questioned, and then sat down at the desk waiting for McHugh to respond.

Knowing it wasn't his place to explain how US security services had obtained the information, McHugh ignored the question. "As you are aware, less than a month ago, President Reagan returned to the White House after an assassination attempt by a single crazed individual who had been able to penetrate the president's ring of security. The president is seriously concerned for the safety of the Holy Father. The information we have indicates the attempt appears to have the substantial backing of Eastern Bloc governments." He pulled a chair up to the front of the desk and faced the commandant.

Pfyffer dropped his head into his hands and said quietly, "Why would anyone want to do this?"

Although McHugh's sympathies were with Pfyffer, he also knew it wasn't his place to further complicate matters by adding that the intelligence concluded that Soviet Prime Minister Brezhnev had personally ordered the Pope's elimination. Even though Brezhnev was aware of the new Pope's contribution of millions in financial support to the Polish Solidarity Movement, he was more fearful that Pope's speeches rallying the Polish people to return to their faith and reject Marxism could also begin to fracture the Kremlins hold on other Catholic countries within the Easter Bloc.

McHugh remembered that one of those that had briefed him for the mission even boasted, "We became aware of the assassination plan at the moment Brezhnev, sitting in his office high in the Kremlin, bellowed, "Silence him," at Yuri Andropov, the head of the KGB, even before they had heard only half of the translation of the new Pope's speech to the reported million Polish people in Warsaw's Victory Square." Another had explained that Andropov initiated the plan immediately by assigning the Bulgarian Durzhavna Sigurnost- the Bulgarian State Security- to carry out the assassination.

McHugh continued, "We are aware that French Secret Service emissaries recently alerted senior Vatican clergy of the assassination plan but were ignored. With all the speculation surrounding the recent death of John Paul I and the conflicting actions of those in positions of power closest to him, it was decided to provide this intelligence directly to you. We believe our information is credible and of the highest urgency. It's all included in chapter twelve of this book."

McHugh placed the book on the desk directly in front of the colonel, who still cradled his head in his hands.

McHugh took a final sip of wine. "Colonel, I understand how difficult this is for you. However, there is a telephone number in chapter twelve that you may call if you are in need. The number is secure and encrypted. It's also time sensitive and will only remain enabled for the next few days." He paused for a few moments to allow the Commandant grasp all he had said, and then continued. "Please keep our conversation and this information in the highest level of security. Chapter twelve cannot be copied. We hope you will find its contents helpful."

Convinced that he had told Pfyffer everything as he had been instructed, McHugh put down his glass. "Thank you for the wine. The president wishes you and the pontiff well. I'll be returning to the United States tomorrow."

The Colonel's face was ashen. He wiped his brow and looked up at McHugh. "Thank you, Professor... if you are indeed a professor. We are grateful for your information. I will review it completely as soon as I am able." He stood and opened a door on the right side of the credenza revealing a gray safe. Pfyffer inserted the book, closed the door and spun the lock. Then with his composure seemingly restored, he came around the end of his desk and placed a hand in the small of

McHugh's back.

Easing McHugh toward the door, the colonel continued, "Now I know why my friend Admiral Stringer asked me to not only to invite you but also to meet with you."

"How do you know the Admiral?" McHugh asked casually.

"Two years ago, when your good Admiral was then the captain of your nuclear aircraft carrier *USS Enterprise* anchored in Naples, he extended an invitation for me to bring a group of my guardsmen on a tour of that amazing vessel. He was most gracious."

Pfyffer extended his hand. "Now, Mr. McHugh, I must go and greet the families of my men."

The Arriaga Villa, outside Rome

3

With the convertible top of her Fiat Spider folded down over the back seat, Claudette Arriaga relished the wind streaming through her glistening long, black hair as she drove along the beach road edging the Mediterranean. She slowed approaching Arriaga drive and turned onto it after the speeding northbound Lamborghini had passed. It was a happy morning; last night on her return flight from Toronto she'd met an appealing man who didn't hit on her. And tonight they planned to have dinner together.

Arriaga Road climbing away from the sea into the hills southwest of Rome was named as a tribute to her family's long history of commitment to the Lazio region. On the right side of the drive up the hill, she passed a line of new single family homes, a new shopping center with four storefronts for lease, and then an elementary school under construction. The left side of the road was covered with olive trees, fruit trees and wheat fields that her family leased to tenant families that had been previously employed by the Arriagas.

At one time, her family farm had covered about forty hectares, around one hundred acres, extending to the Mediterranean Sea with hundreds of olive trees, fruit trees, wheat fields and fenced grass areas for horses and a small herd of cattle. But after the tragic death of her father in an airline crash, the family sold its landholdings to the east and leased the remaining land. Claudette was nine at the time. The short cobblestone drive through the remaining three hectares surrounding the family villa was edged by a low wall of gathered stones fronting the remaining row of olive trees. Although called their Villa, it was really a small one-bedroom fieldstone farm house with multiple sections added over the years. It now stood with six bedrooms, each with an individual bathroom, a formal grand dining room, the large family parlor and a billiards room.

The original house was now a modern kitchen and pantry.

As Claudette approached the villa, she knew her twin brother, Claudio, had not arrived as the parking area under the villa's second story terrace was empty. She continued on around to the rear and parked between the guest cottage and the large double barn. Doors on both ends of the barn were open. It was empty, except for a few gardening tools and the family's two automobiles.

Her father's silver 1950 Chevrolet Bel Aire hardtop sedan sat against the near side wall resting on blocks. She stopped momentarily remembering his words when he bought it, shortly before he died.

"All Italian auto makers are fascists, and Hitler invaded our country, killing many of my friends. I only buy American; they saved us." At the time she hadn't understood. Later she learned he was a proud partisan during the war. Her mother's spotless new black Mercedes sedan was parked only a few feet away from the abandoned Bel Aire. Her mother, Lauretta, had defended the purchase during their lunch last month by explaining that she had selected the Mercedes because the Italian auto industry was still controlled by fascists, and all the bad German Nazis were dead. Claudette and Claudio had just smiled at her rationalization.

Noticing Sergio, the long time family chauffer, tending his garden at the end of the manicured lawn behind the barn, Claudette yelled "Serg..io!"

He didn't seem to hear.

She knew that his hearing was slipping so she walked toward his sunny side so her shadow would alert him of her approach, instead of continuing to call.

He turned, recognized her, dropped his hoe and opened his arms wide.

She walked into his hug.

"How are you, Serge?" Now she called him Serge. When she was young, her family had tried to teach her how to properly pronounce, Sergio.

She always responded with, "Serg…io." Finally the family relented, so as a youngster it became her friend's name. His hair was thinning and although his skin was creased with age, his face still mirrored strength. His eyes were still bright and his hug welcoming.

Stepping back, he studied her and remarked in Italian, "The enchanting child is now a most beautiful woman."

She kissed his cheek.

He went on. "Must keep busy; there's not much to do anymore. Your mother doesn't much go out; the lease holders tend the orchards and fields. And that brother of yours has hired landscapers to care for the terraces and lawns. All I have now is my garden."

"Well, you're part of our family and there comes a time for rest." Then knowing that her friend would usually go into a long explanation about the kinds of vegetables and spices in his garden, she quickly added, "How are the ladies?"

"They talk, always talk about everything: the weather, television, the Roman church, neighbors, and always food, food! My garden is quiet." As usual, as his comments about most things, his answer was pointed and concise.

"Serge, tell me about their health."

"My Natalia nags as always, but she's as healthy as a ..."

Realizing that he was struggling to think of a comparison, Claudette squeezed his hand.

He went on - "And my Natalie says your mother's arthritis is becoming more painful, and she sleeps too much."

A car skidded to a stop. Claudette exclaimed, "Got to run, Claudio's here. Love you!" She kissed him on the cheek again.

The three Arriagas, gathered for their monthly luncheon, stood overlooking their expansive lands, now leased to contract farmers, from behind the low ornate wrought iron railing that edged the wide Tuscan stone veranda their father had constructed years ago. For a long while they didn't speak, and Claudette believed the other two, like her, were reflecting on days past.

Lauretta, now sixty-nine, was dressed in the same pale green housecoat she had worn when the three of them had lunched the previous month. Her thinning gray hair was pulled back into a bun away from the age lines that graced her sun-bleached face. Her eyes, however, still had a youthful sparkle and her smile was playful.

Claudio, at thirty- five like his sister, was the Director of the City of Rome Housing Authority and had arrived alone. His wife, Giselle, and their three children were away on a visit to her family in Cortuna. In his youth, Claudio had been a member of the professional Rugby Roma Olimpic Club. Then at six feet, with 200-plus pounds of muscled body, he was the Hooker in the center of the scrum, much like the *Cen-*

ter on an American football team. Now with the pressures of his job, a growing family and a huge appetite, much of that muscle had morphed into a prominent waistline.

Standing between the two ladies Claudio grasped his sister's hand and winked at her when she turned acknowledging his touch.

Claudette, in a knee-length white linen dress that accentuated her smooth caramel skin, had her long black hair flowing onto a linen scarf wrapped loosely around her shoulders. She was only a few inches shorter then her brother. Although taken by many to be a Vogue model, she was now senior flight attendant for Alitalia, Italy's national airline. Regrettably, she had left college against her family's wishes to pursue a modeling career, which she impulsively cut short by entering into a brief, embarrassingly difficult marriage.

Still holding Claudette's hand, Claudio guided his mother back to the large square table set for them under a wide lime green sun umbrella in the center of the veranda.

"As always, you look gorgeous," he whispered.

She punched him lightly on the shoulder.

"Tell me about your travels."

"Last week I had a wonderful three days in Toronto and last night on the overnight return flight, I spent hours chatting with a rarity."

"What's a rarity?" he quizzed.

"Well..., for me it's a man who can hold an intelligent conversation without hitting on me."

"Must be some guy, Canadian, AY?" he mimicked, as he pulled out a chair for his mother.

"No, he's American."

Once their mother took her place at the table, they pulled out chairs on either side of her, sat down and immediately bowed their heads.

As had become the family custom after the death of her husband, Lauretta began a lengthy prayer thanking God for all their blessings and beseeching a list of her favorite saints to welcome her husband and all of their departed family into heaven. Then after a momentary pause, she continued on, asking the almighty for blessings on the Holy Father, all the missionaries, the poor and a long list of friends, neighbors and distant family members.

Claudio turned his head and winked at his sister when their mother stopped, seemingly out of breath. The two of them knew what was coming.

In a much stronger voice, Lauretta beseeched God to forgive her daughter for divorcing her wonderful husband. Then she invoked the Blessed Mother to bring more children into Claudio's young family. Finally, she crossed herself and smiled at both of them.

Sergio's wife Natalia, their housekeeper, watched the performance from the doorway and knew it was now time to bring the lunch.

Claudio stood and poured their favorite local red wine into their glasses. Then he raised his glass, "Mother, thank you for your prayers; I believe God has forgiven Claudette many times for dumping that gigolo she unfortunately married. And Giselle and I are happy with the three children we have been blessed with. I think you should pray for continued good heath, as Claudette and I pray for you every day." He leaned over and kissed his mother's forehead.

When he had taken his seat, Natalia began to serve lunch; bruschetta, antipasto salad and her special, *Ravioli al Forno*, baked ravioli with fresh tomato, spinach and local Lazio area cheeses. The meal was long and delicious. Conversation was mostly centered on Italian politics, speculation concerning reported conflicts in the Vatican, and hearsay about neighbors and distant family.

Finally, Lauretta's head began to droop; it was time for her nap.

The twins helped their mother stand and each in turn gave her a long hug. Then Natalia walked her through the large open door into the house. As they walked into the sitting room, Claudette couldn't help reflecting how small her mother's world was becoming.

Claudio put his arm around his sister's shoulder and guided her off the terrace onto the expansive front lawn.

"This American must be something. For over a year, you haven't mentioned a man that impressed you, even though I did introduce you to my friend Mario!"

"Mario's an ex-jock who still hears the crowd cheering. He can't hold an intelligent conversation for more than three minutes without injecting football or politics. He was a boor in so many ways."

"Well, tell me about your American rarity," Claudio asked.

"It was a nine-hour flight and I only had an elderly couple and Colin in the first class section of the plane.. The couple slept most of the time. Colin and I just talked; talked like you and I do. We were comfortable with each other - no airs, nothing pretentious, just conversing about life experiences, where we've traveled, things we like and dislike." She paused, "It was easy; the hours passed too quickly."

"Sounds like an academic."

"He's educated, but not what you would describe as an academic. He's slightly taller than you and as handsome, but in an American way. He played a sport called Lacrosse at America's Naval Academy and now manages an international business."

"This guy must be something to have you go on. Will you see him again?"

"I've invited him to have dinner later this evening."

"Sure he's not married?"

She fixed on him. Then pushed him in the chest, "No, he's not married."

They finished their wine and began to circle back toward the veranda.

She leaned into him, clasping his arm with both of hers. "You know how much I love being your sister. You're so good to me, and have always given me a security and support that's been so helpful through my good and bad times. And you're the strength that's carried mother and me since father passed."

She stretched and kissed his cheek. Then added, "And you were monumental throughout the divorce. I probably wouldn't have been able to have survived it without you."

He pulled his arm from her grasp and placed it around her shoulders and whispered, "And dear sister, I will always be there for you; wherever you are."

They took the stone steps onto the veranda two at a time.

At about that same time, McHugh eased his way through the crowd of well wishers and guardsmen in San Damaso Courtyard and walked through the Bronze Doors into St. Peter's Square. He stood momentarily and wondered just what the colonel and his guardsmen could do against a well planned assassination backed by of one of the most powerful countries in the world. "God help the pope," he murmured.

He removed his coat and folded it on his arm. His shirt was drenched. He took the Leica camera from the coat pocket and then flipped the coat over his shoulder.

On previous visits McHugh had acquired numerous photographs of the remains of ancient Rome, Vatican buildings, frescos and statues. And now relieved that his mission had been concluded, he decided to join the crowd of tourists and photograph people.

While weaving his way toward the towering Egyptian Obelisk in the square's center, he stopped and raised the camera to photograph two teenage girls walking hand-in-hand toward the Basilica. One of them looked his way, flashed an annoyed smile and gave him the finger.

American, he thought.

Turning in another direction, he considered photographing a nurse dressed a white hospital dress and starched white cap, who was pushing an elderly woman slumped in a wheel chair, but felt it would be too intrusive. Realizing that the photo might be a relic in just a few years, he snapped two young nuns in long sky blue habits and starched gull-like winged headdresses walking arm in arm toward the basilica.

A small girl in a sleeveless white silk dress stooped gracefully to pick up a lace handkerchief from the cobblestones. A crown of white flowers topped her dark curly hair, as if she had just made her first communion. McHugh raised the camera toward the girl's mother and pointed to the child.

The mother nodded and told the girl, in French, to look toward the camera.

McHugh knelt in front of the child and rapidly snapped three photos then stood and gave a 'thumbs-up' to the proud mother.

A crush of Japanese tourists, scurrying to close the distance to their flag- carrying guide forced their way between McHugh and the young girl.

When McHugh turned back toward the girl, he spotted the same slim man in the black suit who had stared in his direction during the ceremony. The individual was engrossed in a conversation with another taller man with a thick mustache.

"Thank God he doesn't see me," McHugh mumbled. He dropped his coat on the stone façade, knelt and set the aperture on his camera. Then he stood and shot a rapid series of photos of the two.

The taller one, with long sideburns and the thick moustache, saw McHugh and momentarily looked shocked as if he had been discovered in a place he shouldn't have been. Then with a sneer, the man raised his am toward McHugh and pointed a cocked finger. Then he grabbed the arm of his thin companion and pulled him into the crowd.

The intensity of his cold eyes and the-*you're a- dead- man-* gesture sent a shudder through McHugh. Watching the two turn and rapidly walk away, McHugh held the camera ready.

Neither of them looked back.

Now aware that others, probably Bulgarian, knew of his meeting with Pfyffer, it was no longer a simple walk-on performance. McHugh also wondered whether they knew he wasn't a professor. He had to watch his back. Deciding not to remain in the area, but to return to his car, he joined the flow of tourists leaving the square.

For a half hour he walked with the jostling crowd streaming along the sidewalk bordering the Via della Conciliazione; the wide cobblestone boulevard clogged with cars heading toward the Vatican. Twice he edged to the side of buildings pretending to look at the name signs on the doorway alcoves and glanced behind unable to pick out an obvious follower within the bobbing crowd. At a newspaper kiosk he purchased a tri-fold street map with walking tour guide of the city.

Tired of the jostling, he crossed into a narrow cobble stone street lined with small shops. The height of the buildings hugging the narrow sidewalk shuttered the hot sun and made his walk surprisingly quiet and cool. There were few people on the street and no vehicles. He stopped momentarily at a shop window and again glanced back. No one had followed him into the street. Now confident that he wasn't being followed, McHugh began to relax.

At a small coffee bar further on, he ordered a cappuccino and again casually surveyed his surroundings while thumbing through his street map. Only two women with shopping bags draped from their arms and a shop keeper rearranging a table display of shoes in front of his shop were visible. From the map, he realized he wasn't far from the Pantheon, one of his favorite Roman sites. The fact that its unreinforced concrete circular dome still stood after two thousand years continued to fascinate him. He decided to view it again before returning to his car.

It took another half hour to reach the Piazza Dalla Rotonda, the large stone square in front of the Pantheon surrounded by tall buildings, cafes, bistros and restaurants. It was bustling with people dodging the merchant vans moving along its periphery and the horse drawn carriages navigating through it. McHugh took a seat beneath a green and white striped awning outside of a small bistro. A young waiter dressed in a white jacket came forward and offered a menu.

"A glass of red wine and a Pellegrino." McHugh smiled, hoping that the waiter understood English.

The waiter bowed at the waist and placed the menu on the table. When he returned with the wine and bottled water, McHugh ordered an antipasto salad.

Deciding to view the Spanish Steps once again as his final stop of the afternoon, he looked in his guide book and discovered he was only a fifteen minute walk away. He took a large drink of the water, stretched his legs, and thought warmly of Claudette, the tall Alitalia Airline stewardess he met the night before on his flight into Rome from Toronto. It had been awhile since he had been so captivated by such an intelligent, beautiful woman. She had even suggested tonight's dinner and he was looking forward to finding the medieval castle where they planned to meet.

With wine in hand, McHugh sat back and observed the passing stream of tourists and locals, trying to match their nationalities and professions.

A tall elderly gentleman, wearing a black homburg and tailored pin stripped suit, entering the far side of the square caught McHugh's attention. The eccentric had a pencil mustache and coke-bottle glasses and extended a shinny black cane horizontally with a twist of his wrist before each step. Guessing that the eccentric might be a retired judge or a senior member of government, McHugh lifted his camera and shot a photo series of the classic individual. As the man passed, McHugh became aware of another man who seemed familiar sitting on bench across the square reading a newspaper. The man glanced over the top of the open paper at McHugh.

At least he's worth a shot; McHugh placed his napkin on the map, stood and walked into the bistro. The small dining room was empty except for the young waiter leaning against a narrow wooden bar at the rear. Taking a position against a side wall unseen from the street, McHugh focused his camera on the interloper. Appearing confused, the individual put the paper down on the bench and stood, glancing toward the bistro.

Good timing - McHugh thought, recognizing the slim man in the black suit who had watched him during the initiation ceremony and whose photo he'd snapped in the Piazza.

How in the hell did I ever miss this guy? He must have taken a parallel street.

Through the zoom lens, he focused on the shallow face, high forehead and dark trimmed mustache; the guy looked more like a maitre d' in a cheap restaurant than a Bulgarian undercover agent.

McHugh returned to his table, finished the salad and ordered another bottle of Pellegrino to take along. *A CIA field agent would probably lead the little shit down a side street and put a revolver in the guy's ribs to find out why he was being followed. I'm just a walk-on, so I'll just stay the course, and let the damn professionals in Washington unravel this situation. Anyway after dinner tonight with Claudette, I'll be back in the States tomorrow.* He paid his tab and headed toward the Steps.

The famous 256 year-old Spanish Steps, the widest staircase in Europe stood in the center of Piazza di Spagna. Its 138 steps led up a steep slope to the double towered Trinita dei Monti Church at its top. The steps overflowed with clusters of people, young and old, chatting, taking photos or just enjoying the setting. McHugh found a place on the ledge of the Sinking Boat Fountain at the foot of the steps and continued to people-watch. He lifted the camera, snapped a couple of photos and then surveyed the periphery of crowd through its lens. His mustached Maitr d' was leaning against the side of a tall stone building near the south entrance to the square. McHugh took a swig of the bottled water and decided to learn a little more about the man, hopefully without an actual confrontation.

Nearby, a young couple stood facing each other holding hands. Because of their gleaming olive skin, McHugh believed they were either Italian or Spanish.

The boy, in shorts and a white tee shirt, had his back to McHugh. The girl with long dark hair, wearing a yellow print dress and beige sandals, noticed McHugh and whispered in her beau's ear.

When the boy turned toward him, McHugh approached and asked if they spoke English.

Hesitating, they looked at each other, and then turned smiling. "A little," said the boy with an obvious French accent.

"Will you do me a favor? I'll give you fifty dollars American, and it's easy."

They glanced at each other again. "Yes, thank you."

McHugh described his follower without looking toward the man and explained where he was standing. He asked the couple to walk over to the man and ask if he was Italian; if he wasn't, he told them to ask if he was English. McHugh then directed the couple to walk away from the man but not return to him. If the watcher was Italian, he asked the boy to raise one finger; if English, two fingers.

"What if he's not Italian or English?

"If he isn't Italian, French or English, then just kiss your beautiful girlfriend."

McHugh handed the money to the girl. They laughed and began to turn toward the follower.

McHugh grasped the boy's arm.

"Wait; walk away from me. Go to the bottom of the steps for a few moments and then approach him. Thank you."

The couple walked to the base of the steps, hesitated and then raced up the stairs, hand-in-hand.

McHugh watched them climb, but lost sight of them in the crowd half way up. He thought *there goes fifty bucks.*

But at the top of the steps McHugh saw the two emerge and kiss. They turned and ran back down dodging people along the way, and then walked directly to McHugh's follower.

After a brief discussion with the man, they walked away hand in hand toward the Steps without signaling.

When they stopped, the boy leaned over and kissed his girlfriend.

McHugh glanced at the follower, who glared back defiantly.

Turning away from the man, McHugh took a last sip of the bottled water and walked to a waiting taxi on the edge of the square.

"Marriott Hotel, Fiumicino" he said, directing the driver to the hotel where he had parked his rental car.

As the taxi pulled away McHugh glanced out of the rear window and observed his follower talking into a hand-held radio.

Marriott Hotel
Rome Fiumicino Airport

4

The interior of the Alfa Romeo sedan was stifling in the heat of the late afternoon sun.

McHugh opened the front windows and turned the air conditioner on full blast. While waiting for the car to cool, he studied the Eurocar road map and discovered that he was only sixty kilometers from his hotel. The medieval castle, Castello di Santa Severa, where he planned to meet Claudette that evening only added about twenty more kilometers to his return trip. Mentally marking the highway turn-off, he decided to pass the castle on the way back to the hotel to be sure he would be able to locate it later in the evening.

When the car cooled enough to drive, he turned the air conditioner down and closed the windows. Exiting the parking lot, he followed the map directions through a labyrinth of side streets to the San Aurelia Highway. Cars raced by the on-ramp as if it were Memorial Day in Indianapolis. A cacophony of blaring horns from the cars behind, nudged him to accelerate into a short cap in the speeding highway traffic. Even with his foot forcing the accelerator to the floor, it was difficult to keep abreast of the fast moving cars; his speedometer approached a hundred and seventy kilometers, more than one hundred miles an hour. Nervous and unsure, he reduced speed and eased into the slower inside lane. Again horns blared and angry drivers shook their fists as they sped around him.

Suddenly a huge, black dump truck with an imposing square push bumper painted international orange closed from behind, but didn't pass. He leaned forward with both hands on the wheel trying hard to focus on the road ahead. The truck remained only a few feet behind with the orange bumper filling his car's rear window. Fortunately the road ahead began to bear to the right and McHugh knew the cutoff to the castle was only a few kilometers beyond. He flipped on his turn signal hoping the idiot driving the truck would see that he planned to slow down and turn.

The monster truck pulled out and sped past.

Relieved, McHugh sat back into the seat and began to search for the cut-off as he navigated through the sweeping highway turn.

Finally, he eased the sedan onto the one-lane narrow road. Weed, yellow scrub grass and struggling wildflower grew through numerous fractures in the aged tarmac. "Damn, the last vehicles on this road were probably chariots," he commented out loud.

The left side of the aged road was overgrown with weathered hedge and ugly bramble. One the right, a field of wild flowers, gray fieldstone and short grass sloped off into a copse of trees and tall grass about sixty yards away.

Anticipating the cool breeze from the Mediterranean Sea that he knew was just beyond the castle, he lowered the front car windows.

The sudden roar of a large motor and a burst of orange to his left brought McHugh instantly alert. That haunting day three years ago flashed in front of him.

While driving through an intense rainstorm on the M5 motorway in Southwest England, the rear edge of a tandem lorry had swerved in front of his Ford Cortina like a large ship breaking through a fog.

Do now what you did then…

Seconds before the huge truck hit the Alfa Romeo, McHugh released his seat belt and stretched full body, face down, across the two front seats of the car. Then wedging his feet against the driver's door, he gripped the passenger door handle and held it firmly with both hands.

With the rented sedan teetering along the edge of the road, the truck braked abruptly; its angry motor still grinding.

Reaching up with one hand, McHugh pulled the passenger seat belt over his back and locked it. Just as he began to pray, *God let me survive one more time*, the truck released its brakes and sent the car rolling down the slope crushing the brush and high grass in its path.

McHugh struggled to keep his position. He buried his head in the bottom of the seat just as the wind shield imploded, and glass shards showered over him. He struggled to keep his feet tucked under the driver's armrest while his body plummeted with each roll. At one point the car became airborne and his right shoulder bounced against the roof when it partially collapsed on landing; only the seat backs kept the roof from failing completely. The pain in his shoulder was intense. His hold on the locked seatbelt kept him from being thrown indiscriminately while the vehicle tumbled. His head bounced against the dashboard a couple of times; blood seeped into his eyes, glass shards covered his clothes and petrol fumes filled his nostrils.

Finally the crumbled sedan came to rest upside down in a dry riverbed.

Get out of the driver's window and crawl away from the embankment, he thought, jolting himself into action.

Releasing the seat belt, he used his feet and hands to back crablike along the overturned ceiling. Then, rolling his shoulder into his chest, he inched through the compressed opening in the driver's window frame. Finally free, he crawled into nearby tall grass.

Rolling onto his stomach, he raised his head just above the grass and looked back up the slope. The truck faced menacingly down at him; two men stood beside it. *Thank God, I'm on the opposite side of the car; the bastards can't see I'm alive*. While keeping the two of them in sight, he wiped the glass shards from his hair, neck and clothes as best he could. Then he ripped a piece of lining from his coat and wiped the blood and sweat from his face and wrapped the lining around his forehead.

The taller man, dressed in a black T-shirt and black fatigues pointed toward the wreckage and yelled in a guttural language at the other shorter, younger man in a gray coverall. He then lifted a brown leather bag from the truck and placed it on the ground. Taking a stock, barrel and telescopic sight from the bag, he assembled a high-powered rifle. When finished, he said something to the smaller man and threw the rifle to him.

The weapon hit the younger one in the chest, but he caught it just before it touched the ground.

The tall man yelled angrily. The younger then knelt down on his right knee and struggled to place the rifle butt in the crook of his right shoulder. He held it clumsily with his left hand placed awkwardly along the barrel, and then pointed it unsteadily at the upturned wreckage.

The tall man roared; the younger one pulled the trigger.

The first shot landed high in the scrub beyond the car. Scattered shots rang out. A couple hit the car, but most landed in the surrounding grass. One chopped through a tree branch near McHugh.

The erratic shooter stood, dropped the rifle and raised his hands above his head in frustration.

The tall man grabbed the young shooter roughly by the shoulder and rammed him against the side of the truck.

The young man's head bounced off of the truck and he folded into the ground.

The tall one picked up the rifle and in one motion turned and fired a volley of shots directly into center of the sedan's fuel tank. Then he dropped the rifle and picked up the leather bag.

Sensing the danger that the sharpshooter now presented, McHugh moved deeper into a thicket of palm trees and crouched behind a wide tree trunk.

The tall sharpshooter walked nonchalantly down the slope carrying the bag in one hand along his side like a brief case.

The shooter's face was flat like a deflated punching bag; his crooked nose had obviously been broken more than once. A thick scar creased his left eye, and a walrus-like mustache devoured his upper lip.

McHugh memorized the face. Even without the mustache, McHugh knew he could pick that face out of any crowd or police lineup.

About ten meters away, the shooter knelt, opened the bag, and pulled out a flare gun. He tossed the bag behind him, stood and took the shooting position with both hands leveling the flare gun in front of him.

Knowing what was about to happen, McHugh crawled farther into the thicket.

The first flare ignited the fuel spilling out of the petrol tank and the wreckage erupted in a ball of flame. Within seconds a dense pall of black smoke rose skyward. The heat was intense.

The shooter reloaded and fired two more flares into the surrounding brush and the scene became an inferno.

McHugh stayed his distance.

Flipping the bag over his shoulder, the shooter turned and began to saunter back up the hill. Stopping halfway up, he turned and yelled in broken English, "Fock you America. You go ta hell,"

At the top of the slope, he motioned at the younger man now observing the blaze from the driver's seat of the truck. When the trucked backed around, the shooter opened the cab door and jumped into the passenger seat. As the truck pulled away he leaned out of the open window and gave the two fingers -up yours- salute.

McHugh crawled away from the heat and sank into the grass overwhelmed with the knowledge that he was also now the target of a trained assassin. Ignoring his bruised body and the intense pain in his right shoulder, he pulled a fallen tree branch from a clump nearby and rose unsteadily to one knee and surveyed the scene. A funnel of swirling black smoke rose into the windless sky as the expanding circle of burning dry grass inched toward him.

He had to put distance between himself and the inferno. Leaning on the branch, he removed the German camera from his coat and slipped it into his trouser side pocket, and then threw the coat into the flames. After pulling his false passport, driver's license and credit cards from his travel wallet, he scattered them into the inferno. For another moment he watched the burning grass advance toward him and then tossed the empty wallet as far as he could into the blaze.

"The charade ends here," he vowed and turned away. By staying in the tall grass and keeping the road to his left, he knew he would eventually arrive at the castle.

At a small stream a short distance to the west, he doused his face and cleansed the makeshift bandage on his forehead. Blood oozed from a tear in his trousers, so he ripped a piece of his shirt and washed the gash in his thigh as best he could. Then he rinsed the shirt piece in the water and draped it around his neck.

After retrieving the tree branch, he glanced back at the black smoke defacing the calm sky, then turned and trudged on.

That evening, Castillo de Santa Severa, a medieval castle on the Mediterranean coast

5

McHugh stood behind a chin high manicured box hedge in front of the stone wall of the castle. He was drained; he smelled and ached like a soundly defeated boxer. The remaining shreds of his bloody shirt stuck to his body and it was excruciatingly painful each time he tried to raise his right arm, so he let it hang limp at his side.

Last night on the plane, Claudette had suggested they meet at the castle around seven. However like the Italian she was, she hadn't been specific. It had taken him more than two hours to find the castle. His watch was lost somewhere in the turmoil, but he knew it had to be approaching seven. For all but the last thirty meters of tarmac, he had struggled through dense brush, thickets of struggling vine, aging trees and tall scrub grass. Ticks and flies rose with each trudging step, while unseen creatures scurried out of his way. Once, when the terrain became level with the road he took to its center, but after walking only a few meters, he dove into the short grass along the road bed when he heard the clanging siren of a fire truck racing toward him. Berating himself for his mistake, he immediately returned to the security of the thick brush after it passed.

His mind wandered - *I need you Claudette, at least to help me return to my hotel to retrieve my clothes and my true identification. The bastards know I can positively identify three of them and will eventually also learn I didn't die in the crash. They'll hunt me down and they'll kill me if I don't get in touch with Stringer and get the hell get out of Italy and back to the States.*

God damn, I'm not cut out for this shit. Reagan and Stringer can find another actor. I'm done with letter dropping and impersonations...God, Claudette be here.

He was a businessman not a trained field agent. His only defensive training was gleamed as a midshipman during a month long familiarization course with a Navy Seal Team in Coronado, California. But that was over twenty-five years ago and consisted mainly of survival training, physical fitness exercises and hand-to-hand combat techniques. *God, if I need to evade these bastards let some of what I learned during that training rise to the surface.* With the punching bag face of the shooter ingrained in his mind, McHugh knew one thing; at the slightest hint of a threat he would take any initiative he might find available, what ever it might be.

Again, trying to focus, he thought, *I have to tell Claudette something convincing without divulging the real story. I really need her help. She knows her way around Italy. It would be stupid to fly out of either of Rome's airports, Da Vinci or Ciampino. Maybe I can get to Switzerland by train or bus. Shit no, the bastards will have agents watching all the trains and buses leaving Rome. Maybe I can get to Milan and take the fast train to Zurich. I took it two years ago. Now all I need is a way to Milan and a phone to shake-up Stringer. My admiral friend talked me into this, now he has to get off his butt and find a way to bring me back to the States and ferret out whoever leaked the information that I would be meeting with Pfyffer.*

He heard a car approaching. *God, let it be Claudette.* A red Fiat Spider Convertible with its top down pulled through the castle entrance gate.

McHugh recognized her immediately. Her glistening long black hair cascaded onto her shoulders.

She pulled the sports car to a stop near the entrance to the castle parking lot and sat momentarily glancing around. Just as McHugh started to push through the hedge, she eased the car into a space near the side of the castle and parked. She got out of the convertible and began to walk toward three cars that remained along the castle fence. She was dressed for dinner in a sheer white blouse and ankle length dark skirt.

Her presence rejuvenated him. Then, just, as quickly, it brought home his desperate situation. He hesitated to impose on her, but knew he had no choice.

"Claudette," he yelled and stepped through a narrow gap in the hedge.

She turned as he approached. "Oh, God," she cried and then ran toward him. "Colin, whatever happened to you?" She reached out grabbing his painful right arm. He winced and she quickly released her hold.

Backing away, he said, "Not here, let's go somewhere."

Claudette's condominium was one of the two units that ran the length of the top floor of a six suite complex with large front balconies overlooking the Mediterranean a few kilometers south of the castle. After parking the Spider in the underground garage, she guided McHugh to the rear of the garage and into the elevator to her condo.

As the elevator door closed behind them she reached up and brushed a few locks of hair away from the cut on his forehead. "We have to get you out of those clothes and cleaned up; follow me to the bathroom and we'll get to it." She instructed him as if they were in the midst of an airline emergency. She opened the condominium door as soon as the elevator stopped at her third floor door, took his hand and led him directly to her bathroom.

"Take off your clothes and I'll put them in the washer." She helped him out of the remains of his blood stained shirt and then picked glass shards from his hair.

He dropped his trousers and shorts, and stepped out of his shoes.

Claudette picked up the clothes. "I'll be right back."

McHugh stood naked, under bright ceiling lights on an inlayed black and white terrazzo floor in the center of an immense bathroom that glistened in white porcelain and chrome. A clear glass walk-in shower took up the wall to his right; an ornate pedestal sink and a long mirrored dressing table covered the left wall.

With eyes closed to escape the brightness, he was thankful how readily Claudette became involved.

The bathroom door opened.

"Not much to wear; bloody, ripped shirt and torn trousers." She slipped past him, wearing only a mesh bra and brief panty and turned on the water in one of the sinks. Handing two pills and a glass of water to him, she ordered, "Take these pills, they'll take the edge off the pain." Then she opened the shower door and turned on the water. "Now let's get you cleaned up." She took the glass from his hand and led him to the shower. Then she stepped in behind him. After adjusting the water to a moderate warm stream, she gently washed his back with a soft soapy cloth.

"Nice cheeks." She washed his buttocks, thighs and legs. Turning him toward her, she knelt and lathered the gash in his thigh. Then she stood. And after soaping his left arm, stomach and chest, she gently raised his right arm just enough to reach under it and washed as best she could. Finished, she handed the cloth to him. "Now you can do your jewels."

Even with his aching body, the intimacy began to arouse McHugh.

She moved behind him and shampooed his hair. "My conditioner has a lavender fragrance, so we'll pass."

After a thorough rinse of his hair, she whispered. "Stay under the shower and relax. There's a towel on the stand just outside the door." She stepped out of the shower and closed the door.

McHugh indulged himself under the cascading water for a few more minutes, then turned it off and stepped out of the shower. After patting himself dry, he wrapped the towel around his waist and faced the mirror. Using his left hand, he combed his hair, realizing that he now felt much better than the battered face reflecting back at him.

The bathroom door opened and Claudette entered wearing a long white terry cloth robe.

He turned toward her and noticed her glance at the bulge protruding from the center of the towel.

She smiled. "I see you're coming back to life."

"No choice under the circumstances: beautiful woman, soft touch, warm water."

Claudette ignored the comment and placed a plastic bag of crushed ice in the marble sink, and said definitively, "It's best to ice that shoulder right now." Then she wrapped the bag of ice on the top of the sore shoulder and secured it with an athletic roll bandage.

Holding up a bottle of peroxide, she ordered, "Let's see that forehead." After cleaning the gash and covering it with a flesh colored bandage, she knelt and used the peroxide to clean the slice in his thigh, covering it with a gauze dressing.

When she stood up McHugh put his good arm around her waist and kissed her lightly on the cheek. "Thanks."

She smiled coyly and backed through the open bathroom door.

Wrapped in the towel, McHugh sat on a deep white leather couch that took up most of the living room side wall. A glass cocktail table stood in front of the couch. The teak floor was covered by a white shag rug. Small oval glass tables with modern cut glass lamps were placed next to twin white leather arm chairs in the corners of the room facing him. A sliding glass door open to a large balcony on his right brought a fresh sea breeze into the room. A mirrored wall to his left reflected the patio railing and the evening sky beyond. A formal oak dining table with eight high backed ornate chairs stood in front of the mirror.

He leaned back and closed his eyes.

A fresh lavender fragrance swirled into the room.

He opened his eyes and turned to see Claudette leaning against the wall. She wore black shorts and a white tee shirt with the green and red Alitalia Airlines logo splashed across its front. She held up a maroon *Rugby Roma Olimpic Club* jersey with the club's black and white team logo. "I sleep in this sometimes." She tossed the jersey to him. "It belonged to my twin brother, Claudio; he was in the rugby scrum line for five years. You're both about the same size. You're taller, and he's wider."

McHugh caught the jersey with his left hand, "A twin brother. What's he do now?"

He stood and she helped him maneuver into the jersey. Then she handed his trousers back to him. They were cut off at the knees.

He slipped them on, realizing that with the exception of his head bandage, a casual observer might think the two of them had just returned from the beach.

"Claudio's now the director of the City of Rome's building department. He lives with his wife, Giselle and their three children on a small farm about sixty kilometers outside the city."

"Your condo's magnificent."

"Spoils of war," she spread her arms. "As I mentioned on the plane, I had a disastrous marriage; this is my ignominious reward. But let's not get into that now. I'm more interested in hearing what really happened to you. That feeble story you told me during the drive over here about thieves attacking you and stealing your car just doesn't fly. All that I've seen of your injuries paints a more serious picture."

McHugh stood and walked onto the balcony. It hung high above a narrow road fronting a line of summer cottages on its opposite side. A long sandy beach extended from the cottages to the Mediterranean Sea beyond. The sky took up most of his view. The setting sun was magnificent; a myriad of yellow and orange hues bounced off a quilt of low cumulus clouds. But the scene couldn't entice him to ignore his afternoon. He had to disappear from Italy as soon as possible and needed to trust Claudette.

She stepped onto the balcony, touched his shoulder and handed him a glass of red wine. Then she sat down on a metal lounge chair. He leaned against the waist high railing facing her.

"Alright, now tell me the real story," she asked softly.

"You're right, I haven't been completely honest." He paused, "As I told you on the plane, I really am a businessman and have visited Italy many times. One of my clients is just north, near Perazzeta."

"You told me that," she said while studying him.

He held up his hand, "But... on this trip, my government asked me to carry out a special assignment and provide important information to your Italian authorities that might help solve a potentially difficult situation." He had decided to keep the Pope and the Vatican out of any information he shared with her.

"Apparently, my mission was compromised by agents of another not-so-friendly government and they now wish me dead." He paused. "They are serious. This afternoon, a huge truck drove my car off the road into a gulley and a sharpshooter fired a flare into the car and set it on fire. Now they probably believe I died in the inferno. But when a body isn't retrieved from the charred metal they'll come after me. I have to leave Italy as soon as possible."

"If all you did was provided information, why are they trying to kill you?"

"They are aware I can identify some of the individuals involved. And their country will find itself in the center of an international crisis if they are exposed. They can't let that happen. I also believe that they can't afford publicity or the capture of anyone sent after me. It will probably be a one- on-one confrontation. With even an inkling of a threat, I'm going to do something about it."

He sat down on the chair next to her. "Claudette, will you at least help me leave Italy?"

She didn't respond, just took a sip of wine and swirled what remained in her glass. She just stared over his shoulder at the setting sun.

He stood and stepped to the railing, wondering how he could go it alone.

She touched his shoulder and said softly, "Well, what do we do first?"

He turned into her and encircled her waist with his left arm. "Thank you."

That same evening in Rome

6

Dimitar Botev's tiny one bedroom apartment was on the third floor of a four story building above a vegetable market. The dreary brick building seemed like an unwanted appendage squeezed between the two larger stone structures on either side. Like so many buildings in Trullo, one of the poorer sections of Rome, it was in need of substantial repair.

Six years before, at twenty-one, the young Bulgarian received his completion certificate from the Karavelov School in Sofia, Bulgaria's crowded capital city. To celebrate, he booked a room at a small hotel in Bankya during its annual Jazz Festival. Early that Saturday afternoon, he took a bus to Bankya, a resort spa at the base of the Lulin Mountain twenty kilometers to the west of Sofia.

That evening while walking along a tree lined path at the foot of the mountain, he recognized Svetianna, one of his classmates, walking toward him. She was a shy, thin, pretty girl with short brown hair. Her academic achievements made her one the most popular girls in his graduating class.

Her eyes lit up when she recognized him. "Hello Dimitar, what a surprise to see you," she exclaimed excitedly when she approached.

He was happy she called him Dimitar as his close friends did; others, even his teachers, called him Botev.

"Hello Svetianna." He fumbled for what to say next, and then blurted out, "I came on the bus. Do you come here often?"

"Not really. My father is overseas on a business trip, so to get away from the city for a day I caught the early morning bus."

Dimitar recalled that Svetianna's mother had passed away two years earlier and her father often traveled on government business.

They decided to walk together. In a small café near his hotel, they stopped and celebrated their graduation with sandwiches and beer. Then they decided to attend the music festival together.

Later that evening, over more glasses of beer, they danced to a number of groups performing music ranging from Benny Goodman swing to Elvis rock and classic Beatles. The concert ended well after midnight, too late for Svetianna to catch the return bus to Sofia. Dimitar suggested she could stay with him in the hotel for the night and then they could return together on an early morning bus. She readily agreed and they walked hand- in-hand to the hotel.

She was first to refresh in the bathroom at the end of the hall. After Dimitar used the bathroom and opened the door of their small bedroom he saw Svetianna sitting in the yoga position in the center of the single metal bed wearing only her bra and panties. He closed the door behind him and she smiled demurely. When he began to unbutton his shirt, she reached behind her back and unclipped her bra. With a shrug of her shoulders the bra fell into her lap revealing her delicate, pert breasts.

Dimitar unbuckled his trousers and leapt onto the bed. They lay side by side eagerly kissing and fondling each other. Slowly he moved his hand down her back and caressed her petite buttocks.

She traced her tongue along his neck and shoulders.

When Dimitar worked his hand between her legs, she began to scream.

He sobered quickly and took his hand away. He told her he wouldn't go any further and pleaded with her to stop screaming.

She continued to scream hysterically.

He clasped his hand over her mouth.

She bit his hand and ran naked into the hall screaming uncontrollably.

The trial in the City of Sofia's Central Court was swift; Dimitar was convicted of attempted rape.

Afterward, he sat on a narrow bench with his eyes closed and his head leaning against the tile wall of the single holding cell waiting to be summoned back into the courtroom to hear his sentence pronounced. He was dejected and trembled with fear.

"Botev stand up! Move back against the wall," a tall, uniformed guard barked, and noisily unlocked the steel door with one of the large keys dangling from the metal key ring hanging from his wrist. The guard pushed the door inward and stepped aside.

A man of medium height with thinning gray hair, dressed in a dark conservative business suit entered and said in a soft voice, "Botev, please sit down,"

The guard closed the door and moved out of sight.

Dimitar glanced into the man's dark eyes framed by round rimless glasses and slid down to the end of the bench.

As another seat was not available; the man sat next to Dimitar.

"Do you know the *Durzhavna Sigurnost*?" He asked discreetly.

Like all Bulgarians, Dimitar dreaded the Bulgarian Secret Service and responded dejectedly, "Yes sir."

To which the man added, "Well, I'm one of its senior directors."

Terrified, Dimitar again dropped his head into his hands.

The man continued in a conciliatory voice, "I am also Svetianna's father." He paused to ensure he was understood. "And my daughter told me you did not intend to rape her. She explained that you were both intoxicated and she may even have encouraged you. She's very sorry that she panicked and screamed. She asked me to meet with you. She's truly sorry you were arrested."

Dimitar stared helplessly at the man.

Svetianna's father continued, "I've had a long discussion with the judge. However, the verdict has been recorded and it cannot be changed." He looked at the dejected prisoner beside him and continued, "There is an alternative to the twenty years in prison that the judge is obligated to sentence you." He paused, and then asked, "Do you want to hear it?"

Dimitar answered without hesitation, "Yes please."

To his surprise, Dimitar was released the next day and driven to an ominous gray stone building on the outskirts of Sofia and placed in the custody of the Bulgarian Secret Service. He was greeted formally by a gruff plainclothes agent who informed Dimitar he would be assigned to assist a group of agents in the 7th Division. His handler, who spit out his surname Botev, proudly told the young conscript that the 7th Division was dedicated to eliminating Bulgarian dissidents abroad and others inside the country that were harmful to the state.

Three days later, Dimitar was issued a driver's license, a passport and the required travel documents and immediately flown to Rome accompanied by another silent minder. In Rome he was met by Andrei Petcov, a senior agent who immediately confiscated his passport and drove him to the Bulgarian Embassy on Via Pietro D. Rubens.

The young Bulgarian was informed that Petcov would be his direct superior. He was given a hand held radio and ordered to keep it with him at all times. Within a week Petcov found the young conscript a small apartment and menial job with an Italian construction company that was overseeing the construction of a new residence wing within the Bulgarian Embassy compound. Petcov also reminded the young Bulgarian that his mother and sister, still living in Sofia, were under constant surveillance by the agency.

Young Dimitar Botev knew his only alternative at that moment was to work hard at his job and respond immediately whenever Petcov called.

Now at twenty-seven, Dimitar a tall, cheerful, round-faced hard worker, had become one of the drivers of the two heavy dump trucks owned by Lombardi Construzione, the Bulgarian Embassy contractor.

The heat of the day had waned. It was a cool pleasant Wednesday evening in Trullo. People strolled or talked in small groups on the narrow sidewalks while children played kickball and tag in the cobblestone streets. Dimitar sat with his hands caressing a cup of espresso at a sidewalk café mulling over the call he'd received earlier that afternoon.

He had just finished his lunch of bread, sausage and espresso while sitting on the ground in the shade of his truck parked on the construction site of a large apartment building when his radio buzzed.

"Botev, take your truck. Meet Todor Bukhalov in the parking lot of the Airport Marriott Hotel. *Go now.*" It wasn't Petcov; the harsh voice was as much a threat as it was a command.

Dimitar informed the foreman that his truck had an oil leak and he was going to the garage. Then, aware of Bukhalov's brutal reputation, Dimitar drove uneasily to the hotel parking lot.

Tonight Dimitar was still unable to comprehend all that had happened earlier that day or why the 7th Division had been so eager to kill the man in the green sedan. Even after pushing the car clear of the road he had braked, hesitating to shove it down the slope. Bukhalov had then slapped Dimitar in the head and crushed the young driver's foot on the accelerator with his boot. Having never fired a rifle before, Dimitar had even tried to do so in a feeble bravado to escape more abuse from the brute. He wished the events of this afternoon had never happened and prayed that the man in the car had survived. Dimitar knew he must find a way to escape the stranglehold the Secret Service had on him and his family.

He also remembered Bukhalov's words, "Your fat ass better be at the meeting tonight or I'll come after you. *Shiban Petal*, You fucking fag."

The meeting was to be held eight blocks from his apartment in an old tavern that was frequented by Eastern Europeans who drank, talked, smoked, and played dominos and card games.

Two old men rested at a table beneath a faded red, white and green stripped canvas canopy in front of the place. Tattered edges of the canopy hung like pieces of laundry from its rusted metal frame. A wooden board covered with dominos sat on an overturned vegetable box between them. One man, in an aged black fedora, sat away from the table leaning on his cane. The other, in an open-neck gray work shirt, sipped from a cracked white ceramic mug.

Deciding to be a few minutes late in an attempt to show those at the meeting he wasn't one of them, Dimitar made a point to stop and chat. He also believed to fail to appear at all would also mark him for elimination like the car driver this afternoon.

The tavern's long narrow room was dark except for a cloth covered light hanging above a table in the center of an alcove in the rear. A wooden bar with liquor bottles stacked on shelves behind it stood in front of a brick wall to Dimitar's left. Old metal chairs and round tables were stacked along the wall to the right giving the impression that someone planned to clean the worn tile floor. A heavy smell of tobacco permeated the place. He walked cautiously down the center of the room toward the alcove. Four men sat under the light at the square table cluttered with short drinking glasses and ashtrays. Two bottles of Balkan Vodka and a bottle of Bulgarian Brandy stood on a stand next to them. A heavy cloud of gray cigarette smoke hovered above. They spoke in the hard western Bulgarian dialect from Sofia.

Noticing Dimitar standing in the shadow, Bukhalov stood up from the table and grabbed an empty chair a few feet away. "Botev, sit down."

Dimitar accepted the chair and sat down.

Petcov, his contact, and the assistant press secretary at the Bulgarian Embassy, nodded toward him.

Dimitar remained silent.

Petcov addressed the others, "Kalina is one of our most effective agents so I assigned her to the Vatican. She's been fucking the manager of the Vatican printing office for over a year. The guy's like a faucet; every time she turns him on he gushes with information. Although much of what he gives us has turned out to be minor, occasionally there's a useable gem. And after one of their sweaty sessions four weeks ago, her pigeon commented how unusual it was for the Commandant of the Swiss Guard Regiment to personally appear at his print shop on short notice to order a special invitation for a ceremony when all the other invitations had been sent out months earlier. And when her Vatican pigeon added that the invitation was for a Professor Allen from an American military school, it alerted her." He paused, and then continued, "Of course, she relayed this information to me, and as required, I immediately transmitted it directly to the division in Sofia." Pleased with his statement, Petcov sat down.

"Well, then, I guess you and our gallant girl are both heroes!" The speaker glared at Petcov. "But an experienced control agent would have had Kalina turn on her, as you say, *faucet*, until she knew the fucking American professor's blood type."

The gravelly words sent a chill through Dimitar; it was the same voice that had ordered him to meet Bukhalov in the hotel parking lot that afternoon.

The broad shouldered gravely voice with long sideburns and a dark brushed moustache, whom Dimitar had never seen before, stood and eyed the three others at the table, "All it took was for me to have a phone call made to that American WestPoint military school to confirm that a Professor Allen did not teach there; he's fucking CIA."

The others seemed in awe of the individual.

"Well, I did follow the American after he took our picture in the Piazza and I was able to photograph him near the Spanish Steps," Petcov responded anxiously… and then added, "At least we now have a photo of him."

The leader turned on Petcov, "And if you had followed the American as I ordered and not spent you time sniffing the skirts in the square, you would *not* have seen me in the crowd and that bastard wouldn't have had an opportunity to photograph the two of us. And if he was able to survive the crash and fire, he will now be able to identify us."

The other person Dimitar didn't recognize addressed the leader. "Is he really CIA?" The tall, athletic looking man, about the same age as Dimitar, appeared to be making an attempt to dilute the confrontation

The leader sat down and drummed his fingers on the table, then poured a shot of vodka into his glass from the Balkan bottle on the stand. "No matter who he is, he isn't a fucking professor, and he knows about the project."

Knocking his chair over, Bukhalov stood and spoke for the first time. "It doesn't matter who he is. He's dead! Burned to pulp!" He turned and eyed Dimitar. "Botev, tell them what you saw!"

They scrutinized Dimitar as if he had just emerged through the wall.

Shaken by the attention, Dimitar pushed his chair back and slowly stood. "I saw the car roll down the slope and burst into flames."

"But did either of you see the body? The leader slammed his fist on the table and glared at both of them.

They shook their heads and mumbled, "*No.*"

The leader stood and glared at the remaining two seated at the table. "Find out who he is and verify he's dead." He then slammed his glass down on the table and walked over to Dimitar.

Dimitar stumbled backward, bumping into his chair. His fear of this man had escalated rapidly in the last few moments.

"Botev, you were never here tonight." The leader stood directly in front of Dimitar. His dark eyes were fierce and his face was so close that Dimitar was forced to inhale his heavy cigarette breath. The leader reached up and locked a strong hand on the young Bulgarian's shoulder. He spoke so only Dimitar could hear, "Understand me. You were never here tonight, nor did you see that car crash and burn today."

The man returned to the table and Dimitar took another chair further away from the group. Everyone ignored him. It was more difficult to follow their conversation from his new seat, but the few words Dimitar did hear made him extremely uncomfortable: *Papist*, *Turkish shooter*, *find the American prick*, *soft-kill.*

Shifting slightly, Dimitar's chair scraped against the tile.

The leader looked up realizing Dimitar was still there. He growled, "Botev, go home. Forget you were here!"

It had been an exhausting day for Colonel Pfyffer. He had risen well before dawn to oversee the final preparations for the Holy Father's special morning Mass for the guardsmen, their families and their friends in front of the beautiful Grotta di Lourdes in the manicured Vatican gardens. It was also necessary for him to review the precise timing of the initiation ceremony. Then in rapid succession, he had joined those attending the Mass, reviewed the regiment at the sweltering, mid-day initiation ceremony and then met with President Reagan's messenger. For the remainder of the afternoon, he had greeted the guards' families and friends at a reception.

It was approaching five-thirty when he stole time to seclude himself in the quiet of his office. After locking the door, he opened the safe and removed the book that the American had delivered earlier. He turned the seamless plastic container over in his hands, reached into his top desk drawer, took out a pocket knife and slit the plastic casing. He placed the book in the center of his desk and tossed the plastic into the wastebasket. After a few moments staring at the book cover, he walked to the credenza and poured himself a glass of wine. He took a sip of wine, opened the book and scanned a few pages of what appeared to be a history of the West Point Academy. Realizing he needed to be more refreshed to focus on the contents of chapter twelve, he closed the book, took another sip of wine, and sat back in his chair.

The ringing phone woke him instantly. It was his wife, Beatrice, reminding him they had reservations for dinner. He checked the brass encased clock on his desk. "*My God, it's seven o'clock*. He returned the book to his safe and spun the lock.

"What was going through your mind today, Franz, Beatrice asked. You seemed distracted?"

It was eight-thirty and they sat together enjoying their coffees after a light pasta dinner at a sidewalk table under the wide awning of the Ristorante Borgo Nuovo, a short walk from Vatican City's Saint Ann's Gate.

He responded to her question with what was becoming a routine reply for most of the questions he didn't want to answer. "I guess I'm slowing down."

Noticing the disappointed look on her face, he reached across the table and put his hand on top of hers. "Beatrice, I'll be sixty-four at the end of the summer. We've been here almost ten years. Maybe it's time to return to Lucerne, or travel; whatever you want."

"Franz, I know these past three years have been so very difficult for you. Even with all of the rumors and intrigue surrounding the death of John Paul I, you've kept the regiment focused. And now with the animosities that have emerged toward John Paul II, you've never wavered in your devotion to any of the popes you've served."

Much of what Beatrice knew of the problems and intrigue within the Vatican she'd gleaned from others living there.

About the size of London's St. James Park, the Vatican was comparable to a high walled medieval village. Although more than twelve-hundred people of many talents and trades worked daily in the Vatican, only four hundred or so actually lived in it, and the Swiss Guard Regiment and their families accounted for more than a quarter of those.

On many occasions, Beatrice knew more of what was happening within the Vatican than the colonel did. After Sister Vincenzia, the personal housekeeper of Pope Paul I, found his lifeless body slumped in his bathroom around 4:30 am after only 33 days in office, the nun was immediately sworn to silence and quickly whisked off to a monastery by Cardinal Villot, the Vatican senior administrator. Like many working in the Vatican, Beatrice questioned the contradictory statements regarding the pontiff's death that were issued by Villot and other senior cardinals because it was widely known that John Paul I had planned to demote Villot and a number of other cardinals for their membership in an outlawed Freemason Lodge.

Beatrice later learned from one of the maintenance men that a gardener had discovered Bishop Marcinkus, President of the Vatican Bank, in the papal gardens outside the pope's palace shortly after the pope's body was found even though the bishop habitually began his day at the bank much later in the morning. It was also widely known that the deceased pope planned to dismiss Marcinkus and other Vatican Bank officials that were under investigation by Italian authorities for a number of serious banking irregularities. The fact that Villot, Marcinkus and the others remained in their positions after the death of John Paul I whom she admired greatly had Beatrice saddened and discouraged.

Pfyffer, on the other hand, remained as much aloof of Vatican intrigue as he could and focused his energies on his responsibility for the safety of the Holy Father and only confided his goals and plans for the regiment to his wife.

Beatrice reached across the table for his hand and said softly, "It's been a struggle Franz; maybe its time for the regiment to have a younger, more qualified leader."

He wiped his mouth with his serviette. "More qualified?"

"Well, I only mean,....that with today's advanced technologies and the increase in tension and violence in the world, maybe a younger more energetic man well versed in modern police matters is needed. I don't know... I do know I'm tired."

Usually after dinner on such a pleasant spring evening, they would walk through the narrow streets of the Borgo for half an hour or so. They knew most of the residents of this closely knit neighborhood bordering the Vatican. However, tonight Pfyffer begged off and the two of them walked hand in hand back toward St. Anne's Gate.

As they approached the gate, Pfyffer leaned into her. "You know Beatrice, I really miss the warmth of Luciani. As John Paul I, he would have initiated the changes this church desperately needs."

The two Swiss guards, dressed in their informal blue uniforms and tasseled capes, saluted.

"Good Night, Commandant and Mrs. Pfyffer."

The evening was still young when Dimitar fell asleep extremely drunk on the stairway leading up to his apartment.

It was after midnight when someone shook him.

He woke with an aching head and a throbbing pain in the knee he'd cracked stumbling up the steps.

"Dimitar, better get to bed," a gentle female voice whispered. His pretty young Italian neighbor stepped over him and followed her boy friend up the steps to their apartment.

Groggily, Dimitar reached for the banister and hit his head on the wall. One of his shoes was missing. He saw it laying a few steps below. With one hand holding tightly to the banister, he grabbed the shoe and slowly made his way up the stairs and down the hall to the toilet just before he peed his pants. He opened his apartment door and stumbled to the sink attached to the wall next to his bed. He turned on the faucet and cupped cold water over his head and then matted his hair with a frayed towel and fell onto the unmade bed.

Santa Marinella, the Mediterranean coast

7

Just before midnight, Claudette parked the Fiat convertible in the Piazza Trieste in the center of the seaside town of Santa Marinella. She and McHugh got out and looked toward the Hotel. In the daytime, the small boutique Hotel L'Isola's bright orange façade and ocean blue shutters offered a welcoming sight. Featured on the cover of many area tourist guides, it was McHugh's preferred hotel when he had business in the area. And as usual, Mr. Firpo, the long time hotel manager had reserved McHugh his favorite room: third floor, south end, sea view. Tonight, in the dark, the hotel appeared gray and haunting. The only welcome offered were the soft illuminations of the ground lights beneath the hedges and trees in the manicured lawn surrounding the hotel.

They walked up the broad drive and entered the intimate lobby. No one was behind the front desk. McHugh took Claudette by the hand and led her up the three flights of carpeted stairs to his room. He removed the laminated privacy tag hanging from the door knob and slowly opened the door a few inches. Glancing behind the door, he noted the location of his small folded cardboard *flag*. Convinced no one had entered his room since he left; he opened the door fully and followed Claudette into the room. He stopped to pick up the *flag*.

"What's that?" She said.

"Just an amateur security device." He showed her the eight inch by eight inch piece of cardboard that he had folded in half and placed against the door before he squeezed out of the room that morning.

Claudette just smiled and walked over to the window and opened the drape.

McHugh tossed the piece of cardboard on the bed and checked his other two security signs. His hand held calculator sat at the precise angle in which he had placed it on top of his brief case. He picked it up and opened the case. The West Point recruiting brochure was in the exact cocked position on top of the other academic papers he brought to enhance his professor persona.

"It's lovely; now I know why you prefer this room. The palm trees and ocean offer a beautiful view and the sea breeze is wonderfully refreshing."

She closed the drape and turned toward him "But why does a businessman need to make home-made security devices?"

He took her hand. "When I returned to my Johannesburg hotel room on my first business trip to South Africa, I noticed my business papers had been rifled. The next day I mentioned my concern to my clients and they responded nonchalantly that it was probably just a Bureau of State Security agent verifying my legitimacy. Since that experience, I have set signs whenever I feel uncomfortable about a situation or location. Because of my security set-ups I know for a fact that when I traveled to last year to Libya and previously to Argentina my hotel rooms were searched."

She smiled at how serious he sounded and kissed him on the cheek. She released her hand from his and went into the bathroom.

As soon as the door closed, McHugh went to the bed, lifted the mattress and retrieved his real passport, driver's license and credit cards. He opened his suitcase, took off the Rugby shirt and cut-off trousers and slipped into his jogging gear. After placing the Rugby shirt and torn trousers on top of the other clothes he had not worn, he closed the case and set it by the door. To give the impression the bed had been slept in, he rumpled it and then knocked on the bathroom door.

Claudette opened it immediately and handed him a zippered leather case.

He stepped back, surprised. "Oh, I was about to ask you to bring out my travel kit."

Earlier, they had decided it was best not to stay at the hotel. She had invited him to remain at her apartment where they could solidify a travel plan. McHugh picked up the suit case, closed the room door and they walked back down the steps, stealing past the empty front desk.

In the morning, he planned to call Firpo and apologize for not checking out properly.

At a small table near the rear of the Harbor Café, the teenage waiter was so absorbed with the girl sitting across from him that didn't notice Claudette and McHugh take seats at one of the tables on the outside terrace. When the waiter eventually noticed the two of them, he rose, kissed his girl friend on the forehead and brought out a menu. McHugh ordered the local red wine and Claudette selected a medium-size focaccia; a local cheese-less pizza.

It was a clear starry night and the fresh harbor breeze was invigorating. Anchor lights on the sail boats and small yachts moored in the harbor danced on the rippling water.

McHugh felt guilty, not revealing to Claudette all the details of his predicament, particularly since she has agreed to help him leave Italy.

The waiter brought a carafe of wine and the pizza.

McHugh attempted to lift the carafe and stretch across the table to pour her wine with his right arm but put it down immediately wincing in pain.

"You shouldn't do that, let it heal," Claudette chastised.

"Thank God I'm left handed," he said, and pushed the carafe toward her.

He lifted his glass and looked directly into her eyes. "Claudette, I want you to know how much I appreciate your help, but this may become extremely dangerous. Only drive me half way to Milan. Go as far as Livorno or Pisa and return home. That way you'll not be danger. I can then take a bus the rest of the way to Milan and catch the fast train to Zurich. I've taken that train before."

She just sipped her wine, took a small piece of the pizza and looked over his shoulder to the bobbing boats in the harbor.

Finally she said, "Well, Colin McHugh, whether you like it or not, I'm going all the way to Switzerland with you. I know you need me; you just haven't had the time to think through your situation."

He leaned back in his chair and stared at her.

"Your friends will be searching for an American professor traveling alone, right?"

He nodded.

She held up her hand before he could comment. "They certainly won't be looking for a couple…us. And if these people are as serious as you've told me, we should also make some changes. First I'll cut your hair a little, and then I'll change into my jogging gear. They're looking for a single professor-type, not an athletic couple traveling in sport clothes. Maybe ball caps will help. Yours will cover your head bandage." She paused. "And glasses."

She took a sip of wine. "No matter who is after you, by yourself you are easy to spot and follow. You'll not be a match for them… but maybe with the two of us." She stopped, and then continued, "You're a good man. I've been single now for three years and all I get are guys hitting on me. Last night we talked for hours about a number of things just as friends would. Not once did you hint or imply anything further. It was refreshing to meet a gentleman, and that was why I suggested we have dinner tonight. The drive to Milan and train to Zurich will at least let us continue that conversation."

He smiled warmly at her. "As we Yanks sometime say, you knock my socks off."

"Well, it's going to be at least a six hour drive to Milan, so I think we should take my mother's Mercedes instead of my cramped Fiat Spider. It'll make a more comfortable trip."

He extended his hand across the table and put it on top of hers. "Thanks." He sat back. "I like your thinking, but as soon as we arrive in Milan, I insist we part and you head back home. I'll take the train to Zurich by myself."

They drove back to Claudette's condominium and she trimmed his hair with a scissors and then shaved the back of his neck with an electric razor. Handing him a small mirror and planting a warm kiss on his cheek, she asked, "What do you think?"

"I'm a new man….in many ways,"

She smiled, "I'll be right back with my mother's car. I think we should start as early as possible."

At the door she turned, "Now go to bed."

Early Thursday Morning

8

It was drizzling when McHugh heard her return. The patter of rain drops and the smell of the sea drifted through the open bedroom windows. He was nude, and had been sleeping on his back on the far right side of the large bed with his injured right arm resting along his side and his left arm extended across the width of the bed. The sheet lay crumpled at his waist.

He watched her remove her damp clothes, shadowed by the night light. And he pretended to sleep when she slipped under the sheet and curled onto his extended good arm.

"Hi," he said, lifting her onto him with the arm. She hugged him, careful of his right shoulder.

They were eager for each other, yet slow in their initial explorations. Their caresses were mature and caring, as if they were aware of each other's needs. She moved slowly down between his legs, her lips lingering along the length his body. Straddling his left leg, she began to caress and satisfy his erection. Then sensing her need, he gently lifted her head and looked into her wanting eyes. Strands of her long damp hair fell over her firm nipples. He clutched her breasts as she gracefully mounted him. Her movement accelerated into a fury he had never experienced. And when her body exploded, she collapsed satiated onto his chest in a trembling sweat. Then with her arms still around his neck, she caressed his left ear with her lips. He held her close for the longest time and listened to the raindrops, while gently stroking her sweaty backside.

They said nothing; just fell asleep in their own time.

Colonel Pfyffer woke in a sweat with words whirling over and over in his head, "*Let us pray to the Lord so he keeps violence and fanatics away from the Vatican walls. Let us pray…Let us pray…*" He glanced at the bedside clock as he rolled away from his wife, slipped out of his side of the bed and headed to their small bathroom. It was 4:30 am.

While he showered, struggling to wake up, it dawned on him that the Holy Father had pronounced those very words yesterday morning in front of the Grotta di Lourdes. While scrubbing his face and neck with his usual rough pesternal wash cloth, he also knew that the Holy Father had somehow been made aware of the French emissaries visit to the Vatican and the threat to his life they had outlined.

He finished showering and prayed the words of the Holy Father weren't prophetic. He had to read Chapter Twelve immediately.

Dressed in a gray sweater, dark slacks and slippers, he quietly left the apartment and walked down to his office near the guard barracks. He unlocked the door and relocked it after entering. Turning to the ominous task at hand, he opened the safe and removed the book and quickly thumbed through numerous pages, finally reaching chapter twelve. It consisted of a single page. He read it over three times, etching each point in his mind:

An unimpeachable source at the highest level of the Soviet government has confirmed that General Secretary Brezhnev with the approval of the Soviet Politburo has ordered the assassination of Pope John Paul II.

Evidence acquired from secure communications between the KGB and the Bulgarian Durzhavna Sigurnost (Bulgarian State Security) confirms that the Bulgarian agency's 7th Department has been assigned to eliminate the Pontiff. Further verified information indicates East German Stasi ordered to provide financial and logistic support. An unconfirmed, but reliable source points toward assassin to have been recruited from outside Eastern Bloc. Assassin believed to be a Muslim who may have received training in Yemen.

Believe present Vatican internal security capabilities and procedures may rule out assassination attempt within the confines of

Vatican City itself. Believe attempt planned when Pontiff outside Vatican City proper or while traveling outside of Italy.

Recent increase in secure and unsecured communications traffic and personnel movements indicate final planning completed. It appears plotters now awaiting opportunity. Suggest immediate increase in security and vigilance.

Repeat: *This page cannot be copied. It will now evaporate in four hours*

It was obvious that the Americans had employed their most sophisticated intelligence gathering technology to offer such definitive information. It was also clear to him why the American messenger had explained that his government had decided there was a significant risk in providing the same information to the Vatican hierarchy as the French had previously done.

Pfyffer sat back in shock at the magnitude of what he had just read. One of the world's superpowers had not only planned to assassinate the leader of the world's largest organized religion; *but the assassination attempt could happen in the very near future.*

Suddenly the realization that the clock was ticking hit home, even though the timing of the attempt was never mentioned. And even if the Holy Father did believe that he would be protected by the hand of God, at least at this moment, Pfyffer knew that the guard regiment and he must stand alone against the threat.

His hands began to shake; the full burden of this responsibility engulfed him. *My God, this can't happen. Help Me*"

He knelt at his desk and prayed.

After about ten minutes, there was a knock on the door.

"In a moment," he replied, and crossed himself. He rose and tossed the book into the safe, closed the door and spun the lock. He crossed himself again, and then unlocked his office door and opened it.

"Good Morning, Colonel." The sergeant of the guard said, saluting. "May I bring a cup of coffee?"

"Thank you, Geiger that would be nice." As the sergeant turned to go, Pfyffer questioned, "All secure?"

"Yes sir. I' m about to wake the next watch."

Pfyffer left his office door ajar, returned to his desk and opened his leather bound planner. Checking the official Vatican schedule, he verified that the next occasion on which the Holy Father was scheduled to leave the confines of the Apostolic Palace was next Wednesday afternoon May 13th, for his usual general audience in St. Peter's Square.

The style of Pope John Paul II made one hundred percent security impossible. He insisted on being close to *his* people. He didn't have a bullet-proof vehicle surrounded by armed secret service guards. During his audiences in St. Peter's Square, he stood in the back of an open jeep that moved slowly along a prearranged route edged with temporary barricades so close to the Holy Father that he could reach out and touch the people standing directly behind the barricades.

Phyffer was somewhat pleased that his new evacuation plan to immediately transport the Holy Father to Gemelli Polyclinic Hospital, if he was ever injured, during one of the Wednesday general audiences had recently been put in place. However, Pfyffer was also concerned that the Inspectorate General of the Vatican police, who reported directly to the Vatican City Commission, composed of a number of the very cardinals that met with the French emissaries, was also aware of the French meeting but had not shared that information with him.

Deciding to retain the American intelligence, Phyffer realized he had to find a way to discreetly reinforce the Swiss Guard for next Wednesday's general audience.

Normally, two thirds of his guardsmen were on duty assigned to stations in corridors and galleries within the Vatican and in front of the Pope's private apartment in the Apostolic Palace.

However, during Wednesday afternoon general audiences when the pope ventured out of the Palace, the number of manned stations within it were reduced. The Arch of the Bells, the Bronze Doors and St. Anne's Gate entrances to Vatican City were never left unguarded.

On all Wednesday afternoon appearances, senior Swiss Guard officers and selected Vatican police officers in plain clothes accompanied the Pope's jeep as close in body guards. Another group of guardsmen and Vatican police along with a few Italian Secret Service agents, all in plain clothes, mingled in the crowd in the Piazza.

The question now was how to increase the Swiss Guard presence without causing scrutiny from the Vatican hierarchy or questions within the guard itself. Pfyffer needed to talk with someone who would appreciate the situation and decided to call his friend Angelo Macari, a retired Rome police superintendent. Angelo had been the Italian police liaison officer in the Vatican in 1972 when Pfyffer arrived and they had instantly become fast friends, usually sharing lunch two or three times a month.

Now they only lunched a few times a year when Angelo visited Rome from his home in Tivoli, thirty-five kilometers away.

It was early, approaching seven, and McHugh, alone in the large empty bed, was relishing thoughts of the night before. He smelled coffee and glanced up to see Claudette standing naked in the bedroom doorway holding two cups of the steaming brew. The soft light from the hallway outlined her statuesque figure.

"We'll never get to Milan if you continue staring at me"

He sat up.

She handed a cup of coffee to him and sat down on the edge of the bed. "I'll never forget last night," she whispered and touched his cheek.

He returned his empty cup to her, marveling at the nonchalance and uninhibited ease she had with him.

As they showered together McHugh savored their intimacy and knew Claudette felt the same. They dried each other and then affectionately embraced.

McHugh tossed his suitcase into the open trunk of the Mercedes with his left hand and was about to shut it when Claudette touched his shoulder.

"Wait." She tossed in a small overnight bag next to the suitcase.

He turned. "What's that for? You're returning here."

"Well, just in case." She immediately moved to the driver's door.

He closed the trunk and opened the passenger door. When he sat down in the luxurious leather seat, Claudette placed on his lap what looked like a cigar box covered in brown leather.

"Maybe you can use this."

He opened the box and lifted a Walther P38 Lugar out of the green felt lining inside.

He turned and stared at her.

"My father confiscated it from a captured German Major after the battle at Anzio in 1944. He said it was his memento of that dreadful time. He really never talked about the war or his part in it. But, Sergio, our family chauffer, told me years ago that father was a hero and lead the Italian underground forces in our area in support of the American Parachute Regiment during the Anzio invasion. Sergio never told me more than that; probably at father's request. The Luger is in excellent condition. Claudio fired it at a fox last summer and set it on a shelf in the barn near my mother's parked car. He keeps it loaded, just in case. There should be two magazine clips in the box. I thought we should take it with us."

McHugh pressed the release catch and a magazine dropped out of the pistol butt into his hand. The magazine held eight shells. He slapped it back and heard the catch click. Then he locked the safety and placed the pistol back into the box.

"All I want to do is leave Italy as soon as I can and return to the states. We don't need this…but thanks any way." He handed it back to her.

Claudette placed the box under her seat and started the car. Using her remote, she opened the garage door and drove out of the garage into an early morning foggy mist.

Her plan was to drive the initial 420 kilometers to Genoa along the coastal A12 highway and then turn inland for the final 150 kilometers into Milan. She handed a Michelin map to McHugh and pointed out the route. "Depending on the traffic and weather we should be in Milan by mid afternoon."

"If we're lucky…and this weather clears." He answered doubtfully. Then he eased into the soft leather and watched the windshield wipers beat rhythmically back and forth like a metronome urging a struggling piano student.

She caressed his leg. "In a way, we're both lucky…so far. Now put your seat back and relax."

Claudette tuned the radio to Rai 3, Rome's classical music station and adjusted the volume of a Vivaldi concerto to a level just above the quiet hum of the car's purring engine.

The loud pounding on the apartment door shattered Dimitar's sleep. He scowled at his bedside clock. It was five o'clock, at least an hour before he planned to rise for work.

The pounding increased.

He rose, put on his trousers and slipped into his shirt, then grudgingly made his way to the door, "Who's there?"

"Botev open up." It was Petcov. Fear gripped Dimitar. He rubbed his eyes, straightened his shirt, and opened the door.

Petcov didn't enter. "Botev, call your company and take the day off. Tell them anything; you're sick …what ever you want. It doesn't matter to me."

Dimitar, still not completely awake, just stared.

"Wake up, you fool. Meet me in the parking lot of the Airport Marriott Hotel at one o'clock this afternoon." He handed a roll of Lira to Botev, and then turned and walked back down the stairs.

Dimitar closed the door as soon as Petcov's head disappeared down the steps. He threw the roll of bills on the table next to his bed and fell back into it. He knew he was being drawn into something sinister and didn't want any part of it. He also knew he had no choice. Their leash on him was tightening. Reluctantly, he rose, splashed a handful of cold water on his face and changed his shirt, then went down the stairs to make the phone call from the vegetable market.

"Dimitar, you're up early." Emilio, the proprietor exclaimed, while continuing to stack mandarin oranges into a pyramid on a square wooden table in front of the market entrance.

"Have to do private business today," Dimitar responded and paid for the phone call and three of the oranges.

Just after eleven, Dimitar washed in his small sink, changed into a fresh shirt and dark trousers and went down to the coffee bar at the end of the street and ordered an espresso and baguette from Angelo, the blind proprietor.

As usual, Angelo wore his straw boater's hat with the wide ribbon of the Italian red, white and green colors wrapped around its crown. Dimitar had a warm feeling for Angelo. Though blind, he proudly wore Italian colors he couldn't see and cheerfully served people he couldn't identify. Bonifila, his wife, was perched nearby on a stool behind the counter watchful that customers didn't cheat her husband.

"Why you're not working?" she asked.

"Have a meeting," Dimitar answered defensively.

He paid for the morning La Repubblica newspaper, espresso and baguette, making sure Bonifila noticed that he had included a large tip.

He hurriedly scanned the newspaper while eating. The crash and fire of the green sedan wasn't even mentioned. Realizing he could no longer delay he took a final bite of the baguette, discarded the paper on another table, and then walked around the corner to the taxi stand.

While surveying the parking lot, Dimitar stepped out of the taxi and slipped his fare through the driver's open front window. It was familiar now. The space where he parked the dump truck the day before was vacant. The nearby cars were empty and none of those parked farther away moved toward him.

He paced back and forth along the curb that edged the lot wondering why he was ordered to be here. He visualized the inferno he'd seen in the rear view mirror as he drove away from the flaming field and became anxious. He nixed the thought of going into the hotel for another espresso realizing Petcov would be livid if he arrived and didn't find him waiting in the parking lot.

Minutes later, a black sedan similar to those used by Italian government officials sped into the parking lot and headed straight at Dimitar. Instinctively, he stepped off the curb onto the hotel grass. The sedan screeched to a stop a few feet in front of him.

The passenger door opened and Petcov commanded, "Botev, get in!"

When he sat down in the passenger seat, Dimitar noticed an attractive woman, about his age, with glistening blond hair, seated in the center of the rear seat. She wore a sheer white blouse revealing a substantial amount of cleavage. Her blue eyes made direct contact with his and her demure smile told him she was aware she was attractive.

Petcov nodded toward the woman, "Lubanov she works for me."

She smiled discreetly at Dimitar when he turned to acknowledge her.

"Take me to where you killed the American."

"Todor Bukhalov killed the American and…"

"Shut up." Petcov interrupted, "Let's go."

With minimal conversation, Dimitar coached Petcov through the narrow streets and onto the highway and into the turn-off road he had driven. When they drove onto the fractured tarmac, they noticed a light blue car with the white stripe of the state highway patrol parked next to the crushed hedge where Dimitar had backed the dump truck before ramming the sedan. The patrol car was empty. Petcov drove a short distance past it and parked on the edge of the road. He and Dimitar then walked back to the top of the slope. Two state highway policemen, in their recognizable dark blue jackets and sky blue trousers, walked around the burned-out wreckage writing in small notebooks.

Petcov grabbed Dimitar by the shoulder and they rushed back to the sedan. Petcov drove to the end of the road and then doubled back toward the hotel.

Without taking his eyes off the road ahead, Petcov ordered, "Kalina, show Botev the photograph."

She reached forward and dropped a photograph into Dimitar's lap.

He picked it up and saw that it was a color photograph of a tall man in a white dress shirt carrying a brown coat over his shoulder. In the background Dimitar also noticed the Spanish steps.

"Do you know him?" Petcov asked.

"No, I never saw him before," Dimitar said, handing the photo back over his shoulder to the girl who he now realized was the same Kalina he heard discussed in the tavern meeting the night before; the girlfriend of the Vatican print shop manager who printed the special invitation for the American professor.

"He was the man you killed yesterday," Petcov challenged.

Dimitar did not respond but now knew he was here for more than just guiding the two of them to the wreckage. He was being set-up for the murder if the American's body was found.

They arrived back at the Marriott parking lot and Petcov parked the sedan well away from the hotel entrance.

Kalina announced to Petcov, "We're aware the man isn't a professor at that West Point school. Before he arrived from Trieste, Herr Zhelov ordered the school to be called. The school confirmed that a Professor Allen did not teach at the school."

"I know all of that." Petcov growled and glared at her. "What's now important is to find the American bastard."

Now Dimitar realized that the name of the frightening leader of last night's tavern meeting and the voice that ordered him to meet in the hotel parking lot was the same, Herr Zhelov.

Kalina explained that Zhelov had ordered her to call all the American airline companies that had flights landing in Rome during the past three days; none reported that they had a man named Allen on any passenger manifests. All of the American-owned hotels in and around Rome were also contacted by others at the embassy with the same negative results. No airport car rental agency had a record of renting a car to either a Professor Allen or a Mister Allen.

Petcov seemed on edge, "What if he arrived on an airline other than an American airline or he came from another country?"

"Americans are insecure like sheep, Kalina snarled. "They all do the same things. He would have taken one of their airlines; he probably flew under another name."

The two of them seemed to have forgotten Dimitar. The tone of their conversation was becoming testy.

Dimitar appeared aloof but mentally made an effort to remember as much as he could of what they said. He knew it would be easy for them to return to Bulgaria if necessary, while without a passport he was bound to remain, making him the only target for Italian authorities.

"Did anyone show his picture at the hotels or car agencies, or are we going to only rely on phone calls." Petcov challenged.

"Zhelov will have the picture shown everywhere tomorrow." She paused, and then ended the discussion. "I am sure he has made detailed arrangements to do everything that should be done." She opened the rear door of the car and got out.

Dimitar watched her stroll toward the hotel lobby with her hips swaying one way, while her shoulder length blond hair flipped in the opposite direction.

"Fuck, small minds on big heads," Petcov said quietly, but loud enough for Dimitar to hear. He then looked around the car park, and then at Dimitar, "Shit, where is she?"

"She went into the hotel."

Petcov turned on the ignition and drove alongside the walkway leading to the hotel entrance.

Finally Kalina walked out of the hotel smiling.

Petcov opened his door and rounded the car to meet her.

Dimitar lowered his window to listen to their conversation.

"He's been here," she announced triumphantly.

"How…" but before Petcov could finish his question, she continued, "I showed the photo to the bell captain and he told me the American was in the cocktail lounge yesterday afternoon around four o'clock

"Well, go back in and let the bartender see the photo," Petcov ordered.

She snapped, "I did, but he wasn't on duty yesterday afternoon."

"Now go back in and ask him to give you the name of the bartender that was on duty yesterday… and get his address. Use your charm; offer him money, take off your pants, anything!"

She glared. "You animal, I..." She stopped abruptly, and then turned and sauntered back into the hotel.

Dimitar raised his window and Petcov returned to the driver's seat. It was almost an hour before Kalina opened the rear door and slumped into her seat.

"Well?" Petcov turned toward her.

"The bartender's name is Angelo and he lives about ten kilometers away in Ostia Antica," she said, tossing a piece of paper onto the front seat.

Glaring at Petcov, she declared "That's his address. He's leaving on holiday tomorrow for Palermo…and I kept my pants on."

Petcov drove the short distance to Ostia Antica, once the seaport of ancient Rome, now a tourist destination with excellently preserved ancient buildings, frescoes and mosaics. Ignoring the tourist sites he headed through the complex of working class high rise apartments on the city's west side until he finally found the street where the bartender lived.

"There he is." Kalina exclaimed, as they passed a young man loading luggage into an old, rusted Fiat.

Petcov drove around the block. He stopped the car and turned to her, "Well, go back there and use your damn charm to find out more about the American. You have a way."

Kalina gave him the two finger salute and jumped out of the car.

She turned the corner and walked back to the curb side of the Fiat. Picking up a fishing rod lying on the sidewalk, she handed it to the startled young bartender. They soon became engrossed in an animated conversation. With the loading completed and a promise from Kalina to visit the hotel lounge, the young man closed the hatch and walked toward the apartment complex.

Kalina ran back to the sedan, flung open the rear door and fell back into her seat.

Petcov turned to her. "Well?"

"He remembered the man and said that the American was in the lounge for about a half hour. He even remembered that the American had ordered Dewar's White Label Scotch with soda and had also asked for directions to the lobby phones to make an overseas phone call." She paused, then added, "The boy is also proud of the large tip the American gave him."

"Well, get to the point," Petcov growled.

"The boy believes the American may be staying at one of the small hotels along the coast near Santa Severa Castle."

"Why would he assume that?" Petcov snapped

"Just because he's young and a bartender doesn't make him stupid." She replied angrily, and then continued, "He told me that the American would probably have made the phone call from his room had he been staying at the Marriot," receiving no comment from Petcov, she continued, "Also, he said that the American asked how long it would take to drive to a Castillo de Santa Severa. And the bartender believes that the American might have been using the castle as a landmark to locate his hotel. He explained that when Americans ask for directions he usually directs them past a landmark that they remember is near their hotel, because they don't understand Italian road signs and metric measurement. And yesterday he believes that American asked about the castle because it may have been on the way back his hotel."

"Well where's the fucking castle?"

"Along the coast about thirty kilometers away," She answered.

"Now we go to the sea," Petcov said and turned on the ignition.

They dropped Dimitar off near a taxi stand.

Thursday Afternoon,
Milan, Italy

9

At about that same time Claudette eased the Mercedes into the middle of the horn-blaring traffic in Milan's city centre. As the large sedan crawled along with the slow moving mass of metal she and McHugh scanned in all directions looking for a place to park. Finally, they were able to turn into a side street just beyond the city's Duomo di Milano, the magnificent white marble gothic cathedral. Like the Italian she was, Claudette backed onto a curb among a maze of closely parked cars in a small cobblestone square. McHugh was amazed that she was able to fit the Mercedes into the tight space without adding a swatch of color from the two cars on either side of them.

Claudette unbuckled her seat belt and kissed him on the cheek, "I'll be right back, just stay in the car; don't get out." She cautiously opened her door and squeezed sideways between the car next to her and the Mercedes.

Examining his situation, McHugh realized he would have to exit the car the same way that she did. Unlike her, he was less concerned about being cautious here. After all, they were over six hundred kilometers away from the Bulgarians. And they now were looking for a man with shoulder length hair dressed as a businessman. Unable to see around him from inside the Mercedes, he slipped across the front seats and struggled out of the driver's door and stood on the door sill to look over the tops of the parked metal. He stretched and relaxed watching an animated conversation between two drivers standing along the side a classic red Fiat Ghia and assumed they were discussing how the driver of that classic car was going to maneuver out of the maze of vehicles without leaving a memento of red paint on one or more of the vehicles around it.

Twenty minutes later, he spotted Claudette rounding the corner of a nearby building followed by a tall hotel bell boy, in a red high-buttoned coat, pushing an upright luggage cart.

"I found a hotel that I know you'll like; it's only a few blocks from here."

"What about the car?" he asked.

"The concierge agreed to park it in a local garage until I return from Switzerland," she said, quickly turning her back to him and inserted the key into the car trunk.

"Switzerland, what the…?"

Before McHugh could continue, she said coyly, "A traveling couple should spend at least one night on the road together." She opened the trunk.

The boy retrieved their luggage and headed back to the hotel.

McHugh caught her arm just as she was about to close the trunk.

"What's this?" He lifted a piece of steel piping from the floor of the trunk. It was about twelve inches long and two inches in diameter.

"I think Serjio, our family driver, uses it as an extension over the short handle on the tire jack. He's older now and it probably gives him a little more leverage if he had to use it."

In the 'on guard' pose of a fencer, McHugh extended the steel pipe in his left hand and lunged forward thrusting it like a sword toward an imaginary opponent. "Well, maybe I can use it too." He slipped the pipe into the elastic waist band on the left side of his jogging pants. "I guess we're going to see Switzerland together."

She took his good arm and led him out of the square.

Their quiet little hotel was on a narrow street cluttered with antique shops and small art galleries, just behind the cathedral. The room was small, comfortable and very expensive. Claudette insisted on leading McHugh on a short tour of the Milan Cathedral and the Galleria Vittoria Emmanuele, Italy's most famous shopping arcade just off the cathedral square.

"It will ease your mind," she said.

"I'll stay here. I must call Stringer." He didn't tell her he had taken an extensive tour of Milan a couple of years before, including a wonderful evening at the opera at La Scala "Why don't you check the train schedules while you're out?"

She agreed and told him she would also buy athletic bags to replace his suitcase and the overnight bag she'd brought.

He handed his credit card to her, but she rejected it.

"Its better if I use my card, don't you think?"

"OK, but I owe you."

"And I plan to collect," she said and kissed him lightly on the cheek.

After she left, McHugh poured a Dewars scotch from the extensive bar stock and picked up the phone. First, he called the hotel to apologize to Firpo for leaving without checking out. The desk clerk informed him that Firpo wasn't in, but would return in the morning during breakfast. McHugh replaced the handset and made a mental note to call again in the morning. He then took the phone over to the couch and dialed Stringer's overseas number.

The Admiral answered enthusiastically. "Hey got your message. Congratulations. Bravo Zulu," He said, using the naval signal for *well done*.

Before McHugh could interject, Stringer continued. "Colin, where are you? When will you get back here to good old Yankee terra firma?"

"Hold it, Dan. I have serious problems. The Bulgarians in Rome that have been tagged to carry out the assassination know who I am and are trying to kill me. I'm marked for extinction."

"Why? Where are you?"

"I can identify some of those involved…" He remembered the guy with the cruel eyes and brush moustache in the piazza, "Maybe I can even identify one of the leaders.

Yesterday, while I was driving back to my hotel after delivering the book to Pfyffer, the bastards had a huge truck crash into my rental and pushed it off the road into a gully. I made it out of the upturned wreck. Then a trained sharpshooter fired high powered rifle shots into the upturned gas tank and then set the wreck an fire with a couple of shots from a flare gun. The asshole then sauntered back up the hill with a parting, Fuck you…, As soon as they discover that my charred body isn't in the burned out heap, they'll come after me."

"Do you think they know you're still alive by now?"

"Probably not yet. It happened in the countryside outside of Rome late yesterday afternoon. Hopefully, the earliest they might know is tomorrow. I'll be in Switzerland by then."

"Come on, Colin; where the hell are you."

"I'm in Milan and beat up a little. The roll down the hill in that metal hulk roughed me up a bit; I can't use my right arm. We're going to Switzerland tomorrow morning on the train."

"We? Who's we? How'd they know who you are? What are your plans? How can I help?" Stringer's concern was genuine.

"I've had the help of a friend and if I survive and get out of this country, I'm going to book the first flight I can out of Switzerland to anywhere in the good old U-S of A. The only way the bastards could have learned about my professor act was by a leak in Washington, probably one of the bureaucrats you pulled together to arrange this excursion. You have to find the bastard."

The Admiral ignored McHugh's comments. "Colin, my immediate concern is to get you back here. First of all," he continued in a command voice, "watch your back. That Bulgarian consulate in Milan is the main hovering nest for Bulgarian agents from all over Italy. They'll certainly be alert and on the street. Second, disguise yourself as much as you can and keep moving, preferably in crowds. Don't isolate yourself. Lastly, as soon as you arrive in Switzerland, call me and get your butt to the International Airport in Bern. The Swiss Air Force Command is there and I'll arrange to have a Gulfstream waiting for you."

Neither spoke for a few moments.

Finally, McHugh said, "We are disguised… as a couple traveling together in jogging gear. She cut my hair and took care of my cuts and bruises."

"A couple? Who's your female friend?" Stringer paused. "Be smart; don't keep a foreign civilian involved, particularly a female. Send her home now"

"Come on, Dan, she's none of your business. I'll discuss the entire situation when we meet. I'll call you again when we get to Zurich. Arrivederci." McHugh hung up just as Claudette walked in.

Feeling guilty, Stringer let the phone slip out of his hand. He had insisted to the National Security Advisor, and the President, that his friend was the only person for the task.

Maybe he shouldn't have been so dogmatic. He remembered the objection from the CIA member of the group who had compiled the information and put the mission together.

"Do you realize what you're saying? This McHugh is a businessman! He isn't trained; he's vulnerable. We're dealing with the most vicious state security organization in the East Bloc. Admiral, you need an experienced field agent."

Stringer cringed, recalling how he had dissected the CIA position. "First of all, time is of the essence. Second, the fact that McHugh is a seasoned international businessman with a business client just outside of Rome is a definite plus. And..., there is no reason for the opposition to have him on radar. And we don't know which of our field agents they might have under surveillance." He paused to let his comment sink in. "I know Pfyffer, the Swiss Guard Commandant personally and have been able to arrange for McHugh to meet with him discreetly. The Commandant will help, should it be necessary. We're just talking about an information drop and McHugh has been doing that for us for the past couple of years without a glitch.

Now all that the Admiral felt was fear. He picked up the phone and dialed the Commander of Andrews Air Force Base.

Claudette dropped her shopping bags just inside the door. "Your admiral friend?" she asked, pecking him on the cheek.

"It was him all right, and he'll have a plane waiting for me at the Bern airport. He's concerned about your safety." He took her by the shoulders, "He told me to send you home."

"You told him about me?"

"Not really, just that I'm traveling with the most desirable woman I've ever met and who she is, is none of his damn business." He smiled. "I didn't say that really, but maybe I should have. Anyway, he doesn't know who you are, except that you helped me."

"But, he ordered you to send me away,"

"I don't take orders from admirals anymore; my navy days are long gone. Besides, I like traveling with you...Enough, what did you spend your money on?"

He poured a scotch for her and then freshened his.

Claudette laid the purchases on the sofa. There were two black baseball caps with the orange *BWIN* logo of the AC Milan Football Club, two pair of sport sunglasses; one had broad white frames, obviously hers. To complete the look, she had purchased athletic wristbands, a tennis racket and two medium-size canvas athletic bags, one gray, one sky blue.

"Thank God you were only gone for an hour." He put his arm around her waist, "Why the wristbands and tennis racket?"

"Well, I remembered the piece of pipe you took from my mother's car, and thought you might need a way to carry it ready to use. If you could secure it in some way to your left forearm, you might be able to move it into your hand. I saw the wrist bands and bought them to see if they could work, and... I really do need a new tennis racket."

"Are you sure you're just an airline stewardess and not in the Italian Security Service?"

He paused. "I like the way you think, and travel, and smile and...."

"Stop it. Let's try it out,"

It worked; He put the bands on his left arm and worked the length of the pipe under the bands between his wrist and the crux of his inner elbow. The bands held the pipe comfortably in place, and after a few tries, he was able to move the pipe down by rubbing his arm against the side of his body until the pipe end was in his palm. Then he easily worked it into his hand using his fingers.

She handed him a small white plastic bottle. "Pain pills, like your Tylenol."

"As David Niven said in the movie, *Guns of Navarone*, "You're brilliant; you are,"

Early Thursday Evening
Rome, Italy

10

In a top floor apartment above the office of Banca d'Italia, on Via San Valentino Street in Rome's embassy district, Zhelov waited for phone calls from the agents he had set in motion to find the unknown American. The night before sources in the highway patrol reported that a complete search of the burned-out Alfa Romeo sedan revealed no evidence of a body in it or around the site. Whoever had driven the car had escaped.

The apartment had become Zhelov's home and command center since he'd arrived in Rome and he looked forwarded to abandoning it in less than a week. Prior to his arrival, agents dressed as movers had brought in plain metal furniture: a desk, a long table, a few chairs and a filing cabinet. There were no pictures or personal touches of any kind, if the coffee cups and dirty ash trays scattered on the table top were not included. The air reeked of cigarette smoke. A full-length sliding glass door, now covered by a large white bed sheet taped to the wall above it, opened onto a narrow balcony.

Zhelov pushed the sheet away, slid the glass door open and stepped onto the balcony to survey the surroundings. He could observe the tile roofs of the Bulgarian Embassy buildings secluded behind a ten foot-high cement wall half way down Pietro Rubens Street directly opposite the apartment. Tall cypress trees inside the wall further screened passers-by from any extended view of the embassy proper. The wall's peach color was fading, but the peach exterior of the embassy buildings appeared fresh.

Other agents posing as telephone workers had rigged overhead cables from the embassy to the apartment to enable Zhelov to communicate with Sofia and those involved with the project.

Zhelov liked to characterize the plot as a *project* because it implied organization and a successful conclusion. *And*, he thought, *my project had been on track until that fucking American had appeared.*

He recalled the commitment he'd made weeks before when the Deputy Director of the Interior Ministry had phoned him just before the final meeting in Trieste.

" Zhelov, Prime Minister Todorov wants you to have a face-to-face meeting with Horst Steiger and that Turkish fanatic to insure the project will be completed as planned. Make your own arrangements; no notes, no transcripts, no records."

"Where and when?" Zhelov asked.

"Make it quick, somewhere your friend Steiger and the Turkish anarchist can easily attend." Then the deputy director continued emphatically, "The Prime Minister demands your assurance that no matter what happens at the event in Rome, *Bulgaria will not be implicated in any way*. He insists you call me at the conclusion of your meeting and provide that guarantee. I plan to the record your phone call,... of course at his insistence."

Zhelov had easily selected Trieste.

He and Steiger, an East German Stasi agent, had met in Trieste three years earlier to arrange the financing and final plans to eliminate the Bulgarian dissident Markov in London. It had been easy to slip through the porous Italian border from Yugoslavia with their false passports. And even if they had been caught, they knew they could have easily bribed the underpaid Italian border guards. They had spent two days in the luxurious Excelsior Palace Hotel finalizing arrangements before Zhelov flew alone to London to ensure Markov's demise.
Meanwhile, Steiger had remained a few days to avail himself of the Italian and Slavic whores that worked in Trieste's seaport brothels.

Zhelov picked up the phone and dialed the East German's secure phone number.

"You're a fucking genius Zhelov, Trieste it is." Steiger continued, "And this time I insist you join me with one or two of the ladies."

"I'll arrange for your booking at the Excelsior Palace and send the details on to you tomorrow." Zhelov hung up with no intention of joining the Stasi agent on a night of carousing. His concentration had to focus on the Roman Pope. If successful, it would be his ticket to another promotion; if the attempt was compromised, it could mean a stint in a gulag or even a bullet in the back of his head. There were no other alternatives.

Zhelov next had phoned a secure number in Milan. It was immediately answered by Anton Kostov, his protégé, who had custody of the Turkish terrorist.

Young Kostov had been an undercover agent in the Sofia Youth Crime division before Zhelov recruited him. Kostov was a tall, thirty-year-old karate expert with an infectious smile that concealed the fact he'd eliminated a number of young malcontents using his honed martial arts skills.

"Herr Zhelov."

"Anton, I'm going to need you to bring that Turkish asshole to the Trieste safe house. I'll call shortly with details.`" He reminded Kostov of the address.

Zhelov heard the phone ring and took a last drag on his cigarette before flipping it over the railing. He returned to the room and picked up the phone, "Ya."

"Zhelov, we found the American!" Petcov pronounced excitedly.

"You found him? Where is he? Talk to me!" Zhelov commanded, while pouring a shot of vodka into one of the dirty glasses on the table. He circled the table and lit another cigarette, while cradling the phone to his ear with his shoulder.

Petcov continued, "His name is really McHugh and he's in Milano. Kalina and I drove to the coast and showed the American's picture at a number of small hotels. At a hotel in Santa Marinella, she gave the picture to the front desk clerk and he told her the American checked out this morning."

"Where's the bastard?" Zhelov interjected, "Tell me!"

"Our little whore knows how to make men to talk. Before she went in, she opened her blouse and hitched up her skirt. It worked; the clerk probably got a hard-on when he told her the American's name. McHugh's a businessman and has stayed at that hotel a number of times."

"Bik Laina! Toi e na TSRU!" Zhelov screamed in Bulgarian! - *Bull Shit. He's CIA.* - The Americans don't send businessmen. It's just a cover." He continued in a less agitated voice, "Well, tell me where he is now, whoever he is?"

"As I said, he's in Milano, but he is planning to go to Switzerland in the morning. The clerk told Kalina that McHugh had phoned earlier to apologize for not checking out of the hotel properly. He even promised to call and apologize to the manager in the morning. I don't know what Kalina told the clerk, but whatever it was, he also gave her the American's business card from the hotel file."

"You're sure he's in Milano?" Zhelov questioned.

"Ya, the American told the clerk he was calling from Milano."

"Petcov, where are you and Kalina now?"

"We're still in Santa Marinella."

"Stay there; let me think. I'll call you back; give me your phone number."

Zhelov poured more vodka, crushed out the cigarette, picked another from a pack on the table and walked back to the sliding glass door. He ripped the sheet down and stepped onto the patio. Knowing it wouldn't be in his best interest to ask headquarters in Sophia to arrange for the American's elimination in another country, he growled, "I have to silence that fucker before he leaves Italy."

His first reaction was to go to Milan and kill the American himself, but realized his place was here maintaining contact with those involved in the project. He needed someone with field experience that he could rely on to eliminate this businessman, McHugh. Kostov was the proper choice but he had his hands full with the Turkish assassin; Petcov was incompetent in the field and certainly no match for the American if he were to confront him; and Bukhalov was all muscle, who couldn't think beyond his nose. Realizing he had only one option, Zhelov walked back into the apartment and picked up the phone.

"Petcov, I want you to put Kalina on the next flight to Milano. Tell her I'll have someone meet her. Order her to phone me here at the apartment as soon as she arrives. And as soon as that plane takes off, call me. Then you pick up some food and get back here." After ending the call, he dialed a secure number in Milano.

Zhelov pulled a chair to the cluttered table, sat down and took the three-hundred thousand dollar Swiss bank deposit slip out of his leather passport wallet and reflected on the last meeting in Trieste with Steiger.

That afternoon, three weeks before, he'd sat at a table on the balcony of the Excelsior Hotel edging Riva del Mandracchio Boulevard along the Trieste harbor front and watched a lightning shower erupt to the northwest.

"Here you are Zhelov." Steiger announced in English as he stepped onto the balcony.

The two had barely tolerated with each other during their previous planning of the Markov poisoning.

Steiger, a 40 year old educated son of an officer in Hitler's SS Corps, considered Germans superior to all races. He had ascended rapidly through the Stasi ranks by his ability to procure information when others had failed. It didn't matter that the cruel and sadistic methods he used rivaled the worst of Hitler's Gestapo.

Steiger considered Zhelov, the 38-year-old son of a Sofia postman to be just an ignorant killer even though the Bulgarian held a higher position in the 7th Division than Steiger had achieved in the Stasi. It was known that as a teenager, Zhelov had sliced up a schoolmate who had criticized one of the teachers in the Unified Polytechnic School and had been immediately recruited and trained by the 7th Division of the Bulgarian Secret Service.

Steiger glanced toward the harbor. "The storm will wash the streets tonight?"

"Not tonight." Zhelov countered, "The streets will remain dry for your visit to the ladies. The storm's to the north, over Monfalcone and moving east."

Zhelov then grudgingly stood and extended his hand. "Steiger, good of you to come,"

"Did I have a choice?" grunted the newcomer, grasping the outstretched hand.

"No. And neither did I. I also have no choice but to take that Japanese recording device you always carry."

Steiger pulled the slim Sony recorder out of his coat pocket and handed it to Zhelov.

They sat down at the table and Zhelov poured two glasses of German Puschkin Vodka.

Raising his glass, Steiger said, "*Prost.* It seems that when the two of us meet, we're doing the grunt work for those fucking KGB bastards."

"They're smart. " Zhelov responded, "They'll never be caught holding the gun."

Steiger quickly added "Well, let's not be found with one either."

Noticing a steward in a white jacket standing inside the balcony glass doors, Zhelov motioned him forward. "Menus please."

The steward bowed and handed both of them ornate oversized one page menus and set the wine folder on the table next to Zhelov's place setting. He stepped back a few paces, then turned and returned to his position.

"Have you met this crazy Turk?" Steiger asked.

"Not yet, and he's *not* crazy. I have the bastard's dossier. He's a self possessed killer for hire. The KGB, *probably through you*, paid a high price to arrange for Agca to stroll out of that prison fortress dressed in a military uniform after he murdered the Turkish editor two years ago."

Steiger picked up the menu and began to study it. "Do you have any recommendations for dinner?"

"No." Zhelov focused on his Stasi acquaintance. "But a hand written comment in the dossier noted that on the day the Turk escaped he was paid to write a letter to a Turkish newspaper claiming that he would kill the papist if he visited Istanbul." He paused. "Who paid him, you or our friends in Moscow?"

Zhelov then took a sip of water and observed his Stasi tablemate over the top of the glass, "Steiger, it was a skillful ploy that established Agca as…. what were your words? *A crazy Turk*…. Why a Turk?"

The German grinned. "He's also a Muslim; and obviously the Gods of Red Square want the event to be religious, not political." He raised his glass, "*Prost*, let's eat."

Zhelov finally perused his menu and muttered just loud enough for Steiger to hear "The fucking Turk now belongs to me and he'll join the Muslim hereafter as soon as the Papist dies."

After dinner and a discussion of the assassination plan, including the mandate that they had to keep both East German and Bulgarian involvement secret at all costs; they exchanged new secure telephone numbers.

With nothing more to discuss, Steiger turned to look at the angry dark sky to the north.

Zhelov said, "I hope you have the funds."

"As instructed," Steiger responded, turning to him, "I've brought one-hundred thousand American dollars and a Swiss bank deposit slip for another three-hundred thousand for the Turk. I'm now out of this… It's all yours." He reached into the inside pocket of his coat and handed a bulky manila envelope to Zhelov.

Zhelov took the envelope and placed it in his travel case and returned the tape recorder to the German without comment.

They finished their coffees; the Bulgarian picked up the bill and left enough American dollars to cover it and a substantial tip.

Smiling, the waiter held open the balcony doors. Steiger led the way through the grand restaurant and down the wide marble staircase into the lobby. Just inside the massive glass doors, held open by a young bellman, he turned and extended his hand, "Good luck, Zhelov… You have my number if it's urgent."

After the German walked out of the hotel and turned out of sight heading toward the seafront, Zhelov asked the bellman to ring for a taxi.

Later that evening while relaxing in one of the two deep lounge chairs next to the stone fireplace in the safe house sitting room, Zhelov reviewed the Turk's dossier.

There was a knock on the door, and Anton Kostov stuck his head into the room. "May we come in?"

Zhelov nodded and crushed his cigarette out in the ashtray on the table next to his chair.

Mehmet Ali Agca entered the room and Kostov took a position directly behind him.

Although there were numerous photographs of the Turk in the dossier, it was the first time Zhelov had actually seen the assassin in person. Agca wore a dark blue knit sweater and expensive jeans. He was in his early twenties, tall, with cropped hair and high cheekbones. His eyes were dark, deep-set and focused on Zhelov.

Agca spoke in heavily accented English, "I kill the papist, like planned!"

Zhelov ignored the Turk and said to Kostov in Bulgarian, "Get the bastard one of the straight backed wooden chairs in the corner and have him sit facing me."

Kostov placed the wooden chair a few feet in front of Zhelov.

Agca calmly sat down and placed his hands in his lap.

With his eyes fixed on the Turk, Zhelov snarled, "You and I have only one thing in common. We're both murderers. You kill for financial benefit and notoriety. I eliminate those opposed to my country…*And I don't like you.*"

He set the dossier beside the reading lamp on the small table near his chair. Then he leaned forward; his face only inches from the Turk. "I just read your dossier. The champagne, luxury watches and elegant dinners are over. And no more vacations in Spain or Tunisia. The bureaucratic assholes that have entertained you for the past months have now handed you to me. You're a fucking contract killer and I am now your only employer. Understand that!"

Zhelov sat back into the comfortable chair. "You will do exactly as you are ordered to do by me or Kostov, or I will have you eliminated! Only when the papist is dead will you receive your pieces of silver."

The young Turk sat rigidly in the chair with his eyes fixed on his new employer.

Zhelov reached into his coat pocket and removed the envelope. He took out the stack of dollar bills and handed them to his protégé.

Then he turned to Agca. "There's one hundred thousand dollars in that stack and Kostov will provide any necessary funds he thinks you need until you kill the papist."

Then he handed the deposit slip to the Turk and pointed out the name of the Swiss bank and the 300,000 dollar amount of the deposit. "And either Kostov or I will see you that you receive this after it is finished"

Agca handed the deposit slip back without ever taking his eyes off of Zhelov.

Zhelov nodded to Kostov.

Stepping forward, Kostov touched Agca's shoulder.

The Turk made a perfunctory nod, stood and walked out of the room.

Kostov followed.

Zhelov also remembered the phone call he had made to the Deputy Director after Kostov and Acga left the room. "I've held the damn meetings that you ordered and everything's in place." he reported after the Director's terse greeting.

To which the Director had retorted, "We want you to understand one thing. We want the Papist dead. However if the Turkish prick only cripples the pompous Catholic bastard we will accept it. What we will not accept and cannot afford is to be exposed. Let me be clear on this; you are charged to keep Bulgaria out of the assassination at all costs. Eliminate any possibility of exposure. Do you understand?" He'd pronounced each word slowly and precisely.

Knowing that the conversation was being recorded, Zhelov had replied, "I understand."

"Acknowledge you not only understand, but that you are directly responsible to avoid exposure at all costs." the director had commanded.

"I am responsible." Zhelov had answered, with a tinge of irritation.

"You are responsible for what?" the director had then demanded.

Zhelov had slammed the phone down on its receiver, "Fuck off, you bureaucratic ass."

This evening, that phone call from Trieste became very personal for Zhelov. Kostov had Agca in tow and assured his boss that the Turk was never out of sight of himself or the other agents assigned to the project. Now the phony American bastard had to be found and silenced.

Thursday evening, Milan, Italy

11

Colin and Claudette walked hand in hand window shopping the luxury brands and expensive fashions displayed throughout the Galleria Emmanuele II, the two glass-vaulted arcades covering the street connecting Piazza del Duomo and Piazza della Scala, the public squares in front of Milan's Domo cathedral and La Scala. The concentration of indoor shops out dazzled the expensive stores on Chicago's Michigan Avenue, New York's Fifth Avenue and along Causeway Bay in Hong Kong.

They wore their ball caps and tried to look like any other couple on a date. Claudette's shinny black hair was pulled into a ponytail through the opening above the adjustable strap in the back of her cap. McHugh wore his cap down on his forehead covering the bandage and carried the steel pipe comfortably in place along his left arm inside his jacket. They were elated to be out together, yet still watchful.

When Claudette pulled him to a stop in front of the Prada shop, ostensibly to look at a leather hand bag, but only glanced in the window at the man walking behind them, McHugh whispered, "We're supposed to be enjoying this; we're getting paranoid. Let's find a restaurant for a light supper and then head back to the hotel room."

She jogged ahead for a few paces, pulling him along, then slowed and hugged his good arm. They stood under an incredible glass dome.

Ahead, four teenagers stood looking down at something on the floor.

Claudette gestured toward the teenagers and said," It's the bull, let's look."

McHugh watched as each of the teenagers in turn, stepped forward and placed the heal of his shoe on the testicles of the figure of a bull etched in the center of a mosaic coat-of-arms in the galleria floor and spun three times."

He turned to Claudette, "What's that all about?"

"The mosaic is the City of Turin's coat of arms, and tradition says that anyone who puts the heal of his shoe on the balls of the bull and spins three times will have good luck."

"Well, I need luck, but I'm not going to raise my one arm and try to pirouette as a ballerina like that last girl did."

When the group moved away, McHugh completed a clumsy half spin and stepped back to watch Claudette twirl athletically with her arms gracefully extended above her head.

Then at a quiet bistro tucked around the corner from the display of designer clothes and accessories in the Roberto Cavalli shop window, they shared a carafe of red wine, an antipasto salad and roasted sliced pork stuffed with seasonings.

"Colin… May I ask a couple of questions?"

"Of course. I'll tell you why I haven't married." He paused. "The real answer, not the flippant one I usually tell people.

"Thanks." She took a sip of wine.

"It's a long story, but I'll give you the short version. As I told you on our flight here, my university years were spent as a midshipman at the United States Naval Academy; *then* it was an all-male college: all academics and athletics. At graduation, I was awarded a commission as a naval officer and reported to my first assignment aboard a navy destroyer. Shortly I fell in love with a wonderful lady. However, after a whirlwind three months together, my ship was sent on patrol here in the Mediterranean Sea. Six months later, when my ship returned to its homeport in Newport, Rhode Island, my wonderful lady broke off our relationship, explaining that she didn't want to spend her life standing on the end of a pier. It was painful, but the right decision for both of us." He took a sip of wine and continued "Then, after ten years of service, I resigned my commission and again fell hard for someone. It was a brief relationship complicated by an ex-husband and *his and her* children. Now I travel so much, it's difficult to begin a relationship, let alone sustain one."

"Colin thanks for being so straight forward. By the way, why did you leave the Navy?"

Knowing how extremely difficult and emotional it would be for him to explain the Gulf of Tonkin fiasco and President Johnson's ill advised decision to initiate US air attacks on North Vietnam caused the loss of his closest friend and Naval Academy roommate, he just answered "Let's leave that for another time, OK?"

She looked pensive, as if she were about to ask another question, but just poked at her salad.

"So, if you're not going to ask me another question, I'll ask one and don't want you to think I'm prying, it's just….."

"Like you, I'll give the short version of why I divorced my husband."

She put her fork down and pushed her salad dish toward the center of the table. Then she clasped her hands on the table and looked directly into his eyes. "At twenty-two, I studied at Sapienza, University of Rome, and was selected to be a member of the Italian Women's National Volleyball Team. Fabrice, my ex-husband saw a photograph of the team in *la Repubblica*, one of our national newspapers. He was almost fifteen years older then I and owned a modeling school here in Milan that he invited me to attend. As you Americans say, I had a large head then. Against both Claudio and my mother's wishes, I resigned from the university and a few months later left the volleyball team and joined Fabrice's modeling school." She wiped an eye with her serviette. "If only Father had been alive, he would never have let me even consider such decisions."

She glanced around the room momentarily. "I graduated from Fabrice's school and became one of the featured models at a modeling agency he also owned. Eventually, he proposed and I morphed into his trophy wife. We bought the condo outside of Rome that you were in yesterday, a magnificent apartment only a few blocks from where we now sit, and a large studio in London's west end off Park Lane." She paused and dropped her head trying to gather her thoughts. When she looked up at McHugh there was a tear forming in one eye. She rubbed the eye with a finger and continued. "Five years ago my mother had a mastectomy and I spent considerable time with her at our villa…." She hesitated. "And one day I returned to our condo only to find Fabrice indulging a young man on our bed." She looked away briefly. "I later learned that the young man was only one of Fabrice's many boyfriends."

Colin reached across the table for her hand but she pulled it away and continued.

"The marriage had been falling apart for many other reasons, but that destroyed it. I sent him his belongings from the condo, including the furniture, bedding, towels, rugs, kitchen appliances, even the utensils. And for a few more weeks I continued to live with my mother and her repetitious Catholic *sanctity of marriage* lectures; I never told her about his boyfriends. I had the condominium redecorated and moved back into it. This is Italy, and I was required to wait three years before I could officially file divorce papers. I joined Alitalia then. There's much more to tell, but here I am." She seemed relieved, yet another tear appeared and McHugh gently wiped it away.

"Well, even though I am sure it was horrendously difficult, it was also a real blessing," he said as he took her hand.

She wiped her eyes and then took a sip of wine, "Thank you for being here, Colin. Yet I'm concerned that you seem so calm, maybe even nonchalant, about the fact that people are seeking to kill you. Aren't you afraid?"

At first he didn't answer. "I don't know; all I can do is what I can. I'd like to believe that the thugs sent after me will not be told why they've been ordered to make the kill. And they'll probably be instructed to make it look like an accident to eliminate the possibility of police involvement. The guy that followed me in Rome took my picture, so they'll probably have that photo of me as a businessman. It may plant doubt in their minds when they see me as I'm now dressed. It might even give me some advantage of surprise."

He lifted his glass. "It doesn't matter anyway; we'll be in Switzerland tomorrow." He placed the steel pipe on the table without her noticing.

She lifted her glass. "I don't know what to say, but I'm happy to be with you,"

"OK, lady, let's go wrestle." He stood, picked the pipe off of the table and offered his hand.

Friday morning, May 8th
Milan, Italy

12

The phone rang next to their hotel bed. Claudette reached over McHugh, lifted the handset and listened for a moment, and said, "*Grazie.*"

McHugh whispered, "Hello," and kissed her breast. "What a way to wake up." His left hand found the small of her naked back.

She replaced the handset and squirmed away from his probing fingers. "Stop it; that was the concierge with our wake-up call. The waiter will be here any minute with coffee." She rolled out of his grasp and slipped into the bathroom.

McHugh glanced at the antique clock on the night stand. He had to make that call to Firpo. He gathered his clothes from where he had dropped them on the floor beside the bed, walked to the window and dressed. A bright sun filtered through low level stratus clouds warming the morning shoppers heading toward the Galleria. The buzz of car traffic vibrated the weathered glass window pane.

"What's it like outside?" Claudette asked, entering the room, wrapped in a long monogrammed white terry cloth robe.

He turned away from the window. "It's overcast, but the sun is struggling through it. Looks like it may be a reasonably good day to travel."

There was a knock on the door and when Claudette moved to answer it McHugh slipped into the bathroom. He returned to find her standing at a small round table covered with a white linen cloth, pouring coffee into two delicate china cups.

He took the cup she handed to him and sat down on the edge of the bed. After a couple of sips of the espresso, he placed the cup on the bedside table, picked up the phone and dialed.

"Emilio, how are you, is Mr. Firpo there?"

"Mr. McHugh, yes, he's in the office. I'll transfer you." His English was precise.

When Firpo came on the line, McHugh said, "Angelo, I'm sorry for not checking out yesterday evening."

Claudette raised her eyes and McHugh put his hand over the phone. "I've spent considerable time with Firpo and his family on previous visits. We're on a first name basis."

"No problem," said Firpo, "I'll just forward the bill to your company. By the way, how's Milano?"

McHugh slammed the handset against his chest and said "shit" through clenched teeth. He then spoke calmly into the phone, "Angelo, how do you know I'm in Milan?"

"Emilio said you told him you were calling from *Milano* yesterday afternoon, just before the lady inquired if he knew where you were."

McHugh almost yelled into the phone, "What lady?"

"According to Emilio, she was from Yugoslavia and showed him your photograph. She told Emilio you forgot your watch and she wanted to send it to you. Emilio explained to her that you were in Milano and gave her your business card from our file."

"Son of a bitch!" McHugh said under his breath. "Angelo, let me speak with Emilio."

Emilio came on the phone and said, "Mr. McHugh….She told me her name was Kalina and that she was from Yugoslavia. She was young, blond and big… you know."

Frustrated, McHugh pictured Emilio with his back to Firpo's open office door.

"What about the photo?"

"It was a color photograph; you wore a white shirt holding your coat over your shoulder. The Spanish Steps were behind you."

"Emilio, why in god's name did you give her my business card?"

"Well, we had it in our file." Emilio answered guiltily, "and I thought she could send the watch to your company address in the States."

McHugh stared at the phone in his hand, realizing he had forgotten he had even given his business card to Firpo three years ago on his first visit to the hotel. It certainly wasn't Emilio's fault he had been so easily taken with the girl.

"Emilio, tell me everything. What time was it? How tall is she? Anything else you can think of?"

"It was late afternoon, near on six." Emilio continued deliberately, "She had blue eyes; her hair was blonde, short and partially covered her forehead. She had a soft voice and a few of the buttons on her blouse were open, with part of her… you know, plain to see."

McHugh pictured the mousy man of forty, mesmerized by the woman. "OK, thanks Emilio."

McHugh dropped the phone and starred at Claudette. "The clerk handed some woman, probably a Bulgarian agent, my business card I gave Firpo three years ago. Now they know my name and that I'm not a professor. Shit they can even locate me in the states."

Before Claudette could comment, there was a knock on the door. "Room Service"

McHugh pulled the steel pipe from his athletic bag and stood next to the door.

Claudette opened it.

McHugh relaxed when a young boy, in a monogrammed high-buttoned white jacket, wheeled in a breakfast cart. He pushed the small coffee cart into the corridor and set their table for breakfast.

When he finished, Claudette said,"*grazie*," and handed the boy a tip.

While they ate, Claudette again stressed that the Bulgarians were looking for a businessman with shoulder length curly hair traveling alone, not a couple in jogging gear.

"All we have to do is stay together, be alert and maintain our poise. You'll be on that flight home to America tonight, and I'll be on my way back to Rome."

McHugh wished that he could believe her.

Six hundred kilometers away in Rome, Angelo Macari, a chiseled-faced ex-police inspector with thin graying hair glanced at his watch; it was twelve- thirty. He sat at the sidewalk table Commandant Pfyffer had reserved for them under the brown awning of Amalfi, their favorite restaurant in the Borgo District just outside the Vatican. It was a half hour after the time Colonel Pfyffer had arranged to meet him, which was completely out of character for the punctual commandant. The commandant's voice had been strained the day before when he'd called to invite Macari to the meeting, and now Macari's concern was heightened.

After taking a sip of wine he put his glass down on the table and motioned for the waiter. "Would you inquire if there is a phone message for Inspector Macari?

The white-coated waiter acknowledged with a nod and walked into the restaurant proper. He returned shortly. "No sir, there are no messages."

"I'll be right back." Macari rose and walked down the narrow street and stood at the corner, looking toward the Vatican City's St. Ann's Gate, the direction he knew his friend would be coming from.

After five minutes the commandant, dressed in an open collared white shirt and dark slacks, stepped through the open gate. Pfyffer returned the salute of the two Swiss Guards, and began to weave his way along the crowded sidewalk. He appeared anxious and his stride seemed unsure.

Pfyffer saw Macari and waved.

"Franz, it's good to see you," Macari said, and the two of them briefly embraced.

"Sorry I'm late, administrative matters," Pfyffer responded, as they turned and walked back to the restaurant. They sat down at the table and raised their wine glasses to each other, each taking a sip.

Marcari placed his glass on the table. "Franz, are you all right? You seem strained."

"Angelo, as you know, it's been a difficult time since the passing of John I. And our new outgoing Polish traveler has kept us jumping to even remain two paces behind him."

"Franz, you've always have been able to handle things in stride in the past. It's me you're talking to and I know you. Something serious is bothering you; I know it?"

Pfyffer picked up the menu. "Have you ordered?"

"Not yet."

"Then let's order now. I do need your advice on a very unsettling situation."

After they placed their orders, Pfyffer leaned across the table and quietly outlined his position with the Vatican bureaucracy and the contents of the American information. "I need a reason to reinforce the security around the Holy Father next Wednesday without obtaining approval of the hierarchy. And I also need your suggestions for how I might effectively reinforce my guardsmen.

"Well, other than that; how are you?" Marcari questioned sympathetically.

They both sat back as the waiter approached with their pasta dishes and refilled their wine glasses.

Braking off a piece of bread from the small Ciabatta loaf in the center of the table, Macari leaned toward Pfyffer. "First let's talk about a reason to reinforce the guard." Without waiting for a response, he continued, "Remember in the spring of seventy-six, when it was announced in one of those important American newspapers that a group of Catholics planned to travel to Rome and demonstrate about the church's position on birth control. Remember Cardinal Villot, then Secretary of State, ordered you to heighten security during the Wednesday general audience in the piazza that week?"

"You're right, I remember we went crazy that day, and the American group didn't even show up." Pfyffer now very attentive to his friend asked "So how does that apply to this situation?"

"Why don't you just create a radical group and reinforce the security on your own?"

"All right, good idea. Any suggestions?"

"Well, it seems that these days the ordination of women is the latest of the American crusading causes. Why don't you just announce that a small group of American women might be present on Wednesday to protest and just reinforce your security? It would certainly be within the realm of your responsibility to do so."

"Not a bad idea. I'll either find a group or create one."

Somewhat encouraged, Pfyffer also knew that the threat of an assassin supported by one of the most dominant countries in the world could not be compared to a group of well intentioned women. "Look, we're talking about an assassin, heavily supported and financed, not a group of women flying tourist class.

"I know,"Macari mumbled and picked at his pasta.

They didn't speak for a few moments, both reflecting on the gravity of the situation.

"Let's finish up and take a walk," Macari suggested, knowing that their conversation was about to turn sensitive. "Maybe get a coffee in the Piazza del Risorgimento?"

"I'll take care of the bill," Pfyffer said and shortly left his seat and walked into therestaurant.

Seated on a bench outside a coffee bar in the crowded Piazza del Risorgimento, Pfyffer said, "I've brought a diagram of St. Peters Piazza that we can use to determine where to deploy the additional security components."

"Franz, just keep it in your pocket, we don't need to attract attention. Besides, we both know that piazza like the back of our hands." Marcari took a sip of his large espresso. "Do you still provide the plain clothed body guards around the pope's jeep and have a similar guard presence in the crowd?" He thought for a moment. "Also do you still rely on plain clothed police to supplement your guard?"

"It's still the same. All we've added is a procedure to quickly evacuate the pontiff along a planned route to Gemelli Hospital in the event of a serious attack." He sipped his espresso. "As you know our tall Polish Pope in white, standing on a slow moving vehicle is an easy target for either a long range or a close-in shot. I discount a long range shot because access to all Vatican buildings will be secured by my guardsmen and your police always provide a helicopter fly-over of the city buildings before the Holy Father even moves out of the Arch of the Bells."

Macari didn't say anything, knowing the Colonel would continue his analysis.

"The Bulgarians will probably have two alternatives for a close-in shot, a diversion of some sort that would allow the assassin to escape, or a plan to secure his or her silence. Dead assassins don't talk."

Macari took their empty cups back to the bar and returned. "Let's walk."

As they passed a line of pricy dress shops, Macari clasped the colonel by the elbow. "If I were in your shoes, Franz, I'd make damn sure access to the top of the colonnades was secure and install your sharpest men up there. And stagger guards in plain clothes along the west side of the barricade; the shooter will want the sun to his back. Put as many guardsmen as you can, also in plain clothes, among the crowd. Do you have miniature radios with earpieces for those positioned on the colonnades to communicate with the men along the barricade and those escorting the jeep?"

"I have enough."

"Will you arm your guards?" Macari questioned.

"Right now, I don't think so. We're expecting a crowd of about thirty thousand, so it seems our only option is to apprehend the assassin before he or she has the opportunity to take a shot."

"What about convincing the pope to sit instead of stand?"

"It won't happen. The pontiff's stated emphatically many times, "God will protect me."

Macari put his hand on the Commandant's shoulder. "Maybe the American information is premature."

"Let's pray you're right on that," Pfyffer responded.

The two friends shook hands, parting with the agreement to talk by phone before Wednesday.

At that same time in Milan, McHugh and Claudette found their first-class compartment in the front section of the bullet train. Before the overcast weather and the disturbing news from Firpo, they had planned to relax and enjoy the passing view of Italy's famous evergreen fringed Lake Como and its picturesque surrounding sea-side villas, and then the colorful Swiss villages as the train climbed through the Alps. The day before, Claudette had reserved lunch in the dining car and seats in the glass-domed panoramic coach, but now they decided to remain in their compartment for the entire trip. When they boarded, Claudette asked the porter to cancel the viewing seats and their reservation for lunch.

Two comfortable, brown leather bench seats with attached pillow head rests faced each other across the width of their compartment. A sliding door, with a shade covering a head-to-floor Plexiglas window separated their compartment from the corridor. McHugh sat on the couch near the window facing forward with Claudette curled next to him.

When the train began to move, McHugh opened the International Herald Tribune newspaper he purchased at the small kiosk in the hotel.

Claudette moved to the compartment door and lifted the shade. She was determined to scrutinize any passengers who walked past their compartment.

With the city only a few kilometers behind a few passengers walked by stretching their legs.

One man caught Claudette's eye as he headed toward the front of the train. When he made the return trip, he paused momentarily at their compartment and looked directly at them.

"*The bastard isn't eyeing me, he's scrutinizing us,*" She thought, concluding they had at least one pursuer on the train. She nudged McHugh. "I think we have a tail. Some guy in a brown suit eyed us when he walked passed the compartment on his return from the front of the train."

McHugh took the newspaper and moved to her other side closer to the door.

In less than a half hour, Claudette nudged McHugh again and he looked up, catching sight of the back of a brown coat as it passed toward the front of the train.

McHugh clutched the steel pipe and focused on the corridor.

Claudette held on to one end of it. "No, Colin not here. We're not sure."

On his return, the tail stopped and glared at McHugh.

McHugh noted his features: medium height with a wide heavy body, protruding cheeks, square jaw, and tangled eyebrows above dark eyes. He wore a gray sweater buttoned to his neck, under his brown suit.

A half hour later, after the man passed the third time, Claudette left the compartment and followed him. Twenty minutes later she returned, followed by a porter carrying a tray of finger sandwiches and a pot of tea. She sat down and opened the pull-out table under the compartment window. The porter placed the tray on it, and then slid their door closed.

When the door closed, McHugh pulled the shade down.

Handing him a cup of tea, Claudette explained, "I walked all the way through the entire train and didn't see the brown suit, he probably ducked into the *bagno*... sorry, I mean bathroom."

Colin nodded, understanding. "He's one of them. Now he knows we're a couple. In the station we should split up, but stay in sight of each other. That might confuse him. We'll have to watch what he does, and remain alert for others." They worked out an initial plan for their arrival in Switzerland.

Colin kissed her on the cheek. "Let's keep our eyes open. I'm sorry I brought you into this."

"You didn't. So far... I'm happy to be here and remember; *I came willingly*."

She punched him softly in the stomach

The weather cleared as the train began its climb into the Alps.

Friday afternoon, May 8th
Zurich, Switzerland

13

Hauptbanhof, Zurich's massive central train station, is one of the busiest in Europe. Each day there were more than 3000 arriving and departing trains. The station overflowed with travelers on this late Friday afternoon.

McHugh was the first passenger off the train and walked directly to a wide steel column near the center of the passenger concourse. On his previous visits, the station had not been as crowded, nor so full of construction scaffolding. Men in white coveralls and a variety of colored hard hats worked on walkways along the walls high above the concourse. It seemed that the overhead arched glass ceiling and its supporting columns were either being upgraded or going through maintenance inspections.

Following behind, Claudette left the passengers entering the concourse and headed for the ticket booths to check the train schedules to Bern.

Through openings in the scaffolding surrounding the column, McHugh watched the remaining passengers emerge.

Their heavy pursuer, now wearing a light green raincoat walked into the concourse. He stopped and surveyed the crowd. The rain coat seemed to spot someone familiar and walked toward the concession stands, but stopped after only moving a few feet. McHugh glanced in that direction and saw a tall woman with long black hair wearing an athletic suit similar to Claudette's turn away with a bottle of water in her hand. She merged into a crowd walking toward a side exit.

"Thank God, it's not Claudette," McHugh sighed, knowing that she was at the ticket booths in the opposite direction.

McHugh observed Claudette leave the ticket counter and begin to make her way through the crowd toward him.

He caught her eye and pointed toward the heavy man, hoping she would recognize the pursuer, even though he was now wearing the green raincoat.

She nodded, understanding.

The raincoat turned in her direction.

She noticed him turn and glanced back toward the ticket booths, as if she forgot something. She then headed toward the nearest exit, passing within a couple of meters of their pursuer.

The man watched her, but hesitated, not sure of what to do. A swarm of young boys, wearing navy blue blazers and school caps, rushed toward the train platform. The heavyweight pushed through the boys, knocking one to the floor, and followed Claudette.

McHugh fell in behind a group of elderly tourists heading for the same exit. Realizing his height could give him away; he eased to the edge of the group and walked, with his knees bent, along the concourse wall. He stopped inside the glass exit doors and observed Claudette in the crowd outside. The sidewalks were wide and the boulevard traffic seemed light for the time of day.

The elderly tourists stood stoically queued in front of a large Swiss Airlines motor coach.

McHugh didn't see the heavyweight.

Claudette set her athletic bag on the sidewalk, lifted her right hand to shade her eyes and surveyed the scene. She faced away from McHugh. With her left hand behind her back, she pointed to the right.

Glancing in that direction, McHugh saw her pursuer leaning against a large, glass-enclosed information board with postings of train and bus schedules. McHugh continued to watch the two of them, not sure what to do next. It appeared the guy was alone; at least he hadn't made contact with anyone in the station.

While McHugh hesitated; Claudette made up her mind and walked across the bus lane and joined a group of people standing on a long streetcar platform.

The guy did the same. They stood on opposite ends of the platform in front of the wide boulevard. Both looked straight ahead.

McHugh slipped through the glass doors and walked along the outside station wall, contemplating his next move. When a streetcar pulled up to the platform, he made his mind up, dashed behind it, over the tracks and dodged through traffic to the other side of the boulevard. On the sidewalk ahead, he took a position next to a large colorful back-lighted Swissair sign inviting tourists to visit Brazil's Rio De Janeiro's Ipanema Beach.

Claudette stepped from the platform and eased her way across the boulevard into a narrow street forty yards in front of McHugh.

The Bulgarian waited a couple of minutes and lumbered across the boulevard following Claudette.

McHugh dropped his athletic bag near the sign and sprinted to the next street paralleling the one Claudette entered. Tall, aged brick warehouses rose from the sidewalks on both sides of the narrow cob-blestone street. Rows of closed arched wooden shutters lined the wall high above McHugh's head. He ran like a wounded sprinter anchoring the final leg of a relay race with the steel pipe pumping in his left hand, while the right arm hung limp at his side. Halfway along, he stopped and glanced back to see if he was being followed. His side of the street was empty. On its opposite side, a group of school girls, in plaid skirts, gray vests and white blouses, walked in his direction.

McHugh turned the corner and quickly closed the distance to the intersection of Claudette's street. He stood with his back against the corner building trying to catch his breadth.

The two lane paved road in front of him was empty. To his right, a playground and a school building stood on the opposite side of the road near its far end.

He saw the flash of Claudette's jogging suit, grabbed her arm and pulled her next to him away from the corner. Waiting for what he thought was the proper time; he stepped out in front of her pursuer.

They were only five feet apart. Startled, the man initially froze, and then fumbled for his rain coat pocket

Before he even saw the pistol, McHugh lunged through the dis-tance between them and drove the pipe into the man's chest.

Bone shattered.

The heavyweight jerked upright, eyes bulging. He dropped a silenced revolver on the sidewalk and opened his mouth to say some-thing but only careened forward, blood curling at the edge of his mouth.

McHugh stepped back and the Bulgarian crumpled to the pave-ment.

McHugh turned around the corner to Claudette.

She hugged him, pinning his arms to his side and kissed him pro-fusely.

Between kisses, she said, "I didn't know where you were but I knew you'd be close."

"Mr. McHugh." It was a female voice.

Glancing over Claudette's shoulder, McHugh observed the blond. She stood fifteen feet away. The sun reflected off the revolver pointed in their direction.

He whispered, "Don't look around, just take the pipe out of my hand and remain here."

Claudette took the pipe and held it down along her side.

McHugh moved a few paces laterally away from Claudette and faced the girl.

"Kalina, from Yugoslavia!" He exclaimed, and focused on her eyes. They were deep blue, but where the Italian hotel clerk had observed enticement; McHugh saw hate and determination.

"Mr. McHugh, or whoever you are; you put your foot where it should not be." She moved closer to him.

McHugh stepped a few more paces away from Claudette.

The girl's eyes and gun barrel moved with him.

He had to keep her attention. "Kalina, you don't want to shoot me or be captured by the Swiss police. They'll take you to a place where you'll spend the rest of your life looking from behind steel bars at snow covered mountains. You're so young; do you want that?"

He saw hesitation and a glint of doubt in her eyes, but the gun remained steady and pointed at his stomach; his suggestion of prison seemed to have lost its effect.

She stepped closer and tightened her grip on the pistol.

He needed to keep her talking. "Who are you Kalina? Are you really Yugoslavian? The clerk at the hotel said you had my watch."

She smirked. "You're stupid, like all Americans. It doesn't matter where I'm from…."

Loud talking and laughing arose from behind them. The school girls turned the corner and began to walk in their direction.

Kalina glanced toward the noise.

McHugh only saw a blur, as the steel pipe crashed down and shattered Kalina's wrist. Her shriek of pain came just before the explosive sound of the gunshot, and the sting of the bullet that grazed his right side.

Kalina lunged for the gun that fell to the pavement.

McHugh kicked the revolver away and punched her in the face. She collapsed with blood streaming from her broken nose.

The screaming school girls turned and ran toward the school at the end of the block.

Knowing they had only a few minutes before the gun shot and the screaming girls attracted a crowd, McHugh urged Claudette to pick up her athletic bag and run back down the side street to the train station.

In shock, Claudette didn't move; she stood holding the pipe away from her as if it were contaminated.

He yelled, "Go, Claudette!"

Finally, throwing the pipe across the street, Claudette picked up her athletic bag and disappeared around the corner.

"I'll be right behind you!" McHugh picked up Kalina's gun, put it in the pocket of his athletic jacket, and then turned the corner to follow.

Claudette was halfway down the block.

Her bludgeoned pursuer groaned and reached up to trip McHugh. McHugh pulled his foot away and reached for the gun in his pocket. After shooting the brute in the leg, he turned around the corner and fired another into Kalina's foot. *Can't let the bastards follow us!*

Rounding the corner again, he saw Claudette at the end the block, turn and race back toward him. He picked up the heavyweight's revolver and stuffed it in his jacket pocket.

"Go on!" he yelled, and sprinted to catch up.

"Why'd you kill them?" she screamed, tears rolling down her checks.

He grabbed her wrists, "I didn't! I only put a bullet in their legs so they can't follow us. Come on let's find a taxi."

She stood frozen, momentarily resisting. Then she grabbed his hand tightly and they both ran. At the corner, they slowed to a walk.

McHugh led her past the Swissair sign, tossed both guns into a waste-bin and picked up his athletic bag.

They eased their way through the boulevard traffic.

McHugh opened the boulevard side rear door of the first available taxi and Claudette told the shocked driver to take them to the Hotel Baur au Lac.

In the backseat, she collapsed into McHugh's arms and began to cry.

There was nothing to be said. He just held her.

Fifteen minutes later, their taxi pulled through a gray portal into the forecourt of the Baur Au Lac Hotel.

As soon as the taxi came to a stop, McHugh opened the door and offered his hand to Claudette, well before the tall hotel porter, dressed in a high white collared coat with two rows of brass buttons, descended the hotel's royal blue carpeted steps.

May I help you?" The porter tipped his captain's cap and inquired condescendingly.

"Is Herr Schwartzenbach in today?" Claudette asked from behind McHugh.

The porter turned to her. "No madam, he's in Spain for the week."

"How unfortunate." Claudette remarked and slipped between the two men and strode up the steps into the hotel vestibule.

McHugh glanced at the stunned porter, picked up his bag and followed.

"Who's Schwartz...what's his name?" he whispered when he caught up to her.

"Andy Swartzenbach's the assistant manager. His sister, Astrid, flies for Lufthansa. They're both very good friends of mine.

She marched straight through the opulent welcome room, resplendent with Persian carpets, carved pale oak woodwork and plush lounge chairs, into the terrace lounge.

McHugh stood at the entrance and looked around. An elderly, hatless bellman in a white, high buttoned coat, stood at attention on one side of the room, and a young clerk wearing a double-breasted navy blue coat and monogrammed tie leaned against the marble-covered front desk. McHugh inhaled the luxurious silence and realized that in his condition it was evident he was out of place. None-the-less, he held his injured right arm over the dried blood and bullet hole in his jacket and mimicked Claudette's march through the room into the terrace lounge.

Claudette led him to a square glass top corner table with a tall crystal vase holding a single orchid.

Two other couples were chatting at a larger table near the far open end of the lounge leading out to the garden.

When the waiter arrived at their table, Claudette ordered ice water. And for a time, they just sat and stared at each other, relieved to still be together.

"Colin, I'm so sorry. I thought you'd killed them and I hated you for it. For a few minutes I never wanted to see you again. And now I feel terrible because I know you could never out- right murder someone."

McHugh took a sip of his water and reached across the table and touched her arm, "It's been a long day." He raised his hand to attract the waiter and ordered two large glasses of Dewars White Label Scotch with sides of soda.

"Are you seriously hurt?" She asked, pointing to the blood on his jacket.

"Only a scratch," he began to unzip his jacket but Claudette shook her head.

The waiter returned and set their drinks in front of them.

Claudette said to the waiter, *"Ci torno subito....* We'll be right back."

She stood, picked up her bag and motioned to Colin. "Come on."

He followed her into an alcove, but stopped when she entered the ladies' restroom.

Shortly, she opened the door. "Come on in, there's no one here." He entered and she locked the door behind him.

The room was long and bright under recessed ceiling lights. A row of white marble sinks beneath continuous mirrors along one wall faced closed toilet stall doors along the other. A plush rose color carpet ran between them.

She said, "Take off your jacket and shirt." The superficial wound, just a few inches above his right hip was still seeping blood.

Claudette opened her athletic bag and took out a small plastic container holding peroxide and a tube of ointment. She removed a hand towel that was neatly folded on one of the white marble sinks and cleaned the bullet wound. Removing her jacket, she took off her tee shirt, ripped it and wrapped it around his waist.

McHugh stood watching her performance through the mirrors. She was ravishing in her net sports bra. "Should I suggest we stay the night?" He said and quickly stepped back when she feigned a slap at him. His remark seemed to ease the seriousness of their situation.

She put on her jacket and hugged him, "You've only one thing to do. Get to Bern. *Do not worry about me.*"

Returning to the lounge, they picked up their drinks and walked out to the garden overlooking the canal.

She clung to his good arm. "The Bern airport's about 95 kilometers, so why don't you just take the hotel limousine?"

He nodded in agreement. "Great idea, but what about you?"

"I'll spend the night here and call the Alitalia station manager in the morning to book a flight back to Rome."

They watched the city lights reflecting on the water both knowing they couldn't escape the reality at hand.

"You can't stay here! They know you're with me, and as soon as either Kalina or her fat friend gets access to a phone, others will also know about you."

"How?" She shook her head.

"The girl will certainly realize we ran back toward the train station and will rightfully assume we took a taxi. It won't take long to find out that we were driven here. Don't stay here. I can't let them find you. If you don't have any other options, fly to the States with me."

She thought for a moment. "No, I'll stay with one of my stewardess friends and have my brother meet my flight in Rome."

"Call someone now; I'm not going to Bern until I know you'll be safe. He led her back to the terrace lounge and Claudette asked the waiter for a phone.

"I really don't think this is necessary." She smirked, as she dialed a number.

"Maia, its Claudette. Are you flying tonight?"

Silence for a few moments. "Great, can I stay with you?" She glanced at McHugh. "Just for the night" Claudette gave a thumbs-up. "Thanks, the futon will be fine. I'll be over shortly. I'm planning to fly to Rome tomorrow morning."

Before Claudette could hang up, McHugh touched her arm and whispered, "Ask if she can meet you in a café or restaurant near her apartment. I'm going with you in the limousine and I don't want the driver to know Maia's address…just in case."

While Claudette continued on the phone, McHugh walked toward the front desk to arrange for the limousine.

A group of about thirty men and women dressed in formal attire were gathered in a corner of the welcome room having cocktails. Waiters, in white coats, moved through the group with trays of hors'd'oeuvres. The chatting came to a stop when McHugh passed by.

McHugh ignored them and approached the front desk.

"Good evening," he addressed the clerk; the same twenty-something young man he noticed when he entered the hotel.

"Can I help you?" the clerk questioned authoritatively and glanced toward the group in the welcome room.

"Well…I would like to arrange for the hotel limousine to take me to the airport in Bern."

The clerk looked McHugh up and down. "Are you a guest, Mister…?"

"My name is McHugh." Then remembering that most luxury hotels reserved the use of their limousines exclusively for guests, he quickly added, "And I would like to check in now, and then schedule the hotel limousine to drive me to the Bern airport to pick up my brother; we'll both be staying for the weekend. Do you have a suite available?"

"Of course, Mr. McHugh, "The clerk's reply was now courteous. Turning the registry book to face McHugh, he smiled.

"Mr. McHugh, would you please sign in?"

He picked up the phone. "Bertrand, would you please come to the front desk?" He then checked McHugh's passport and processed his credit card.

"Mr. McHugh, your suite has balcony views of both the lake and the canal. Do you have luggage?" The clerk handed McHugh a brass key attached to a medallion with the hotel logo and the suite number embossed on it.

"Thank you, I only have an athletic bag, the rest of my luggage is in Bern."

McHugh turned and bumped into an elderly man in a dark chauffeur's uniform holding his cap.

The chauffer extended his hand. "Sir, my name is Bertrand, and I'll be happy to drive you to Bern Airport."

McHugh grasped the hand. "Thank you Bertrand, the name's McHugh. I'll be with you in a few minutes."

McHugh returned to the lounge and dangled the hotel key in front of Claudette, "I had to check in so I could use the limousine. I told the front desk clerk I planned to meet my brother in Bern and we'd be staying through the weekend. I can't wait to see Stringer's face when the bill arrives; he'll probably piss his pants. What did you arrange with your friend Maia?"

Claudette explained that Maia had agreed to meet in the lounge of Hotel St. Gotthard in a half an hour. It was only three blocks from her apartment.

With everything seeming to be coming to an end, Claudette receded into herself.

McHugh noticed and touched her arm. She looked up with a bland smile.

He took a sip of scotch. "I'll be right back."

Returning a few minutes later and he handed her a sheet of lined hotel paper and a pen.

"I want you to write down all your telephone numbers; your condo, your mother's villa, your brother's home, Maia's apartment, Alitalia Rome, Alitalia Milan, Alitalia London, Toronto everywhere.... even your hairdresser."

Her expression didn't change, but she took the pen and began to write. After listing a few numbers she raised her head to see McHugh holding a single long stemmed red rose. "I want you to keep this until I bring you the other eleven."

She stood and folded into him with both arms around his neck.

He held her as tight as he could with one arm, but couldn't help wondering who Kalina and the fat man might be calling.

On the way to the Hotel St.Gothard, Claudette explained to McHugh that Maia had taken an apartment nearby because she liked *fishing* in the hotel. Before he could ask her to explain what fishing meant, she added, "Unlike me, Maia couldn't handle her divorce, and now she fishes for love in the hotel lounge. Unfortunately, the fishes are only looking for sex, while she continues to hope she might land one who might know difference between the two."

McHugh waited.

"And, no, I don't fish. I dance, and I assure you Maia won't be bringing any fish home tonight."

Bertrand stopped the black Rolls-Royce where the St. Gotthard Hotel doorman could open the rear door with ease.

"Bertrand, I'll only be a few minutes, keep the motor running," McHugh said, and followed Claudette into the hotel.

Claudette waded through the Friday after-work crowd and found Maia in front of a long mahogany bar chatting with a tall, athletic-looking executive-type. She introduced McHugh.

McHugh was surprised that Maia, in her late thirties, was tall and full-figured, not the pixyish image that her name had conjured up in his mind.

Maia introduced her companion, Mark, and suggested that the four of them find a table.

"Unfortunately, I have a plane to catch, so I must be on my way," McHugh responded.

"Oh, sorry you can't stay; I hope you have a safe flight." Maia turned to Claudette. "I'll find a table for the three of us." She led Mark by the arm through the crowd toward a cluster of small square tables along the far wall.

Claudette walked into the lobby with McHugh. They stood, toe to toe, looking into each other's eyes, and then kissed like the couple they knew they could become.

He broke the embrace. "I'll see you soon." Then paused and said, "Stay away from Mark; he fixed on you as soon as you said hello."

He started to walk away, and then abruptly turned back. "Don't stay here for more than an hour, no matter how long they do. The chauffer knows where he dropped you off. I'll call you at Maia's apartment when I'm airborne."

Claudette kissed her finger and touched it to his lips, "Be safe, Colin."

She turned and walked back into the club.

"Mr. McHugh, we'll be arriving at the airport shortly," Bertrand said, over the limousine's intercom.

"What? Who?" McHugh was confused, waking from the nap he'd succumbed to as soon as the comfortable leather backseat had enveloped him.

"Mr. McHugh, we'll be at the airport shortly. There's water and libations in the console, if you're interested."

"Oh, thanks, Bertrand." McHugh struggled to focus through the window into the diminishing twilight. The headlights of the Mercedes fixed ahead on a large sign-*Flughafen Bern-Belp-10KM*

"Bertrand, what's *Bern-Belp*?"

"Sir, the airport is located in the town of Belp."

"Oh, Thanks, by the way, could you pull over before we enter the airport? I'd like to explain something." McHugh took a bottle of water from the console bar.

Bertrand pulled the limousine into a lay-by. Needing to stretch his legs, McHugh opened his door and walked around to the driver's window.

Apprehensive, Bertrand didn't lower the window and only opened the car door enough to enable him to turn toward McHugh. He kept his feet inside the car and hands on the steering wheel.

"Bertrand, when we enter the airport, I'd like you to drive to the Swiss Air Force Headquarters Building, which I am told is on the opposite side of the runway from the commercial terminal."

Sensing that the chauffeur was suspicious, having been asked to stop for such a simple direction, McHugh continued amiably "I also need you to do me a favor."

Bertrand took his hands off the steering wheel and faced McHugh. "Yes sir?"

"I'll be flying to the United States tonight. Would you do me a favor and delay returning to the hotel for about an hour. Here are my remaining Swiss francs; it's close to five hundred dollars US."

He handed the francs to the chauffeur. "Wish I could explain more, but for important reasons I can't."

The chauffer took the francs and extended his hand. "Good luck, sir."

"Thanks," McHugh shook hands and returned to the rear seat.

"Welcome, Mr. McHugh. I'm Captain Deubel, the night duty officer. Your flight crew is aboard the plane, but before we let you join them, your Admiral Stringer asked to have one of our doctors take a look at you." The Swiss Air Force Captain led McHugh through a set of double doors and down a narrow hall to a small dispensary.

"This is Major Fahr, our headquarters' saw-bones, as you Americans say."

The doctor, a thin distinguished looking man with dark hair graying at the temples, wore a white medical coat. He smirked at the joke, and, with a slight British accent, said "Thank you, Captain. I'll take it from here."

When they were alone the Major said, "I understand you've had a tough go of it."

He removed the bandage from McHugh's forehead, "This football scrape seems to be healing well. Now take your shirt off and show me the other damages!"

McHugh removed his shirt and unwrapped Claudette's tee shirt.

"Your Admiral told the duty officer something about your arm also."

McHugh winced trying to raise his right arm above his shoulder.

The doctor observed the struggle. "We'll get to that shortly." Then he made a cursory examination of the bullet wound.

"I'd say you've had some medical help along the way. I'll just clean this up and put on a proper dressing."

"I met a Florence Nightingale."

"Well, whatever her name is, she's damn good. Now, let's try that shoulder. Don't give me any resistance when I take your hand and move your arm."

When the doctor moved McHugh's arm laterally, he winced several times. However, when Fahr tried to raise the arm above McHugh's shoulder; he pulled the arm out of the doctor's grasp.

The doctor stepped back. “It looks like a neuropraxias.” In other words, you have a severe shoulder contusion. I believe its nerve damage and not structural. You should have an x-ray taken as soon as you arrive in the States. In the meantime don’t sleep on that shoulder or lift anything. I’ll give you an injection for pain. It should last through most of your flight.” He handed McHugh a small bottle. “Take these pills only if you need them.”

The doctor helped McHugh put his shirt on, and then led him back to the reception area. The duty officer was talking with a US Navy Commander in flight gear.

Spotting McHugh, the Navy Commander approached and extended his hand. “McHugh, Dan Banks. I’m your bus driver tonight. We’re ready to roll when you are.”

McHugh shook the pilot’s hand with his left. “Let’s fly, Commander.”

Both shook hands with the duty officer and doctor, thanking them for their hospitality and walked out to the plane.

McHugh felt relieved to see the rotating red light on the Gulfstream’s fuselage and the American flag illuminated on its finned tail. *Thank God, this damn mission’s over; no more theatrics for me. Hopefully the information I gave Pfyffer will preserve the life of a good man*, he thought.

At the top of the extended metal staircase, he stopped and looked back vowing, “Claudette, I’ll be back.”

At about that same time
Rome, Italy

14

Zhelov looked at his watch: seven o'clock. He had lumbered throughout the small apartment the entire day like a caged bear. As the day wore on, the pile of cigarette butts grew in and around the four ashtrays on the long table. Smoke hung like a fog over everything; nauseating cigarette smell permeated the room.

Zhelov went into the bathroom and washed his face pouring water over his head.

"Why doesn't she call?" he yelled at the unshaven reflection in the mirror. He hadn't heard from Kalina since the night before when she had arrived in Milan and he'd given her the specific instruction to call when she located the American bastard.

He opened the sliding glass door onto the balcony and stepped out for some fresh air. The scene in this part of Rome's embassy quadrant was quiet, compared to the Friday evening traffic and noise reverberating from other parts of the city. The breeze was refreshing, but his uneasiness made it difficult to relax in the moment.

The phone rang; he turned, stumbling over the door sill, caught his balance, ran back into the room and picked up the receiver.

"Ya, Kalina, where are you? What's happened?"

"It's Kostov."

"Shit. I've been waiting all day for that bitch to call me," Zhelov answered dejectedly.

"I saw her this morning with Videnov near the consulate. They were about to catch a taxi to the train station to follow the American."

"When? Who's Videnov?"

"It was about eight o'clock and I've been told Videnov's one of the most experienced agents we have in Milano."

"Well, at least I know she's carrying out my orders. Now, what do you want?"

"You told me to report at the end of the week."

"OK, OK. Bring me up to date."

Kostov explained that he and Agca had stopped going to St Peter's Square for fear of attracting Vatican security. The Turk knew where to stand and what to do. "I now have him in an apartment in Milano a few blocks away from via Paolo Surpi. The area's overrun with European immigrants. A young Italian whore is keeping him very satisfied. I'm doling out money slowly and have an agent on watch twenty-four hours."

"When do you plan to bring him back to Rome?"

"Well, we have less than a week. We'll be in Rome and ready Monday night and stay out of sight all day Tuesday." Kostov said confidently.

Before Zhelov could ask anything else, there was a loud crash in the street outside the apartment; people began to shout.

"Kostov, something's happening outside." He hung up.

Zhelov went to the balcony and looked down. It appeared that a large Fiat truck had grazed the front fender of a black Mercedes limousine. Zhelov knew the Mercedes was an embassy car because the miniature nationality flag usually attached to its front bumper lay in the street between the two vehicles. The damage to both vehicles appeared slight. The assembling crowd seemed out of proportion for a simple fender bender. However, Zhelov knew an accident with an embassy car usually brought a swarm of onlookers. The truck driver argued theatrically with the limousine driver, a burly man, who took off his chauffeur's cap and placed it on the hood of his car as if preparing for a more physical confrontation. By now all traffic had stopped and the scene began to resemble a crowd at a local soccer match. Two *Polizia Municipale*, in white custodian helmets arrived on their white motorcycles and tried to separate the two combatants. Only when two *Carabinieri*-Italian paramilitary police arrived on their dark blue BMW motorcycles did the crowd began to disperse.

Glancing down Pietro Rubens Street, Zhelov saw Petcov walk through the embassy gate and stepped inside the apartment to watch.

Petcov seemed agitated; first he jogged up Pietro Rubens Street and then slowed to a walk, glancing behind. When he reached the accident scene, he initially attempted to push through the crowd. However, as soon as he saw the *Carabinieri*, he slipped around the fracas until he was directly below the apartment balcony. After a quick glance toward the police, he entered the building.

Zhelov opened the door as soon as he heard footsteps on the landing and asked impatiently, "What's happened?"

Startled, Petcov stepped back and tripped on the top step. Recovering, he said, "Kalina called the Embassy."

Zhelov closed the door and cursed. "Shit! I told everyone not to make contact with the embassy under any condition."

"She didn't make the call; it was made for her from a hospital. I recorded it all." Petcov's voice was defensive. He put a tape recorder on the table.

"Wait." Zhelov walked over and closed the balcony door.

They pulled up chairs, with the recorder on the table between them, and sat back to listen.

Petcov hit play.

A woman's voice said in Italian, "Bulgarian Embassy, can I help you?"

A female voice responded, "I have a phone call from one of your staff, a Kalina Lubanov."

The Embassy voice replied, "Yes, thank you."

There was muffled discussion.

Finally they heard, "Its Kalina. I need to talk to Zhelov or Petcov. It's urgent."

There was a series of beeps.

"Kalina, its Petcov. Where are you?"

Her voice had a whimper, "I'm in a hospital in Zurich. The door to my room's open with a policeman outside. I'll speak softly, even though I don't think he understands Bulgarian. I need to get a message to Zhelov."

"Go ahead, I'm recording our conversation. I'll take it to Zhelov as soon as we're finished. Petcov continued, "How are you? What happened?"

"I've been shot in the foot and have a broken wrist, I'll be all right, but Videnov is dead."

Petcov said, "What?! Go on!"

She continued slowly. "Videnov and I followed McHugh and his girlfriend onto the bullet train in Milano. Our plan was to double shadow them until they arrived at their destination in Zurich. Then we planned to eliminate them quietly as Zhelov ordered. I let them see Vedenov on the train while I remained out of sight."

After a slight pause she went on, "When the train arrived in Zurich we split up. I told Videnov to follow them so I could make a quick phone call to Zhelov. He kept the girl in sight but lost McHugh. I didn't have time to call because I saw Videnov follow the girl toward an exit. As I started to go after them, McHugh stepped out from behind a column and edged his way behind Videnov. So I followed that bastard McHugh. The girl crossed the boulevard outside the station and walked down a narrow street. Videnov gave her a head start then followed.

McHugh ran down a parallel street so I followed him behind a group of school girls on the other side of the street. When he turned the corner, I moved quickly ahead of the girls."

She stopped and took a couple of deep breaths.

"Go on, Kalina," Petcov urged.

"When I got to the corner, I saw McHugh and his girlfriend near the far end of the street. I didn't see Videnov, so I drew my Makarov and confronted them. McHugh moved away from his girl, but I kept the gun trained on him. The next thing I know, the bitch broke my wrist with a club or something. My gun fired when I dropped it. I tried to pick it up, but McHugh knocked me out. When I started to come around, the bastard shot me in the foot. I couldn't get up and a damn crowd gathered. Someone called an ambulance and it brought me to this hospital. The bullet went through flesh; there's no bone damage. I have to stay for observation. They've given me pain pills. The police took my diplomatic identification, but I insisted that I be allowed to call the Embassy. Finally, they put this call through." She seemed out of breath.

Petcov said, "Kalina, I need to ask some questions. It's important. When did you arrive at the hospital and what's the name of it?"

"I guess about two hours ago. I don't know the name, but when I asked the ambulance orderly where we were, he said in the Alstadt district."

"What happened to Videnov?"

"He's dead. He bled to death on the sidewalk. The nurse said he was stabbed in the chest and apparently an artery was severed. That bastard McHugh killed him. They've asked me all kinds of questions about Videnov. They told me he had a Russian 6P9 silenced pistol and a Polish passport. Why wasn't I issued a silenced 6P9?" Her voice was agitated.

"What did you tell them about Videnov?"

"I haven't told them anything. I think the inspectors that questioned me left the hospital and stationed a policeman outside my door.

"Where's McHugh?"

"I don't know. He and the girl probably went back to the train station and took a taxi to wherever they planned to stay."

"Kalina, why do you think they split up in the train station?"

"They probably thought Videnov was their only tail and were setting a trap for him."

A series of chimes rang, followed by a garbled announcement, then a door slammed shut.

"There's a medical emergency. The policeman just closed my door."

Petcov continued, "Let's go on. What were they wearing? What does the girl look like?"

Kalina described Claudette as a tall Italian model with long dark hair. Then she detailed the differences between McHugh's photograph and what she had observed. She said his hair had been cut and he had a bandage on his forehead. She described the athletic outfits and the baseball caps they were wearing.

"That McHugh bastard is hurt. His right arm hung limp when he ran down the street." Her voice was fading.

Then she added, "I think the pills are beginning to take effect."

"Wait. One more question. Do you have any idea where they went?"

"Probably to a hotel. His girlfriend's a stunning bitch."

At this point, another voice came on the line and said in English, "I'm sorry but Miss Lubanov needs rest. I'll let her phone later if she wants to make another call."

Zhelov stood knocking over his chair. He threw the ashtray against the wall scattering cigarette butts over the table and Petcov. He paced the room. When he stopped, he kicked the wall and said, "Fuck, that bastard American. Petcov, get back to the Embassy. Get the descriptions of those two sent to our people in Zurich. Then get your ass back here. Pick up some take-out food and don't return up Pietro Rubens, go over a couple of blocks. It's going to be a long night."

Petcov brushed the cigarette butts from his jacket, pocketed the tape recorder and headed out the door.

Zhelov went into the bathroom, washed his face then wiped his neck with a cold, wet towel. He changed his shirt, cleaned the butts from the table and floor and opened the balcony door. There was no trace of the accident.

He wondered whether he should inform Sofia of the situation, but decided against it; he might still have an opportunity to eliminate the bastard if he was still in Zurich. Videnov's death and Kalina's hospitalization would certainly bring repercussions.

He picked up the phone and called the Bulgarian Consulate in Zurich. He insisted on speaking with the duty security officer.

Meanwhile in Bern, a smiling, olive-skinned Philippine stewardess in a white coat embossed with the presidential seal took McHugh's bag as he entered the plane and led him to a lounge seat on the right side of the luxurious cabin.

The pilot, Dan Banks said, "Petty Officer Cruz will look after your needs during the flight.

We're pretty informal. Co-pilot's Air Force Captain Mike Boyle. Up front we're 'Dan and Mike,' back here Petty Officer Christine Cruz prefers, Chris. We'll lift off as soon as we obtain clearance from Swiss Military Air Control. This bird cruises at about 550 knots. With the six hour time difference, it's now only fourteen hundred in Washington; I mean two o'clock in the afternoon."

McHugh raised his hand. "That's OK; I'm an ex-naval officer."

"Our flight path is just over 4000 air miles, so with good winds over the *'pond'* we should be landing around twenty hundred. Once we get airborne and clear of the continent I'll stop back and bring you up to speed on our flight path."

When the Commander turned toward the flight deck, McHugh asked, "Dan, can I place a call when we're at altitude?"

"Certainly, I'll have Chris give you an open line. And I've told her you had a serious go of it. She'll make your flight as comfortable as possible."

Although it had been a long harrowing day and he was extremely tired, McHugh decided to write his report to Stringer before he had a drink and attempted to relax.

He pushed the call button and Chris came forward.

"Yes, Mr. McHugh?" she asked, standing next to his seat.

"What about Colin? Dan said first names are the norm aboard."

"He only says that to relax our guests. I must still call you Mr. McHugh. I'm Chris."

"Well Chris, could you bring me some paper and a pen?"

"Yes sir. Would you like a drink? We have a complete bar, or maybe you'd prefer tea or coffee?"

"Maybe a cup of tea will settle me down."

He wondered if it was kosher to write an official report to Stringer without including Claudette. With a snake in the Washington woodpile, I'll be as vague as possible and fill in the blanks verbally to Stringer; he can handle any flack.

Chris returned with a pad of paper, pen and a cup of steaming tea. McHugh thanked her and began his report. He really didn't know the proper form, so he reverted to what he recalled from his Navy days:

Date: Friday, May 8, 1981
From: Colin R. McHugh, Civilian
To: Rear Admiral Daniel P. Stringer, Deputy Director, National Security Staff

Subject: Delivery of Information, as directed.

As directed, I delivered a package of information to Colonel Frantz Pfyffer, Commandant, Vatican Swiss Guard Regiment, at the conclusion of the initiation ceremony of Swiss Guard candidates in the Vatican on Wednesday, May 6, 1981.

From the time I arrived in the Vatican I was followed by what I believe to be Eastern Bloc agents, probably Bulgarian. (Photos to be provided)

While driving a rental car on the way back to my hotel, I was forced off the road by a large truck and my car rolled down an incline. I suffered a shoulder contusion and other minor injuries, but was able to move away from the upturned vehicle into the surrounding trees. A military-type professional, (I can describe him) fired thee shots from an automatic weapon at long range into the upturned car's gas tank. He then ignited the leaking gas with a flare.

McHugh stopped writing and tried to visualize the end of the incident. He saw the truck pulling away and the name on its side, *Lombardi Construzione*, immediately came to him. He also remembered the shooter bullying the young truck driver. Maybe the driver wasn't one of them. *When I call Claudette I'll ask if her brother can look into the Lom-*

bardi Company and find out who that young driver might have been; with the way the shooter treated him, he may also be in danger. He took a sip of tea and continued:

> I walked away from the scene. An Italian citizen cleansed my wounds as best *he* could and then drove me to Milan.

Stringer was already aware he had met an unidentified Italian female, but at this juncture McHugh didn't think it important for anyone else to know.

> I boarded the train to Zurich yesterday morning, May 7th, at 1155 and arrived in Zurich at approximately 1545. In Zurich, I was followed by two people I believe to be East Bloc agents. (Probably Bulgarian)
>
> I eluded the two agents and, as directed, reported to the Swiss Air Force Headquarters at the Bern-Belp airport and boarded a special aircraft for a flight back to the United States.

He put the pen down and closed his eyes. The report was short, *probably too short.* If Stringer wanted more, he would receive it verbally, not in writing.

McHugh recalled the news reports when Navy Warrant Officer John Walker was convicted of spying for the Russians. It was reported that Walker had even recruited his young son, an ordinary navy seaman, as a spy. Shit, McHugh had no idea who the leak in Washington could be; it could even be the damn typist.

Anyway, this was his last assignment for Stringer; it was time to go sailing. For the first time since he'd left the states, he thought about his boat. He closed his eyes and pictured *WayWard*, his 34' Sloop nestled alongside its dock in the Vermillion River. By now, Archie Rhodes, his friend and retired navy boatswain's mate, would have put her in the water, rigged and ready.

"Mr. McHugh."

He stopped his day dreaming, and looked up to see Chris standing next to his seat.

She smiled, "Sorry to interrupt but Captain Banks wanted me to alert you that we are about to leave the European continent and head over the Atlantic. We should be passing over the southern coast of Ireland in about ten minutes."

"Thanks for the head's up, Chris. Now would you please bring me a scotch and soda, and perhaps arrange for that phone call?"

When she returned, he lifted the glass from the tray she held out to him. "Thanks, Chris; you're a dear."

From a console next to his seat, she handed him a phone. "You can place that call now."

He sipped his scotch as he watched the blinking lights of Ireland fade behind them, and then dialed Maia's apartment number.

Claudette answered on the first ring. "Hi Colin, where are you?"

"We just passed over Ireland and I miss you. How did things go after I left?"

"Well, I really don't know. I left about twenty minutes after you. There wasn't any dancing; only fishing." She paused and he pictured her smiling at the reference to their conversation in the limousine. "Maia didn't come home yet, but it's only nine-thirty. Hopefully she'll find a fish."

He took a sip of his scotch. "By the way Claudette, the name on the large truck that drove me off the road on Wednesday came to me while I wrote my report to Stringer. In English, I believe it was the Lombardi Construction Company. Maybe you can ask your brother if he can find out who the driver might have been. The shooter intimidated the young driver throughout the ordeal."

"I'll ask him tomorrow when he picks me up at the airport."

"Tell Claudio to give a vague reason for his inquiry, like he needs the names of drivers for some city survey or such. We don't want to raise any suspicions at the company or of the driver."

"Yes, I understand, so will Claudio. I'll let you know what he discovers when we talk next.

McHugh glanced out of his window. Only the red flashes from the rotating beacon on top of the plane's fuselage interrupted the dark universe.

"I'll call you as soon as I get settled tomorrow. Love ya."

"You too, Colin. Be safe."

Bertrand pulled the Rolls-Royce into its assigned parking pace in the Baur au Lac Hotel courtyard, and checked his watch. It was nine o'clock; he had worked a twelve hour day. With over-time at double his normal wage, and the Swiss Francs McHugh had given him, it had also been a profitable day. His wife would be overjoyed with his contribution to the savings account they had recently opened for their winter holiday in Faro, on Portugal's southern coast. He turned off the ignition, got out of the car and locked the door.

Before he could turn he felt cold metal against the back of his neck.

A gruff voice said, "Mr. Bertrand, where's Mr. McHugh?"

"I...I don't know." His voice trembled. He tried to turn.

"Don't move!" Then the voice continued, "The front desk clerk told me you were to bring McHugh back to the hotel. He has a reservation. Where is he?"

Bertrand hesitated, his mind racing for an answer. The metal object moved down to the base of his spine. Finally he said, "Mr. McHugh asked me to take my time returning to the hotel."

"Well where is he? He has a reservation." The voice was increasingly agitated.

Bertrand began to sweat.

"Do you have a family?" The voice didn't wait. "You'll never see them again if I don't hear the proper answer."

Bertrand's mouth was dry, "No please. Mr. McHugh told me he was flying to the United States."

Bertrand first felt the pain when the butt of the gun came down on the back of his head and then everything went black.

Friday evening,
Andrews Air Force Base, Washington, D.C.

15

McHugh gave Chris a hug and shook hands with Banks. Then he stuck his head into the cockpit and waved to the co-pilot, who was going through the post-flight check list. He opened the umbrella Chris handed to him, stepped through the hatch into a chilly spring shower and walked down the short metal gangway to the waiting limousine. The driver, in a hooded black rain coat, took McHugh's umbrella, and opened the rear door for him.

"Welcome home," Admiral Stringer said as McHugh eased into the backseat.

The limousine moved away from the plane and headed slowly toward the airfield's exit gate. An Air Force guard in a white helmet and yellow rain gear, carrying an M-16 rifle stood next to the open gate. He saluted as the limousine passed.

"Dan, it's good to see you and be back. But damn it, your *piece- of-cake* letter drop almost got me killed. I've barely survived and now the bastards know who I really am and where I work. And you can certainly bet they will shortly know where I sleep."

"Slow down. What the hell are you talking about?" Stringer looked stunned.

"Three years ago I gave my business card to the manager of a small hotel outside of Rome where I stay when I call on one of my Italian clients. To make a long story short, one of his clerks took it from the hotel file and gave it to a Bulgarian bimbo agent sent out to find me after they discovered my body had risen from the ashes of the burned-out car. She flashed her big tits at the guy and he just handed her the card."

"Ok, Ok, as I said welcome home." The admiral slapped McHugh's knee. "Take a breather. First of all, we're going to make a stop at the Bethesda Naval Hospital and let one of our good doctors take a look at you. Then we'll have dinner and get you on a plane back to Ohio. I can assure you there will be no Bulgarians looking for you here and I will know if and when they even consider pursuing you."

McHugh put his head back against the seat, "Yeah, well, how sure are you of that?"

"How sure do you think I am about the information you gave to my friend Pfyffer?

"Touché," McHugh responded, somewhat assured at Stringer's confidence. Handing Stringer his report, he added, "And I'm positive you'll have many questions when you read this innocuous report. I don't know who will have access to it, so I left out specific individuals and the circumstances involving them."

"Do you mean your Italian angel?" Stringer took a brief glance at the report. "Obviously, this won't fly upstairs, but you knew that." He folded the report and put it in his coat pocket.

"Well, I guess I did. What I don't know is what will fly, or who will have access to the damn thing. Dan, I'm prepared to detail everything that happened these last three days to you directly, or dictate a full report for you only. You can decide what to shove up the chain. After all, I think we both agree there's a leak in Washington. How else would those bastards know about my visit with Pfyffer?" McHugh stopped, believing he had said enough.

"Colin, I tend to agree about the leak, and I have an idea of how we might expose the individual or individuals. First, we'll stop at the hospital and have a look at your injuries. Between the two of us though, we need a credible story for my boss and Rawhide." He handed McHugh a tape recorder.

"Rawhide? Is that what you Washingtonian insiders call Reagan?"

Peering at his friend, Stringer added, "I thought maybe you were up to speed, now that you're one of us."

"Shit, Dan, I'm not one of you guys. I'm a businessman, and I like it that way. There's too much bureaucracy and bullshit in Washington for me. But I'll dictate a report as soon as I have a few moments to myself. You can filter out what you think shouldn't be in it. I'm not going to identify my Italian angel in any report." Deciding to change the subject, he asked, "By the way, how are Amy and young Daniel?" referring to Stringer's wife and son.

"Amy's not too ecstatic about being in Washington; she's not a party-type. It seems that all that the senior officers' wives do is have teas, theatre parties, silent auctions and other showboat benefits. She sticks to her jogging and painting. And the time we have together, we spend quietly. After all, my next duty assignment will probably be a major sea command. That is, if you and I don't screw up this situation."

"And Daniel?" McHugh prompted.

"Dan's a first classman at the Academy and captain of the Navy Lacrosse Team this year. He's on the first midfield line and scored the winning goal against John Hopkins last week..."

Before he could continue, the driver announced over the intercom, "Admiral we're at the Hospital. What entrance do you want me to pull into?"

"John, they'll be waiting for us under the side portico."

McHugh mouthed. "John?"

Stringer responded, "Master Chief Gunner's Mate John Dahlen's been with me for the past ten years. He's one of the good guys."

They pulled under the portico and Dahlen opened the door. They stepped out, and Stringer introduced McHugh to Doctor Matt Ellison, who directed him into a wheelchair nearby held by an orderly.

"Doc, don't take any crap from this guy; he can be a real pain in the ass." Stringer said.

He then shook McHugh's left hand and said, "Matt's one of our finest orthopedic surgeons; calm down and listen to him. I have to run. Chief Dahlen will be back shortly to pick you up for dinner. By the way, we have new clothes for you. Obviously you've been living in that outfit for more that a week."

Doctor Ellison slipped the X-ray film onto the screen. "No bone damage or cartilage tears. You've probably severely bruised the muscles and tendons covering your humerus where it attaches to your scapula. The bursa, the sack of lubricant fluid allowing movement of the shoulder is most likely inflamed. In layman's terms, you've injured the soft supporting tissues of your shoulder, not the bone structure itself.

"The report I have from Doctor Duebel said you had some friendly medical attention after the injury to your arm. That probably minimized the swelling. My recommendation is for you to take it easy for a week or two, no lifting and minimal movement of that arm. Be smart, Mr. McHugh. Take the time to let your body heal. I'll give you an injection for the pain now and pills for later, if you need them. Limit your alcohol intake until you've recovered."

An orderly stuck his head in the door. "Mr. McHugh?"

The doctor opened the door and the orderly handed a pile of neatly folded clothes to him.

"Well, looks like the Admiral wants you to change. There's a wash room down the hall. Maybe you'd also like to clean up; there's a shower."

McHugh took the clothes and went down the hall. After a long, hot shower, he changed into the clothes Stringer had provided, sat down on the toilet and dictated a complete report. He made it short and sweet without naming or even describing Claudette. Now in a button-down beige shirt, brown slacks and slippers, he opened the door.

The doctor and Chief Dahlen were conversing at the end of the hall.

"I see you're dressed for dinner." Doctor Ellison extended his hand.

"Thanks, doc." McHugh shook with his left and followed Dahlen out of the hospital.

After a cordial dinner with the Admiral and his wife, Amy, in their Arlington condominium, McHugh stood looking at an array of photographs and citations hanging on the navy blue wall of Stringer's den. He picked Stringer out of the framed photograph of the Navy Football Team and easily found the two of them in a framed photo of their Lacrosse Team.

McHugh pointed to the collage. "I see your butt cheeks are still blue and gold."

Stringer, standing next to the sideboard bar of a floor-to-ceiling oak bookcase, handed McHugh a large snifter of Glenfiddich, twenty-one year old single malt scotch. "I was born on a crest of a wave," Stringer began, quoting a line from the poem plebe midshipmen were obligated to recite when academy upperclassmen asked, "*How long have you been in the Navy?*"

McHugh laughed. "I know Dan, but your wave crested just outside the main gate of a Pittsburgh Steel Mill. And you've come along way, Cheers," He raised his snifter in admiration.

Stringer acknowledged raising his. "Thanks. The last time I tapped this scotch was three years ago when we were stationed in Norfolk. Daniel and I had a short sniff before he left to begin his plebe year in Annapolis."

"Thanks for including me," McHugh raised his glass again.

"Colin, Let's get to things at hand." Stringer sat down in one of the two coffee colored lounge chairs straddling the sides of a glass cocktail table in front of the stone fireplace.

McHugh slipped into the other chair and before Stringer could go on, interjected, "Dan I understand the reasons that the President mistrusts the Vatican cardinals and the risks he took by providing the Intel directly to Pfyffer, I just wish he would just give the order to put the damn Bulgarians out of business."

"Well Pfyffer does have our telephone number. And if he calls, we may have to consider other options." Then to change the subject, Stringer continued, "But for now let's focus on the situation at hand. First don't concern yourself about any Bulgarians pursuing you here. As I said in the car; before Prime Minister Todorov would even consider giving that approval, I would know about it."

"OK, so they *also* have a security leak in Sofia. And we certainly have at least one here in Washington. It's the only way the bastards knew of my professor gig."

"What makes *you* so sure the leak's in Washington?"

McHugh took a sip of the scotch and then continued, "First of all, the only people that knew I had even planned to fly to Rome and go to the Vatican *are* in Washington. Bill Williston, my company president, and Rhonda, my secretary were the only people that even knew I was flying to Italy, and all they were told was that I had a business meeting with a client in Perazzeta. Shit Dan, neither of them has any clue where the hell the town of Perazzeta might be."

McHugh put his glass down on the cocktail table and stood behind his chair. "Also, you did tell me the CIA was against my selection. Who knows, they might have leaked the whole damn thing just to discredit you and your staff. I've heard about some pretty sordid interagency crap over the years. Also, remember two years ago when you asked me to carry out occasional letter drops? You said you were replacing marine officers from Quantico who previously handled the drops because you felt they were too visible." He paused. "Actually, what you really said was, "No matter how you dress 'em, you can't disguise a marine." At least at that time, you believed to continue to use marines might compromise Reagan's initiative with some new contacts.

Well, maybe one of the marines may have fingered me to get back at you. Who the hell knows?"

McHugh walked to a bay window overlooking a manicured green lawn behind the condo.

"I just don't see how anyone in the East Bloc, Bulgaria or even in Italy, except of course Phyffer, would know why I arrived at that ceremony."

Stringer joined him, and opened the window. They inhaled the refreshing scent of newly cut grass.

Finally, Stringer said, "I asked Pfyffer to invite you. I'm sure he couldn't be the source. I only told him you were a friend and would be in Rome. I didn't even mention you would be bringing anything for him. What I haven't told you is why I also think the leak's probably here in Washington."

McHugh interjected, "OK, lead on."

Stringer continued. "On your last letter drop in the Carlton Hotel in Johannesburg, the person for whom the drop was intended observed another guy leaving your room just as he was about to retrieve it. He found the letter intact and the assignment was completed. After that incident, our South African friend also questioned the security in Washington."

McHugh smiled knowingly. "Dan, what you do not know and what your South African friend should have known is that, *BOSS*, the Bureau of South African State Security, routinely checks the rooms of overseas business people. That apartheid government is totally paranoid. My South African clients and I don't discuss business in hotels; we only converse in their cars, on the golf course and at their homes. I would bet it was a guy from BOSS that came out of my room after rummaging through my luggage. It's happened numerous times before."

Stringer took a sip of his scotch. "Well, anyway, in a couple of weeks, when you feel up to it, I'd like to schedule a dummy drop in England. You know the country pretty well; having lived there after you resigned your commission. Maybe we can arrange some things to shake the snake out of the trees."

McHugh walked away from the window and stood looking at the wall of photographs.

"Dan, why not right now, before the snake has a clue or there are any other slip-ups?"

Stringer closed the window and followed.

"Doc Ellison said you need two to four weeks to properly recuperate."

"Shit, Dan, my arm's not a problem. In fact, traveling would probably be better for me now than working on my boat. It'll be another routine drop, not face-to-face or a phony persona; I've done a dozen of 'em. Besides, I owe a visit to my company's English licensee. I'll have Rhonda arrange a meeting in London for Monday and be back here on Wednesday. Anyway I'm not too enamored with being pushed off the road and shot at." He walked to the fireplace. "Listen Dan... After this drop, whenever I make it, I'm hanging it up. It's sailing time in the Great Lakes.... And it's time for me to take a serious breather from this traveling; I'm not getting any younger. So right now would be an opportune time for us to plug the damn leak, before you have to initiate another search for a new mailman."

Stringer's face was expressionless.

McHugh had no idea whether Stringer was pissed or pleased.

"As usual, you're full of surprises. I'd like a cognac, how about you?" The admiral lifted a bottle of Hennessy XO from the bar. "A fine cognac always complements the Glenfiddich."

Stringer refreshed both of their glasses, and added, "Only this time I'm ahead of you. I already have a dummy package arranged and an itinerary prepared. If you're serious about next week, I can have everything delivered to your condo tomorrow afternoon. The drop will be in Cheltenham, about an hour or so west of London by train. GCHQ, the British Government Communications Headquarters is located there. And a good friend of mine is in charge of the contingent of our defense department people assigned to the center. He'll be helpful if you need him."

Stringer sat down in the closest lounge chair. "I also have a few chips to cash in at Century House. I'll arrange to have you shadowed by a capable British agent while you're tramping around her majesty's property."

McHugh took the other chair. "Century House?"

"It's MI6 Headquarters in Westminster. One of their directors owes me a considerable favor. I'll let you know what I arrange. And next Wednesday we can discuss this crazy sailing idea of yours."

"Dan, can I use your phone?"

Stringer pointed to the phone on his desk. "Don't call Italy. It's three in the morning; she's asleep. I'll go and see what Amy's up to." Stringer took the two empty brandy snifters and placed them on the bar, then left the room and closed the door.

McHugh lifted the phone and dialed. "Rhonda, I hope I'm not intruding."

"Mr. McHugh, no, not at all, where are you?"

"I'm in Washington; I'm just back from Italy and I need a favor. Can you to go into the office tomorrow morning and make some arrangements for me?"

"Of course, sir." she responded.

He outlined the itinerary he wanted her to arrange and asked her to have the company driver deliver his English client's file and the itinerary to his condo the next afternoon.

He concluded by saying, "I'm sorry for the late call, I'll make it up to you."

"No problem. See you when you return. Have a safe flight home."

He thought for a moment. "By the way, I'm also going to need to have Malcolm drive me to the airport at noon on Sunday, can you arrange that also?"

Rhonda said, "Yes, sir."

"Thanks so much, good night and give my best to Gideon." McHugh walked into the living room. Stringer and his wife sat on the couch chatting.

"My itinerary's all arranged."

Stringer looked astonished. "Who did you call?"

"My secretary; she'll take care of everything in the morning."

"God, Colin, its Friday night and awfully late. Don't you ever give her a break?" Stringer questioned.

McHugh responded matter-of-factly, "Well, yes. Most of the time I'm not even in the office to pester her, and she runs the place like a tight ship when I'm away. I only intrude when I need her. And I always make it up to her. Last year, I arranged for a week at Disney World for her, her husband Gideon, and their children."

"Gideon, that's unusual." Amy said.

"They're a wonderful couple; farmers. He was raised Amish. They have six children. Their oldest son's in the army stationed in Korea." McHugh wanted to say more, but the doorbell rang.

It was Chief Dahlin. "Sorry to intrude." He nodded, "Mrs. Stringer, Admiral, we have just enough time to get Mr. McHugh to National Airport for his flight."

McHugh bid good-bye to the Stringers, thanking them for their hospitality and then left with the chief.

It was approaching midnight when McHugh arrived at his third-floor condominium overlooking the west bank of the Vermilion River. The small town of Vermilion, on the edge of Lake Erie was located halfway between Cleveland and Toledo, Ohio.

The note attached to the door read: *Call me for breakfast whenever you get up. Archie*

McHugh dropped his athletic bag just inside the door, walked straight through the living room and unlocked the sliding glass door onto his balcony. He stepped out and looked down to see *Wayward*, his 34' sloop nestled at her dock. Archie Rhoades, his friend and retired navy boatswain's mate, had rigged her ready to sail. As a welcoming touch, Archie had even turned on the flood lights on the spreaders near the top of the tall mast to illuminate *Wayward's* deck.

McHugh stepped back into the small kitchen and took a bottle of Dewars and a glass from the cupboard. He poured a short two finger nip into the glass and returned to the balcony.

He raised his glass, "Salute, *Wayward.* I'm ready to sail, no more Bulgarian agents, guns, impersonations or car crashes; only a simple letter drop in the Queen's backyard and we'll get underway." He swigged the scotch and tossed the glass into the river just off the port side of the sloop.

Early Saturday,
Vermilion, Ohio

16

In the dream, McHugh was pushed into the center of a circle of Vatican Swiss Guardsmen standing at attention on the manicured lawn in London's Hyde Park. The top of the Marble Arch could be seen just above the tree line. The Guardsmen wore their tri-colored red, blue and yellow uniforms, with their white honeycomb collars and steel breast plates. Their Medici helmets were topped with bright orange plumes. Their halberds were extended horizontally toward the center of the circle. It was late afternoon. The cacophony of the traffic noise along Park Lane and Oxford Street was intrusive. Water began to swirl from nowhere, rising above his shoes and the guards' ankles. He stood rigid as the traffic noise slowly abated and the Guardsmen began to blur. Three guardsmen directly in front of him disappeared, opening a gap in the circle. A cloaked figure with only cold menacing eyes and a brush mustache visible moved through the gap toward him.

McHugh screamed, "Claudette," and awoke instantly soaked in sweat.

He lay still, drained, staring at the ceiling. He struggled to recall details of the dream, but only saw swirling streaks of reds, blues and yellows circling around a pair of dark piercing eyes.

He rose and walked through the entire condominium touching everything, the dining table, chairs, pictures on the walls, books, even the front door; as if to assure himself that he was where he was.

He slid the patio door open and stood on the balcony. It was early. The morning was cool and damp. The sun, struggling to appear from behind the water tower beyond the tree line to the east, outlined a parade of fishing boats and skiffs plying their way down river toward the lake.

After a few minutes he regained his composure and went back into the kitchen and started a pot of coffee. It was half past six, just after noon in Italy. He reminded himself to call Claudette as soon as he finished his shower.

That same Saturday, just before noon in the Rome apartment, Zhelov prepared to begin his meeting. The table was clean and he had swept all the dirt and cigarette butts from the tile floor. A pot of coffee percolated on the stove in the kitchenette.

Bukhalov, dressed in dark fatigues, was the first to arrive.

"Looks serious," he commented, and dropped his leather duffle bag next to the door and extended his hand.

Zhelov shook the hand and pointed to the coffee pot.

Bukhalov poured a cup of black coffee, walked to the sliding glass door, opened it and stepped onto the balcony.

Petcov arrived shortly afterwards, in a dark blue suit, white shirt and conservative striped tie, dressed as if he intended on going to an afternoon cocktail party.

"Where in the fuck do you think you're going?" Zhelov asked, inspecting the suit as if it hung on a store mannequin.

"There's a reception for the new Australian ambassador at three o'clock at their Embassy and I've been ordered to attend by the ambassador."

"Let's hope we're finished by then. Did you bring the recorder? I want these fuckers to hear Kalina."

Petcov took the recorder out of his brief case and set it on the table. "The place looks good; did you hire a maid?"

"No, I cleaned the damn place myself. Where's Kostov? I told you to have him here." He glared at Petcov.

"His plane was due in at ten. He should be here shortly,"

"Have your coffee. Bukhalov's on the balcony." Zhelov went into the bedroom and closed the door.

"What the fock is going on?" Bukhalov asked, as Petcov joined him on the balcony.

"Well, for one thing, you should've eliminated the American Wednesday afternoon before you left the crash scene. Now all our asses are hanging on the line."

Bukhalov glared. "Fock you. I should'a shot the bastard in the hotel parking lot. You're the one who told me to make it look like an accident. That kid and I couldn't spend the entire afternoon beating the bushes for the American prick. The goddamn smoke and explosion probably had the police there right after our focking truck pulled away. It's all bullshit, this no noise, no press, soft kill crap." Bukhalov emptied his cup into the bushes below and stepped back into the apartment.

Petcov sipped his coffee and murmured, "All we need now is for Kostov to say that the arrogant Turk absconded to Muslim land."

Zhelov opened the sliding glass door. "Kostov's here. Let's get started."

They all shook hands with Kostov. Bukhalov handed him a cup of coffee.

Zhelov said in a calm voice, "Take a seat."

Surprised at his tone, they glanced at each other and pulled out chairs.

Zhelov remained standing. "There's a lot at stake here for all of us." He looked deliberately at each of them and then continued. "We only have a few days until the fucking job is done and the papist is eliminated. Then we can close this place. I want to be sure each of you understands his role." He stopped and again eyed each of them. "We also have a serious situation that I intend to take care of personally; Petcov, play the tape."

They leaned back in their chairs and listened to Kalina without comment.

When it ended, Bukahlov said, "I shoulda shot the bastard in the hotel parking lot."

Zhelov focused on him. "You weren't ordered to shoot him then. It's past. Still the American must be eliminated. We can't let him live to expose us to any inquiry after the papist is dead."

"I'll cut out the bastard's tongue. That'll silence him." Bukhalov announced.

Zhelov starred at the brute and barked, "Put it behind you!" Then he turned to the other two. "It's important that we focus on the next few days. We'll discuss the American later. Now I want to make sure our plan to eliminate the Vatican Papist is clear and understood."

He nodded to Kostov and sat down. "Outline the plan."

Kostov stood and unfolded a sketch of the Vatican's St. Peter's Square and the surrounding area. They stood to look at it.

"We've been ordered to make the assassination attempt now to send whatever fucking message Brezhnev needs to send to the world.

So we go with it next Wednesday afternoon in the Vatican piazza. We have no choice." He paused then pointed at the sketch. "The crowd will be in this area." He traced his finger along a gray area outlined on the sketch. "This red line shows the path the Papist's jeep will drive between a series of low barricades shortly after five o'clock. I've arranged for the Turk to stay Tuesday night in a small pension a couple of blocks from the square. One of my men will be with him. The next afternoon when the crowd begins to build up, I'll pick the Turk up in a stolen car and park in an alley a few blocks off the square. I've bribed a hotel doorman to make sure the parking space is available. I'll explain to the bastard that the car will be used for our get away. I'll also show him a hand grenade and inform him I'll explode it as a diversion."

He pointed to a small circle along the jeep's route. "When the Papist's jeep begins its route, the Turk will be about here, well within pistol range. The low barricades along the route will allow the crowd to get close to the Jeep. The papist will be standing in the rear of the vehicle; an easy target for the Turk. I've instructed our assassin to shoot at the papist's body and not the head. The bastards in Sofia don't want a miss even if the papist lives."

"What about the hand grenade and escape?" Zhelov asked.

"There will be no hand grenade for him. He will not escape. After he shoots the papist, I will take him out him and make my way out through the panicking crowd.

"What if someone sees you shoot the bastard?" Petcov asked.

"I'll be close enough to him to allow the shot without attracting any attention and I'm confident that my disguise will allow me to ease through the crowd. If necessary, I will explode a real grenade in the crowd."

"How will you get out of Italy in case you are spotted by cameras or television?" Zhelov asked. To insure Kostov's survival, Zhelov had agreed with his protégé not to discuss the escape plan with anyone.

"You and I have discussed the escape a number of times."

"I know we have, but *now* I want you to explain it to Petcov and Bukhalov."

Kostov glared at his mentor.

Before Kostov could address the other two, Bukhalov asked, "What about the Turk's gun? Can it be traced to us?" He gleamed as if he had found a slip-up.

"I'll give Agca a Browning semi-automatic pistol with the manufacturer's serial number still on it. If it's traced, they'll find it to be missing from a collection of guns that have been smuggled into Austria by a Nazi zealot. We're clear."

When Kostov explained that a TIR truck would transport him over the boarder into Yugoslavia in case someone in the crowd might have recognized him or a photograph or television tape could identify him; Bukhalov's face went blank.

Believing that Bukhalov had probably never heard of a TIR truck, Kostov explained, "The TIR on the side of a truck stands for *Transport Internationaux Routiers*, and means the content of the truck is bonded and sealed. It's allowed to cross through borders without re-inspection at the next border."

"Where's the truck? Who's going to drive it?" Bukhalov picked up his coffee cup and walked into the kitchenette not waiting for an answer.

"It'll be parked in a warehouse about six blocks from here and Petcov's going to arrange for young Botev to drive it and..."

Zhelov interrupted. "No! He's fucking weak and knows too much. Maybe he's even told someone about the *accident* with the American. He can also identify each of us. He must be eliminated."

Zhelov turned to Bukhalov standing in the kitchen alcove with a cup in his hand. "Bukhalov, I want you to eliminate Botev. If it's necessary you will drive the TIR truck to Yugoslavia."

A smile lit up Bukhalov's face. "Yes, sir."

Zhelov looked at Kostov. "Is that it?"

Kostov nodded.

Zhelov then glanced at the other two, "Questions?"

No one responded.

Petcov asked Zhelov for a break to use the bathroom. "OK, but we still have more to talk about"

"Let's sit down," Zhelov said when Petcov returned.

When the three of them took their seats, their leader continued to stand. "To kill the Catholic Papist is only one of our two orders. The other, and probably more important, for the three of us and Kalina, is to not expose Bulgarian involvement in the assassination.... *our involvement*. Bukhalov, that's the reason you were ordered to make the American's death look like an accident. And why I had Kalina tail the American for a soft kill."

He went into the kitchen and opened a bottle of his special Balkan Vodka and brought it and four shot glasses back to the table. "At one-thirty this morning I received a phone call from one of Prime Minister Todorov's bureaucratic ass-lickers reminding me for the third time that any exposure of Bulgarian involvement will have serious consequences for us. You know what that means, or do I have to explain it?"

The three nodded.

"Sofia's aware of the botch-up in Zurich. What they're not aware of is that McHugh has flown to the States. They're also not aware that I'm going after the bastard and will silence him for all eternity. He will never be able to describe any one of us." He paused, and watched their stunned faces. "Each of you will continue with your assignments. Petcov will be in touch with me. No one, I repeat, *no one* outside of the four of us is to know that I have left or where I might be. I will eliminate this McHugh."

He handed glasses to them and poured each to the top. "Na zdrave."

They raised their glasses, "Na zdrave."

Zhelov looked directly at each. "Comments?" Questions?"

They just stared, not knowing what to say.

Zhelov glared. "Now get on with it."

As they began to leave, Zhelov grabbed Petcov by the arm. "Leave the tape recorder, I may need it. Go to your party and say hello to the new Aussie ambassador, but send that other female agent, Reina something or other, to the apartment at three. I'm told she speaks English."

"Reina Veneva; she works in my office. She attended school in England for four years."

"Well, have her here on time. I need her to make a phone call for me."

Petcov made no move to leave.

Zhelov glared at him." Do you have a problem with anything that's been said?"

"Are you free-lancing on this?"

Zhelov picked up a cigarette. "Can you think of any other way to save our asses?"

Petcov extended his hand. "Be sure."

Zhelov nodded and walked into the bedroom.

At about the same time as Zhelov's meeting was ending Claudette, in a bikini, lay on a lounge chair on the balcony of her condo sixty kilometers away reading a book. Well, trying to read the book. She had her watch set to US east coast time eagerly anticipating McHugh's phone call. She needed to tell him the name of the truck driver who had pushed his car off the road. And more importantly, she wanted him to know that she would be flying into Chicago next Friday morning. She checked her watch; seven o'clock. Laying the book aside, she went into the kitchen and put on a pot of tea. Her kitchen clock showed Italian time, one o'clock.

The phone rang just as she slipped out of the bikini intending to refresh in a quick shower.

Picking up the receiver, she said, "Hello, Colin."

"Well, with all of your other talents, you also have ESP. OK, what was I doing before I called?"

"You were in the shower; it was only six thirty there."

"What was I doing in the shower?"

"You were thinking of me."

He said, "Touché."

"How are you? How's your arm?"

"The arm's feeling better. Had it checked out at a naval hospital. I finally arrived at my condo last night about midnight." He paused, trying to decide if he should tell her about his dream or that he was going to England. All he said was, "I miss you.'

"Me too," she said, touching herself.

Walking to the open balcony door, she continued, "I called my brother. The general manager of Lombardi Construction told him that the drivers assigned to their two heavy dump trucks are an Italian by the name of Fialko and a Bulgarian immigrant named Botev. The general manager said Fialko's been with the company for over twenty years and although this Botev has been with the company for seven years, he's only driving the truck for the past three. He also told Claudio both men were good, reliable workers."

McHugh realized she had actually confirmed for the first time that a Bulgarian was involved in the attempt on his life. He also realized this Botev might have significant inside knowledge of the assassination plans and could positively identify those involved.

"Did you get this Botev's phone number or address?" he asked.

"Claudio found their addresses, I wrote them down. They're on the patio table. Wait I'll get them."

"Never mind, I need you to do me a favor. Ask Claudio to verify this Botev's address and confirm he actually lives there. Maybe he could have one of his staff talk with a neighbor. Ask him not to contact Botev directly, OK?"

"I'll take care of it. By the way, I'm scheduled on a flight into O'Hare next Friday afternoon, with lay-over until Sunday night. Maybe we can spend some time together, that is, if you don't have other commitments."

Knowing he would be back from England on Wednesday, he said flippantly, "I'll have to check my schedule and get back to you on that."

The silence was unexpected, she had taken him seriously.

He quickly added, "Hey, I'm only kidding. I love Chicago and I'm becoming kinda fond of you too. I'll be at the gate when you arrive. Look for the guy holding eleven roses. Call me after Claudio checks out the address."

"I'll call as soon as I can." She paused, and then added, "Colin, I miss you much."

"Miss you too." He held the phone, not knowing what else to add… then hung up.

Zhelov heard the knocking on the apartment door and stepped out of the shower, grabbed a towel and looked at the clock, Two-thirty. Not expecting anyone, he wrapped the towel around his waist, picked up his silenced pistol and walked to the door.

"Ya, who's there?"

"Mr. Zhelov, its Reina Veneva."

While drying himself, Zhelov yelled, "Well, you're early. Why don't you go for a walk for a half hour? Pick up a pizza,"

Later when he opened the door, he found Reina to be the opposite of Kalina, the only other female agent in Rome. She was tall and athletic, in her early thirties, wearing jeans and a tight bra-less tee-shirt that drew his attention to her taut, small breasts. She wore no make-up and her short brown hair accentuated her child-like face.

"Mr. Zhelov, here's your pizza. I understand you wish me to make phone calls for you," she said with a proper English accent and handed the pizza to him.

"Ah, yes." He was surprised at her precise English and forthright manner. He set the pizza on the table.

"Whom do you wish me to call?" She sat down in the chair directly in front of the phone.

He rubbed his jaw and said in a commanding voice, "Spirane durzha! Stop, hold on, Miss Reina. I will tell you exactly what I want you to do."

He outlined the strategy for the phone call he intended her to make without providing her any reason for it. Then he handed her McHugh's business card that Kalina had received from the clerk in the hotel and pointed to the telephone number. He sat down in the chair next to her and placed a sheet of paper on the table in front of her with a list of statements and questions.

"I want to hear the other side of the conversation, so we have to hold the phone together." He pointed to a telephone number and handed her the phone.

When the phone was answered, they both heard, "Security."

Zhelov pointed to a question on the sheet.

Reina asked, in her proper English accent, "Is this the Williston Pump Company?"

"Yes, Ma'am"

"I'm calling from Europe. May I speak with someone in the International Department?"

"Ma'am, its Saturday morning and the company is closed… but hold on and I'll see if anyone is in that department."

After a moment he came back on the line. "Rhonda, the department secretary is here. I'll transfer you."

"International Division, Rhonda speaking."

Zhelov pointed to another question.

"Good morning, my name is Reina; I'm calling from Europe and if it is convenient I wish to make an appointment for my company president to meet next week with Mr. Colin McHugh."

"I'm sorry, but Mr. McHugh will be in London next week. May I ask the name of your company?"

Smiling at his good fortune, Zhelov pointed to a statement, and Reina said, "Of course, it's Edgewere Trading Limited. We do business in many Middle Eastern countries."

Zhelov put his hand over the phone. "Tell her Mr. Lester can be in London on Monday and ask if it's possible to meet Mr. McHugh there?"

Reina asked as he directed, and Rhonda told her McHugh would arrive in London on Monday and would be staying at the Carlton Tower Hotel.

Zhelov mouthed, "Thank you" and Reina said, "Thank you. I'll advise Mr. Lester. Have a good day." She hung up.

Zhelov started to hug the girl but backed off, and said, "Join me for pizza?"

Reina stood, "No sir, I'm already late for the picnic and tour."

"A picnic and tour?"

"It's for the junior staffs of all the embassies. It begins at four o'clock in the Castel Sant'Angelo museum. It was once the mausoleum of Roman Emperor Hadrian," she said authoritively and walked out, leaving the door open.

Later Saturday morning, Vermilion, Ohio

17

After talking with Claudette, McHugh took his coffee onto the balcony and sat down on one of the two wicker lounge chairs to watch the early morning action on the river. A shrill whistle from below brought him to his feet and he leaned over the waist high wrought iron railing.

"Hey Colin, you're up. Why didn't you call me?" Archie Rhodes yelled through cupped hands from the sidewalk below that ran between the condominium building and the boat docks. He was a burly man of sixty, with a neatly trimmed white beard and a head of flowing white hair that just touched the collar of his denim fisherman's work shirt. His sleeves were rolled up to his elbows revealing strong forearms covered with faded tattoos. Skinny legs dropped out of a pair of khaki shorts held up by red and white striped suspenders.

"Arch, I just got up."

"No excuses. Get some clothes on. Let's go to Captain Larry's for a real breakfast."

"I'll be right down." Then realizing he was standing in his underwear, McHugh ducked into the condo to dress. Not wanting Archie to know about his shoulder contusion, he struggled into a white sweatshirt with ocean blue *SAILING* across the front, by first easing his sore right arm into it and then ducking his head through the neck opening. Anticipating they would take a short shakedown on *WayWard*, he slipped on a pair of khaki shorts, laced up his boat shoes and headed for the door,

"Boy, you look beat up. Where have you been?" Archie delivered a soft punch to McHugh's right shoulder.

McHugh grimaced. "Hey."

Archie stopped and regarded his friend with genuine concern. "Shit. You're hurt. There's even an ugly bruise on your forehead. You didn't leave with that last Sunday."

"Let's get to Larry's. I'll explain there," McHugh responded, wondering how much he should tell his best friend.

While walking to Liberty Avenue, the village main street, McHugh decided to bring Archie into as much of his situation as possible, without mentioning the Pope or the Vatican. Letter dropping would soon be finished anyway, then he was going sailing.

Captain Larry's was a no-frills restaurant facing Liberty Avenue in the historic section of the lake front community, labeled Harbourtown 1837.

During the Lake Erie summer boating season, visiting boaters swelled the usual numbers of breakfast-goers. However, today it was mostly the local crowd, as the season had yet to get into full swing.

Archie and McHugh waved to those on the stools at the counter in the rear of the place and said good morning to the few sitting at a cluster of small tables in the middle of the room. They took seats across from each other in a booth along the wall near the front window. The white walls were punctuated with framed fading photographs of early village life. There were photos of steamboats, sailboats, the old fish house, the Inland Seas Maritime Museum, the lighthouse, the water tower, early settlers and bygone homes.

The waitress, a chunky girl in her late teens, brought coffee and took their orders. When she left the table, McHugh said, "Arch, what I tell you is between us, OK?"

Archie, nodded. "You really didn't have to say that."

"Yes, I know. Sorry." McHugh then explained that on business trips abroad during the past two years he acted as a courier for a federal security agency. He didn't identify the agency.

Archie just sipped his coffee and listened as McHugh described two letter drops he had made in South Africa and Ecuador.

"But last week I ran into a bit of difficulty in Italy."

Archie leaned across the narrow table, "Bit of difficulty, my ass; you were beat up. Be straight. What happened?"

McHugh described what happened after he made the letter drop in Italy. He mentioned the drop was at a hotel instead of the Vatican.

He described his cuts, the shoulder contusion and the shooter as vividly as he could. He included meeting Claudette and the drive to Milan, the train to Zurich and the confrontation with the girl, Kalina, and her overweight partner. In glowing terms, he also told Archie, how Claudette saved his ass with a steel pipe. Finally, he decided not to mention that he planned to leave for England the next day, knowing Archie would insist on going along as his bodyguard.

Just as he finished, the waitress brought their breakfasts and refreshed their coffees.

Archie waited until she left. "That Claudette's sweet. Obviously there's someone in Washington that's out for your ass, or maybe your boss's. Maybe there's a mole in your boss's agency? So, tell me you've quit this mailman shit."

McHugh didn't answer and looked away.

Archie picked up his fork, pointed it at McHugh and whispered, "You're supposed to be smart and all that shit, academy educated, business executive, world traveler, been everywhere. You're sitting on your brain! You've always talked of going sailing. Well, now you have the sailboat and met a beautiful woman. Be smart. Get the hell out now!"

McHugh looked directly at his friend. "You're so right, but the guy I work for is a classmate and very good friend. He's an Admiral and pretty close to Reagan. He and I agree the leak's in Washington. He needs my help, so I'm going to make one last dummy letter drop next week to entrap the snake. I'm leaving tomorrow afternoon and will return on Wednesday. Then Arch, I assure you my mailman role is finished."

Taking a last bite of toast, Archie sat back, folded his arms and stared at McHugh, "Well, smart ass, I hope you're going to be better prepared this trip. How'll you defend yourself? Take a gun?"

"You can't carry a gun on the airlines; they X-ray everything. Hell, it's a simple letter drop in a small town west of London, like the others, No sweat." McHugh looked at his watch: ten-thirty. Hoping to close the discussion, he added, "Anyway, why don't we meet on *Way-Ward* at four and take her out for a couple of hours? Now I have to get back; I'm expecting my business files to be delivered from my secretary."

Archie mimicked a seaman's response. "Ay, Ay, Captain."

McHugh left a twenty dollar bill on the table, more than enough to cover the breakfast and a generous tip and they left the restaurant.

He shook Archie's hand with his left as they stood on the sidewalk outside the restaurant and Archie strolled around the corner toward his small cottage two blocks beyond the railroad tracks.

When the traffic light changed, McHugh waited for a semi-trailer to pass, then crossed the street and walked to the edge of the river. He was a member of the Vermillion Boat Club and sat on one of its green wrought iron benches facing the river.

The sun was bright with only wisps of cirrus clouds dotting a vivid blue sky. The warm temperature had brought out large numbers of winter weary boaters. Boat Club members worked on their sailboats moored alongside the club's finger docks jutting into the river.

He relished the scene and tried to clear his mind of the past week. Then Doug Steven's bikini clad wife, Michelle, stepped into the cockpit from the cabin of their 34' Catalina sloop and wrapped her arms around her husband, who had been coiling one of the sail lines.

Their embrace brought back the void he always tried to ignore in such idyllic settings. *He was usually alone*. However, now pleasant thoughts of Claudette quickly filled that void. He rose and walked back to his condo.

The phone rang in a small apartment only a few blocks from the massive Ministry of State Security *(Stasi)* Headquarters in Lichtenberg, an East Berlin borough.

"Scheibe *(shit)*" Steiger said, lifting himself from between the legs of the naked girl lying on the small cot next to the apartment's single window. He looked at his watch, four o'clock, and then at the girl illuminated by the hazy light filtering through the dirty window. She lay there starring blankly at him with her legs splayed and her arms crossed over her small breasts.

His erection shriveled.

Knowing it was his secretary calling, he picked up the phone. "Was willst du, Gretchen?"

She was the only one with the apartment phone number. A year before she also knew the apartment well.

"Herr Steiger, you received an important phone call from Herr Zhelov in Rome. He needs you to return his call as soon as possible. He didn't leave a message, but said it is extremely urgent."

"I'll be there as soon as I can." He growled, threw the girl's dress at her and motioned for her to leave.

She stood and faced him with her eyes downcast holding the dress modestly in front of her, not knowing her next move. She couldn't have been more than sixteen, obviously not one of the twenty thousand female employees who worked in the massive Stasi building nearby.

Recognizing her indecision, Steiger opened the folding door to the commode. The smell of urine permeated the small room. Holding the dress like a shield, she walked past him sideways and pulled the door closed behind her.

Steiger slipped into his shorts and glanced out of the window. This afternoon was just another of the one or two Saturday afternoons each month that he escaped from his wife and worked in the office. He didn't care whether or not his wife was aware of his liaisons. They had no relationship. His senior position dictated an appearance of marriage. He didn't have to live it.

The toilet flushed and the girl emerged wearing the faded colorless dress. She didn't look at him, just picked her torn panties from the cot and pulled them up under her dress. Then she slipped into her flat shoes and faced him. He handed her the flimsy brown woolen sweater she had worn when she arrived.

"Helena, you don't have to come again." He handed her a few DDR marks, and continued, "Your father will be released Monday; take care of him."

The girl nodded and left.

She was one of numerous young girls Steiger used, leveraging sex against the release of a family member from the numerous cells in the basement of headquarters building. Many innocent people were routinely rounded up on spurious charges and interrogated and abused principally to amuse their captors. Initially, Steiger used his senior position to impose himself on a number of female employees in the Stasi headquarters, but was reprimanded by the director. Now, he just arrested individuals when he became aware they had young daughters.

He glanced about the room before leaving. It was devoid of anything human: gray walls, a cot with soiled sheets, not even a coverlet or pillow. No chair, table or picture. A half-empty vodka bottle on the window sill mirrored his soul.

When Steiger walked into the large office on the twelfth floor of the Headquarters Building, Gretchen immediately began to dial the phone. Just as he closed the door to his private office and he sat down at his desk, the phone rang.

He picked up the receiver and barked, "Zhelov."

"Steiger, we've got a serious problem."

"Ya, what?" Steiger propped his feet up on top of his desk.

Zhelov explained how the American, McHugh, aware of the assassination conspiracy, could positively identify at least him and Petcov. "And he killed one of my agents and put another in the hospital."

"Well, where's the bastard now?" Steiger demanded. "Why is he still alive?"

Zhelov explained how they failed in their soft-kill efforts to eliminate McHugh who then flew to the States and would be traveling to London on Monday. He also told the Stasi agent that he was going to London to eliminate the American.

"Who authorized the London kill?" Steiger asked.

"I'm free-lancing. No authority from Sofia. I need your help. If this bastard lives to expose our involvement, not only will both of our heads roll; blood's going to flow from Sofia through Lichtenberg, all the way to fucking Moscow."

"I can't come to London; tell me what sort of help you need and I'll make it happen."

Zhelov explained what he needed.

"I'll arrange it; call me back in an hour." Then almost as a command, he bellowed, "Zhelov, kill the fucking bastard!" Steiger slammed the phone down.

At Five thirty, that same afternoon in Rome, Fialko asked Botev to stop for beers at the bar down the street from the company yard. The two heavy dump trucks drivers of the Lombardo Construction Company had been called into work that morning, their off-day, to haul gravel from a pit near the company storage yard to a construction site thirty kilometers away.

It had been a long, dirty day for both. Between hauls they didn't have much of an opportunity to talk.

Fialko, a big burly guy in his late forties, with a Marlon Brando godfather face, and arms like pool table legs, yelled at the bar maid as soon as he and Dimitar Botev walked in, "Two Peroni, Jolanda."

They took seats near the front window on either side of a long worn oak table covered with cigarette burns. The dark, grimy place smelled of stale beer and rancid tobacco. Dimitar swept an empty cigarette pack and ashes from the table to clear an area to lean on. The place was empty, except for the woman who rose from a chair at the rear of the narrow room and walked behind the bar.

Jolanda, a heavy woman with unkempt, streaked blond hair and more makeup than a fiftyish woman should wear, walked toward them and set the beers down on the table, then turned to walk away.

"You look inviting tonight," Fialko said.

She kicked him in the shin and raised her hand in jovial threatening gesture.

"Only kidding. Pour yourself something, and bring us some pretzels and two more beers."

When she had her back to them walking toward the bar, Fialko raised his bottle, "Salute"

"Salute." Dimitar returned the toast and they took long draws of their beers.

The burley driver focused on Dimitar, "Botev, remember when Mr. Lombardi radioed at lunch, and asked me to stop back at the yard?"

Dimitar nodded and took another sip.

The older driver continued. "When I pulled into the yard, Mr. Lombardi came out to the truck and told me he had received a call from an administrator in Rome's Housing division asking for our names and how long we've been driving the trucks. When the old man asked why they needed our names, the person said he believed it was for some sort of list. The old man is concerned because the caller seemed unsure of why he was calling. Lombardi asked if you or I had done anything that would bring the Company to their attention. I told him not me."

To hide his anxiety, Botev raised his bottle near his face as if he was about to take another swig.

Fialko continued. "I said, if anything unusual happened I would've reported it."

Dimitar thought quickly and said, "I had an oil leak that afternoon and took my truck to the garage for repair. Maybe there was oil on the road." He watched Jolanda put the pretzels and beers on the table. "Did the person say what kind of truck it was?"

Seemingly unaware of the question, Fialko wrapped his arms around the bar maid's waist and pulled her onto his lap.

With her hands clasped on the back of the Italian driver's bald head, she pulled his face into her large bosom.

The two of them didn't notice Botev slip away from the table and leave the bar. He walked to the bus stop at the end of the block. Then realizing Fialko might come out to look for him, he rounded the corner and began the long walk to his apartment. He had made the hour-long walk only once before, at the end of his first week of work. His money had been low then, and he needed to save what was left for bus fare to work until he received his first pay. Today he just needed to think.

Even though it was a mild day, Dimitar began to sweat. Removing his light jacket, he flung it over his shoulder and wondered if someone was pursuing an investigation into Wednesday afternoon's attack on the American. Was it the Italian police, or even the Americans?

Dimitar was unnerved. If he went to the authorities and told them of the assassination plan, he could possibly save the life of the Pope, but Zhelov and the others would claim diplomatic immunity and leave Italy. He also knew his name would be prominently added to Division 7's kill list. He thought of his mother and sister back in Sofia being dragged out of their small apartment at four in the morning by agency thugs and sent to a work camp or prison, maybe even executed. Also, if the boss checked with the garage about the hydraulic leak, he could lose his job and be arrested as an accomplice, and he had no diplomatic immunity. He didn't know what to do or to whom he could turn.

Ahead, he saw the white and green awning of a small market he recalled from his previous walk and knew coolers of soft drinks and bottled water lined its rear wall. He entered the store and purchased a bottle of water, sat down on the stone sidewalk outside and leaned against the wall next to the market. He put his head down and sobbed. He was alone, isolated and helpless.

Dimitar felt a touch on his shoulder and looked up. It was the shopkeeper.

"Better be on your way, and pick up the water bottle you dropped in the street." It was an order, but the man's voice had a tone of concern.

Botev scrambled to his feet. "Sorry, I must've dosed off." He wiped his hands on the sides of his coveralls, reached down, picked up the empty bottle and walked on.

"You look terrible," Bonifila said when Dimitar walked into the coffee bar at the end of his street.

"It's been a long day," he said and sat down at one of the tables. "Where's Angelo?"

Bonifila didn't look up from wiping down one of the tables. "My Angelo, he's not feeling good this afternoon. I will close; we have some pizza slices left."

Dimitar looked hungrily at the three pizza slices remaining on top of the display counter. "I'll take the lot." He paid her and asked her to give his best wishes to Angelo. Then he walked up the short street to his apartment building.

Dimitar ate a piece of the pizza with the remainder of the bottled water and put the other two slices in his small refrigerator. He then stripped off his coverall and under shorts. After grabbing his only towel from the closet and a bar of soap from the shelf above the sink, he glanced out of the apartment door.

The hall was empty.

He wrapped the towel around himself, walked to the bathroom at the end of the hall and took a long, hot shower. Refreshed and extremely tired, he pulled on another pair of shorts and crawled under the flimsy sheet on his bed.

Precisely at noon that Saturday in Vermillion, Admiral Stringer's messenger delivered the courier package to McHugh.

While the courier waited outside the condo door for the signed receipt, McHugh sat down at his desk, opened the package and perused the included list of contents. He checked each item.

There were two passports and driver's licensees with his photo; one in the name of Matthew Carroll from Toronto, and a similar set in the name of a Ray Ingram with an address in Glen Bernie, Maryland. Additionally, there were Master Card, Visa and American Express cards in both names. A verification of a confirmed one-night reservation for a Suite in the Queen's Hotel in Cheltenham Spa in the name of Carroll for Monday night, was also included. An early hotel check-in was requested. A manila envelope held a map of Cheltenham, twenty thousand US dollars, and five thousand British pounds. To his surprise, it also contained a first class round trip rail ticket to Cheltenham Spa for an early Monday afternoon departure from London's Paddington Station with a return Tuesday morning. The note attached to the rail ticket explained that Stringer had made the reservations to aid the MI6 shadow to *catch up with* McHugh.

McHugh had told Stringer he planned to do the letter drop as soon as he arrived in England and had Rhonda arrange his business meeting for Tuesday.

At the very bottom of the packet, he found a manila envelope with his name on it marked *personal.* The envelope was sealed with wide red adhesive tape with Stringer's signature scrawled across it. McHugh ripped the seal, opened the envelope and dumped the contents on top of everything else on his desk. A hand-written note wrapped around a couple of photographs said: *One thing you're not is a photographer. The other photos were not clear either. Dan.*

McHugh scanned the first; it was the color photograph he'd snapped last Wednesday near the Pantheon. His follower was standing with a newspaper in his hand; his head was turned slightly to the side. The photo was in focus but only the follower's profile was visible. The other photograph was shot earlier that day in St. Peter's Square. He remembered the exact moment he took it. However, the photo of the two men was out-of-focus. It didn't matter; he would not forget the glaring face of the taller one.

Rome was over. He put the note and photos in his desk drawer and walked toward the balcony to clear his mind of the experience. After a few moments watching the activities on the river he remembered that the courier was still outside his condo door. He signed the receipt, sealed it in the accompanying envelope and returned it to the anxious courier.

Later, as he packed, McHugh thought of how much happier his arrival in London would be if Claudette were there to meet him. Usually on his international trips, he walked directly through the throng of waiting family and friends greeting and hugging new arrivals, to meet a driver from the company he came to visit or to take a taxi alone to his hotel. He pictured himself exiting the customs hall in London's Heathrow Airport and dropping his bags as Claudette ran into his arms, …maybe someday.

The doorbell rang. He opened it and Malcolm stood outside holding a large envelope.

"Malcolm, it's good to see you. Sorry for rousting you out this morning and also again tomorrow."

"It's OK, Mr. Mack; my wife will have to wait a while longer to have her to-do-list completed. Besides, it's a wonderful day for a drive." The thin, old man with white hair had retired from the Williston Pump Company accounting department two years ago at sixty-five. He now worked on a part-time basis driving company executives or clients to and from Cleveland Hopkins International Airport.

"Malcolm, how about a coffee?"

"No thanks, Mr. Mack." Again Malcolm used the familiar nickname McHugh had acquired at Williston. It started when a new hire in the international department pronounced his name, McHuge, and was summarily corrected by Rhonda.

"By the way," Malcolm continued, "Rhonda asked that I remind you to read her note about the phone call she received this morning."

"Thanks, see you tomorrow around noon." McHugh shook the old man's hand before closing the door. He then took the envelope and his coffee onto the balcony and sat down in a lounge chair.

Rhonda's envelope contained his two airline tickets, an Air Canada round trip from Cleveland to Toronto, and a British Airways first class ticket to London from Toronto with an open return flight. A confirmed reservation at the Carlton Tower Hotel, and a lean file of his client's information were also included. In her neatly handwritten note Rhonda advised McHugh that she had received a call earlier this morning from the secretary of a Mr. Lester of Edgewere Trading. She advised McHugh that she had told Lester's secretary that he could contact McHugh at the Carlton Tower Hotel on Monday.

With his frequent travels and changing itineraries, the last minute arrangement Rhonda made with Mr. Lester occasionally happened. He put the note with the tickets and the hotel reservation in his travel wallet, and then scanned the file Rhonda had compiled on his client, Pumping Engineers Ltd, a company specializing in reverse osmosis systems design located in Peteborough, just north of London. Rhonda had even arranged for him to have dinner with its managing director in London Tuesday evening.

When McHugh climbed aboard *Wayward* at four o'clock, Archie was standing in the cockpit holding the end of the yacht's stern line in one hand and a can of Labatt's Blue Beer in the other. The engine hummed. Only the stern line in Archie's hand and the bow line tied to a cleat on the dock held the yacht to it.

"In a hurry?" McHugh took the offered can.

"Welcome aboard, Captain. All lines singled up, ready to get underway." Archie handed the stern line to McHugh and moved forward to the bow.

McHugh took the helm, gave Archie a thumbs-up and they tossed both lines onto the dock. The river was clear behind, so McHugh shifted into reverse and slowly backed into the middle of the river. Once clear of the dock, he headed toward the lake hugging the right side of the channel.

When they were clear of the break wall, McHugh took a northwesterly heading and pressed the set button on the *Autohelm* to automatically maintain the compass heading.

"Hey, you're injured. Stay in the cockpit and take care of that arm; I'll handle the rigging and sails," Archie said, while standing on top of the cabin, removing the tie-down straps securing the mainsail to the boom. "Colin, you handle the beer and the helm.

It was a beautiful refreshing day. From the offshore wind and the rippling waves and occasional white caps, McHugh judged the wind to be about six to eight knots. When Archie had the mainsail up and the Genoa flapping in the wind, Colin disengaged the *Autohelm*, and changed course to the west. He turned off the engine and the sails billowed. Under mainsail and Genoa they made a comfortable headway of five knots. Sandusky's Cedar Point Amusement Park loomed twenty miles ahead off the port bow and Kelly's Island sat thirty degrees to starboard at about twelve miles. The 350 foot tall Admiral Perry Monument commemorating the Battle of Lake Erie in the war of 1812 towering over the island of Put-in-Bay lay dead ahead on the horizon.

"Well, are you all set with your dummy drop Monday?" Archie asked, as he climbed into the cockpit. After opening another beer, he sat down on the starboard storage locker waiting for McHugh's answer.

McHugh took his sun glasses off and wiped them with his handkerchief. "Everything's a go."

"Well, you seem uneasy about something." Archie took a sip of his beer.

"Well, here is a deviation to the schedule I usually make on letter drops. Maybe it's because my friend is trying to uncover the bastard causing the leak."

"Tell me about it," Archie stood next to McHugh and took the helm.

McHugh moved away and sat on the port storage locker. "In all my previous drops, I made my own in-country travel arrangements, principally because business appointments sometimes change. It seems my admiral friend has made specific train reservations for me next week probably to help someone he planned to have watch my back while I'm in England."

"What backup?"

"Well… As a precaution, because of the leak and the Bulgarian bastards that tried to eliminate me, my classmate is arranging with the British Secret Service to have an agent shadow me while I'm in England."

"Don't tell me your Admiral friend makes arrangements for you. Bullshit. He gives the order. Someone else, a clerk or secretary made those train reservations. That someone might just be setting you up for a fall. You better get hold of your Admiral friend, ASAP."

"Come on Arch, aren't you getting a little over dramatic, My friend moved some heavy timber to arrange for a backup in England, I trust he had an excellent reason for the train reservations and covered his bases making them.

"Who knows. Be smart. Call him as soon as you arrive in London and straighten everything out. And watch your back when you get there." As soon as he said it, Archie realized it came across like an order.

"Any more suggestions?" McHugh snapped. Then he quietly said, "Sorry, I didn't mean that."

"No offense. But I do have something that may come in handy." Archie reached into his pocket and pulled out what looked like rolled up sail cloth about ten inches long.

"What the hell?" McHugh remarked.

"It's a *fish-kill;* I made it special for you this morning. Here hold it."

It had a heavy feel, like a black jack, six inches of rolled sail cloth with a pocket sewn on the end that contained a heavy weight.

"What's in the pocket?" McHugh swung the fish-kill against his leg, "Jesus that could crush a skull."

"I took weights from the lead line I use to determine the water depth beneath my skiff. You said you can't take a gun. Well, maybe it'll come in handy. Who's to know?"

At that moment, McHugh relished the friendship he had with Archie. They were shipmates in the truest sense of the word.

They talked about the round trip sail north to Canada's Georgian Bay they might take when he returned from England.

While Archie took down the sails, McHugh brought Wayward into the wind and turned on the engine. With the sails secure, he set a course for the Vermillion lighthouse.

Outside Rome, Sunday Morning

18

On Sunday mornings when Claudette was home, the alarm went off at six. However, this morning she was already up at five-thirty and stood at her patio door watching a heavy rain pound on her balcony. Thunder and lightning exploded to the west over the Mediterranean. She savored her coffee, fresh from the espresso machine on her kitchen counter, happy within the security of her condominium.

Later, after she showered, the storm had faded into a drizzling rain.

Mother will not be pleased riding in my Fiat Spider this morning with the top up, she thought. I can hear her first words when I pick her up for early Mass: "Why don't you get a real car instead of this toy? With the top up, I can't even see through the windows."

Father Angelo, the elderly pastor of St. Rocco's, the small village church her mother still religiously attended on Sundays and holy days, always said the early Mass even though he could have ordered his young curate to take the assignment.

At first, Claudette didn't understand why there even was a seven o'clock Mass on Sundays. Each time she brought her mother, only the two of them and one or two others were in attendance. Sergio, their chauffeur, took her mother to the Mass when Claudette was away and she had asked him about it months ago.

As usual, his answer was short and to the point. "Your father and the reverend were classmates and best friends in school. When Mussolini led Italy into the war on the German side, the two of them joined the partisans and together fought both the Fascists and the Germans. They both idolized your mother." After a pause he concluded, "After the war, your father married your mother and Angelo joined the seminary. Since your father died, Father Angelo has said the early Mass for your mother and, as you know, invites her to breakfast afterward."

With another espresso, Claudette stood in front of her closet trying to decide what to wear: rainy day, small car, Mass, and then a venture into one of the seedier parts of Rome to find the address of a Bulgarian truck driver. Her brother, Claudio was out of town, so she decided she would pass by and verify the Bulgarian truck driver's address. She chose a lightweight beige turtleneck sweater, dark slacks and jogging shoes. She grabbed her rain slicker and umbrella from the hook by the door, took the rear elevator to the garage and drove in the drizzling rain, south along the shore toward Arriaga Drive.

Her mother paced back and forth under the wide overhang outside the villa kitchen. Even before Claudette turned off the car's ignition, her mother was at the passenger door fidgeting with its handle. Claudette reached across the passenger seat and unlocked the door.

The sandstone wall of the small church was framed by white stone columns. An oversized wooden cross stood above a bell tower centered on an orange tile roof. Two thick wooden doors stood open inside a shallow archway under a circular stained glass window.

The interior of the church was dark, except for the faint glow of two flickering candles on each side of the altar; Claudette shuddered in the cold, damp place. An elderly man, hunched at the far end of the last pew, looked up as Claudette and her mother entered. They walked down the aisle and knelt in the front pew.

Father Angelo walked slowly out of the sacristy onto the altar, without an attendant altar boy, and began the Mass. He conducted the entire Mass in Latin facing the altar. There was no sermon.

Kneeling at her mother's side at the communion rail, Claudette observed the warmth in the priest's eyes as he placed the host on her mother's tongue. When he approached her, he whispered, "I hope you can join us for breakfast,"

She murmured, "I have to be in Rome."

He nodded and whispered, "I understand. I'll see Lauretta home." He placed the host on Claudette's tongue, and then put his hand on her head. "God bless."

The Mass ended quickly. Father Angelo didn't even remove the chalice or the water and wine cruets from the altar as he normally did.

In the church vestibule, Claudette hugged both of them and walked out into the drizzle.

An hour later, just as the rain cleared, Claudette found Via Della Lungara, the road leading into a maze of narrow streets in one of the poorer sections of the city. After a number of wrong turns between graffiti-covered stone buildings, she found the street she was looking for and almost rammed a police car that blocked entry into it.

When she stepped out of her car, she saw a crowd of people holding umbrellas farther down the street. Reflections from a rotating blue emergency light on top of a white ambulance bounced off the rain-soaked buildings. Anxious, she slipped back into the car and drove a short distance farther along the road and squeezed her small Fiat into a tight parking spot in front of a locked garage door. She jumped out and sprinted back to the police car.

Working her way through the crowd, she approached a young police officer standing rigidly in front of the first line of onlookers and touched his arm. "Officer, what's happened?"

Glancing at her, the young officer snapped, "You can't go any further."

"I understand." She asked again, "What happened?"

The officer turned to her and responded apologetically, "Miss, there's been a shooting. Unfortunately, I can't tell you more. Maybe you should talk with my sergeant." He pointed to a tall policeman standing in front of a vegetable market talking with a smaller rotund man wearing a full length white apron.

Claudette watched the animated discussion between the authoritative police sergeant and the vegetable man and decided to wait for a more opportune time to approach.

The ambulance was backed to a doorway next to the stand. Two emergency medics in lime green coveralls pulled a gurney out of the ambulance and carried it into the building.

The vegetable man noticed a man in a yellow workman's raincoat making his way through the small gathering at opposite end of the street and pointed toward to him. The police sergeant glanced up from writing on a small note pad and motioned the man forward. The three then became engrossed in an animated conversation. Finally the man in the raincoat handed what appeared to be a small leather billfold to the sergeant and took a few steps back

The crowd gasped as the medics wheeled a gurney out of the building with a body covered by a white sheet on it. The medics lifted the gurney into the back of the ambulance and closed its doors. One of the medics then handed a sheet of paper to the police sergeant and climbed into the passenger side of the ambulance. The blue lights stopped flashing and the ambulance slowly eased its way through the crowd gathered at the far end of the street. The crowd began to quietly disperse.

The sergeant returned the billfold to the young man and then pointed a finger at him in a scolding fashion. The young man shuffled side-to-side, with his head down and his hands in the pockets of his raincoat. The sergeant stopped talking. The young man nodded, turned and walked into the same doorway that the medics had brought out the gurney.

When only a few onlookers remained, Claudette approached the sergeant.

"Sir what happened?"

Taken back by the direct approach, the sergeant scrutinized Claudette. "Miss, there's not much I can tell you. It appears that a young couple has been murdered."

She glanced toward the building, "But I only saw one body carried out."

"That was the second ambulance. The first carried away the body of the young woman." The sergeant touched the front of his cap in an informal salute, "I must make my reports." He then walked toward the police car.

Claudette caught up with the vegetable man inside his stand, "I'm looking for a Mr. Botev. Was he one of the victims?"

"Oh, no, Botev's upstairs in his apartment. It's directly above my stand. The police sergeant finished questioning him and told him not to leave the city until the investigation is completed."

"Does the sergeant think Mr. Botev was involved in the murders?"

The man quickly replied, "No, I don't think so; Dimitar is a good man."

"Dimitar?" she queried.

"Dimitar is young Botev's given name. He's Bulgarian." The man picked up a plump Valencia orange and offered it to her.

Claudette accepted the orange and returned to the empty street. After convincing herself McHugh wouldn't be too upset if she just met briefly with the young Dimitar Botev, she walked into the building.

The small vestibule was dark and smelled musty. Steep, narrow, time-worn wooden steps rose in front of her. The only light came from the open door behind her. Blood streaks remained on the wood grain of two steps where someone had tried to clean. She walked cautiously up to the first floor. An apartment door was on the left of a narrow hallway. The stairs leading up to the next floor were blocked off with bright yellow police security tape.

She knocked softly on the door. "Mr. Botev... Dimitar are you there?"

Silence.

She repeated herself and pushed on the door. It opened easily. The room was dark.

She edged into it and asked again, "Dimitar, are you here?"

A slight movement near the window caught her attention. She worked her way cautiously toward it, but stumbled against a bed.

She held on to a bedpost, "Dimitar, my name is Claudette. I'm here to help you."

A shadow rose against the far wall.

"I'm....I'm Dimitar," he turned on a soft light near the bed.

Claudette noticed a light switch on the wall to her right and reached for it.

"No, don't. He's still out there." There was fear in his voice.

Claudette pulled her hand away, "Dimitar, who's out there?"

"Bukhalov, they sent him to kill me. By mistake the stupid animal murdered Emesto and his girlfriend."

They stood in the shadow of the room next to each other and peered out the window.

"Over there, the large man in the dark raincoat. See the mustache."

Claudette saw a large man in a dark raincoat leaning against the doorway of the building across the street. He had an overgrown tangled mustache and wore a fedora on his head. While she watched, the man turned away to light a cigarette and then looked back toward the apartment. Two women carrying baskets walked past the building where he stood and approached the vegetable stand.

She turned to Dimitar. "Listen to me; we must leave now. I know you drove the truck that rammed Mr. McHugh off the road last Wednesday. He's alive and believes you were forced to do it. He wants to help you. We have to get out of here now. Is there a back door?"

"Yes, there's a back door in the basement, but it's always locked and the building owner has the key. He doesn't live here."

"Well, collect what you want to bring with you. I don't believe you're coming back."

Claudette peeked out of the window. The man was nowhere to be seen.

"He's gone. Let's go." She gripped the leather bag Dimitar had finished stuffing with clothes.

"Wait." Dimitar opened a dresser drawer, pulled out some papers and stuffed them into his pockets. He lifted the picture of his mother and sister from a small shelf over his bed and followed Claudette through the door and down the steps. He stood behind her inside the doorway while she scanned the street.

She took his hand, "Let's go."

They ran behind the women standing at the vegetable market talking with the proprietor and up the street to the corner. Claudette stopped and glanced behind them. The fedora was nowhere to be seen. She grabbed Dimitar by the arm and they hurried to her Spider.

"Dimitar," she tossed the orange over the car roof to him and unlocked the car doors with the remote.

Dimitar didn't hear her gasp when she witnessed the mustached killer turn the corner behind them.

She ducked into the car, slipped it in gear and sped away.

Commandant Pfyffer, in plain clothes, stood on the right side of the nave inside St Peter's Basilica next to one of the marble columns on the side of the Chapel of the Pieta. Dressed in a brown cardigan sweater, dark slacks and leather slippers, he was observing the faces of the faithful as they poured into this largest Christian church in the world for the eleven o'clock Mass. The small side chapel contained Michelangelo's renowned marble sculpture depicting the Virgin Mary holding the body of her dead son, Jesus.

Pfyffer easily recognized the Asians and Africans as they passed by their skin pigment and unique facial characteristics. In numerous other cases he realized his conclusion of an individual's origin was mostly determined by their clothes; particularly the Americans, who included all nationalities.

Maybe the Muslim might be disguised as an American, how would I know?

Last night, awake in bed, Pfyffer realized that when he followed the jeep or walked in front of it, during the Pope's General Audiences, he seldom focused on the faces in the crowded piazza. He principally had watched for unusual movements of the crowd near the barricades.

Now he realized how futile his late night idea was observe the faces of the men entering the Basilica might in some way help him to recognize the assassin if he were to appear the Piazza next Wednesday. And to continue would only contribute to his already heightened anxiety and further loss of sleep

Turning to leave, he bumped into an elderly lady in a faded blue print dress carrying an oversized leather bound prayer book. "Mi, scusi, signora," he apologized in Italian, and directed the lady's attention to the woman following a few steps behind her.

"Mother, wait for me," pleaded the fortyish woman pulling a small boy as she caught up to the lady and nodded a thank you to Pfyffer.

Pfyffer smiled at the two of them, and immediately realized that in this morning's exercise he had only focused on the male faces that had entered the cavernous church. He thought *What if the assassin was a woman or even a child? God forbid!*

The commandant eased his way through the throng entering the nave and out through the 'Door of the Sacraments' to the grotto outside.

London,
Sunday Afternoon

19

It was almost two o'clock when Zhelov stepped out of the drizzling rain and dialed the Rome apartment from a phone box outside The Dog and Duck Pub on Bateman Street in London's Soho District. With the phone held away from his ear, he impatiently counted the number of times it rang.

After the twelfth ring he heard a soft; "Ya."

"Who the fuck are you?"

"Io sono, Madelene"

"Get Petcov now! It's Zhelov."

"Si...Si, Signore."

After a long silence and a few grumbles, he heard, "Zhelov where are you?"

"Petcov, what goes on? Who's the girl?"

"It's Sunday afternoon. She's a friend."

"You shit. I know what fucking day it is! Get rid of her now. And don't you ever bring any of your whores near that apartment. I'm going to call you back in five minutes. You *better* be sober and she *better* be gone." He slammed the phone against the booth door.

At noon Zhelov had met with his Stasi contact in the lounge of the Strand Palace Hotel, as Steiger had arranged and they had finalized their plans. In the morning, armed with photographs of McHugh, a number of Stasi agents planned to meet the flights arriving at Heathrow Airport from the U.S. east coast. Once McHugh was spotted, he'd be followed; and a motorcycle courier would immediately be dispatched to meet Zhelov in the park across from the Carlton Tower Hotel.

Zhelov dialed the number again. The phone was answered on the first ring.

"Herr Zhelov?"

"Ya, it's me! What the hell do you think, bringing an outsider into the apartment?"

"Well, it'll all be over in a couple of days. Kostov has the Turk prepared. Kalina will be on her way back to Rome tomorrow and Bukhalov's holding both McHugh's girlfriend and Botev. He took the bitch's license number and now we know where she lives."

"Dammit, you're not telling me everything. What's going with on with Kalina and where's McHugh's whore?"

"I used your authority to arrange to have Kalina extracted from the hospital tonight and brought back to Rome." Petcov then explained how Bukhalov had erroneously killed the young couple, but copied McHugh's girlfriend's license number when the car pulled away from him. "I called our friend in the Carabinieri and obtained the address of the bitch's condominium. I sent Bukhalov to take care of her and Botev."

"Well at least you're also using the head on top of your neck, not just the one on the end of your dick. I'll be back on Tuesday. Kalina and I will greet Botev and McHugh's bitch in that condo. Tell Bukhalov that if he kills them before we get there; he will join them. I'll call with my flight number. You be there!" He slapped the handset into its holder and stepped into the gray wet afternoon.

The room in the Zurich hospital was small and tucked away in the corner of the third floor surgical ward. White walls and dark floor tiles only actuated the room's chilly temperature, so Kalina kept the light blanket wrapped tightly around her shoulders. The blue privacy curtain hanging from a track on the ceiling was folded back behind the head of her bed. She could only glimpse a narrow sliver of sky outside her window when she raised the head of the bed using the hand held remote, as a tall, red brick hospital power plant chimney took up most of her view. The Sunday news programs on a television screen hanging from the ceiling at the foot of her bed continued to stream video of the ambulance attendants bringing her into the hospital. Earlier that afternoon, a scene had flashed of the police investigators examining the site where McHugh killed Videnov.

She was pissed. And even if she was only able to understand little of the Swiss-German language, it didn't matter what the television commentator said, or how long the investigators spent at the scene, she remembered it all... *And when I get out of this damn place, McHugh, I'll find you and your bitch.*

The policeman stationed in the hall guarding the room knocked on the door and without waiting for an answer, opened it. "Miss Lubanov, you have a visitor."

She moaned to herself, *I don't need another damn visitor. The only ones I've seen are Zurich police and Swiss Federal Police. Their translators asked the same questions, even though I told then over and over that I didn't know the gunman who attacked me. I know they don't believe me. They're not stupid; they've had a policeman stationed outside my door since they left. No one from my damn embassy or consulate has even called.*

The guard stood aside and a heavy set, middle-aged woman wearing a dark raincoat entered.

Kalina turned off the television with the hand-held remote.

The woman's dark hair was cut short in a man's style. She wore no makeup. The deep lines etched in her face and the overwhelming smell of her clothes told Kalina the woman was a heavy smoker. Without speaking, she walked to the end of the bed and eyed Kalina. When the guard closed the door, the woman took off her coat and pulled the only chair in the room to the side of Kalina's bed.

A brittle smile crossed the woman's face when she noticed the cast on Kalina's right wrist. Then she leaned on the edge of the bed and said quietly, "Lubanov." Surprising Kalina by knowing her surname, she continued, "I'm Stoyanov. I'm a technical assistant in the embassy in Berne. We must talk. Have you said anything about your work?"

Knowing state security when she saw it, Kalina answered "No, I only told them I was attacked by someone I did not know."

Stoyanov sat back in the chair and said in a formal voice, as if relaying a message from one in authority, "Your job is not done. Your supervisor needs you back at your post," Then she woman stood and walked around the room, obviously looking for any sign of a listening device.

Kalina thought, *she doesn't have a clue about what's going on; she's just a messenger.* "The doctors say I'm only in here for observation, but with all the visitors I've had, I know they're holding me while they investigate my attack. Can they do that?"

Standing at the window with her back to Kalina, the woman responded, "We have lodged a complaint." She then unlocked the window and returned to the chair. "How are they treating you?"

"Fine; the food is good and my foot is healing. It was a flesh wound."

"How's your wrist?"

Kalina lifted the small cast covering her wrist and most of the palm of her hand. "It's fine. I could hit someone with it."

They conversed about recent events in Bulgaria for about fifteen minutes. Finally, her visitor stood and put the chair back in its place, and then extended her hand to Kalina.

Kalina took the hand and the piece of paper in it.

"Now get some sleep." Stoyanov turned and left the room.

"Lubanov!" In the dark room, Kalina heard her name whispered and sat up.

"Lubanov." The voice repeated. It came from a shadow at the end of her bed.

Kalia pushed a button on the pendant attached to the side of the bed and turned on a soft overhead light.

A figure dressed in black stood at the foot of her bed and removed a dark ski mask. The young man with a bald head, high cheek bones and strong jaw, tossed a small backpack on top of the blanket that covered her.

She sat up clutching the blanket around her shoulders and stared at the man apprehensively.

"I have been told to call you Kalina. Now lie down and call your guard." He ordered quietly in Bulgarian, and stepped to the side of the door.

Relieved, Kalina reached up and pulled the cord hanging from a console above the head of her bed.

The door opened and the policeman walked in.

With a quick chop to the back of the neck, her intruder brought the policeman to his knees. Another chop knocked him to the floor, unconscious.

"Take the clothes out of the backpack and get dressed. We're leaving," the intruder ordered while he removed the policeman's coat. He then tied the officer with a length of nylon and taped his mouth with adhesive.

Dressed in a Swiss policewoman's blouse, black slacks and dark slippers, Kalina sat on the edge of the bed and noticed the time on the wall clock; it was three a.m. Her rescuer slipped into the policeman's coat and placed the policeman's cap on his head.

"Follow me. Stay close." Her rescuer opened the door and glanced in both directions.

She followed along a dark narrow hallway close behind his strong shoulders. Small edge lights along the base of the wall guided their way.

After only ten meters, the rescuer stopped and turned to her. "This door is alarmed. We move fast. Stay close."

He pulled out a silenced 6P9 revolver and pushed the door open.

A screeching claxon froze Kalina.

"Kalina move!" her rescuer whispered and pulled her through the doorway. They ran down three flights of steel stairs and pushed through another door onto a loading dock shrouded in a misty drizzle. The man jumped off the platform and extended his arms up to her.

She hesitated, but when a siren wailed close by, she jumped without hesitation. He took her hand, and they ran along the side of the hospital in the opposite direction from the siren and turned onto the narrow street.

Through the drizzle Kalina saw two blue lights flashing ahead. As they approached, rear accordion doors opened, revealing a bright white ambulance medical compartment. Her rescuer bounced over the rear bumper into the compartment and pulled her in, closing the doors behind them.

"Kalina, we have more than an hour run to Bern, so just lie down on the gurney and relax until we arrive." He lowered the gurney's side gate.

"Where are you taking me?" Kalina asked, and jumped onto the gurney.

"The driver knows." He handed her a sweater and pulled a swing stool away from the wall, turned off the interior lights and sat down.

As ambulance moved out without displaying its emergency lights or using its siren, her rescuer said, "Give me the police blouse and slip into the sweater."

Dawn was approaching as the ambulance pulled up to the curb beside a gray stone apartment building directly across from the palatial Bulgarian Embassy on Bernastrasse Boulevard in Bern.

Without saying anything, her rescuer took Kalina by the hand and led her down an alley at the rear of the building and pounded on the solid metal door.

"I go now." He said quietly and sprinted back to the waiting ambulance.

No one answered.

For almost fifteen minutes, Kalina stood in the alleyway. She wasn't frightened, just anxious, believing something may have gone wrong with the rescue plan. She thought about taking the only recourse available to her and breaking the standing rule for all Bulgarian field agents: Do not approach the embassy without obtaining prior clearance.

Five minutes later when she turned to leave, the door opened.

A heavy-set woman fidgeting with the buttons on her wrinkled house coat stood in the middle of the doorway and barked hoarsely, "You, Lubanov?"

Kalina brushed past the woman and entered a large room that smelled of stale cigarettes. She stood just inside the door scanning what seemed to be a combination storage room, sitting room and kitchen. Cardboard and wooden boxes of various sizes were piled from floor to ceiling along one wall. A battered leather couch was backed against the center of the wall of boxes. Two worn lounge chairs stood on either side of a tattered rug in front of the couch. A small television sat on a vegetable crate in the center of the rug facing the couch. An antiquated stove butted against an industrial sized metal sink at the far end of the room. The only lighting came from three fluorescent light fixtures that hung from the ceiling along the room's centerline.

Disappointed at being dumped, Kalina clenched her fist and glared at the woman. "Who the fuck are you?"

Without responding, the woman brushed a length of gray hair away from her forehead and handed Kalina an envelope. She then disappeared into a side room.

Kalina sat down on one of the chairs next to the couch and ripped open the envelope. The decoded telex was from Petcov:

> *Zhelov in England to eliminate American—— Bukhalov holds McHugh's woman and Botev secure in condominium near here——*
>
> *Arrangements made for you to be escorted back to Italy ——I will meet you on arrival in Rome.—— your guide—— code name HAMMER will see you to Rome—— Petcov.*

She read it again and mumbled, "OK, Zhelov, you kill the CIA bastard McHugh…And I will settle with his fucking bitch." A toilet flushed and Kalina stood anticipating the woman's return.

A bald heavy-set man of sixty entered the room wearing brown trousers held up by dark leather suspenders. His armless undershirt was stretched over a stomach paunch, revealing strong shoulders and muscular tattooed hairy arms. As he approached her, his eyes lit up and a smile appeared on his face.

"I am Hammer. Tomorrow we travel to Rome together as father and daughter. Now you will eat and sleep. Later my wife will change your identity. We give you a new passport and credentials. Relax, we know what we do." He smiled and walked over to an open box near the laundry sink and returned shortly with a bottle of vodka and two glasses. He filled both glasses and handed one to her. "Prost. We will succeed."

While he talked with Kalina, his wife passed behind him and began to cook breakfast.

Later Monday morning, London, England

20

British Airways overnight flight 92 from Toronto touched down at London's Heathrow Airport' at nine-twenty, only fifteen minutes late.

McHugh had declined the glass of champagne offered by the stewardess as soon as the Boeing 747 became airborne and pushed the control lever to ease his first class window seat back to horizontal. He curled up under the thin airline blanket and turned off the world, awaking only once during the night to use the bathroom and drink a glass of water.

"Where are we?" McHugh asked when the stewardess nudged him awake offering a morning coffee.

"We've just passed over Glasgow," she responded, offering a small tray holding the coffee cup and a croissant.

He leaned over to view the city only to find it covered in cloud. As they descended through the gray fluff, he was finally able to watch lush green countryside pass beneath the aircraft. Just as he finished his coffee, the fasten seat belt sign came on. The plane rocked into a gentle turn before its steady descent into its final approach into London's Heathrow Airport.

He was first off the plane with his suit carrier over his shoulder and duffel bag along his right side. While the other passengers gathered around the designated conveyor waiting for it to dispel their baggage, he walked directly to passport control and presented his disembarkation card and his own passport to the matronly official at the desk.

Looking up from his passport, she asked, "Mr. McHugh why are you visiting England?"

Knowing to answer that he was on a business trip could result in extensive questioning about the nature of his business, McHugh responded, "I'm just visiting friends for a few days."

How long do you plan to be staying in England?"

"I'll be staying in London tonight and then I'll visit a friend in Cheltenham Spa. I plan to return to the US on Wednesday."

Handing his passport back to him, she smiled and said, "Well enjoy to your visit."

He accepted his passport and then walked through the customs control portal and placed his bags on the table and presented his passport and his customs declaration card stating he had nothing to declare to a young newly minted customs official. The young official unzipped the leather suit carrier and carefully worked his hand around the clothes it contained. Then he rummaged through the duffel bag, never looking into the ditty holding McHugh's toiletries and the fish-kill.

Relieved, McHugh lifted his belongings from the table and walked into the crowd in the arrivals hall awaiting other passengers. He headed directly out through the terminal glass doors to the taxi queue ending third in line, just ahead of a rush of other new arrivals.

When the Pakistani cab driver came around the rear of the taxi, McHugh handed his travel bags to him and said, "Carlton Tower Hotel, Lowndes Street across from Cadogan Place."

As the taxi found its place in the parade of other taxis slowly moving away from the terminal, the driver asked. "Sir, have you been to London before?"

To let the driver know he knew his way around London and insure the cabby took the fastest route to the hotel, McHugh said, "I lived here for few years."

"Welcome back," the driver mumbled and concentrated on driving.

The doorman tipped his brown felt top hat and opened the passenger door as soon as the taxi stopped beneath the glass chandeliers of the Carlton Tower Hotel's off-street covered portal.

"Welcome, sir, I'll retrieve your luggage. The front desk is just inside to the right."

McHugh palmed the doorman a five pound note and walked into the hotel.

"Welcome, Mr. McHugh," a smiling front desk clerk said, perusing his passport. She had raven hair and an olive complexion. Dark framed oval glasses accentuated her large brown eyes. McHugh guessed her to be Egyptian.

"Your room overlooking the park is prepared. May I order you a welcome coffee?" she asked, handing a brochure and a room key to him.

McHugh noticed her brass nametag. "Thank you, Ramia. By the way, do I have any messages?"

"No, sir, but a half hour ago a gentleman asked if you had a reservation."

McHugh inquired, "Did he phone or ask in person?"

"Sir, he came to the front desk."

"Can you describe him?"

"Well, I did have a number of check-outs at the time." She thought for a moment, "But I do remember he placed his bowler on the desk when he inquired. He wore tinted glasses and a dark pinstriped suit. He seemed to be a proper businessman."

McHugh thanked her, and walked through lobby area, into the Chinoiserie, the coffee lounge, on a chance that the tinted glasses with the bowler hat might be waiting for him. No one met the description, so he took an elevator to his room.

As his secretary, Rhonda, always requested, McHugh had been reserved the same room he had stayed in on his previous visits to London. Opening the floor length tan drapes, he looked out over Cadogan Place. During most other visits he would usually take an early morning jog along the park paths and down Lansdowne Street to a small coffee bar. In good weather he'd buy a coffee and a copy of the London Times and return to the park to read and watch the other early morning walkers and joggers. Today the park seemed empty; the regular number of bicycles and scooters were secured in the metal racks outside its entrance.

There was a knock on his door.

"Yes," he said approaching it.

"Sir, your luggage." McHugh opened the door and a bellboy entered and hung the leather suit carrier in the closet and placed the duffel bag on the luggage stand.

"Thank you." McHugh gave him a healthy tip. Before he could close the door, a maid arrived with coffee and scones.

While showering under tepid water he thought of the many nights he spent in this room and others with only an occasional liaison with a secretary or lady he had met at the theater or in a club; occasionally a relationship progressed beyond the moment, but it never lasted. Realizing that after the train trip today and the simple drop tomorrow and a business dinner, he would spend the next weekend with Claudette in Chicago; he decided to call her.

"Hey, how are you; I can't wait to see you in Chicago."

"Oh, Colin, I'm so glad you called. Guess who I have staying with me."

He was about to ask, but she interrupted excitedly, "Dimitar Botev's here with me."

"Dimitar?"

"It's his first name. He's the Bulgarian driver of the dump truck that forced you off the road last week."

"What! What's he doing there?"

Claudette excitedly detailed how she arrived at Botev's apartment and rescued him.

In a lower her voice she added, "Dimitar doesn't know this, but I'm afraid the murderer saw us drive away. He probably recorded my license number. He was an awful looking man."

"God, Claudette, you have to get out of there. They'll be after both of you. Where's the car? I'm so, so sorry I brought you into this. I don't want anything to happen to you. Can you go to your mother's or call Claudio?"

"Oh, I don't know. Claudio's out of town and I don't want my mother or our home involved."

McHugh looked at his watch: eleven-twenty. "Darling, let me think, I'll call you right back."

He checked the train schedule. It was over an hour before he had to be at Paddington station.

Picking up the phone, he dialed Stringer's office number and walked to the window. The phone rang a number of times before he realized it was only a quarter to six in Washington.

As he was about to hang up, a panting voice answered, "Admiral Stringer's office."

"Ginger, its Colin McHugh. Is he expected in?"

"Mr. McHugh, he's down the hall. I'll fetch him."

McHugh noticed a messenger in dark leathers and a white hard helmet park his motorcycle in front of the park gate and approach a man sitting on a park bench reading a newspaper. The man put the paper down and rose to meet the driver. The guy wore a bowler hat, tinted glasses and a pinstriped suit. The pinstripe shook hands with the messenger and pointed across the street toward the hotel.

"God damn it," McHugh said out loud, "I'll be a son of a hedge hog."

"Well stay away from the zoo." Stringer chuckled, and then asked," What's going on, Colin."

"Dan, I'm just a businessman. I'm not cut out for this crap."

"Hold on, tell me what's happening?"

"I'm in my room at the Carlton Hotel. That train you reserved for me to Cheltenham leaves in an hour. I just hung up from talking with Claudette in Italy, who's with the Bulgarian truck driver who drove me off the road. He's in her apartment."

"Hold it... Who's Claudette, your anonymous Italian heart throb?"

McHugh answered the question and told the Admiral about the circumstances Claudette found herself in. "I have to call her back. Her situation's extremely serious. And now I'm standing at my hotel room window watching a man who appears to have asked the front desk clerk if I had a reservation just minutes before I arrived at the damn hotel. He's now standing in a park across the street talking to a messenger who just arrived on a motorcycle."

"OK, one thing at a time. I put you on that train and arranged with my friend at Century House to have you shadowed. I transmitted your photo, your hotels and the train schedule to him for the shadow. My contact assured me that his guy's a chameleon; you won't see him, but he'll be there if you're in need. The security guys at GCHQ will monitor the Cheltenham hotel tomorrow morning when you check out and pick up whoever removes the dummy letter. That guy across the street isn't your friend, whoever he might be. Watch your back; crowds are your best friends. Also call Claudette and tell her to move now to a hotel or somewhere else out of the area. And then have her ditch the car. Call me when you get to Cheltenham. And one thing, be smart." He ended with a command. "And Colin, keep me in the picture!"

"OK, coach, I'll keep you up to date as best I can." McHugh hung the phone up, turned away from the window and immediately redialed Claudette.

She answered immediately. "Colin."

"Claudette, you must move to a hotel or somewhere else out of the area, and get another car. And you have to do it right now. I'm so sorry about this. The last thing I ever wanted was for you to be in danger. Don't alarm your mother, but I'll need a phone number to keep in contact with you; maybe your mother's chauffeur?

"His name is Sergio." She gave him the number.

Claudette, I miss you. Now get going."

"Miss you too, Colin."

McHugh then dressed in jogging gear and placed his casual clothes in the duffel bag and left the leather suit carrier with his business clothes in the closet.

As his taxi pulled away from the hotel, McHugh observed that the guy in the stripe suit standing across the street at the park entrance immediately hail another taxi. The taxi did a u-turn and followed three cars behind. As his taxi weaved through the Monday morning clogged traffic past Hyde Park Corner onto Park Lane, McHugh watched his follower's taxi try to maneuver unsuccessfully through congestion; the separation continued even when they turned into the sluggish traffic on Edgeware Road.

Two streets before his taxi turned onto the East Bourne Terrace entrance to Paddington Station, McHugh dropped a twenty pound note on the driver's seat. When it pulled to the curb under the canopy, he pushed open the passenger door and ran into the station without looking back. Once through the foyer, he turned right along the interior station wall and stepped into a W. H. Smiths book store and joined a cluster of people perusing magazines in a rack along the side wall.

Over his shoulder, McHugh saw his follower rush past the store entrance into the main concourse. McHugh positioned himself along the terminal wall and watched his follower in the center of the crowded concourse. The pinstripe turned full circle looking through the crowd. Obviously confused and upset, the man threw the rolled-up the newspaper he held onto the floor and barked something. Those nearest to him backed away.

There was a familiarity about the man, but McHugh couldn't place it. Deciding to remain the observer, McHugh skirted the edge of the concourse to a coffee bar.

His pinstripe follower's face was curled in frustration. Finally, with a purposeful stride, he moved to the entrance to the train platforms. For a few minutes, he scrutinized the passengers entering the platforms, and then paced back and forth scanning those milling in the center of the concourse. Then he walked past a queue of people waiting at a food stand near the Hilton Hotel station entrance and then stepped back again to survey the crowd. Finally, the pinstripe stopped and talked with a station attendant, who pointed to an opening along a far wall.

Realizing that his follower had asked for directions to the men's washroom, McHugh decided it was time to head for track four, where the fast train to Cheltenham Spa stood waiting. As he started to move he noticed his follower exit the stairway and walk straight to a nearby phone kiosk and lift the receiver. He dropped a few coins in the coin box and began to dial.

With his follower's back to him, McHugh walked as casually as he could to track four and slipped his ticket into the automatic ticket machine. Without looking back, he boarded the last car on the Cheltenham Spa train.

Zhelov dropped the phone when he glanced over his shoulder and saw McHugh making his way through the crowd. The Bulgarian raced through the concourse and caught up to a group of youngsters entering platform four.

Standing just inside his first class compartment discreetly away from the window, McHugh watched those passing by to board the train. It was twelve-thirty; five minutes before the train's scheduled departure.

In a last minute rush, a group of teenagers passed his window; his follower trailed behind.

McHugh focused his attention on the conductor standing on the platform along the middle of the line of passenger cars. When his follower entered the train, the conductor waved ahead to the engineer.

McHugh stepped off the train and stood on the platform watching it leave.

From the shadow of a narrow space between two of the seaside cottages across the street from the condominium building, Bukhalov was becoming increasingly agitated. He had found the address of the condominium at half past eight. He looked at his watch; it was approaching eleven-thirty and his stomach rumbled.

He wore an olive green tee shirt, khaki fatigue shorts and beach sandals. A dark baseball cap covered his head; his black fatigues, boots and silenced revolver were in a canvas duffle bag at his feet. Even though he wore a pair of wrap-around sunglasses to cover the scar near his left eye, the passengers on the bus he had taken to the area still stared at him.

He had not seen anyone leave the building's front door. However, in the last hour a couple of women he deduced to be maids had entered the building. A number of luxury cars had exited the underground garage and the door closed immediately behind each one.

He started to cross the street and ring one of the condominium buzzers when the garage door opened. He moved into the shadows. A gleaming white Lamborghini rose to street level and stopped allowing its leather convertible top to open and disappear into a compartment in the vehicle's rear. As an elderly driver slowly turned the Lamborghini into a right turn on the street, a tail-gating red fiat convertible screeched into a left turn behind it and sped away.

"Fock you bitch." He yelled and leapt to his feet grabbing his duffle bag. Just as he started to run across the narrow road, the garage door closed. "Bitch, you will return. I will wait," he muttered.

In the lobby of the Hilton Hotel adjacent to Paddington Station, McHugh phoned Claudette's condominium. To his relief there was no answer. *Thank God she took my advice and got out of the place.*

Deciding to have breakfast, McHugh took a seat at a small square table in the center of the hotel restaurant just off the lobby lounge. It was empty except for a couple in a booth along the side wall with luggage stacked near their feet.

A copy of the London Times sat next to his place setting. An elderly waiter in a white coat approached with coffee.

"Thank you," McHugh said as the waiter poured his coffee. "I'll have the English breakfast, with whole wheat toast."

McHugh glanced up when a middle-aged man in a gray double-breasted coat passed his table and took a seat in rear of the restaurant. *Maybe he's my chameleon*, he thought, sipping his coffee.

When McHugh completed his breakfast, he left a generous tip on the table and returned to the lobby phone. While continuing to observe the restaurant entrance to see if his chameleon would follow him out, he called Sergio, Claudette's chauffer.

"Ciao"

"Sergio, its Colin McHugh. Is Claudette there?"

"No sir, she left her Spider in the barn and took her mother's Mercedes." His English was clipped and clear.

"Thanks, Sergio. If she calls let her know I called." McHugh hung up; relieved Claudette was putting distance between her and the Bulgarian murderer. He left the phone booth and glanced into the restaurant. His has-been chameleon was now fixed on a fashionably dressed young woman sitting across the table from him.

A short time later Bukhalov was shocked when the black Mercedes sedan pulled up to the garage door of the condominium building and stopped. McHugh's girlfriend got out of the car and ran up the steps to the condominium entrance and retrieved mail from a metal box at the side of the door. When she got back in the Mercedes, he quickly covered the distance to the car and followed it into the garage.

After parking the Mercedes in her assigned space, Claudette opened her door and turned into the barrel of the silenced revolver held in the Bulgarian killer's hand.

"Welcome home Bitch." he snarled, and then waved the revolver at Dimitar who had just emerged from the passenger door. "Take us to your condominium," He pulled her close and put the revolver to her head. "Botov, you go ahead." He growled in Bulgarian.

When Claudette opened the door of her elevator in the rear of the garage and pressed the third floor button, Bukhalov pushed her against the elevator wall and slapped her across the face.

When Dimitar stepped toward Bukhalov, he received the butt of the revolver across his shoulder.

Claudette nodded at Dimitar and mouthed, *No!*

As soon as the condo door opened, Bukhalov demanded, "Where is phone?"

Claudette walked into the living room and pointed to the phone on an oval table near the front door of the condo.

"Where is other phone?"

"I only have that one." She said defiantly.

The killer grabbed Dimitar by the collar and flung him onto the lounge chair next to the table. "Bitch, get some food, while I use phone and put gun in focking Botev's mouth."

When Claudette went into the kitchen, Bukhalov overturned the chair Dimitar was sitting in and sent the young man sprawling onto the carpet. He kicked Dimitar in the ribs and said in Bulgarian, "You move against me and I will put a bullet in your brain!"

He picked up the phone and dialed. "Ya, its Bukhalov," he answered in Bulgarian and continued, "I have McHugh's bitch and the fag Botev in her condo."

After a few moments, he responded, "Ok, I will play with them until then."

Claudette entered the room carrying a tray of hastily put-together food.

Bukhalov smiled ay her. "Bitch we will play until big boss comes tomorrow."

Across from the Bulgarian Embassy
Berne, Switzerland

21

In the far corner of the basement apartment in Berne, Kalina, wrapped in a large white Turkish towel, sat in a hair dresser's chair facing a mirror propped up on a make-shift dressing table covered with bottles, scissors, combs and jars of make up creams. Although the smell of stale cigarettes on the woman fussing behind her was annoying, Kalina chose to ignore it knowing that that disguise would help her escape Switzerland and repay McHugh's girlfriend for breaking her wrist. *You will get yours, bitch!* She vowed

The woman announced proudly in peasant Bulgarian, "After I cut hair, I color it brown, even make curls. You look like school girl, teenager."

Kalina didn't respond, but thought, *Ya, a teenage girl smelling of cigarettes. I'll shower for a long time after you're done.*

After applying the dye into Kalina's short hair and eyebrows, the woman coiled a towel over Kalina's head and handed her a newspaper.

"Now read while we let dye work," she said and walked to the sink and washed her hands.

Twenty minutes later the woman snatched the towel from Kalina's head. "Now come to sink."

At the deep industrial sink, she took the large towel from Kalina and pointed to the stream of water flowing from the rusted faucet.

"Now rinse hair."

Only covered in her bra and panties, Kalina glared at the woman, then leaned over the sink edge and worked the cold water into her hair using her left hand, keeping the cast on her right hand on the edge of the sink.

When Kalina finished the woman placed a small worn towel on her wet hair and led her back to the seat at the table. After roughly drying her hair by hand and applying a conditioner, the woman handed Kalina a large fresh towel. "Now I make coffee for us. You sit and watch stupid TV."

Wrapped in the large towel, Kalina curled into the side of the old couch, ignored the movie, and tried to visualize the moment McHugh's girlfriend had broken her wrist causing her to loose the revolver. Not able to recall how it had happened, she got up and turned off the irritating movie, promising, *Bitch, you will know everything I do to you!*

Half an hour later, the woman picked up Kalian's empty coffee cup from the top of the TV and touched her shoulder. "Now take a shower in other room. Stall is small, but the water is hot. Take time. Girl clothes are on table near shower."

Kalina slowly uncurled from the couch and went into the bathroom. First, she unwrapped the dressing from the wound on her foot and tucked a plastic bag around the plaster cast on her wrist. She dropped the towel, took off her bra and panties and tested the water. With both shoulders rubbing against the shower walls, she was forced to stand directly under the shower fixture in the ceiling above her head. She indulged in the hot water until it began to cool.

Each piece of clothing she donned seemed a step toward her transformation into a teenage school girl. Struggling to squeeze into the tight undersized bra, she knew it and the frilly white blouse and gray school sweater were necessary to minimize her cleavage. The short pleated dark blue skirt, gray knee-high wool socks and laced black walking shoes completed the picture. After wiping the dust from the mirror on the metal medicine cabinet door, she reflected on her disguise. Now, with trimmed brown eyebrows, short brown hair and no make up, she realized that she might be able to pass as a teenager. *Bitch, I only dress like a fucking little girl just to come for you..* After fidgeting with the tight bra and a final adjustment to her new clothes, she left the bathroom and returned to the large room.

Hammer, dressed as a typical working man in a dark coat, open gray shirt and black trousers, took off his the flat wool cap and applauded her entry.

Kalina glanced around the room for the woman's reaction, but she wasn't there.

"Now father and daughter will go for a walk and find understanding. He stepped back and opened the door to the alley. Noticing the cast still on Kalina's wrist, he slammed the door closed and said, "Wait, we must do something before we go. Come." He led her to a small workbench along the far wall. "Give me your hand, the right hand with the cast." He lifted what looked like an electric mixer from the workbench.

Kalina pulled her hand away.

"No, daughter, I will cut the cast away to make your disguise complete. We will put it back together when we return to Italy. The motor hummed, and he demonstrated how the cutting blade rotating on the end of the device worked by cutting a thin piece of wood that was on the bench. Reluctantly, she extended her hand and Hammer carefully cut the cast into two pieces.

"Good, I will put the pieces in your school backpack until Italy."

After rubbing her wrist and stretching her fingers a number of times, she followed Hammer out of the basement.

Hammer grasped her left hand as they walked across Bernstrasse Boulevard. When they reached the other side, he said, "I was bodyguard for many important Bulgarian officials. Do not mistake my age and fat belly for weakness; I will be a strong bodyguard for you until we arrive in Rome. You be a young girl without worry." He squeezed her hand slightly.

She pulled her hand away and responded, "And don't you forget that I am only dressed as your teenage daughter so I can get back to Italy and finish my business."

Further along, they took seats on the sidewalk terrace of Restaurant Waldeck. Hammer ordered croissants, with coffee for him and milk for her.

She frowned.

When the waiter left the table Hammer said, in a low voice, "Now I will call you Ana after my mother. We must know the plan." He pulled a brochure from the inside pocket of his coat and opened it. Before he could continue, the waiter brought their croissants and drinks.

Hammer lifted his coffee cup and smiled at her.

She still frowned.

After a sip of the fresh coffee, he put his cup down. "Our train will leave Bern tomorrow at half past two and will arrive in Milano at six in the evening. Even though you are eager to carry out your business,

Swiss police and other security groups are looking for…" he paused and looked directly at her, "for someone I have been told is one of our best field agents; you, Kalina. But now you must play as young daughter and stay close to me. We both must carry out our roles. On the train, put in your earplugs and listen to the music on the portable tape player I will give to you, or read one of the school books from your backpack. At least pretend to be into the music or the books. I will have sandwiches, so we don't need to move from our seats. You sit by the window and I will be at your side in the aisle seat. Look out train window at the scenery, and…, don't stare at anyone. Do not draw attention to yourself in any way. Now finish your croissant and milk."

Don't lecture me, old man. I've been a field agent for five years, and in situations you probably could not handle. She thought, but only said, "Sounds good, but I also want a silenced revolver in that back pack."

Cheltenham Spa, Gloucestershire, England

22

It was four o'clock when McHugh's train pulled under the glass canopy of Cheltenham Spa Railway Station. The platform was crowded with school children and business types. With only a cursory look, he spotted his follower leaning against one of the steel girders supporting the canopy. The guy still wore the bowler hat, pinstriped suit and tinted glasses but had removed his tie. His shirt collar was open and his coat was unbuttoned. It was obvious that he to wanted to be seen.

Remembering Stringer's advice, *Keep moving and stay in crowds*, McHugh surveyed the parking lot and noticed a bus about to close its doors, preparing to depart. He quickly walked to it and stepped on board, handing the driver a ten pound note and took an inside seat halfway down the aisle. He placed his travel bag on his lap and put his head down, hoping his follower would not be able to locate where he sat.

"Sir, are you all right?" asked the lilting voice of his seatmate.

He studied the woman beside him; in her sixties and dressed for an evening on the town.

"Oh, I just rushed from the train." He said and glanced around the bus realizing at once that he was sitting with a group of elderly women similarly dressed.

As the bus pulled away from the station, his seatmate nodded toward her companions and continued, "We're in from Bristol on a night out; a shopping stop at the Cavendish House department store, dinner in the Marinades, and then Agatha Christie's The Mousetrap at the Everyman Theatre. We'll be on the train by ten o'clock and back home within an hour." She dropped the names of their evening venues as if she believed he knew of the places. "Why don't you come along?"

"Unfortunately I have to meet a friend," he responded quickly, "but thanks very much."

The bus stopped in front of the Cavandish House on the tree lined Promenade in the town center. McHugh joined the group leaving the bus and walked through the store's revolving doors. He stopped at a perfume counter and asked if there was another exit. The clerk pointed to a sign in the rear of the store. He smiled at one of his companion shoppers and walked out of the rear door onto Regent Street and caught a taxi to the Queen's Hotel.

When the taxi let him off at the Imperial Gardens across from the hotel, he understood why the tourist guides heralded Cheltenham as one of England's finest garden towns. The flower beds, in early stages of bloom, created a collage of color. The hotel brochure mentioned that the classical white columns of its massive façade were modeled after the temple of Jupiter in Rome, but they reminded McHugh more of the south façade of the White House which quickly brought to mind the realities at hand.

He walked through the hotel's arched main entrance to the front desk. The bell captain made a move toward him, but McHugh lifted his duffel bag and waved him off. He then checked in as Matthew Carroll from Toronto.

His suite was on the top floor overlooking the Gardens. He double locked the door, placed the dummy envelope between the mattress and box spring, and collapsed on the king size bed.

There was a knock on the door and then a woman's voice announced, "Evening service."

Immediately alert, McHugh checked his watch: nine-thirty. He slipped out of bed, pulled the fish-kill out of his travel bag and walked to the door.

"Yes, what is it?"

"Sir, evening turn down and towel exchange," a pleasant female voice answered.

"Thank you, I don't need a turn-down tonight." He listened at the door until he heard her make the same announcement farther along the hall. Then he relaxed and put the fish kill away.

In case his follower knew he would be staying at the hotel, McHugh decided to move. He took the local telephone directory out of the desk drawer and leafed through the accommodations section, selected a bed and breakfast and called.

"Good evening, Wystone House."

"Good evening, would you have a room for the night? I know it's late."

"Yes sir, but only our Montpelier Suite is vacant at this time."

"Good I'll take it, my name's Ingram. I'm at the train station, and should be there shortly."

He hung up and checked the location of the Wystone House on the city map inside the front cover of the directory. It was only three streets away. He took his second set of clothes from the duffel bag and dressed: navy blue sport coat, blue denim shirt, dark cargo pants and black walking shoes. *No sense leaving the note. GCHQ security guys will be watching the hotel in the morning.* He reached between the mattress and box spring and pocketed the note.

McHugh opened the door. The hall was empty. He slipped out of the room and hung the DO NOT DISTURB sign on the door knob. At the end of the hall, he took the stairway down to the basement. There were two doors at the foot of the stairs. One had an exit sign over it with a red ALARM ENGAGED sleeve on its push arm. The sign above the other door read EMPLOYEES ONLY. It opened into a storage area. The smell of disinfectant filled his nostrils. Along the left side wall stood floor-to-ceiling metal shelves filled with cardboard boxes marked by their various contents: soap, pens, ashtrays, cups, and glass. Two large overhead doors took up the wall to the right.

He peered through the narrow glass window on the metal door between the overheads. It opened onto an empty loading dock. He pushed the door open and walked out.

After a few blocks, he turned a corner onto Parabola Road. Above a picket fence halfway along the road, he saw a spot light shinning on a white sign hanging from a pedestal pole. The words reflected in gold leaf:

Wystone House
62 Parabola Road

McHugh rang the bell. The door was opened by an elderly rotund gentleman with white hair wearing a maroon waistcoat, open white shirt with an untied black bow tie hanging around his neck.

"Good evening, Mr. Ingram."

McHugh hesitated, at first not understanding how the man knew his name, and then remembered he was told on the phone that only one room was available. Obviously, he was the last guest expected.

Handing the man the Ingram American Express credit card, he said, “Thank you, I apologize for calling so late.”

“Not to worry; have you no luggage?”

“No sir, I have a meeting at GCHQ tomorrow and the colleague that I planned to stay with is out of town.”

“All’s well, Mr. Ingram, the Montpelier Suite is at the top of the stairs.” He pointed toward a stairway a short distance down the hall. “Would you like a tea or coffee?”

McHugh said, “No thanks. I’m just going to turn in.”

“Make yourself to home. There are biscuits and fruit on the bureau and a complete bar in the sitting room of the suite,” he said and handed McHugh a brass ring with two brass keys dangling from it. “Can I schedule a wake-up for you?”

“Yes please, six thirty will be fine.”

About the same time that McHugh entered the Wystone House, Zhelov walked out of a pub a few streets from the train station, livid and talking to himself. *That American bastard disappeared again this afternoon, and in such a small fucking old town. It was like he knew his way around. And fuck me; it wasn’t to smart to stand on that platform in full view and let him know I’m after his ass. Thought the bastard would run and I could put a bullet in his back from the silenced 6P9. The CIA trained the bastard well; his slip into the bus was good. Checked the town’s three hotels; no fucking McHugh. It cost me fifty pounds for that bitchy barmaid to find out that a man with the fucker’s description checked into a Queen’s Hotel a half hour after the bus left the station. And now McHugh, you meet your maker.*

At the corner of the street Zhelov opened the rear door of the waiting cab and ordered, “Queen’s Hotel.”

The cabby turned, “Hey mate, it’s only a few blocks, why don’t ya walk, so I can have a go at a decent tip?”

“Shut up and move,” Zhelov ordered and dropped a twenty pound note on the seat beside the driver.

As the taxi approached the hotel, Zhelov ordered the cabbie to pull into a narrow alley behind the hotel and drop him off. After the cab departed, he walked to the rear of the hotel and located the staff entrance. He stood against the dark side wall and waited.

Shortly after eleven, a maid pushed the door open and hurried away.

Slipping an empty cigarette pack between the frame and the door, the Bulgarian followed.

The street was empty. He remained at a discreet distance behind her.

Three blocks away, probably sensing her follower, the maid glanced over her shoulder, and then began to run.

Zhelov closed the distance quickly and grabbed her around the neck cutting off any chance of a scream. She kicked him in the knee and scratched at his neck, but he wrestled her through a hedgerow onto the grass behind it.

With a hand over her mouth, he jerked her face toward him and whispered in broken English "Listen, I will not hurt; I need room number of the tall man checked in late this afternoon."

Her eyes were wide and wild with fear. She tried to move but his body weight kept her subdued.

"Tell me and you go home now." He flashed a fifty pound note in front of her. "I take hand away, you talk."

Terrified, she nodded.

He moved his hand just enough for her to speak. "He's on the top floor in Suite Three."

"Thank you," Zhelov put his hand back over her mouth realizing she could easily identify him. With his free hand he pushed the button on his stiletto. The blade clicked open and he slit her throat. He ripped her blouse off as he stood up and wiped the knife blade on it. Then he threw the blouse under the hedge, pocketed the stiletto and looked down at her open dead eyes. He pocketed the fifty pound note, then dragged her body under the hedge and walked calmly back to the hotel.

Zhelov smiled at the DO NOT DISTURB sign on the door of the suite. He glanced back at the empty hallway and slipped on his gloves. He held the silenced revolver in his left hand by his side and picked the lock silently with his right. The door opened easily and he walked in, leaving it ajar. With the revolver extended in both hands, he scanned the room professionally and listened; no sound, not even breathing. He backed toward the door and ran his hand along the wall to the light switch. With the overhead light on, he saw that the room was empty and the bathroom door was open.

Training the weapon ahead, he looked into the bathroom. It was empty. He uttered, "Fuck it," and fired two shots splintering the door frame. He tossed the bed, throwing the sheets and pillows against the wall and the mattress toward the windows. Back in the bathroom he rummaged through the clothes McHugh had left behind and pitched the empty duffel bag into the toilet. Using the butt of the revolver, he shattered the glass wall of the shower. Returning to the bedroom he pulled the empty drawers out of the dresser and threw them randomly around the room.

A tall hotel security guard stepped into the room. “Sir, are you having difficulty?”

Zhelov shot him in the head, stepped over the body and walked out.

Tuesday morning in Cheltenham

23

The last two locals put their beer mugs on the bar of the *Stirrup Inn* and left shortly after midnight. The hard-pressed old inn struggled to remain standing at the end of a rarely traveled short street only a couple of blocks from the train station. While he cleaned the pub, the bartender, a thin old man, allowed Zhelov to remain with his bottle of vodka at one of the tables along the back wall.

Zhelov fumed. He knew he had no choice but to eliminate the hotel security guard. Had he not, the guard would have sounded an alarm and brought the local authorities, possibly compromising the mission. The hotel maid was another story. It was an unnecessary kill; an impulsive reaction to her terrified eyes staring up from beneath him. He carried leather ties and tape with him as he always did on a kill mission and should have bound and silenced her with out the kill. His training and the instruction he provided to other Division 7 agents strictly prohibited killing unnecessarily. He had no remorse only regret that he had made the serious mistake. And it was a serious mistake; he wasn't wearing his gloves when he wrestled her to the ground. *My fingerprints, hair and other clues could ultimately place me in this out-of –the-way town if British Intelligence Services were brought in.* He was thankful he had the gloves on and never came in contact with the hotel security guard.

He sipped his vodka and thought about his present situation. On all other kill missions he had received a detailed analysis of his target: its daily routine down to the minute, preferred restaurants and food, unusual habits, even its sex life and quirks. Smiling, he remembered one assignment where Division 7 agents had tracked a Bulgarian mole who had absconded from London with hundreds of thousands of English pounds from the international account he managed at a British investment house. They had traced the target to Cascais, a coastal village catering to Europe's jet set only a few miles outside of Lisbon. The agents not only had provided Zhelov with the details of the accountant's life in the village, they also included explicit information about the accountant's Portuguese mistress and his collaborator, a prominent Lisbon Banker. The information enabled Zhelov to stage the assassination of the banker and the Bulgarian dissident in such a realistic manner that the Portuguese authorities concluded that the mistress had killed them both. He chuckled remembering how he had planned the meeting with the mistress in the hotel bar and had convinced her he was a German movie producer. After their night in bed and the drug he placed in her glass of wine, she was unable to remember the evening or how she acquired the thousand British pounds and the murder weapon the Portuguese police had found in her apartment. He took a sip of vodka and relished his accomplishment.

McHugh was another story. All the information Zhelov had was the belief that McHugh was CIA. The phone call Reina placed Saturday to McHugh's company only told him that the American would be returning to London tomorrow for a meeting with a client. He didn't know any more about his prey.

Zhelov pushed the vodka bottle away resolving to eliminate McHugh in the morning before he reached London. Now he needed sleep.

"Hey, boss," he yelled.

The bartender stopped sweeping the floor and stared over the top of the broom handle at the Bulgarian now walking toward him.

"Could you be sure to wake me early? I have a train to catch in the morning." Zhelov asked, almost pleading.

"Ya, what time? Not too early, I hope."

"Could you do eight?"

The bartender nodded, "OK," then he pulled a wooden bench away from the wall and began to sweep under it.

"Thanks." Zhelov mumbled and then eased himself up the rear stairs to his small rented room on the second floor.

It was seven thirty. A matronly woman with a warm smile wearing a floor length maroon dress with a white lace collar met McHugh at the dining-room door. Her white hair was pinned in a bun on top of her head and a white half-apron was tied around her waist.

"Good morning, Mr. Ingram, aren't you the lucky one? Our other four guests left earlier. I'll have a proper English breakfast for you in a jiff; tea or coffee?"

"Coffee please."

He took the seat at the only place-setting at the head of a long rectangular table with four high-backed oak chairs evenly spaced on either side. An arrangement of spring flowers sat in the center of its white linen table cloth. A copy of the local newspaper, The Gloucestershire Echo, was folded to his right. He opened it.

"It's been on the radio now, but it won't be in the paper or the *Telly* until this afternoon," the lady said, while pouring his coffee from a sterling silver coffee server. She placed the coffee server on the table next to a similar sugar bowl.

"What with the murder at the Queen's Hotel, it's been a difficult morning." She stopped abruptly and then said, "Oh how terrible of me. I failed to introduce myself. I'm Mrs. Eggers. My husband and I are the proprietors. Oh, and there's a selection of fruit, cheeses and cereals on the sideboard." She pointed toward the far the end of the room. "Certainly my apologies are in order."

McHugh glanced up at the woman apprehensively. "What happened at the hotel?"

She sat down on the chair next to him and watched him pour cream into his coffee.

He was about to say get on with it when she continued. "Apparently, in a room on the top floor, an intruder shot one of the hotel security guards. The police found the room in quite a disarray. Mrs. Atterton, next door, said a Canadian man had checked into the room and gave a Toronto address; the police are checking the credit card."

She paused momentarily, and looked directly at him, "Where are you from Mr. Ingram?"

"Ma'm, I'm from Maryland, in the States... Where's the Queens hotel? Is it in the city?"

"Oh, it's only a few blocks from here, at the top of the Promenade." She went on, "It's also been reported that one of the maids didn't return home last night after her late shift. There's talk she and the Canadian may have slipped off together. Oh, I've gone on so that I forgot your breakfast."

Zhelov didn't sleep well. He sat on the edge of the narrow cot in his shorts holding his aching head. Dry phlegm from all the cigarettes seemed to be stuck in his chest. His mouth felt as if it was lined with sheep's wool. The BritishRail train schedule between Cheltenham Spa and London's Paddington Station sat unfolded next to him. There were five departures that morning beginning at 05:54, arriving two hours and seven minutes later at Paddington. The last train before noon was scheduled to leave at 11:42. Perusing the schedule details, he concluded that in all probability McHugh would catch one of the trains leaving between 09:45 and 10:24. "And I'll be at the station to welcome you, Mr. McHugh, he said out loud.

There was knock on the door.

"Ya!" Zhelov responded, and reached for his revolver on the side table.

"Sorry, I'm late. It's just after eight o'clock," called the old bartender's screechy voice. "I put a clean towel in the washroom at the end of the hall."

"OK, no harm." Zhelov slipped the revolver under the BritishRail schedule.

Mrs. Eggers placed a plate of eggs, sausage, ham, mushrooms and half of a tomato covered with melted cheese on the table in front of McHugh. "I'll leave you to your breakfast; more coffee?"

"No thank you, ma'm."

Mrs. Eggers backed through the kitchen door.

The story of the murder eroded McHugh's appetite, but he knew he couldn't show concern so ate most of the meal and stepped into the kitchen. "Thank you, Mrs. Eggers, the breakfast was wonderful. May I take the newspaper?"

"By all means. Can I arrange transportation?"

He asked for a taxi.

"May I tell him your destination, GCHQ?"

He hadn't decided what to do, so to stay in character he replied, "Well, I would like to shop for a gift first."

"Splendid. Might I suggest the Cavendish House on the Promenade? It's a proper department store."

There were only a few people in the Chletenham Station cafe on Platform One. Talk was minimal as most were reading newspapers and drinking mugs of tea or coffee. Zhelov was seated with his coffee at a table next to the window overlooking the platform, pretending to read a copy of the London Times.

"Going to London?" a sweet voice asked.

Realizing that a woman had taken the chair across the table from him, Zhelov lowered his paper.

"Yes," he responded straight-faced to the middle-aged woman with dyed blonde hair smiling over a steaming cup of coffee.

"So am I. I haven't been for more than a year. Six months ago my sister took a flat on Luxor Street across the Thames in Lambeth. Do you know it?"

"No I don't." Zhelov snapped. Ignoring the woman, he lifted the paper but turned to observe the passengers standing outside on the platform. Unaware that the woman had left his table until he saw her approaching the window from outside on the platform, he immediately focused on the paper.

While in his room packing, McHugh took a chance and called Claudette's condo.

The phone rang a number of times. He was relieved she wasn't there, and was about to hang up.

"Oh, H...Hello." Her voice was low and unsteady.

"Claudette, are you all right."

"Y...Yes, I, I'm just not feeling well. My...My brother, *Mario's* not in town."

"Claudette are you in trouble?"

The phone went dead.

Mario,...her brother's name is Claudio. Shit. The bastard's got her. Overwhelmed with the thought of Claudette now in the clutches of the Bulgarian murderer, he sat down on the edge of the bed and put his face in his hands. It was his fault, thinking all she would do was ask her brother to check the damn address; not go there herself. *I have a killer stalking me and Claudette in the hands of that animal.* He had to do something.

He decided to try and contact Claudio and dialed his office in the Rome Building Department.

"Buon giorno, l'ufficio misterArriaga," a female voice said.

McHugh spoke slowly, “I’m calling from England and would like to speak with Mister Arriaga.”

“Arriaga mister e’a Cortuna.”

Shit, he thought to himself, *Cortuna is only about three hundred kilometers from Claudette’s condo; only a three hour drive or so from her.*

“Do you have a phone number for him?”

“No sir, but he plans to be in tomorrow.” Her English was labored.

McHugh said thank you and hung up.

With a killer stalking him, there weren’t too many options available. He had to get out of this town and call Stringer.

“No baggage?” the taxi driver asked when McHugh came down to the lobby.

Seeing Mrs. Eggers at the desk, McHugh answered, “I’m only visiting for the day.”

Then he turned to her, “Good-bye, Mrs. Eggers.”

When they were in the cab, the driver questioned, “You Canadian?”

McHugh glared in the rear view mirror and said, “No, I’m American. I work with GCHQ, but I need to do some shopping first. Just drop me at the Cavandish House.”

“Do you require that I wait?” Before McHugh answered, the driver continued, “I’ll be parked across the street for about twenty minutes.”

McHugh entered the Cavandish House through the revolving door and walked down the main aisle. Two clerks arranging perfume bottles in a display case stopped their work and conversed. One picked up a phone and the other walked from behind the counter toward a security guard on the far side of the store.

Realizing they were probably aware of the murder in the hotel, McHugh walked directly to the rear door. It was time to get out of town. He looked at his watch: nine-fifteen. The next train to London was due shortly. He had to call Stringer before catching it.

He hailed a taxi parked outside the door, “Train station please.”

The driver didn’t say anything, but scrutinized McHugh in the rear view mirror as he pulled away from the curb.

McHugh returned the stare without saying a word. He also realized the police would certainly be at the train station checking all males of his description. He had to come up with an alibi. Thankfully, he could use his own passport.

Two police officers wearing white shirts, black ties and black trousers stood chatting next to a white Land Rover, with the blue lettering of Gloucestershire Constabulary on its door. The Rover was strategically parked across of the entrance to the train station.

As soon as McHugh stepped out of the taxi, the younger of the two officers approached.

"Good Morning, sir, could you show me your identification please?"

The older officer took a position behind McHugh.

"Good morning, officer, of course." McHugh handed him his passport.

The policeman glanced at the name in the passport and looked up. "Mr. McHugh, may I ask how long you've been in Cheltenham?"

"I've been on a special assignment at GCHQ for the past three days, and I now have a meeting in London," McHugh answered, then immediately realized that the latest arrival stamp into England was dated yesterday.

The officer scanned the pages in the passport.

McHugh tried to think of an acceptable response should the officer notice the entry stamp.

With an informal salute, the officer handed the passport back to McHugh. "Have a safe trip, sir."

"Thank God," McHugh said to himself, and turned toward the station platform. He slipped the passport into his pocket, silently berating himself to be more careful.

Businessmen, school children and others in groups of two or three stood outside the cafe in the center of the platform waiting for the London train to arrive.

Seeing McHugh pass his window, Zhelov dropped the paper on the table and left the cafe.

McHugh walked quickly to a red telephone booth on the far end of the platform and entered. Glancing across the small station's two sets of tracks, he noticed that Platform Two was empty.

Lifting the receiver, he inserted a twenty pence piece into the coin slot. When the operator came on the line he gave her his international calling card number and asked to be connected to Stringer's priority phone number in Washington. Before the connection could be completed, he heard the London train approaching and looked toward the sound.

Zhelov watched McHugh pick up the telephone and decided to put an end to it all before the American could make a call to summon others. He edged along the wall behind the passengers on the platform and lifted the silenced revolver from under his coat.

"Sir!... Sir... What is that?"

Zhelov glanced to his right.

His screaming middle-aged woman friend was waddling toward him.

Startled, McHugh looked toward the confrontation and saw his follower still in the pinstriped suit. The tinted glasses were gone. Even without the thick mustache and long sideburns, McHugh immediately recognized the piercing eyes of the bastard from St. Peter's Square.

The Bulgarian's arm came up.

The revolver, lengthened by a silencer erased any doubt McHugh may have had. He dropped the receiver and pushed the phone box door open. A square glass panel in the door exploded above his shoulder. Then another window in the opened door shattered near his head. Without looking back, he jumped off the platform, just as a piece of the stone facing on the station wall splintered.

McHugh ran head down, zigzagging along the railroad tracks as bullets kicked up the cinder bed around him. A chilling ping sounded as a bullet ricocheted off a rail and pierced his leg just below the left knee. It felt like an ice pick speared his flesh. He continued zigzagging, head down.

The shots stopped.

Briefly looking back, McHugh noticed the Bulgarian had stopped and was slapping a second magazine into the butt of the revolver.

The London train stood at the station.

Gravel began to explode along the track bed as the shots became more rapid.

Again McHugh looked back and noticed the London train beginning to move toward him on the same track he was straddling. He crossed over to the second track. The Bulgarian did the same.

Wrenching his ankle on the edge of a wooden rail tie, McHugh rolled over the cinder track bed and crawled directly away from the tracks into a side field of tall grass. After about twenty yards he raised his head above the grass and looked back.

The London train was passing behind the Bulgarian, who knelt on the outer edge of the second track with his revolver pointed in McHugh's direction.

McHugh rolled to his left and buried his head in the dirt as another volley of bullets spattered around him. Suddenly the ground began to shake and he raised his head. Through the tree line on his right, he watched the shadow of an approaching freight train barreling toward the station.

With the noise and vibration of the passenger train passing behind him; the shooter only realized his danger when the oncoming freight was less than four hundred feet away. His attempt to dive out of the way of the monster was too late.

McHugh looked away.

The screech of metal as the train braked and the thunder of cars pounding against each other confirmed the inevitable.

McHugh saw a piece of arm resting near the Russian revolver on the edge of the gravel bed. He put his head down and vomited.

A policeman and a station attendant were running along the tracks toward the carnage.

McHugh wiped his mouth and most of the dirt and sweat from his face, turned away from the scene and sprinted through the tall grass. Splinters of pain shot up his right leg every time he landed on it. With his left arm covering his face, he put his head down and crashed through a dense hedge onto a side street running parallel to the railroad tracks. A couple of yards to his left an intersecting road led away from the station. He turned onto it. Trying to walk calmly, he removed his coat, straightened his shirt and dusted his trousers as best he could, realizing each step was a step away from any pursuers.

His left leg stung and his right ankle ached as he walked. Droplets of blood marked the sidewalk behind him.

Middle-class homes, some behind low yellow Cotswold stone walls and others hidden by tall green hedgerows, lined both sides of the two-lane road.

He heard a siren ahead and slipped behind a row of hedge fronting a home of Cotswold stone. He found a garden hose hanging from a fixture on the side of the home. While he rinsed his mouth he watched a police car, lights flashing, speed past toward the station. Then he rolled up his trouser leg and cleaned the superficial bullet wound with his handkerchief. He was thankful the dark cargo pants camouflaged the blood stain.

He had to get off the street and reach a phone. The police were probably looking for him from the description obtained at the Queen's Hotel, now reinforced by those at the station. His heart pounded like a piston pump fighting a fire. Stepping out from behind the hedge, he continued down the street hoping that the traffic light three blocks ahead indicated the intersection of a major cross street.

At the corner, he ducked under low hanging tree branches that extended over a wall of the yellow stone and scanned up and down the wide street in search of a taxi. The few people who did walk past him didn't seem to be aware that he stood there. Finally, a taxi stopped at the curb a few feet in front of him. He opened the rear door relieved to find it empty and sat down in the seat.

The elderly driver, wearing a tweed cap and a tattered woolen sweater, turned toward him.

"Where to, Gov?"

McHugh said, "The nearest phone booth, I need to make a call"

"A yank, aye?"

Realizing the driver certainly had heard about the hotel murder, McHugh quickly replied, "Yes, I'm American, from Maryland. My name's McHugh."

"Name's Foyle," the driver responded with a heavy brogue, "Live just ahead, first turning on the right. I can drop you at the telephone exchange in the city center or you can use my phone if you like. Wife makes a grand cup of tea and it's time for me morning break."

It was an easy answer. "Great, I could use a cup of tea."

The taxi pulled onto a gravel drive next to a small white cottage. It had a large leaded glass front window with a green window box beneath it full of small white pennycress. A vegetable garden took up a large portion of the area in front of the cottage. A group of young mothers sat on benches watching their young children play in a grassy park beyond a low hedge to the left of the cottage.

"Mary, meet our new American friend, Mr. Mc..." He looked at McHugh.

"Name's Colin McHugh," he said, smiling toward the woman.

Mary, a large woman about sixty shook McHugh's hand as if she were jacking up a car.

"Welcome, McHugh's Irish. John's from County Kerry and my family's of Donegal." Her lilting brogue had a musical ring.

A teapot whistled somewhere in the rear of the cottage as they entered. When he stepped into the small foyer McHugh knew he had to make his call immediately and leave or he would probably have to spend considerable time with this gregarious couple.

"John, I have to make that phone call, it's extremely important. I'll pay for the call."

"No problem, phone's right here in the sitting room." He opened a glass door. "Kitchen's down the hall. Join us when you're finished."

McHugh entered the room and checked his watch, 10:20: after 4:00 am in Washington.

I don't care what time it is there; I need his help now. He dialed Stringer's secure number.

It rang three times before McHugh heard a groggy, "Stringer here."

McHugh said, "Dan, sorry to wake you but I'm in deep shit; they think I killed someone."

Stringer coughed a couple of times, and then said, "OK, slow down, just give me the details."

McHugh summarized what he knew about the hotel murder and the fact that the bastard following him was killed by the freight train. He also emphasized that the follower was the same Bulgarian he had photographed in St. Peter's Square."

"Where are you now?"

McHugh didn't answer the question. "Claudette's also in trouble. She and the young truck driver are in her condominium.

Puzzled, Stringer asked, "So what about Claudette and the Bulgarian. That doesn't seem as urgent as your situation."

"It may be more urgent. This morning when I called, she was distressed and said her brother Mario would stop by."

Stringer said, "So?"

"Dan, she doesn't have a brother *Mario.* His name's Claudio. I'm sure the bastard who tried to kill me outside Rome is there in the damn condo. We have to save them both."

Hoping to help the admiral with Washington bureaucracy, McHugh added, "That young Botev can positively identify the Bulgarians in Rome that are planning the Pope's assassination. He might have information that could tell us when it's planned. He could even lead us straight to the organizers and financiers."

"OK, OK, let me see if I can get Rawhide to move some mountains. Where are you?"

"Hold on, I'll be right back." McHugh put the phone down and went into the kitchen and asked John for their address.

When McHugh relayed the address, Stringer said, "Stay there, have some tea. I'll have someone come by shortly." He hung up.

All the while McHugh listened to John tell stories about growing up on the Dingle Peninsula in County Kerry and savored the tea and the cucumber sandwiches Mary had prepared, he churned inside worrying about Claudette.

Mary said, "Tell him about Liam, your best friend."

The doorbell rang; just as john was about to reluctantly begin another story. Seeming relieved, the Irishman stood and went to the front door.

McHugh almost remarked, "Thank you, God," but only stood and went into the sitting room and looked out the front window. A white Land Rover was parked behind John's taxi. It had block letters, GCHQ in the middle of a gray ring centered on the passenger door.

McHugh placed a fifty pound note on the drawing room table and joined John and Mary in the driveway.

A square-jawed man with gray hair, wearing a dark brown coat and open necked white shirt conversing with the Foyles, extended his hand to McHugh. "Ken Mitchell, I'm your ride."

McHugh shook his hand with his left and said goodbyes to Mr. and Mrs. Foyle.

Mary bear- hugged him. Standing beside her, John offered a slight wave.

While driving through Cheltenham, Mitchell identified himself as a US Navy four stripper, commanding the American contingent at GCHQ, and began to give McHugh a dissertation on the mission and importance of the place.

Relieved to be beyond the reach of the local authorities and concerned about Claudette, McHugh only heard snippets of the captain's explanation.

The huge GCHQ complex was the successor to the British Code and Cipher School which deciphered the German military codes encrypted by the ENIGMA machine, providing a major turning point in WWII. Captain Mitchell then rambled about the development of an asymmetric key encryption scheme. When he heard *asymmetric*; McHugh tuned out.

Finally Mitchell said, "I served under Admiral Stringer aboard the nuclear carrier *Enterprise* and I'm looking forward to another sea assignment with him."

As they passed the Cavendish House, he turned to McHugh, "The admiral has arranged for the GCHQ helicopter to fly you out of Cheltenham."

"Fly me where?" McHugh asked.

The captain shrugged. "Damned if I know. That's all the information the good Admiral gave me."

When they drove through the headquarters' main gate, Mitchell returned the wave of the civilian security guard and turned to McHugh. "I believe your chopper's arrived."

The gray Royal Navy Sea King helicopter sat on a cement pad behind the main building in the center of the large headquarters compound. The cockpit and tail areas were painted tomato orange. McHugh hoped the black block letters, ROYAL NAVY RESCUE painted on the side of the fuselage just ahead of the recognizable Royal Navy red, white and blue roundel, would hold true in his case. When the Land Rover approached the pad, the pilot, in flight gear, jumped out of the chopper and ducked under its idling blades. When he cleared the blades he, took off his hard helmet and walked toward them.

Mitchell extended his hand to the navy lieutenant. "Chip, here's your package, Mr. Colin McHugh. He's ex-navy; take good care of him."

McHugh shook Mitchell's hand with his left, and said, "Thanks Captain."

The pilot saluted McHugh. "Lieutenant Chip Davies. Your taxi's ready to roll, sir."

He turned back to the chopper and McHugh followed.

The co-pilot turned toward McHugh as he buckled in, "John Bird."

"McHugh," he said, and watched the two pilots work their way through the pre-flight check list. It was 12:15 when they lifted off.

McHugh asked over the intercom, "Chip, where are you taking me?"

"Our orders are to drop you at the Royal Air Force Base, Mildenhall, in Suffolk County. It's about an hour's ride. By the way, there's a thermos of hot tea and a tin of biscuits behind you if you care for some vittles."

"Thanks, maybe later." McHugh took off the intercom headset, made a pillow of the life jacket next to him, and tried to relax. *God, I hope Stringer knows what he's doing.*

John Bird yelled, "It's pretty noisy in here, so I would suggest you keep your head phones on. If you don't want to listen in on our chit-chat, just pull the plug." McHugh gave him a thumbs-up and slipped the headphones back on, pulled the plug and watched the landscape as they flew. He immediately recognized the village of Moreton-in-Marsh and was reminded it was Tuesday, Market Day, by the crowd in the town center milling around numerous farm stalls. Ten minutes later, the helicopter's shadow passed over the dome-like chimney of the 18th century Bliss Tweed Mill and he knew they would shortly fly over Chipping Norton. Both towns brought pleasant memories of his visits to the Cotswold's during his time in England.

After handing cups of tea to the pilots and pouring one for himself, he sat back, and watched the shadow of the chopper glide over the colorful fields and quaint villages along the route.

An hour later, with the magnificent Gothic buildings of Cambridge University fading off to their right, John Bird pointed ahead to a number aircraft hangers and single story buildings clustered near a long, wide runway.

Royal Air Force Base, Mildenhall, Suffolk, England

24

Shortly after one o'clock, the helicopter dropped into a momentary hover, then descended onto the cement pad next to the RAF Mildenhall control tower. Nearby, an officer wearing a black beret and a leather flight jacket over camouflage fatigues stood next to an open jeep.

"Thanks for the lift," McHugh said, as the rotor came to a stop. The two naval officers gave a "thumbs up" as McHugh opened the chopper's sliding door and jumped out.

An American Air Force Colonel walked toward him. His jacket had a patch on the left chest representing a gold eagle holding a sword in one of its talons and a gold lightning bolt in the other hovering above a blue world globe. A banner below the patch declared "7th Air Commando Squadron."

The colonel exuded a commanding presence; six feet tall, broad shoulders, square jaw, resolute brown eyes and the posture of a ceremonial guard.

"Vic Vitucci." The colonel offered his hand.

"Colin McHugh." His left hand and fingers groaned under the colonel's iron grip.

"Admiral Stringer said you had a tough time of it in Cheltenham. That left hand attempt at a handshake and your bloody trousers tell a story. Looks like you rolled around in a construction site."

Hoping not to have to relate the entire story, McHugh said, "You're pretty close. I had a run-in with a Bulgarian agent who didn't take a liking to me; had to crawl around a grassy field dodging bullets."

Before getting into the jeep, Colonel Vitucci stopped. "Well, we have two choices. You can clean up and get out of those grubby clothes now, or we can go to the officer's club, relax with lunch and discuss the problem you are facing in Italy. I have the green light to help."

"I'm not really hungry, but I do agree we should talk first," McHugh said and sat down in the passenger seat.

On the short ride to the club, Vitucci explained that he was the commanding officer of the U.S. Air Force 7th Special Operations Squadron stationed at Mildenhall. He described the make-up of the squadron, concluding, "Our mission is to deploy and extract troops and other friendlies from hostile, sensitive or otherwise undesirable situations, under all weather conditions." He stopped momentarily and then went on. "My friend, Stringer, said you're classmates from that canoe club in crab town," he said, referring to the nick names of the Naval Academy and the city of Annapolis.

"Sometimes it seems a millennium ago. Are you a Falcon?" McHugh asked, referring to the Air Force Academy.

"Na, no academy for me, my real learning was in the Bronx. And after working day-time in a small iron foundry, I put in nights at Fordham, finally eking out a BA in Education. Dad was an Air Force sergeant in a search-and-extract squadron in Europe in the war-to-end-all wars." He smiled at the obvious irony of his remark, "And after the heroic stories he told me about those he served with in France and Italy; I had no choice but to follow him."

McHugh felt a genuine admiration for the Colonel. No bureaucracy here, just a strong down-to-earth leader doing his job.

Vitucci turned the jeep into a parking space outside a single story white lap-board building with a peaked green shingled roof. A wooden sign near its front entrance announced:

BLDG 218- OFFICERS CLUB.

Vitucci shrugged. "It's not much, but it's home."

A small nondescript foyer opened into a single room just smaller that a basketball court.

A long bar, television and cluster of small round tables were to the left, divided by a half wall display of faux greenery. To the right was a formal dining room with a spattering of officers eating lunch at square tables.

Vitucci led McHugh into a corner of the oak paneled barroom. A waitress appeared at the colonel's side as they sat down.

"How about a beer, we have a broad selection: English, American Belgian, German…" He looked at the waitress. "Ellen, I'll have a Dortmunder and bring us two specials."

McHugh glanced toward her. "Ditto."

The wall behind them sported colorful air squadron insignia plaques.

McHugh said, "Looks like all NATO's been here."

"Almost; even our competitors stopped by. That one in the far corner is from the Russian 320th Search and Rescue out of Teoisk.

"How'd that happen?"

"One of their M8 helicopters with a ruptured fuel tank got lost in a fog over the North Sea and was flying on fumes. We heard their *May Day* and vectored'em in. Shit, they were so happy and had such a good time with us, they almost defected."

To change the subject McHugh asked, "What's my friend Stringer told you?"

The colonel pulled a cigar out of his shirt pocket and unwrapped it. "Well, your Admiral friend told me about your run-in today and that your girlfriend and the young Bulgarian with sensitive information for his National Security Staff are being held hostage somewhere along the Mediterranean coast near Rome." Vitucci glanced around them, and then went on. "Stringer also told me to let you know that even though he never received a phone call from his Vatican Swiss friend, we now have an opportunity to do something more than just deliver a book to him." Understanding the message, McHugh nodded.

The Colonel continued, "Colin, the admiral explained all the details to me. He's aware that this Botev can positively identify the Bulgarian conspirators and may have more Info about their plans; maybe even the precise timing of the assassination attempt. And we have been ordered to rescue him pronto and retrieve that information for the Swiss Guard commandant and President Reagan. As I said earlier, we've got the green light. Now, let's talk about the situation, and then while you shower and change, I'll pull things together with my staff."

McHugh stared at the colonel. "And Claudette… is she expendable?"

"God no. Don't you even think about it! Maybe I didn't phrase it properly. First we rescue her and the kid, and then you and I turn to the job of pulling as much Info as we can out of the Bulgarian bastard."

McHugh sat back in his seat. "And who else knows about the assassination attempt?"

"Stringer said only you and I are aware of it and he wants us to keep it that way."

Vitucci put the cigar in an ashtray and focused on McHugh. "OK... let's get down to specifics."

The waitress arrived with two large mugs of beer and set a plate with a sandwich and fries in front of them. Each beer mug had a different air squadron logo on one side.

Vitucce picked up a fry. "Thanks Ellen. Could you bring some writing paper and a pen from Eric's office?"

He pointed to his sandwich, "Tuesday; it's probably ham and cheese. Our time is short. The regular lunches here are hot and heavy."

Ellen returned and placed a pad of paper and two pens in the center of the table.

With his mouth full of sandwich, Vitucci gave her a thumbs up. He then turned to McHugh. "Have you been to your girlfriend's condo?" Before McHugh could answer, the colonel went on, "If so, I need you to draw a schematic of the place. Try and locate it on the coast and identify any possible sites near it where we could land a couple of choppers, but far enough away so we won't be heard or detected ...if it's at all possible."

McHugh took a sheet of the paper and began to draw a sketch of the condominium complex, including a layout of the interior of Claudette's condo. He also added the underground garage and the location of the two elevators to the rear entrance of each condo.

"As the Brits say, 'Good Show!' I couldn't draw a better schematic myself; your damn lines are even straight." Colonel Vitucci took a sheet of paper and a pen, "What do you know about the surrounding area, the buildings, land, anything?"

McHugh took a sip of his beer and tried to picture the setting. "Well, the building sits on a hillside across from a two lane narrow road running along a sandy Mediterranean beachfront. A group of beach houses face the road across from the condo." He drew a diagram of the setting.

"What about the roof?" the colonel said while making notes.

"It's flat. Sorry, I've never been up there, but Claudette has a large balcony with a sliding glass door onto it." He pointed to the sketch and continued, "As you face the building from its front, her condo's on the left side of the top floor; her balcony faces the sea." McHugh waited for the next question.

"OK, what about my choppers?"

McHugh recalled the parking lot at Castello de Santa Severa and said "I only know of one place. It's about fifteen minutes north of her condo by car. Is that too far?"

"Not really, we'll have vehicles. Is there good cover?"

"I believe so. It's a medieval castle right on the coast about twenty kilometers north of the condo. The road going by the castle also runs straight past her condominium building." He stopped and recalled the castle surroundings, then continued, "There's a large parking area north of the castle that's not visible from the road. I believe the castle is open to visitors until five in the evening."

"When does the damn thing open?" the colonel asked.

"I'm not sure; probably around ten each morning for visitors. I don't know when the help arrives."

Realizing that they had covered the information he needed, but had hardly touched their food, Colonel Vitucci, stood and lifted his glass. "Didn't get much grub, but we're good for now. Let's get you cleaned up. Bring your beer."

When the two of them walked toward the door, Ellen ran up.

"Colonel, you know better." She took the mugs and poured their remaining beers into plastic cups.

The colonel took his cup from her and said, "Just testing, I knew you'd never let us walk out of here with the mugs."

At two o'clock in the Bern train station, Hammer and Kalina, disguised as father and daughter sat in the middle of the second class section of the train to Milano. The conductor ignored them as he walked through the compartment counting the number of passengers as the train pulled out of the station. The others in the compartment, mostly tourists, were watching the scenery, absorbed in reading or engaged in quiet conversation. The ride was smooth and quiet on the well maintained track beds.

Kalina watched out her window as the quaint Braggasse section of Bern disappeared into open fields fronting distant gray mountains. Finally she opened the book Hammer had given her and tried to read. After what seemed like only minutes the train began to slow approaching the outskirts of another city.

Kalina nudged Hammer, who appeared to be asleep.

"I'm awake, only my eyes are closed." He grinned.

The train slowly worked its way through a maze of converging rail tracks and came to a stop in front of a long stone building that Kalina thought looked like a city administration building. In the center of the building a large sign announced THUNE.

Kalina became uneasy when she observed the conductor step off the train with the few exiting passengers and walk across the platform to a tall man in a dark suit standing outside the building entrance. The two shook hands and after a brief conversation, both boarded the train.

She nudged Hammer and whispered, "A tall man just boarded; he looks like police."

"I see him. Eat your sandwich and read your book."

Kalina lifted her back pack onto her lap and touched the silenced revolver inside.

A short time later the conductor walked through the compartment checking passports.

The man followed a few paces behind surveying each passenger.

"Passports, please," the conductor said in French and extended his hand toward Hammer.

Hammer handed over both of their passports.

"Ah, Romanian. Where are you going?"

"My daughter and I are going to visit my brother, a professor at the Politecnico Universita in Milano.

"Where do you work?

"I drive a truck for a paper company. He handed the conductor a company photo identification card.

"Your daughter?"

Kalina looked directly at the conductor and smiled, ignoring the other man.

"She will stay with the wife of my brother, until baby arrives maybe in the week."

"Well, good wishes to your brother and his wife." The conductor returned the passports and identification card to Hammer.

Hammer said, "Thank you."

The conductor moved on and the other man followed.

Kalina resisted a sigh of relief and kept her head down.

When the two men left the compartment Kalina whispered, "When do we arrive in Italy?"

Hammer told her he didn't know the exact time they would cross the boarder into Italy, but the train was due in Milan at five o'clock, just before supper. He checked his watch, "We have another hour and a half to Milano. Relax and look at the mountains."

But Kalina didn't see the mountains. She only saw Vedenov's glazed eyes peering up at her from the sidewalk when the medical technicians lifted her gurney into the rear of the ambulance. He was dead, she knew that. But she was also sure his eyes were pleading her to avenge his death. She vowed, *Bitch, whatever your name is, you will also be ugly dead as soon as I get free of this fucking bra and find you in Italy,.* To conserve her energy for the confrontation, she closed her eyes.

Sensing the train begin to slow. Kalina sat up and watched the train enter a switching yard and stop in front of a maintenance office sandwiched between the two main track lines. Two official looking men stood next to a black Mercedes parked along the side of the office.

Hammer, who was watching the scene whispered, "Turn to me, don't show your face at the window."

"I know that," She murmured, and closed her hand around the butt of the revolver in her back pack.

To his relief, Hammer observed the man in the dark suit leave the train and join the two men standing near the car.

As the train began to move Hammer said, "They're gone."

Kalina watched the Mercedes drive away and whispered; "Now I can get out of this fucking bra." She lifted the backpack and began to rise.

Hammer held on to her wrist and said quietly, "Kalina, no, we may have another aboard, possibly undercover. Wait till Milano."

She smirked and crumbled back into her seat and turned toward the window.

A tall airman with a narrow face and cropped blond hair came from behind a nondescript wooden desk just inside the door of the Bachelor Officers Quarters, the BOQ.

"Welcome, Mr. McHugh. If you'll follow me, I'll take you to your suite."

'Thank you." McHugh took the set of keys the airman handed to him and followed down a long corridor with single doors lined on each side of the gray walls. The name and rank of an officer was printed on a plastic card held in a metal holder in the center of each door.

The airman stopped at the last door on the right with the nametag: Transient Officer.

"Mr. McHugh, the colonel said for you to take your time. There's a set of clean clothes and toiletries on the bed. There's also a safe for your valuables and a coffee bar and snacks. One of our medics will be by shortly to check on you. Should you need me just pick up the phone and dial 11." He saluted.

"Thanks, Airman…?"

"Nichols. I'm from Indiana, outside Fort Wayne, sir."

The room was time-worn with an overwhelming smell of lemon, as if it had just been cleaned. McHugh found this suite had an attached bathroom. Other BOQ rooms he'd previously stayed in had community bathrooms usually located as far as possible from the room assigned to him. A set of neatly folded camouflage fatigues and underwear sat in the middle of a single metal bed. The coffee bar consisted of a small one-cup, plug-in carafe with packages of coffee and condiments. McHugh stripped off his clothes and headed to the shower. The hot water was refreshing. He completed the shower and lay down on the bed wrapped in the towel and closed his eyes.

A half hour later, a knock on the door brought him awake.

"Mr. McHugh," a pleasant female voice announced.

"Yes," McHugh replied as he rose from the bed, pulled the pair of shorts on under the towel and opened the door.

"I'm Corporal Madison, an AirMedic/PJ. I'd like to take a look at your wounds." A thin young woman in fatigues with short auburn hair and large round glasses brushed past him and set a gray duffel bag on the bed.

"The colonel said you have a bad shoulder, a bullet wound in your leg, and an ankle that's giving you trouble. It might be difficult for you at Saturday night's dance." She regarded him with a playful smile and opened her bag.

Confused he asked, "I understand Airmedic, but what is PJ?"

"Sir, I'm also a qualified parachute jumper."

Before he could compliment her, she continued, "Let's look at that leg first. It might be easier if you removed the towel and slipped into some shorts."

She began to turn her back to give to give him privacy, but McHugh dropped the towel and faced her in his shorts.

Ignoring his bravado, she said, "Certainly doesn't look too serious, but it does need cleaning and a proper dressing." She cleaned the wound and dressed it professionally, then wrapped his ankle with an elastic athletic tape. "Now about your arm?"

"Doc in Washington said it's a contusion." He lifted his right arm cautiously, surprised that he was able to raise it forty-five degrees above his shoulder without any serious pain. "It's becoming more functional, but I still have occasional shooting pains."

Madison handed him a small plastic container of pills. "Use these sparingly; they're not M&M'S.

"Thank you. Is it Mary Madison?"

"No, Courtney, but you can call me Mary if you come to the dance." She smiled coyly and closed the door behind her, just as the phone rang interrupting his plan to return to the bed.

Airman Nichols announced, "Mr. McHugh, your driver's here."

Six olive green UH-60 Black Hawk helicopters were backed to the side walls facing the center of the cavernous aircraft hanger. Each had an M60 machine gun mounted above its side doors. The front fuselages reminded McHugh of the heads of barracudas he had watched circling the stern of his navy destroyer while anchored off the coast of the Dominican Republic a few years before.

A group of technicians in gray coveralls worked on two other Black Hawks in the center of the hanger.

Colonel Vitucci moved away from a group of commandos gathered in front of a podium in front of a large white board in the rear of the hanger and approached McHugh. "Colin, we're just about to begin the briefing. I hope you can help."

McHugh noticed that an enlarged view of his sketches of Claudette's apartment complex and a contour map of England and Southwestern Europe were attached to the white board.

Vitucci addressed the commandos who were in camouflage gear, sitting on low benches facing the podium.

"Gentlemen, remain seated. I want to introduce Mr. Colin McHugh the man responsible for our overnight excursion and tour of the pizza capital of the world. I don't want anyone to disparage him for the fact he's ex-navy."

There were a few chuckles and muffled comments.

The colonel continued, "It's a serious matter. A Bulgarian killer, who by the way has already made an attempt on Mr. McHugh's life, is holding a female US agent and a young Bulgarian ally who has sensitive information, captive in a condominium along the Italian coast a short distance outside of Rome." He glanced toward McHugh, who nodded that he understood the characterizations.

"We're going in light and fast. The information we have indicates they're being held by only one Bulgarian agent and, as I said, he's a killer. We've obtained a flight clearance over England and France for a NATO training exercise. We'll be over French airspace for more than three hours so we've also had to obtain special French approval for a long distance test flight of our new Black Hawks. All in all, the flight will take about six and a half hours; that's a long time in a vibrating machine." He paused and looked deliberately through the group to insure each man had an appreciation of the length of time they would be airborne. There were nods of understanding.

"In Italy, we'll technically be participating in a joint training exercise with a contingent of the Italian Special Air Brigade led by Colonel Matteo Sezzi."

He reached for a coffee cup on the podium and took a sip. "Matt is a friend of mine and a solid guy. We worked together on a hostage situation on the outskirts of Milan a few years ago. His guys will provide perimeter security, ground transportation and any necessary translating. They'll also run interference with any inquisitive Italian locals or bureaucrats. We'll meet Matt and his group when we land in Pisa. One last thing before I turn this meeting over to Lieutenant Murray who will provide all the flight details. We're flying light: fatigues, soft hats and issued athletic shoes. All weapons, body armor, hard hats, personal items and communications gear will be stowed in your carryalls; nothing else goes." He pointed to the two helicopters nearby. "The techs are completing the change out of the M-60's on our choppers for long range fuel tanks."

McHugh watched two mechanics push a portable crane holding a fuel tank toward one of the choppers.

Vitucci walked over to a lieutenant sitting in the first row. "John, you're on."

Lieutenant John Murray picked up a pointer from the podium and moved to the white board.

"Gentlemen…, and lady. He nodded to AirMedic Madison. "First of all; we'll probably be in rain and dense fog over England but it should clear once we hit the French coast. The first leg of our excursion is to Pisa." He pointed to a spot on the map just inside Italy's Mediterranean coast. "We plan to cruise at about 150 knots and maintain an altitude between 2000 to 3000 feet."

"Our flight plan is to head directly south over Margate, staying well to the east of London." He pointed to Margate. "We'll cross the channel and head inland over Calais, then south, to the east of Paris, continuing on south over Troyes." He moved the pointer along the route. "From Troyes, we'll follow the Rhone River valley, clear of the Alps to the east on down to Toulon. Our flight over France should take a little over three hours.

The last hour of the flight will be from Toulon over this short slice of the Mediterranean into Pisa." He pointed to the flight path over the Mediterranean. "The entire flight from here to Pisa is well within the flying range of our Black hawks, as they'll be configured. With departure at 1900, we should be landing in Pisa about 0100. As the colonel said, we'll meet the Italians share a glass of wine, rest and be ready for a brief early morning flight to the event. Any questions?"

A commando in the back stood up, "Blankets and pillows?"

Vitucci stood. "We'll be flying only seven to a chopper, including the two pilots up front, so there should allow plenty of room. In Pisa, we'll offload what's not needed for the event and pick up everything on our way back. So bring them, but don't overdo it. We will inspect everything before we board." He moved to the podium and turned to Lieutenant Murray, "John, take your windmill jockeys over for a short beer and review your flight plan."

After the pilots left, he continued, "I'll lead the assault team, Captain Kyle is number two. The rest of you all know your assignments."

He walked over to McHugh and whispered, "Its 1430 and the team's reasonably prepped. We've gone over a preliminary assault plan that we'll refine as we go. Now I'm going to let these guys go until about 1830. Why don't you, Kyle and I head to the club and clear up any questions you might have?"

McHugh agreed and the colonel discharged the group with the admonition to go and get their gear together. "*And rest, no booze or grab ass!*"

"Be back here at eighteen-thirty sharp; ready to roll."

In the officer's club, the colonel accepted his beer from Ellen and leaned toward McHugh. "You must have a question or two?"

McHugh thought a moment. "Well, there are a couple of things that concern me. First, the Bulgarian bastard holding Claudette and the young truck driver is really out to kill me; they're only bait. Don't you think I should let them know I'll be returning tomorrow? Secondly, what do we do if the bastard moves them somewhere else before we arrive?"

"Good questions," the colonel said, then took a sip of beer and looked over the edge of his mug at Captain Kyle.

Kyle turned to McHugh. "Maybe you should call her now and tell her you'll be arriving in the morning. If she answers, we know she's there, and if the Bulgarian knows you'll be arriving in the morning he'll keep them in the condo."

"Good idea, Larry. Vitucci interjected. "By the way, earlier this afternoon I asked Matt Sezzi to put the condo under surveillance. I don't know if he's been able to set it up yet. Maybe there's something else we can have done in case the bastard moves them." Vitucci rose and walked to the office next to the bar. He returned shortly. "I've put in a call to the Italian Air Group, and as soon as the duty officer locates Matt, he'll return my call. What kind of car does your Claudette drive?" he asked McHugh.

"She has her mother's car, a year old black Mercedes four door sedan."

"Well, there are only six condos in that building so it shouldn't be too hard to find her car in the garage. And damn it, if they all drive a Mercedes, I'll have Matt's guys put a transponder on each of them."

McHugh stood. "Maybe I should call her now and let her know I'll be there in the morning."

"OK, The colonel said. "Tell her you're coming in on the early morning flight and hope to be there shortly after eight. With the bastard believing you won't be there for another hour, we'll hit the place around seven; let's hope we catch him off-guard." He looked at his watch: 1545, and then glanced at McHugh, "Now's as good a time as any. Use the phone in the dining room. My Italian friend's going to return my call on the office phone."

McHugh went into the dining room, picked up the receiver and asked the operator for an outside line. He then gave the commercial operator both his credit card number and Claudette's phone number.

After only four rings Claudette answered the phone. "Colin."

"Hi, darling, is everything all right?"

After a hesitation that seemed too long, she replied, "Sure, everything's fine."

McHugh heard a guttural-like sound in the background and quickly said, "Claudette, I'll be on the early morning flight tomorrow and should be at your condo shortly after eight." He repeated, "*Shortly after eight in the morning*. Love you."

She repeated what he said very slowly in a louder voice.

Then she whispered, "He understands when you're coming. Bring help. Love you, too."

McHugh heard a slap and she cried out.

The phone went dead.

He looked at the receiver in his hand. "You son of a bitch!" He kicked a chair next to the table nearest him and a startled cleaning woman dropped her broom and ran out of the empty dining room. He smashed the handset down on the top of the counter. It cracked and the mouthpiece insert dropped on the floor.

The Bulgarian's punching bag face and walrus mustache flashed in front of McHugh's eyes. He stood shaking with a knot in his stomach and vowed: *If you rape her I'll kill you!*

A strong hand landed on his shoulder.

He turned into Vitucci, who planted both hands on his shoulders.

"Colin, what happened?"

Shaking his head, McHugh said, "She's there and terrorized. The bastard slapped her hard. She cried out, but she also made sure the bastard now knows I'll be there in the morning I'll kill him myself."

Vitucci released his grip and slipped his arm around McHugh's shoulder, "I understand your feelings and would react the same if it were my wife, but now it's our show. Our prime mission is to rescue your Claudette and the young Bulgarian. And I assure you that I'm not concerned about taking prisoners. Stay focused and help us!" He kept his arm around McHugh's shoulder while leading him back to the table.

Kyle rose and pulled out a chair for McHugh.

Vitucci looked toward the bar, "Ellen, another round" He glanced at his two companions, "OK?"

McHugh stood up, "Not for me colonel. I'm going back to the BOQ."

Turning toward the bartender, Ellen raised two fingers and pointed to the two sitting officers. The bartender made a gesture of holding a phone to his ear.

"Colonel, I believe your phone call has come through."

McHugh headed to the door.

Kalina and Hammer were standing beneath the one hundred foot high arched ceiling of the crowded main ticket hall of Milan's Central Station.

Hammer, you wait here. I'm going to the ladies room and take off this fucking bra.

"I will follow and wait outside. Too many beggars and thugs in this place."

"OK, follow." She shrugged and eased her way through the crowd.

With the bra removed, Kalina's teenage profile evaporated. The buttons on her blouse were stretched to the limit so she pulled her sweater completely across her chest.

Hammer watched her fiddling with the sweater when she came out of the restroom. "Now you look, not much of a young girl any more."

"Do we have time to find me other clothes?

"Come, we have more than an hour before the train leaves for Rome. We will get coffee and find a new sweater." Hammer turned and walked toward the station's massive arched main entrance.

Kalina walked close to her bodyguard as they entered Piazza Duca d'Aosta, the large square outside the station.

Hammer's stride lengthened.

"Do you know where we're going?" Kalina asked, trying to keep pace.

"Ya, years ago I was bodyguard to the Premier Zhikov's wife when she visited Milano and she bought clothes at a shop on a street near here. Maybe it's still there."

They turned down a side street flanked with cheap restaurants, currency exchanges, and clothing shops. "There it is, but now it's a sports shop. Over there."

They crossed the narrow street.

Kalina selected a properly sized sports bra. Then looked at a number of V-neck jumpers and jogging pants. She picked one of each and entered the fitting room.

The sales ladies watched awe-struck at the speed with which Kalina made her decision. They surely had questions of whether or not the working man standing near the door would be able to pay for any of her purchases.

Leaving the schoolgirl's clothes in the fitting room, Kalina walked out to the shocked faces of the two salesladies and picked up an oversized gray warm-up jersey and put it on over the jumper she had selected. The jogging pants fit perfectly.

Focusing on the shocked senior clerk, Kalina handed her sufficient American Dollars to pay for the clothes and provide a generous tip.

"I will meet friend." Kalina said in broken English, then picked up her backpack and marched straight out of the shop.

Hammer followed.

The station's twenty-four train platforms that ran beneath massive steel girders supporting the canopy of embedded clear glass panels served more than a hundred and twenty million passengers each year.

Their train for Rome was scheduled to depart on track fourteen at six o'clock. While Kalina waited for Hammer to return from the men's room, she dumped everything out of her backpack into a trash container except the silenced revolver and the two pieces of her cast. Realizing they had only fifteen minutes before their scheduled departure, she turned to call into the men's room for Hammer and bumped into him. "We must go. The train is eight tracks away."

Hammer decided that they would sit in the lounge car for the trip and paid the conductor the required additional lira. They faced each other at a window table and chatted in Bulgarian.

Hammer asked Kilana how she became a field agent.

She snapped, "I do not talk about me."

They sat and stared at each other for a few minutes, both realizing that their real lives were so divergent and compartmentalized that they really had nothing in common.

Kalina turned away and stared out of the window.

Without looking at her, Hammer stood and walked to the toilet. When he returned to the compartment he bought two glasses of vodka at the bar.

He handed her a glass and sat down. "Nazdrava."

"Nazdrava." Kalina put her backpack on the table between them and took out the two halves of her wrist cast. "I don't need these." She placed the halves on the table in front of Hammer.

"Daughter, sorry, I mean Kalina, maybe you should wear cast a while longer."

"No, my wrist needs exercise, I will not let it become weak," She slipped the revolver into the pocket of her jogging pants. "I have an assignment that I must complete." She placed the two halves of the cast into the back pack and kicked it under the table.

Kalina sipped the last of the vodka and stared out of the window at the passing vineyards as an ebbing sun slipped behind a distant line of cypress trees.

When McHugh returned to the BOQ, he found his clothes cleaned and folded neatly on the metal bed next to the carryall. The blood stains on the pant leg were gone. He placed the carryall on the chair next to the night stand, set his folded clothes on top of it and lay down on the bed with his hands behind his head. He needed to calm down and contain his anger; anger he had never before experienced. He reached over to the bedside table and turned on the radio.

A tenor in the middle of a romantic aria brought warm thoughts of the first night he and Claudette spent together. Then, just as quickly visions of the flat-faced Bulgarian animal abusing her shattered his emotions. He turned off the radio and buried his head in the pillow. His muscles were taut and his stomach was twisted in knots. He now understood how people could lose control.

Calm down. Relax. Maybe you're magnifying the situation. He won't abuse her; he wants to get to you. Maybe the slap you heard was for Botev. No it was there; she cried out. Claudette's just a beautiful, vulnerable lady caught up in a whirlwind of intrigue because she willingly stepped into my life. If only she had asked Claudio to have one of his staff verify the truck driver's address and hadn't gone there herself. He felt helpless.

His mind raced, one moment coiled in anger, the next searching for calm and focus. In all, he had never experienced such an overwhelming concern for anyone. In less than a week Claudette had totally captivated him. She had to be rescued quickly

This morning in Cheltenham McHugh couldn't think of what he could do to save her. Now he couldn't even help the commandos who were going to make it happen. The idea of being on the sidelines gnawed at him. He felt insignificant among these men who took on the task and its risks without blinking an eye.

There was a knock on the door. "Mr. McHugh, its Airman Nichols. Captain Kyle's here."

"I'll be right there." McHugh responded, rubbing his eyes and sweating profusely.

"He said to bring your gear."

"Give me a minute to wash up." He yelled and slipped out of his shorts. The cold shower kicked him into reality. He half-dried, slipped on the fatigues, then stuffed his civilian clothes into the carry-all and slammed the door behind him. McHugh glanced at his watch as he raced down the hall: 1830.

A rolling fog with a drizzling rain greeted Mchugh when he opened the BOQ door. He ran to the covered jeep and Kyle leaned over and opened the passenger door. "The weather guys say we'll be out of this soup as soon as soon we hit the French coast, maybe in a half hour or so."

"Let's hope so," McHugh said and tossed the carryall into the rear seat.

They didn't speak during the short drive to the hanger. As soon as they entered, Kyle left McHugh and walked over to the commando team lined along the side of a wooden table. They were now dressed in the same chocolate chip uniforms worn in Vietnam, with soft hats and dark athletic shoes. Kyle inspected each person meticulously, including the contents of each carryall opened on the table. When Kyle concluded his inspection of the troops, he did the same to the colonel and his gear.

The colonel immediately reciprocated.

Although McHugh was dressed like the others, neither officer moved to inspect him, confirming that he was only a bystander in the operation. He was pissed, and then just as quickly subdued that anger, realizing Claudette's rescue was finally underway. It renewed his vow to stay focused and help from the sidelines if he was asked.

Standing next to the colonel, Kyle announced, "Gather round."

Everyone moved toward the two officers.

The colonel said, "We're going to fly through some shitty weather over England and the channel."

Someone muttered, "As usual."

The colonel stared down the individual, and then continued, "It could be a rough ride for a while but should clear once we head inland over France. You may not be able to see your companion chopper in the dense wet soup but the flyboys will have each other on radar. For safety purposes they plan to maintain an altitude separation of two hundred feet in poor visibility. Once over France, and the visibility improves, we'll fly side- by- side. You're all familiar with the rock and roll of these beasts, so get comfortable, put on noise reduction or your music headsets and relax." He stopped and looked through the group, then at Captain Kyle.

Kyle mouthed, "Questions."

"Thanks Larry." Vitucci then asked, "Are there any questions?"

Someone asked if they could order their pizza now instead of waiting to land in Italy. It took the edge off.

Captain Kyle announced, "OK, piss call, no food aboard, put everything in the containers near the heads. We lift off in twenty minutes."

Commandant Pfyffer signed the last requisition and placed it on top of the stack of the other completed requisitions on the edge of his desk. In the morning the supply sergeant would retrieve the approved requisitions and issue formal purchase orders to the regiment's Italian suppliers. Most were for food and other necessities to restock the regiment's store room. However Pfyffer had included one special requisition for six miniature radios with ear pieces to be purchased directly from Motorola, the American manufacturer.

He ate the last bite of the generous slice of quiche that Beatrice had brought to him before she left for her Tuesday night book club.

It was the Pfyffer routine on Tuesday evenings. While he finished his accumulated paperwork, Beatrice would bring him a light supper and then join the other members of her book club to help the Sisters of Missionaries of Charity serve meals to Rome's homeless gathered in the Domo di Maria Hostel. Located behind a small door in the Vatican wall, the Hostel entrance is open to all in need. Usually after eight o'clock when all had been fed and the club members had finished the discussion of their book selection in one of the hostel's anti rooms, Beatrice would join the commandant in their apartment.

Pfyffer placed the empty dish on his credenza and lifted the West Point book that the American professor had delivered to him out of his open safe.

He opened the book to chapter twelve to again read the two sentences that had been puzzling him:

> *Believe present Vatican internal security capabilities and procedures may rule out assassination attempt within the confines of Vatican City itself. Believe attempt planned when Pontiff outside Vatican City proper or while traveling outside Italy.*"

Do the Americans realize that Vatican City includes St. Peter's Square or are they just suggesting they believe that *only* the Vatican buildings are secure?" He questioned softly, glancing at the framed photographs of his predecessors covering the wall in front of him.

It really doesn't matter. "I have done what I had to do."

He closed the book, tossed it into the open safe and spun the lock.

Sipping the last of his wine, he placed the glass on top of the empty quiche dish and opened the folder containing the regimental schedule and security assignments for tomorrow's general audience. After spending a few moments reviewing the assignments of the guardsmen he had available, he closed the folder, satisfied they were prepared as best they could be.

Night flight to Italy

25

McHugh struggled to get comfortable in the low canvas backed aluminum seat just behind the copilot. The smell of oil and aviation fuel permeated the damp cabin. Except for the eerie mint-green lights on the instrument display system in front of the pilots, it was pitch dark inside the chopper. He put on the headset the copilot handed to him, saw Vitucci plug his set into a control panel above their heads and he did the same.

After obtaining permission to start engines, Lieutenant Murray gave a thumbs-up to the rain soaked airman standing security to the right of the helicopter, pushed the start button and the main rotor began spooling on its pylon. The entire fuselage vibrated as if it might come apart.

The beast lifted off the tarmac shimmying into the weather with its red and blue night flying lights on the fuselage and the tail pylon piercing the wet haze.

Finally the Black Hawk transitioned nose down into level flight toward Margate.

The commandos stuffed cloth and cardboard where ever practicable to muffle the metal-to- metal banging of the side doors and secured the other loose gear in the cabin.

McHugh leaned forward trying to decipher the radar picture and the indicator lights on pilot display system.

Unlike the other helicopters, both civilian and military which he had flown in; this beast with its head down and powerful jet engine seemed to slice through weather like a cutter plowing through a heavy sea.

The rain dissipated as they crossed the English Channel, and McHugh was able to pick out flashes of white from the rotating beacon on the lighthouse above Calais harbor. When the rain cleared, the dark, starless night made it easy to pick out city lights and even the headlight beams of cars moving in the countryside.

Twenty minutes later Lieutenant Murray announced over the intercom, "That mushroom of light off to the right is Paris."

Their chopper now flying on the right side of its companion gave McHugh a bird's-eye view of the white halo on the eastern horizon above Paris. A cold chill overshadowed the euphoria of the moment as he envisioned the Bulgarian brutalizing Claudette. He leaned forward, head down, elbows on his knees with his hands behind his neck trying to erase the picture.

The Colonel touched his shoulder and handed McHugh a pillow, "Sit back and try to relax."

McHugh gave a feeble grin and slipped the pillow behind his back, leaned back into the seat, closed his eyes and crossed his arms over his chest.

Kalina and Hammer stood in the waiting area of the Piazzale dei Cinquecento in front of the modern Aluminum façade of Rome'sTermini Train Station. The station's interior lights blazed through the building's clear glass wall blending with the high intensity street lights of the large square welcoming the arriving passengers into the city's dark night.

It was ten o'clock, more than an hour since their train had arrived, and Kalina wasn't enamored with the setting. In fact she wasn't even aware of it. She was pissed.

Petcov hadn't met them on arrival, as agreed.

After two unanswered phone calls to the apartment, she now weighed whether she should take a taxi to it. She paced back and forth in front of Hammer, who stood silently by, giving her space. She knew Zhelov would fume if she brought Hammer to the apartment. But what alternative did she now have? She decided to take on Zhelov's wrath.

"Hammer, let's catch a taxi." She led him toward the taxi queue on the other side of the large square.

A black Mercedes sedan skidded up to the curb ahead of them.

Kalina lifted the revolver out of her pocket and held it along her side and scrutinized the driver when he stepped out of the car. His dark chauffeur's coat was much too small for his weightlifter's torso.

"Hammer, its Genkov." The chauffeur extended his hand.

"Genkov, I remember you from the old days." Hammer shook the driver's large hand vigorously in both of his.

Kilana put the revolver back in her pocket and approached the two friends.

Genkov glanced toward Kalina, "Lubanov, I am told to bring you to Petcov. Please get in."

Genkov pulled the Mercedes to the curb three blocks from the apartment.

"Lubanov, you are to walk to the apartment. I will bring my friend Hammer to my place and he will return to Switzerland tomorrow. Good luck."

Kalina put her hand on the back of Hammer's wide neck. "Hammer you are a first class bodyguard. Now I will go and take care of my business." She opened the car door and walked toward the apartment without looking back.

Standing on the dark landing outside the apartment door, Kalina collected herself, anticipating a deluge of venom from Zhelov. She knocked on the door.

Petcov cautiously opened the door with a silenced revolver in his hand and pointed it at the dark haired woman standing in front of him.

"Yes, what do you…"

"Petcov, put down that weapon. It's me, Kalina."

"Oh Kalina, come in things have happened."

Kalina moved past him. After her eyes adjusted to the bright light in the room, she became aware of another man standing near the kitchenette holding a cup of coffee.

"Sit down Kalina we must talk." Petcov continued, "I don't believe you have met Anton Kostov."

Kostov nodded toward her and lifted his cup. "Coffee?"

"With sugar," she acknowledged and sat down at the table, cluttered with ashtrays and cigarette butts.

Kostov brought coffee and sat down between the two of them.

Kalina surveyed the room. "Where is"…

"Zhelov is dead!" Petcov interrupted, "I received a phone call two hours ago from Steiger, the Stasi agent. He said Zhelov was killed yesterday by a train while chasing McHugh along railroad tracks outside of a small town in England."

Petcov went on to explain that Stazi agents in England confirmed the death and had contacted Steiger. "I have no further details. Now the three of us must decide what to do about the papist and the American, McHugh."

Kalina glared at Petcov and then stood knocking over her cup of coffee. "I need to know where that bastard McHugh is; I'm going after him! Where is he?"

"McHugh's in England, but will soon be on his way to his girlfriend's condominium here outside Rome," Petcov answered. "He phoned her that he will arrive later this morning.

Bukhalov is holding Botev and McHugh's girlfriend in her condo."

"I know that," Kalina said and then turned to Kostov. "And who the hell are you?"

Before Kostov could respond, Petcov interjected, "Kostov is one of us. Zhelov assigned him to keep the assassin in tow and make sure the papist is eliminated."

Kostov stood and picked up Kalina's cup and went into the kitchenette. Returning, he handed the refilled cup to Kalina and said, "You and I have the work to do, and I don't need our friend here to speak for me." He turned on Petcov. "Now Herr Petcov, I think you should go back to your Embassy duties. Kalina and I have much to discuss."

Petcov stood, kicked his chair against the wall and picked up his cup and saucer. He walked into the kitchenette and threw both toward the sink. The saucer fell on the floor and broke into pieces. He grabbed the tape recorder from the table, glared at Kostov and stomped out of the apartment, leaving the door open.

After closing the door Kostov said, "Now we must make plans for tomorrow afternoon."

The two Black Hawks were cruising east of Lyon, France at an altitude of 2500 feet when a twister wind rolling down the west side of the Alps caused the chopper to lurch violently and loose altitude.

McHugh almost slipped free of his seat belt and fell out of his seat.

When Lieutenant Murray brought the chopper back on its course and altitude, he announced over the intercom, "Sorry guys, we caught the wash of a down draft from the Alps to our left. We now have control.

Vitucci took off his headset and turned to the rear, "OK, now's a good time to break out the chow."

Someone tapped McHugh on the shoulder. "Sir, could you pass these to the pilots and the colonel?" He handed McHugh four small boxes.

The colonel looked over his shoulder and said, "Sergeant, four coffees up front. Give me the cream and sugar and I'll do the honors."

How much longer to touch down?" asked Vitucci.

Lieutenant Murray answered, "We'll be crossing over the Mediterranean and into Pisa in a little over two hours. I'll raise your friend Sezzi's frequency as soon as we pass over Toulon."

At 0145 Wednesday morning, the two helicopters swooped low with their landing lights reflecting off of a calm Mediterranean Sea on the final approach into Pisa's Galileo International Airport. Although McHugh knew better, the view through the front windscreen gave the appearance that the chopper was almost skinning the water and the flashing control tower beacon and the bright white runway lights ahead were rushing directly toward them.

The two Black Hawks landed simultaneously side by side on the tarmac in the far south- west corner of the airport near an Italian Air Force helicopter.

Five men in camouflage fatigues stood near the Italian helicopter watching them land. When the rotors were shut down, the Americans disembarked and stood by their choppers.

A broad shouldered officer of medium height, whom McHugh assumed was Colonel Sezzi, approached with his arms open wide. The other Italian commandos followed a few paces behind their leader; the Americans huddled behind Vitucci.

After a warm hug to Vitucci, Colonel Sezzi turned to the Americans and raised his arms in a welcoming gesture, saying in near perfect English, "Welcome to Italy, my friends. We will meet for a few moments and then have a bite to eat before resting."

The groups began to intermingle, shaking hands and greeting one another.

Sezzi turned toward an arriving Alitalia Airlines luxury bus. "Our limousine has arrived."

The bus took the group across the airfield toward the main airport terminal and stopped in front of an Alitalia arrivals door. A tall attractive stewardess in the familiar airline blue and green uniform led them into the Alitalia First Class Lounge. Along one wall of the room, a table covered in a white cloth held carafes of wine, bottles of Peroni beer, a large coffee urn and plates of pizza and sandwiches. Lounge chairs and metal cots filled the room's center.

With a nod to Courtney Madison, Colonel Vitucci said, "Gentlemen, and lady, Go easy. Eat light, Coffee's OK, Only one glass of wine. It's almost 0130. We take off at 0500." He turned to Colonel Sezzi. "Matt, thanks for your hospitality."

After the two Colonels, Captain Kyle, McHugh and two other Italian officers selected their food and retreated to a table in the far corner of the room, the mingling group of American and Italian commandoes approached the table.

"I will bring you up to date on the condominium situation," Sezzi said, and explained that at the suggestion of Colonel Vitucci, he had one of his men had attach a transponder to Claudette's Mercedes and it still remained in the garage. He also pointed out that he had assigned a team to reconnoiter the building and from their report concluded that there were only two ways into the condo if the planned initial assault was to be a surprise: through the front condo door or through the glass patio doors. The two elevators at the rear of the garage leading directly up to her private rear condo door probably couldn't be used for such an assault because the motor and the cable noise would alert those in her condominium.

The possibility of climbing the elevator cables, remained an option, but he believed it might also be difficult to open the rear condo door without alerting the Bulgarian. He concluded by advising the group that four of his men, dressed as policemen, would be assigned to isolate the other building residents by securing the hallways and the garage.

Sezzi pointed to one of his officers. "Lieutenant Guira has made a test-landing at the castle and he will now brief us."

A thin lieutenant, with the darkest eyebrows McHugh had ever seen, stood and explained that the parking lot at the castle had only enough space to safely land two choppers and still allow sufficient room for the vehicles they would require."

The lieutenant then looked directly at Vitucci, "So, Colonel, one of your Black Hawks will have to remain here in Pisa."

Vitucci glanced at Kyle, who gave thumbs up. "I guess we can work with that.

Sezzi stood and turned to Colonel Vitucci, "Vic, we will support your rescue, but it's your operation to carry out. Any questions?"

Vitucci glanced at McHugh and Kyle. Both shook their heads.

Vitucci raised his cup. "I could use another coffee."

He and Sezzi both stood and walked to the food table.

After the other Italian officers left, McHugh and Kyle sat alone.

McHugh said, "Larry, how do you plan to actually carry out the rescue?"

Kyle played with his empty coffee cup, and then looked directly at McHugh and answered, "Let me assure you, we'll assess the entire situation before we do anything. Two guys have been assigned to the roof to position miniature cameras and highly sensitive microphones on the bedroom windows and balcony door to enable us to observe and listen to everything that transpires inside the condo. Another will check out her elevator. Our senior sergeant will attach a similar microphone to the condo door and also determine if it's possible to slide a mini-camera under the door. These initial operations will take about half an hour. All the Intel that can be gathered by the cameras and microphones will be transmitted to a portable control console which Burns, our electronics guru, will have set up in one of the Italian vans they are providing to us."

"Sounds good."

"We'll formalize our plan and move in only after evaluating all of the gathered information. So I can't give you a definitive answer right now. However, the colonel has given me his assurance that we will include you in the final decision-making process.

Noticing a puzzled look appear on McHugh's face, Kyle asked, "Colin is something still bothering you?"

McHugh wiped his mouth with the back of his hand. "I'm glad you're including me, but how will you be able to specifically identify those in the condo? After all, there are *two* Bulgarians! And we only want to eliminate the bad guy."

"Damn good question. Any suggestions?"

"Have your men identify their location in the condo by their names, Claudette, Botev… and Bastard!" McHugh stood.

At 0445, McHugh, like the others, slipped on the lightweight, bullet-proof vest he'd been provided. After assuring himself that the chamber of the Colt forty-five that Vitucci had given him was clear, he holstered it.

Raising his voice, Vitucci ordered, "Load up, no extra gear. Everything that's not essential stays here."

After the commandos took their places in the lead chopper, McHugh followed the colonel and again took the seat behind the copilot.

The colonel turned to him. "Colin, leave the carryall. You really don't need it"

"Colonel, my civilian clothes are in it, and I plan to stay with Claudette when this is all over."

The colonel gave a thumbs-up. "And I assure you… you will."

To McHugh, the flight along the Mediterranean coast to the castle seemed shorter than the hour it took, probably because he was observing the traffic on the A12 coastal highway, and remembering the drive he and Claudette had taken less than a week before. That Wednesday, they were traveling north in the rain and they were comfortable in the intimacy of the Mercedes.

On this flight south, he was confined in a vibrating metal barracuda and a tangerine sun was inching into a cloudless sky that hinted at a bright afternoon. He prayed it was a good omen.

Burns, the electronics guru, sat on an aluminum stool in front of his portable control console set up in rear compartment of a black unmarked Italian van in a field to the north of the condominium building. McHugh, Vitucci, Kyle, Sezzi, and the Italian pilot Guira stood huddled a few steps outside the van's open rear doors.

Burns yelled in their direction, "Shit, Colonel, the curtains are closed over the bedroom windows and the drapes are drawn inside the balcony doors. Gonzalez rappelled down to the two bedroom windows; they're locked, only way in is to cut. Same for the balcony door. We can't get a look inside. And the disc microphones attached to the windows and the balcony door aren't picking up any conversation. It's quiet as hell in there. And Sarge reported that something's wedged against the bottom of the condo door, so the mini-camera's out. We're flying blind."

Colonel Vitucci looked stunned.

Sezzi eyed Vitucci, "Vic, why not go in with force? Your commandos can easily overpower one Bulgarian."

McHugh stepped in front of the two of them. "That's bullshit. Don't even consider it. If you go in full throttle; you'll only recover corpses. I know that bastard; he had no reservation about killing me last week. Even though he thought I was either dead or trapped in the car, he *still* blew the fuel tank and ignited to the entire area. No, you can't use force!" He stepped back, adding softly, "There'd be no lives to save."

"Well, maybe we can wait him out," Burns suggested.

McHugh ignored the comment and addressed all of them, "I can't tell you the details, but the bastard in that condo is a Bulgarian agent and part of a group planning something disastrous that's maybe only days or a few weeks away. They know I'm aware of their plan; that's why they tried to kill me only a few miles from here, then later in Switzerland and yesterday in England. That bastard's only holding Claudette to get to me. He already killed an innocent couple in Rome thinking one of the victims was the young Bulgarian Botev he now holds hostage... Botev may even be dead already." He stopped momentarily, and then added, "That murderer has nothing to live for except a Bulgarian labor camp, prison or maybe a bullet."

McHugh turned to Vitucci, "Colonel, I have to go in; yesterday, you told me to tell Claudette I would arrive this morning on an early flight. I brought my clothes."

Vitucci looked away, but didn't answer. After a minute or so he turned and put a hand on McHugh's shoulder. "OK... we have no other choice." He turned to Burns, "Let's get him wired."

McHugh picked up his carryall and climbed into the van.

The colonel motioned to Kyle and the two walked a short distance away. "Larry, when McHugh goes in, I want one of the guys on the roof to rappel onto the balcony and be prepared to blast through that condo glass door. Keep another in the garage, geared up and ready to climb the elevator cable prepared to blow the rear door. And have the sergeant prepare for a forced entry through the front door. But nobody, *nobody* makes any move until I give the order. Make sure they understand that no matter what happens in there. And double check all communications gear, *Now.*"

Kyle nodded, turned and walked away, talking into his headset microphone.

Burns was about to attach a sticky wafer microphone to McHugh's chest when the colonel sat down on the sill of the van's open door.

"Hold up, Burns." He said, "Colin, do you think the bastard will search you, or make you strip?"

"He'll make me strip; he can't take chances. He has to keep a gun on one of us at all times; he has no back-up."

"I agree. Let's cover all bases. No vest for sure." The colonel looked at Burns apprehensively. "Where can we hide a wafer so it won't be discovered?".

"If Mr. McHugh doesn't have to take off his underwear or shoes, we can put one in either place.

"The shoes!" McHugh said, "The bastard may just want to embarrass me by ordering me to strip. Maybe if you stick it in my socks I can still get rid of it if I'm forced to take them off. Or attach it to a shoe so it won't come loose. God, do these things really work in shoes or socks?"

"Yes, sir, they're very reliable and extremely sensitive."

"OK. One in a sock and one in the other shoe; let's get on with it."

Vitucci added, "Burns, let's give him a backup just in case."

"Why, sir?" the young technician asked, and then added, "Sir, we only operate one mike at a time to eliminate noise interference, so one will be a backup for the other."

"OK, when you're done, give me a couple minutes with Mr. McHugh.

When Burns finished, McHugh walked over to Vitucci standing twenty feet away.

"Colin, I know you have strong feelings for Claudette and how hard it must have been to stand by while we put this show together. Now the show's yours, and the most important thing you can do in there is to keep your cool and stay focused. No matter what condition you find Claudette or the young Bulgarian to be in, remember why you're there."

"To aid you to rescue them, right!"

The Colonel continued, "And *not* get yourself and your two friends killed in the process. Keep your cool. Let us know what's happening. Communication will be one way; from you to us. We *will not* do anything unless you tell us to do it. When we come in; it will be through the front door, the balcony, and up the rear elevator. And I will not give that order unless you tell me to."

He put both hands on McHugh's shoulders. "And now, my friend, how are you going to tell me to give that order?"

"Colonel, that's heavy. I don't know what to expect. I'm pretty sure Claudette will be alive, but I'm not sure what condition she'll be in. I guess I'll just say, 'Colonel, time's up,' and you guys come fast. Botev's probably dead, so I'll hit the deck and hopefully bring Claudette down with me. I'll try to give you hints about where the bastard is located in the condo. Use my sketch regarding the layout and location of furniture. If it's changed, I'll attempt to let you know." He looked at his watch. "It's 0700." They turned back toward the group and McHugh leaned into the colonel. "By the way, maybe you should have a taxi drop me off in case he's watching the street."

Vitucci shook McHugh's hand and gave him a soft punch in the chest. "I'll see what I can do. Remember, keep your cool."

"Thanks, give me a few minutes." McHugh turned and walked about ten yards away, knelt down on one knee and lowered his head.

Claudette Arriaga's Condominium

26

McHugh stepped out of the taxi and glanced at the top floor of the condo hoping the bastard would get a good look at him.

A commando on the roof gave a wave.

McHugh nodded and entered the building.

After shaking the hand of the Italian commando/policeman in the third floor hallway and receiving a pat on the back from the American sergeant, McHugh paced up and down the corridor a couple of times and then rang the doorbell.

Claudette opened the door.

"Oh, God," McHugh exclaimed.

The American sergeant standing with his back to the wall beyond the door lifted his SIG 226 pistol and started to move toward McHugh.

McHugh put his hand out toward the commando; the sergeant halted, yet still ready to respond.

Claudette's face was contorted, her right eye was severely bruised and her left eye was swollen shut. Her white blouse had blood on it and was torn in shreds. Her bra was ripped down the center exposing her breasts. A tear appeared in her right eye.

McHugh's jaw tightened and his hands closed in fists.

"Come, Mr. McHugh, your bitch looks to see you. My silenced pistol is back to her head, so don't be hero. We talk much before you both go to your maker." The Bulgarian's English was poor but understandable.

The Bulgarian, dressed in the black outfit he wore a week ago, pulled Claudette slowly back from the door by her hair. He then shoved her onto the couch. Her leg just missed hitting the glass cocktail table in front of it.

Claudette slid to the far edge of the couch, put her head down, and clasped her hands in her lap with her knees together.

The Bulgarian sat down in the middle with his right hand resting on the back of the couch pointing the gun at Claudette's head. He eyed McHugh and beckoned him forward with his left hand.

Realizing any rash move would result in Claudette's death, McHugh entered slowly. He was relieved to see Claudette lift her head toward him with resolve in her right eye.

McHugh glanced around the room and said, principally for Vitucci, "Well, at least you haven't rearranged the furniture."

"You CIA pig, you don't go it alone, so I think you have friends outside."

"Bukhalov, I believe your name is Bukhalov, I'm not CIA. I'm a businessman who happened to be in the wrong place at the wrong time. You and your friends made a big mistake."

The Bulgarian waved the revolver at McHugh. "Take off clothes. You have gun?"

"No, I don't have a weapon." McHugh said and unbuttoned his denim shirt, and then tossed it toward at the Bulgarian's feet.

"Now pants." Bukhalov reached down and retrieved the shirt from the floor.

McHugh unbuckled his belt, slipped off the cargo pants and tossed them in the direction of the Bulgarian. They fell on the floor a foot away.

When Bukhalov stretched to retrieve them, McHugh glanced toward Claudette and mouthed, "It's going to be OK."

Even with her face mirroring pain, she responded by lifting a thumb.

McHugh asked, "Do you want my shoes?"

"No CIA, keep on feet," he threw the clothes back at McHugh.

"Where's Botev, the young man you forced to push my car off the road and into the river bed?"

Bukhalov bellowed, "He's a pig."

"Whatever he is; where is he?"

"Go look in bathroom. I sit on the couch and play with your bitch."

McHugh took a step toward the Bulgarian; Claudette shook her head. He stopped. *Stay focused*, and went into the bathroom.

Botev was alive, naked and hog-tied on the bathroom floor. His hands were bound behind his back with a brown leather woman's belt. His bare feet were tied together with a thin cloth wrap and both hands and feet were pulled together with a bath towel. His ankles, forced back against his buttocks, were causing him obvious pain. His forehead was discolored just below the hairline and his swollen lip was crusted with dried blood.

The young man looked up with pleading eyes and whispered painfully, "He's going to kill us."

McHugh reached down and touched his shoulder. "Not today, he's not." He untied the bath towel, allowing Botev to stretch his legs, then released his hands from the belt. "Stay quiet; untie your feet while I look around."

McHugh checked each drawer in the credenza hoping to find something he could use as a weapon, but only found female necessities and towels. He thought of opening the medicine cabinet but decided against it believing the noise of the door catch might alert Bukhalov.

"Hey, focking American, come out."

McHugh threw a bath towel to Botev and whispered, "Stay here, be quiet. Wrap yourself in this towel."

When he returned to the living room, McHugh glared at Bukhalov, "I remember you used those same words when you shot up my car." Then he glanced at Claudette hoping she understood he was stalling. Her eyes reflected strength and defiance. A hint of a smile gave McHugh an incentive to push the bastard.

"Why do you have young Botev tied on the bathroom floor?"

"The pig doesn't know the fun I have with your bitch." He squeezed Claudette's right breast and twisted the nipple. She whimpered softly.

McHugh took a step forward and Bukhalov shifted the revolver in his direction.

"You sit there on the couch with a gun to a woman's head, torture her and call yourself a man; you're nothing but a piece of shit!"

With the revolver pointed at McHugh's midsection, Bukahlov bellowed, "And you could be easy dead."

McHugh stepped back, realizing he had to defuse the moment, "Don't point that gun at me. I'm probably your only way out of Italy alive. You should be good to me and lay off hurting Claudette if you want to survive."

There was a thud on the balcony.

Bukhalov turned and shot two holes in the glass door and then pointed the gun barrel at McHugh.

McHugh glared at the Bulgarian "You're right. Commandos are out there, and they don't take prisoners. *They will kill you.*"

McHugh watched Bukhalov's eyes glance again toward the balcony and realized that the Bulgarian killer was beginning to understand the seriousness of his situation. It was also clear to McHugh that remaining in the condo offered no chance of survival for any of them. Bukhalov was so wound up that he would shoot at least the two of them as soon as any assault began. McHugh had to get them all out of the apartment.

"The only way you will stay alive is to listen to me."

"What the fock do you do?"

"I won't do anything until you let Claudette go into the bathroom and clean herself.

Keep your Russian revolver trained on me. When she gets up, I will tell you how I can help you."

Again the Bulgarian turned toward the balcony. Then he said, "Bitch, get the fock up."

Claudette rose unsteadily and slowly shuffled past McHugh.

"The bitch is up. Tell me what you do." The revolver was pointed at McHugh's chest.

With hope that his face reflected confidence, McHugh said, "If we can find a car, I will drive you to Anacona; it's only three hours away. There we will take the ferry across the Adriatic Sea to Dubrovnik in Yugoslavia. I've done it before."

"You lie."

"No, I don't lie; I do business in Dubrovink. It's only a few miles inland from the sea." Then he added, "You know the Italian police also want to arrest you for killing that young couple. I *am* the only chance you have to get out of Italy."

The bastard's eyes diverted again to the balcony and McHugh sensed a decision was about to be made.

Bukhalov turned and said defiantly, "No CIA car! Your bitch has Mercedes down in garage. You drive it."

Gotcha, McHugh thought and took the initiative. "We only go if Claudette and Botev go with us."

"Botev dies."

"No. He goes with us or we wait for the commandos…and the Italian police."

"Call your bitch out here."

McHugh turned toward the bathroom.

"Stay," Bukhalov walked over and put the gun to McHugh's head. "Call her."

Before McHugh said anything Claudette walked into the room. She had cleaned her face, applied a blush cream on her sore eye and fastened the two remaining buttons on her blouse.

Bukhalov pointed the revolver at Claudette. "Sit down on couch."

"CIA, you bring Botev, give him clothes. Keep his hands tied."

McHugh went into the bathroom and gave Botev his clothes and let him wash. When the young man was dressed McHugh tied his hands loosely together in front of him with the belt.

Bukhalov yelled in an agitated voice, "CIA, I want you to use phone… tell commando leader not to stop us or you all die."

In the living room, McHugh picked up the handset and dialed a random number. Not wanting the bastard to know that every word they had said previously was heard and recorded, he announced into the receiver, "We're coming out. Have the commandos back away."

To McHugh's surprise, Vitucci answered the call. "Colin, we tapped the phone. Good Job… at least so far so good. You're not out of this mess yet, stay focused. We'll be out of sight following you. Be careful."

McHugh dropped the phone and turned to the killer, "The commandos will not stop us."

In a loud voice, Bukahlov said, "Botev, diode tuk sega!" Botev come in here.

The young Bulgarian walked into the room with his head down.

McHugh glared at Bukhalov. "From now on we speak English. Let's go." Then he looked at Claudette. "Darling, where are your car keys?"

Bukhalov threw the keys at McHugh.

McHugh was the first off the elevator.

Behind him, Claudette whispered, "The Lugar."

He nodded and glanced around the garage. Vitucci's commando was no where to be seen. There were parking places for eight cars; five were occupied by expensive sedans. Claudette's Mercedes was parked in a space near the garage door.

McHugh led the three of them toward the Mercedes, and unlocked its doors with the remote. Claudette opened the rear door behind the driver's seat.

Bukahlov pushed her all the way across the seat. "Bitch, I sit behind CIA McHugh."

He waved the revolver in McHugh's face. "I blow your head to many pieces you fock with me." He then yelled at Botev in Bulgarian, "Pig, you sit in front by CIA."

McHugh waited until Bukhalov entered the back seat and then opened the driver's door. Before entering, he reached down and pulled the box containing the Luger from under the driver's seat where Claudette had placed it the week before when they drove to Milan. As a cover, he dropped the car keys on the cement floor.

"Oh, shit, the keys," he said loud enough for Bukhalov to hear.

"CIA, pick up damn keys, we go now or...." He waved the gun towards Claudette.

As he stooped, McHugh opened the box and lifted the Lugar out with his left hand while picking up the keys with his right. His first thought was to put a bullet in the Bulgarian bastard, but his revolver was still pointed at Claudette's head.

"OK, we go now." McHugh sat down in the driver's seat, sliding the Lugar under his left leg

When he started the car, Claudette said, "The garage door opener is above the visor."

Bukhalov slapped her.

McHugh punched the door opener and turned off the ignition. He turned and faced the Bulgarian, "You touch her again and I'll stop this car for good. You will never leave Italy alive." He thought again about using the Lugar.

Bukhalov leaned forward and pointed the revolver in McHugh's face.

"Go, CIA, no focking stop!"

Outside the condominium

27

A half hour before, Kalina had the taxi driver drop her on a corner behind and three blocks south of Claudette's condominium. Her plan was to survey the area before approaching the condominium building. She was dressed in the beige V-necked jumper and jogging pants she had purchased in Milano. The Russian silenced 6P6 revolver was in the cloth back pack hung between her shoulders.

She walked around the corner and was surprised to see an Italian military ambulance parked along the curb on the opposite side of the street. She hesitated, not knowing what to do. When the two paramedics standing next to the ambulance turned in her direction she decided to continue down the block.

"Caio Bambino," one said, as she approached.

Although unnerved, Kalina returned an engaging smile and offered a friendly two finger salute. To give the appearance of belonging in the area, she then waved and jogged ahead to the corner.

Two policemen stood to the north of the condominium building talking with a soldier dressed in camouflage.

Kalina turned away from the group and jogged further south. Then crossing the road onto the beach, she melded into a group of joggers heading back north paralleling the road in front of the condominium building.

As the joggers approached a line of beach houses Kalina peeled off and headed to a two story flat roofed house directly across from the condominium. She walked casually onto the narrow front porch and rang the doorbell. There was no answer. A glance in the wide bay window told her that the first floor was empty. She removed the silenced revolver from her joggers pack, kicked in the door and raced up the stairs to the second floor.

From a back bedroom window she surveyed the condominium building. A soldier in camouflage crouched on the roof was talking into a hand held radio. Another, cradling an automatic rifle, stood on a third floor balcony with his back against the building wall.

The underground garage door was open.

The two policemen she observed earlier now stood in a side street to the left of the building.

Pointing her revolver toward the garage, Kalina decided to watch what might unfold.

A black Mercedes rose to street level from the garage and stopped at the cross road.

McHugh was the driver and Botev sat next to him in the passenger seat.

Just as she took the shooter's stance with the crosshairs centered on McHugh's chest, the car accelerated and turned to the south. When it passed she noticed McHugh's girlfriend in the rear seat with Bukhalov next to her.

A minute later, a black van appeared from the side street slowly following the Mercedes. The military ambulance followed the van.

Three policemen walked out of the front door of the building and stood at the curb. One glanced toward the beach house and Kalina quickly backed away from the window into the shadows. A soldier jogged out of the garage and joined the police contingent. The soldier on the roof slid down a rope to the balcony, and then the two of them descended hand-over-hand to the group at the curb. A black van picked up the contingent at the curb and drove off to the North; opposite to the direction that the Mercedes was heading.

Kalina sat down on the floor with her back to the wall trying to sort out her predicament.

She was furious that her opportunity to kill McHugh and avenge Vedenov's death had passed, yet relieved she hadn't blindly walked into the American trap. With Zhelov dead, his plan to eliminate McHugh and keep the Bulgarian involvement suppressed was quickly unraveling. Yet, if Kostov still had the Turk under control, the Papist would die.

All at once she realized that she and Kostov would be the only scapegoats when the Bulgaria's involvement was exposed. Petcov could submerge in his embassy cover and, from what she just observed;

Bukhalov would be dead or a guest of the Americans. Allegience in the *Druzhavna Sigurnost* was a concept that flowed up, not down, and she knew both herself and Kostov would soon become priority targets of their own 7th Division. She stood glaring at the open garage door.

Why not, I don't have many options. Placing the silenced revolver in the pack, she slipped it over her shoulder, left the house and walked across the street.

There were two Mercedes, a Maserati and an Alfa Romero remaining in the vast garage. Kalina knew she would soon drive one of them, but now she needed to find how the owners were able to get to their apartments directly from the garage. Finally she found the two elevators. The one on the right had to be the one to be the girlfriend's apartment; the one with the balcony with the soldier on it. She pushed that button and entered. To her surprise the third floor condominium door was open.

"Rich bitch." she mumbled, and walked through the luxurious condo. She rifled the drawers in each bedroom. And just as she found what she had been looking for, the front doorbell rang. Without answering, Kalina sprinted down the hall to the rear elevator and returned to the garage.

An elderly woman stood beside a maroon Mercedes with a car key in her hand.

Kalina approached. "Good Morning."

Before the she could turn, Kalina had the woman's mouth covered and an arm around her waist. She dragged the overwhelmed woman back into the elevator and closed the door.

When McHugh had pulled out of the garage, he stopped at the main road trying to decide which way to turn. Glancing into the rearview mirror, he saw Claudette tilt her head to the left, so he turned the Mercedes in that direction and accelerated away from the garage. *Smart lady, to the right is toward Milan, and you said your family lives to the south, so now you have us driving in a direction you obviously know well*

He drove at a reasonable speed along a narrow two-lane paved road. To his right, joggers and strollers moved along the beach enjoying the sun. A deep Caribbean blue sky hovered above the hills on the left. The road was dull and straight for thirty kilometers and then eased into a meandering turn left toward the hills.

Five kilometers beyond the turn they came to the intersection of Arriaga Drive. In the mirror, McHugh saw Claudette give a painful smile and glance left into the hills.

McHugh returned an understanding nod. However, to gauge Bukhalov's awareness, he pretended to be unsure which way to turn and glanced left and right.

Bukhalov shouted, "Otidete lyay."

McHugh raised his hands in an I-don't-understand gesture, and watched Bukhalov in the mirror.

The Bulgarian's dark eyebrows furrowed in exasperation, "Go lyay! Pig tell CIA."

Botev turned to McHugh. "He wants you to turn left."

In his side mirror McHugh noticed a black van reversing back around the turn.

The climb into the hill was gradual and McHugh stayed focused on both the road and his outside mirror. To the left, halfway up the hill, he noticed a weathered sign with the lettering ARRIAGA hanging from a tall post above a wall of fieldstones.

As they crested a hill farther on, a helicopter, with the logo *RAI-TV1* on its fuselage, flew overhead in the opposite direction.

Bukhlov banged on his window. "What is that? CIA?"

Botev turned, "He, hpocto Italia RAI-TVI."

Only three cars passed by them going the opposite way since they had turned onto the hill and none passed in the same direction. McHugh hoped that indicated that the commandos had complete control of everything behind them.

Through the rearview mirror, McHugh noticed that Bukhalov had begun to frequently turn to look back through the rear window, while nervously shifting the revolver from one hand to the other.

They passed a road sign: A12-10KM.

The four-lane highway was ten kilometers ahead.

Realizing that the drive could easily end at that intersection, McHugh thought, *the bastard is probably coming to the same conclusion; this charade can't go on much longer. I must create an opportunity to use the Luger.*

Hoping he might be able to escape, Botov had been concentrating on the landscape as they drove. However, sensing McHugh's predicament, he turned toward McHugh just as the American lifted the German WWII revolver onto his lap.

Their road ended at the highway intersection. Ahead, cars streamed by at high speed north and south.

McHugh stopped the car and shifted into park.

Counting on Bukhalov's urgency to leave of Italy, McHugh decided to again chance the I-don't- know-which-way-to-turn card. He raised his hands in frustration, "I don't know."

Lowering his hands, he gripped the Luger in his left and released the safety.

Bukhalov moved the revolver from Claudette and shoved the barrel squarely against the back of McHugh's skull.

"You die, American CIA."

Botev turned and pleaded, "Todor, ne! Da ni nakarat- *Todor, No! You lead us.*"

Bukhalov pulled the gun away and shot out the driver's side window next to McHugh.

McHugh turned his head as glass shards splattered over him. While brushing glass out of his hair, McHugh concentrated on the Bulgarian killer in the rearview mirror.

Looking haggard, Bukhalov fell back into the seat; the gun hand resting in his lap.

With a tight grip on the Luger in his left hand, McHugh inched into the side of his door and started to turn, but stopped.

Even though Bukhalov was glancing back and forth along the highway, he still held the revolver pointed at Claudette.

Seemingly resolved, the Bulgarian edged away from Claudette and surveyed the highway to the left.

McHugh tightened his grip.

Bukhalov yelled, "Go!"

McHugh turned, "Which way?"

Exasperated, Bukhalov pulled the revolver away from Claudette and cracked the window next to him with the gun barrel. "Otivamv tasi posoka. - *Go in that direction.*"

Without hesitation, McHugh rammed the muzzle of the Lugar into the center of his seat back, and pulled the trigger.

The explosive flash erupted like a volcano. The sound was deafening. The recoil almost fractured McHugh's wrist but he held on and fired again.

Claudette screamed.

The pungent smell of cordite filled the car.

McHugh's eyes watered.

Holding his ears, Botev opened the passenger door and fell into the road.

McHugh dropped the Lugar on the seat and wiped tears from his stinging eyes. Then he saw Claudette leaning against her door. Her eyes were closed. His first thoughts were that a bullet had hit her. But when he saw her eyes open and her smile, his heart began to pump again.

The Bulgarian killer was pressed against the rear seat, wide eyed, with blood oozing from his chest. McHugh forced his door open, leapt out of his seat, opened the rear door and dragged the dead Bulgarian onto the street. Then slipping across the seat, he held Claudette, rocking back and forth.

The black van screeched to a halt at the rear of the Mercedes and a military ambulance pulled in front of it.

There was a gentle touch on McHugh's shoulder and a compassionate female voice said, "Mr. McHugh, let me."

He didn't move.

"Mr. McHugh." The female voice commanded, and the hand tugged on his shoulder.

McHugh eased away from Claudette and glanced back, "Mary Madison, thank you."

He lifted the Russian revolver off of the seat and backed out of the car, just as Vitucci approached.

Taking hold of McHugh's shoulders, Vitucci asked, "Are you all right?"

With his head down, shaking back and forth, McHugh said, "Thank God it's over."

Then he pulled out of the colonel's grasp and threw the silenced revolver into the knee-high grass along the side of the road.

Vitucci turned to Captain Kyle approaching from the van, "Larry, retrieve that weapon and secure it."

An Italian paramedic opened the two rear doors of the ambulance and Airmedic Murphy guided Claudette out of the car and into the ambulance.

McHugh turned toward them, but Vitucci grabbed his arm. "Colin, not now, let the professionals do their job."

McHugh turned just as the TV helicopter landed in the field on the right side of the road. "Damn it. What we don't need now is the press."

Vitucci ignored him and turned to watch Matt Sezzi climb out of the chopper.

McHugh observed the Italian colonel walk toward them with his arms in the air. He was followed by the two of his commandos outfitted as Italian police officers.

The powerful engine and whirling beat of another helicopter's blades alerted McHugh to the arrival of an American Black Hawk landing in the field on the opposite side of the road.

"I'll be a son of a hedge-hog; looks like it's about to get crowded. McHugh punched Vitucci lightly in the shoulder. "You guys had us completely covered."

The Italian Colonel extended his hand to McHugh, "As you Americans say, Mr. McHugh you have, ah, balls. I thought the Bulgarian was going to shoot you at the first intersection."

Shocked, McHugh asked, "How did you...?"

Vitucci, interrupted, "This morning, after you went into the condominium, Burns had our guy in the garage install a highly sensitive microphone under the seat of the Mercedes. And if you waited a couple more minutes at that first intersection, one of our snipers might have had an opportunity to decapitate the bastard." He paused, "but woulda, coulda, shoulda doesn't hack it. The way you played the Bulgarian took a lot of guts."

Kyle approached carrying the Russian revolver.

Vitucci turned to McHugh. "By the way where did you get the damn pistol you shot the bastard with? It sounded like a cannon in the confines of that Mercedes."

Claudette stepped out of the ambulance wearing a large white jersey over her torn blouse.

"Well, that's a long story. And I'd like to reserve it for later Colonel; let's take a rain check on any more questions." McHugh turned away from them and ran toward Claudette.

It was difficult for him to look at her without thinking that her pain might be deeper than the bruises on her face and the cruel mauling he witnessed. "Did he...?"

Claudette wrapped her arms around his shoulders and rested her head against his neck. "No, he didn't rape me, but the way he eyed me last night I thought he was going to try. He just beat up Botev in the kitchen and tied me to a chair. Then he wedged a chair against the rear elevator door and slept on the couch with his revolver cradled in his lap."

McHugh hugged her. "Do you want to go to a hospital?"

"No hospital, I'm just shook-up. I need time."

"How about your family villa?"

"God no, my mother would have a heart attack if she saw me. And don't ask if I want to go back to the condo." She stepped away.

He eyed her, "Well?"

"Call Claudio; we can go to his farm?"

"I called Claudio's office yesterday afternoon. He's in Cortuna."

"His wife Giselle's family lives in Cortuna. If he's there; his farm will be empty." We can go there. It's not far. I'll call him along the way."

Vitucci approached them. "I think we should have your courageous lady and the young Bulgarian checked out at a hospital, and Colin when you're up to it we should make that report to your friend Admiral Stringer."

"No hospital for Claudette. She wants to go to her brother's farm and would like to call him along the way. Before we transmit our report to the Admiral, I think we have to check Botev's condition and include what information he may have." McHugh looked at his watch: 11am. It's six in the morning in D.C. Let's wait a couple of hours before we call Stringer. What's the plan for your troops?"

"Matt Sezzi wants to return to the castle, his guys can relax and get their gear together while he and I manufacture an appropriate report to send to NATO Headquarters and his senior commander."

Vitucci rubbed his hands together. "OK, here's the drill. Claudette, I don't think you deserve another ride in your car now so the three of you can fly to the castle with me and AirMedic Madison in the Black Hawk. When we arrive I'll arrange transportation to your brother's home. Give me your brother's phone number and we can patch the call into the chopper. I'll have Kyle arrange to bring the ambulance, your car and rest of my troops back to the castle. Get a hold of Botev and wait here while I start the ball rolling." He turned and walked back to the commandos.

McHugh put his arm around Claudette. "Maybe we should find young Botev, I mean your Dimitar"

She turned inside his arms and looked into his eyes. "Are you CIA?"

"No darling, I'm just a businessman as I explained to you."

"Dimitar told me the Bulgarians are planning to kill the Holy Father but you discovered their plan and can identify those involved."

"Well, that's partially true. There are those that may be planning to assassinate the Pope, and as I told you I just delivered information to someone who may be able to derail those plans. However, we don't know when or where they plan to carry it out. Only Vitucci is aware of the plot, so you and I must keep the Pope and the Vatican out of any conversations we have with anyone else."

"Then we should also tell Dimitar not to mention it."

"Right… but I haven't seen your Dimitar lately, have you?"

She shook her head and sat down on the rear bumper of the ambulance.

McHugh glanced into the ambulance driver's compartment and then walked to the Mercedes. Both were empty. He continued on to the van. It, too, was unoccupied. Finally, he eased his way through the group of commandos surrounding Colonel Vitucci and announced, "I can't find Botev."

Across the highway,

28

Dimitar sat on the ground with his back leaning against the front tire of the Mercedes trying to clear the ringing in his head and the searing irritation in his eyes. Then he stood and watched the soldiers surround McHugh and the medical attendants help Claudette into the ambulance.

Everyone ignored him. He felt uncomfortable and fearful. No one seemed to care if he needed medical attention or even glanced in his direction.

His fear heightened when the Italian policemen jumped out of the helicopter and joined the group. Claudette knew he wasn't a Bulgarian agent and was forced to push McHugh's car off the road. He also knew that she certainly didn't have time to tell that to the Italian police.

He remembered how he tried to explain to the police in Sofia that he didn't mean harm to Svetianna, the high school classmate he met at the Bankya Jazz Festival. Yet he was arrested and sentenced to prison. Maybe he would be imprisoned again.

When the American military helicopter landed and the troops, in battle dress, ran forward Dimitar again recognized the uniforms as those worn by the American soldiers in the scenes on Bulgarian television he had watched as a young boy. The commentators reported that Americans killed hundreds of innocent villagers in Vietnam, and brutalized their prisoners. The memory sent a cold chill though him

He even anguished about the Pope. Everyone in his Italian neighborhood believed the Pope was a good man, even though many he knew ignored most Catholic rules. Dimitar had been told by Petcov that the 7th Division only eliminated dissidents or others plotting against Bulgaria. He could not understand why the Pope was a target of his government. Why would they even consider killing such a person? He was totally confused and at the same time terribly frightened. If he told the Americans about those planning to kill the pope, he would be a traitor. And treason had only one punishment, a bullet in the head from Zhelov or one of the other Division agents. It would also mean banishment for his mother and sister. He needed time to sort things out. He needed someone to talk to. He was tired of recycling the same thoughts over and over.

Through the window of the Mercedes, he noticed the Luger on the front seat. He reached in and put it in his pocket. Then on a whim, he walked to the highway and made his way through a break in the oncoming south bound traffic onto the grassy median. He stood in the median and watched the activity around the Mercedes. No one even glanced in his direction. Then he picked his way through the northbound traffic and jogged through the knee high grass edging the road to the tree line beyond and leaned against the trunk of a tall cypress.

Watching McHugh hug Claudette when she stepped out the ambulance, Dimitar realized that even though he was ignored, he had been rescued and saved by Claudette. She cared for him and would certainly talk to the Italian police on his behalf.

Maybe he did have two friends. Then as quickly, he realized Claudette and McHugh would insist that he tell what he knew about the plans to kill the Pope. Zhelov would then find him. There was no solution to his dilemma.

He observed two commandos place Bukhalov's bloody body into a black bag and lift it into the rear compartment of the ambulance. Other solders began to gather their equipment.

They seemed to be preparing to leave.

The commando leader gathered everyone around him. Shortly thereafter Mr. McHugh walked into the group circle and they all turned and began to move in his direction.

However, just as they were about to cross the highway their leader shouted a command and they all stopped.

Claudette and McHugh held an animated discussion with the leader.

Finally the leader gave another order and the commandos removed their jackets and dropped their weapons.

The Italian policemen stopped the traffic in both directions.

Dimitar backed further into the brush.

McHugh and Claudette then led the commandos across the highway.

When they were all on his side of the highway, they fanned out in a single line and walked toward the tree line.

Dimitar didn't know what to do. And why was Claudette with them? Bukhalov had beaten her; she should be with a doctor.

The soldiers and policemen continued toward him.

"Dimitar, where are you?" It was Claudette.

He held his ground.

"Dimitar, we are your friends, come and join us." Again, it was Claudette.

The commandos were very close; in fact two had actually passed his position.

Realizing he had no choice, Dimitar stepped out of the brush and walked toward Claudette. Tripping over an exposed tree root, he fell face down on the ground and the the Luger fell out of his pocket. He retrieved it and stood up.

Behind him, someone shouted, "Weapon."

A commando plummeted into Dimitar's shoulder, drove him into the ground and placed a knee in the middle of his back. Another stripped the Lugar from his hand, cleared it and held it up for the others to see.

"Let him up!" Colonel Vitucci commanded.

McHugh ran forward and helped Dimitar to his feet. "Are you all right?"

Dimitar nodded and wiped dirt from his shirt.

Claudette cleaned Dimitar's face with her handkerchief and then put her arm around him, "Why did you leave us?"

"I have many questions… and I have much fear of the soldiers and policemen."

"They are here to help us. Let's go. We will answer all of your questions. For now just come, OK?" She gave him a hug, then took his hand and led him through the ring of commandos.

Behind them, they heard Captain Kyle order, "OK, everyone mount-up."

Two Italian policemen ran ahead and again stopped the traffic.

Later that same afternoon, May 13, 1981

29

Shortly before three o'clock, Commandant Pfyffer, dressed in a black suit, white shirt and black tie, walked through the Arch of the Bells into Saint Peter's Square after stopping by his apartment to change clothes and share a cup of coffee with his wife Beatrice. She was full of questions about his early breakfast meeting with Cardinal Casaroli, the Vatican Secretary of State, and the other senior staff concerned with Holy Father's security. The cardinal had asked for the meeting to review the arrangements for the afternoon's general audience.

Pfyffer wasn't two feet inside their apartment door when he heard her. "Well, Franz, what happened when you told them you were increasing the guard on the security detail this afternoon?" Although Pfyffer had never confided the information he had received from McHugh to her, all week she sensed his anxiety about the security plans he had arranged for this afternoon's general audience.

"Beatrice, you're too full of questions. Anyway, I didn't actually tell them. I mentioned to the cardinal that a small group of women from Detroit, Michigan might be in the square to demonstrate against the Holy Father's reluctance to listen to their cause for the ordination."

"Is that true?"

"Well, who knows?" He shrugged and smiled shrewdly. "Casaroli was surprised, but when the others at the meeting pointed out that his predecessor had ordered security to be reinforced three years ago at the mere thought that protesters might be in the square; he directed me to use my off-duty guardsmen to bolster our security this afternoon."

Beatrice smiled lovingly at her husband and offered him a gateau. "You worked the cardinal like you were in a Lucerne courtroom."

"Maybe, maybe not… My plans were detailed to the regiment on Monday. Now, my loving wife; I have to make sure everyone is in place."

Beatrice helped him on with his coat and gave him a hug. "Franz, maybe it's time for us to travel."

Pfyffer stood between the two rows of white wooden interlocking barricades that edged the narrow path through which the small white jeep would carry the Holy Father in less than two hours. He remembered the phone call he had received that morning from his friend Macari reminding him that the assassin would want to have the sun at his back. The phone call caused Pfyffer to reinforce the plain-clothed guardsmen at the barricades to his right. And as he walked the route he was pleased to see the guardsmen mingled in the crowd along the barriers as he had ordered. He made eye contact with each as he passed.

Many parents held small children waving white and gold miniature papal flags; each hoping the Holy Father would touch their child or even lift it into his arms. Pfyffer nodded an acknowledgement to a few hopeful faces that he had observed at previous afternoon audiences. He scanned each face along the western barricade hoping to see one that appeared uncomfortable or out of place. Only anxious, innocent faces gazed back. And he realized that he really didn't have any idea how the assassin would appear, or if he would even be in the piazza this afternoon.

The crowd was subdued for its size, which by his estimate had grown to at least fifteen thousand, with more pilgrims arriving by the minute. He stopped momentarily to survey the top of the north colonnade directly in front of him and confirmed that the two guardsmen were stationed as he had ordered. A turn to the south colonnade verified that his other team was also in place. Realizing that he had to quell his anxiety and let his guardsmen do their jobs, he walked up the steps to the Bronze Doors and he made his way into the cool of the Vatican palace, then walked the short distance to the small Swiss Guard's chapel and knelt in a rear pew.

The three of them were sitting at one end of the long oak dining room table in Claudio's farm house at the base of the Alban Mountains sixty-four kilometers from St Peter's Square. The double doors to the stone patio were wide open allowing a gentle mountain breeze to cool the house. The smell of fresh cut grass drifted through the large open windows along the side wall of the dining room. Beyond the manicured lawn, Claudio's farm consisted of a small field of grape vines and two large pastures that he leased to neighbors to graze sheep and a few dairy cows.

Vitucci, sitting at the end of the table, lifted a cigar from his pocket and waved it at Claudette standing in the doorway.

She nodded approval. "It's a habit my brother also enjoys."

Cradling a large cup of coffee with both hands, McHugh sat next to Colonel Vitucci and observed Claudette, grateful that she was emerging from her ordeal and regaining her charm.

Dimitar Botev, sitting on the other side of the colonel, silently observed the other three, thankful he was alive and safe in their company. Periodically he glanced over the colonel's shoulder to watch the tennis match on the television screen in the sitting room. Claudette had turned the sound down on the television set as soon as they'd entered the farm home.

"Well, if you gentlemen will excuse me, I'm going to indulge in a long overdue shower," Claudette announced, and left the room.

While she prepared lunch in the kitchen, Mariella, Claudio's family housekeeper, sang softly along with an aria on the radio.

"Choppers are the way to get around Italy; beats the hell out of driving in its mind- boggling traffic," McHugh said, and then added, "I enjoyed the way Sezzi's pilot scattered the sheep on that the low landing approach into Claudio's pasture.

"My guys would have remained at altitude and then made a vertical landing. Less dramatic, but appropriate when flying in someone else's country," Vitucci added, chewing on the unlit cigar.

The colonel touched Dimitar on the wrist. "Lad, you can watch the tennis later. Now we need your help to make a report for the President of the United States. Your information may even save the life of the Pope.

Dimitar turned to the colonel. "I will help, and thank you for you call me Dimitar."

"I'll take notes," McHugh said, opening a notebook and placing a small tape recorder on the table that Claudette had given to him from Claudio's study. For the next hour, Dimitar and McHugh reconstructed the assassination plot as they had each observed it develop.

Dimitar provided names and added to the descriptions of the Bulgarians involved. He was also able to provide a description of the fourth unidentified man he had seen at the meeting in the tavern. Vitucci prompted them and asked questions to clarify specific points in their observations.

"Escuse, panini e vino!" Mariella announced from the kitchen doorway. Not needing a translation, the Americans cleared space at the table for her to serve the late lunch.

They dove into the antipasto salad and finger sandwiches as if they hadn't eaten for a week. Mariella returned with a carafe of red wine and tall glasses. Their conversation centered on the dramatic events of the past two days.

The colonel put his hand on the young Bulgarian's shoulder. "It's over, lad. I know it's difficult, but try to put everything behind you."

McHugh pushed his glass of wine away and stood up from the table "Thank God we're alive. I had no idea what the bastard was going to do, in either the condo or the car. He's where he deserves to be." He picked up the notebook, declaring, "I need to call Commandant Pfyffer with these descriptions."

Vitucci interrupted, "Wait, the Bulgarian descriptions may not be important to the commandant now: At least two of the group are dead and from all you've mentioned; the other three, Petcov, this Kalina and the unidentified guy certainly don't seem that important." He turned to Dimitar, "Are you sure you never saw or heard the name of someone else that might have been helping those bastards?"

Dimitar put his head in his hands but didn't respond.

"Dimitar, there is something else, isn't there?" Vitucci rounded the table and stood next to the young man.

"I don't know, but at the meeting in the tavern, I maybe remember Zhelov ask something to that man I didn't know, about where he had the Turk holed up."

"Damn, that's it," McHugh said and walked into the bedroom.

Claudette was sitting on the edge of the bed with a white terry cloth bathrobe wrapped around her. McHugh walked to her and she rose into his open arms.

"Darling, I need you to connect me with the Swiss Guard office in the Vatican. I have the direct phone number. I need to talk with the commandant. It's urgent."

She turned to the bedside table, picked up the phone and dialed the number. "You may not be able to reach him now; he's probably in St. Peter's Square preparing for the pope's general audience."

"What's a general audience?"

"The pope enters into the square standing in the back of his open white jeep and blesses the faithful gathered there and addresses the gathering." She handed the phone to him.

"When?" he said and took the phone.

"Around five o'clock." She glanced at the bedside clock, "In an hour or so."

"Hello, do you speak English?"

To McHugh's surprise his answer was in English, "Swiss Guard office, duty clerk speaking."

"My name is Professor Allen and it is of the utmost urgency that I talk to Commandant Pfyffer immediately."

"Sir, the commandant is in the chapel."

"Go and tell him that Professor Allen, the messenger from the United States is calling and it is extremely urgent."

"Sir I..."

"Do it now! The commandant will recognize my name!" McHugh heard a chair slide and the phone being placed down.

Moments later... "Professor, the commandant isn't in the Chapel." It was the duty officer.

"Well find him now; tell him the pope is in danger! I will stay on the phone...Go."

McHugh waited for what seemed like an hour, but in reality was only ten minutes, "Professor Allen?"

"Commandant, we met last week."

"Yes, yes...The Pope?"

"Commandant, the Bulgarians have engaged a young Turkish man to assassinate the Holy Father this afternoon. I don't have a description of the bastard, but the assassination *will* be attempted this afternoon."

"Thank God, I reinforced my security. I must go and alert all the security forces. Thank you... Pray, Professor Allen." Pfyffer had dropped the phone.

Frustrated at having to drive the large Mercedes through the crowded narrow streets of the Borgo, Kalina finally found the alleyway off Via dei Penitenzieri and the empty parking space next to the hotel Kostov had described. She backed the maroon car into it, noticing that the narrow street was empty except for an old man rummaging through a trash bin further along. It was already half past three, and she sat there pounding her fists on the steering wheel, fuming that she had missed the opportunity to put a bullet in McHugh that morning. *Where are you Kostov, and your fucking Turkish wannabe killer*?

Kostov had told her to be there at three and to stay in the car. *To hell with that.* She opened her door. As she turned to get out, she noticed a tall young man in a gray suit walking toward her. She slammed and locked the doors, pulled her jogging bag across the seat and removed the silenced revolver. When the man reached for the rear door handle, she noticed Kostov a few paces behind. She slipped the revolver back into the bag and remotely unlocked the car doors.

The young man she assumed was the Turk sat down in the rear seat directly behind her.

Kostov opened the passenger door and sat down next to her.

"Kalina, meet Agca."

She turned and nodded.

Agca didn't acknowledge her.

Kostov placed a shopping bag on the floor between them and turned to face the Turk.

"This beautiful lady is one pissed off bitch." He paused to let the Turk digest his words. "This morning she missed a chance to kill an American CIA agent and she's furious about it. She will walk with you into the square. Don't upset her; she carries a silenced pistol. Good looks or not she'll put a bullet in your spine and laugh about it."

Agca sat stone-faced, looking straight ahead without a glance at either of them.

Kostov raised the shopping bag and lifted a hand grenade from it. "As I explained during our rehearsals, I will be in the crowd to throw this hand grenade in a direction away from you as soon as you shoot the papist. When it explodes, join the panic and make your way back here to the car. Kalina will be here and will drive you to meet me." He put the hand grenade back in the shopping bag and focused on Agca. "Do you understand everything?"

Agca nodded affirmatively.

"Do you have any questions?"

Agca shook his head and murmured, "No."

Kostov put the shopping bag on the floor under the dashboard. "OK, then let's get on with it." He nodded to Kalina.

She opened her door, got out and walked around the rear of the car to wait on the sidewalk.

Kostov fixed on Agca. "It's about time for you to walk to the square and make your way to the area as we rehearsed. A number of uniformed and plainclothes security people will be around. Ignore them, just keep going. Kalina will walk with you until you are in position.

For a minute Agca didn't say anything, but when Kostov turned away, he asked, "You will meet car with the Swiss deposit paper Herr Zhelov promised?"

Kostov pulled the deposit slip out of his wallet and turned to the Turk. "Of course! It's here."

Agca nodded and reached for his door handle.

As Agca was about to open the rear door, Kostov grabbed him by the arm. "No matter what happens don't panic and run."

When Kalina and Agca disappeared around the corner of the narrow street and into the crowd flooding down Via del Conciliazone, the wide boulevard leading to Saint Peter's Square, Kostov pushed the hand grenade under the front seat, locked the car doors and carried his shopping bag into the hotel.

It was a festive atmosphere. The faithful streamed into the square. Many bought flavored Italian ice in paper cups and a variety of other cold drinks from street vendors. Others, anticipating the presence of the Holy Father, just walked along gazing at the dome of St. Peter's Basilica and the massive Tuscan Colonnades encircling the large square. Tourists and pilgrims were dressed in the garb of different countries: African blacks in long ornate flowing robes, blondes from Scandinavia enjoying lightweight summer clothes, and Americans in a kaleidoscope of loud colors. Young priests and nuns in black, brown and white robes walked together in small groups. Parents held the hands of small children waving miniature papal flags. An Italian cycling club walked in a single file maneuvering their bicycles carefully through the advancing throng. The crowd had mushroomed to thirty thousand people eager to glimpse the pontiff and receive his blessing.

At the appointed time, a cacophony of languages rose like musical instruments tuning for a grand symphony. Many in the crowd along the barricades, wedged closer in the belief that to touch the pope's hand or even receive his glance would absolve their sins and solve their problems.

Finally, screams and shouts erupted from those nearest the Arch of the Bells as the front of the white jeep came into view. Applause rippled through the crowd when Pope John Paul II appeared, standing statuesque in a flowing white cassock in the rear of the white jeep. He appeared to glide above those standing deep in the crowd as the small white jeep carried him slowly along. His captivating smile and outstretched arms welcomed them all.

Pfyffer walked behind the white jeep and focused on those standing near the outstretched hands reaching toward the Holy Father. Realizing he had no idea what a Turkish assassin would look like, he watched for unusual movements in the crowd near the barricades to the west.

After about fifteen minutes into the route, the jeep stopped and the Holy Father lifted a young girl from the outstretched hands of her father. She clutched the strings of two blue balloons floating above her head. Smiling, the Holy Father embraced her momentarily and kissed her forehead.

As the girl's father reached to accept his daughter from the Pope, Pfyffer gasped. The sun reflected off the barrel of a revolver rising above the crowd near the child's father.

"No, Dio, non! No, God, no!" Pfyffer yelled, and ran toward the jeep just as the pistol shots erupted and John Paul collapsed into the arms of his secretary, Monsignor Dziwis sitting next to him. The Holy Father's white cassock oozed red.

Pfyffer yelled at the driver, "Vai,Vai! - Go,Go!" and ran ahead ordering those alongside to clear a path as the small jeep increased speed.

Observing the turmoil, a guardsman in civilian clothes standing under the colonnade near the Bronze Doors jumped over the barrier and joined Pyffer and the others escorting the jeep. The jeep skidded to a stop in front of the Bronze Doors. They carried the bleeding Holy Father around the Basilica and helped to move him into the hall in front of the Health Services Office and from there into the waiting ambulance.

When the shots rang out, Kostov, wearing a black priest's cassock and a black wide-brim hat was standing only six feet from Agca. He lifted the silenced revolver from the cassock.

Agca, immediately tackled by a nun, fell onto the cobblestones and was overwhelmed by others in the crowd.

With no opportunity for a kill shot, Kostov lowered the revolver into the folds of the cassock and slowly backed away.

"Mi scusi padre!" an Italian young man in a dark suit shouted as he bumped Kostov's shoulder knocking the priest's hat to the ground. While talking into a hand held radio, the man surged past Kostov and began to issue orders to those surrounding Agca. As the crowd backed away the man waved an arm in the air, signaling his position to those on the top of the colonnades.

Kostov knelt down, slipped the pistol inside the cassock, picked up the hat and struggled to stand amongst the jostling bodies around him. Finally on his feet, he placed the hat back on his head and slowly eased his way through the sea of shocked faces toward the entrance to the square.

Kalina, waiting near one of the cement traffic bollards that blocked vehicles from entering the square, motioned to the priest as he walked in her direction.

The housekeeper Mariella screamed, "Oh, Dio, non, ucciso il Santo padre!' and fell on her knees in the kitchen doorway wailing, "No, Dio, no! no, Dio, no!"

Dimitar leapt from his chair, ran to the housekeeper and helped her to her feet.

She folded into his arms.

Shocked, Claudette and McHugh stood in the sitting room doorway watching the horrific scene unfold on the television. Claudette increased the volume and announced, "The pope has been shot." She slumped into a chair. Her face was ghostly white.

Vitucci glanced at the television and slid off his chair onto one knee blessing himself.

McHugh pounded his fist on the wall and then walked through the open double doors onto the patio and circled like a boxer waiting to enter the ring. Then he stomped off into the field yelling, "Why? Why? We told them it was going to happen. Did they believe God would stop the bullet?" Finally, he whispered, "Oh God, save him."

Claudette gathered the robe around her and walked onto the patio looking for McHugh. She saw him in the field walking along the crushed ground of a tractor trail. Walking fast and gingerly in her bare feet she caught up and grabbed him around the waist.

"Colin, stop!" she yelled and held on, refusing to budge.

When he turned to her his face was contorted in a mix of sorrow and anger. "We warned them... Maybe they did their best. Who knows? ...God, Claudette, we survived this morning." He paused, "Now, dear God, let that good man also live." He wrapped her in his arms and pulled her closer than he had ever held anyone.

Emotionally drained and saddened, the four of them sat in chairs pulled into a semi-circle in front of the television and watched reruns of camera scenes of the earlier chaos in St. Peter's Square. Claudette did her best to translate the words of the Italian commentators into English. Occasionally the network would shift to London or Washington for commentary and various political or religious dignitaries expressed their outrage at the assassination. All of them made appeals for prayer and calm.

Claudette turned the sound down, and with relief in her voice, announced that the Holy Father was now in surgery at Gemelli General Hospital. "They say he lost a considerable amount of blood and has been given a number of transfusions. Doctor Crucitti, the head surgeon at the hospital, is preparing to operate."

The television camera panned the crowd. Many knelt and prayed; others stood rigid and wept. One elderly woman, wearing a black handkerchief on her head, knelt with her arms extended upward. Two nuns in white held each other and cried profusely. The camera scanned along the Vatican buildings and back into the crowd. It stopped and focused on a priest in a black cassock placing a black, wide brimmed round hat on his head.

Dimitar stood, pointed to the television and yelled. "That's one! That's one!" Dimitar looked at Vitucci. "He's the name I did not know at the meeting in the tavern."

"What is the commentator saying?" McHugh asked Claudette, who had turned the volume up slightly.

"He's explaining to the audience that the priest's hat is called a cappello."

"Well, that's really damn important to know," McHugh muttered.

Grabbing McHugh by the shirt, Dimitar again pointed to the television. "Look, its Kalina."

The priest was walking toward a woman with dark hair.

"No, she's a blonde!" McHugh glanced at Claudette for confirmation. She shrugged.

"It's Kalina. It's her; I know it." Dimitar was vehement. "They're getting away!"

A series of rapid beeps came from the dining-room table. Vitucci walked over and picked up his radio. "Vitucci, go!" He glanced toward them and nodded a couple of times. "Roger, sounds good."

"That was Kyle. My chopper will be here shortly. Apparently the news of the Holy Father's attack has the president in an uproar." He put the unlit cigar in his shirt pocket and eyeballed McHugh. "Colin, I suggest you get on the horn to your friend Stringer pronto." He picked up a finger sandwich and looked at each of them. "I can't tell you how grateful I am to have been with all of you." His face registered admiration. "Now we must all pray for the Holy Father." He stuffed the sandwich in his mouth, hugged Mariella and walked onto the patio.

They followed.

The American Black Hawk came in high, hovered momentarily and then descended in the nearby field. Vitucci gave a quick hug to each of them and then sprinted toward it.

When the chopper disappeared over the tree line, McHugh put his arm around Claudette's shoulder and led her back into the house. "I better call Stringer."

Washington, D.C,

30

"Where the hell are you? The pope has been shot!" Stringer yelled into the phone when the operator announced who was calling.

McHugh stood alone in Claudio's small home office. "Dan, slow down. I know he's been shot. I've been watching it all on television. We finished the report as you asked. Vitucci just flew out to join his commandos in Pisa."

Stringer lowered his voice. "It's almost midnight and I'm in the oval office with President Reagan, Vice President Bush and my boss, National Security Advisor, Richard Allen.

I' m going to put you on the speaker and you can summarize what happened."

McHugh heard a click and then President Reagan's distinctive voice. "Colin, how are you and the lady, our friend Admiral Stringer calls your Italian angel, OK?"

"Yes sir, Mr. President. She's slowly returning to herself. She was humiliated and brutalized by a murderous Bulgarian bastard, whom we have sent on to the *hereafter* he deserves. She's here with me now, along with the young Bulgarian we rescued from the condominium."

Reagan said, "Thank God. Just give us a brief of what happened and then take care of your lady and the Bulgarian lad"

"Well, very briefly, Mr. President... McHugh quickly summarized the events of the last few days as best he could and concluded, "I phoned Colonel Pfyffer and advised him that we believed Turk was in the crowd, but I was too late... By the way, young Dimitar believes that the television we were watching showed two of the Bulgarian conspirators escaping from the square after the shooting. He can positively identify them and the others involved.

"We'll certainly get copies of the videos and have them analyzed."

McHugh heard whispering in the background

"We've just been informed that the chances of the Holy Father pulling through this horrendous ordeal have improved significantly. And a large amount of the credit is being given to Commandant Pfyffer for establishing a rapid evacuation procedure to respond in such a situation. The doctors believe that had the pope been delayed reaching the hospital for even fifteen minutes more, he might not have survived." He paused, then added quietly, "I for one know how important it is to have dedicated people watching one's back."

McHugh sighed. "Yes Mr. President."

"George, Richard, Dan," Reagan addressed those around him; "Do any of you have a question for Mr. McHugh?"

Vice president Bush said, "After the day they've had, I would suggest we let them hole-up in Italy for a couple of days and then get them back here. We should arrange for an immediate pick up of their report?"

"Great idea, George. Maybe I can shove the info in McHugh's report up the ass of the Bulgarian ambassador."

"Mr. President, Allen interjected, maybe we ought to..."

"Hold on George, it was just a thought. Of course we will review everything." The President raised his voice, "Colin, give our dear Admiral all the details. Take a breather, and when you're up to it, I would like to meet the three of you here in the White House."

"Thank you, Mr. President." McHugh heard a click.

"Well, you heard the man. Colin, where are you?" It was Stringer.

"God, Dan, I don't even know; let me get Claudette."

After a few moments, Claudette lifted the handset. "Admiral Stringer, its Claudette."

"Claudette, take care of yourself and get some rest. By the way, I need your brother's address and phone number."

She gave him the address and telephone number and added, "It's a small farm about sixty kilometers north of Rome."

"Tell that new American friend of yours that a courier will pick up his report within the hour... And Claudette thanks for saving his butt. He's a true friend and a good man."

"I know, Admiral."

The Drake Hotel, Chicago
Days later

31

Claudette and McHugh stood next to each other looking out of the window of their sixth floor hotel room watching the rain pounding on Michigan Avenue along Chicago's Gold Coast. Occasionally they were able to glimpse a colorful umbrella fighting the fast moving westerly wind sweeping along the street as the person holding it struggled through the snail-paced traffic below.

They stood wrapped in the white terry cloth bathrobes provided by the hotel with their wet jogging gear piled on the plush blue carpet at their feet. Even after having worked a towel through their hair an occasional drop of water would still inch down their faces. They cradled cups of hot coffee in their hands.

Having arrived exhausted late the previous night on a direct Alitalia flight from Rome, they had taxied from O'Hare International Airport to the Drake Hotel and immediately retired.

This morning, they were up with the sun jogging along the sandy shore of the Lake just to the west of the famous landmark hotel when the storm hit. From the security of their room they contemplated their plans for the rest of the day while waiting for the fast moving storm to pass

McHugh turned to his new soul mate. "These upstart storms are quite frequent in the spring along the Great Lakes. They pass quickly, so after it moves on, why don't we catch the brunch in the Oak Room on the mezzanine then take a taxi to the aquarium as a start to our tour of the town?"

Just as Claudette was about to respond the phone rang.

McHugh put his coffee cup down on the windowsill and walked over to the bedside table and picked up the receiver. "Hello"

"Good morning, Colin, I'm glad you're finally on good old American terra firma," Admiral Dan Stringer responded in a welcoming voice."

"And good morning to you, Dan. It's pouring like a banshee here in Chicago."

Claudette put her cup down next to McHugh's, blew him a kiss and closed the bathroom door behind her.

"Colin, if you have a couple of minutes I'd like to bring you up to date on your Bulgarian friends."

"Sure." McHugh said, just as the shower turned on in the bathroom.

"By the way, the pope is doing fine. He's now out of intensive care and sleeping comfortably." Stringer went on to explain that President Reagan had ordered him to meet with the Bulgarian Ambassador and he had done so the previous evening. "As Rawhide ordered, 'Have dinner with the bastard at the Plume restaurant on 16th street where you both will be noticed by his Russian Embassy henchmen who usually dine there.' And I met him there last evening." Stringer paused.

"Well, Dan, don't stop now. What's happening?

"I informed the ambassador that we can positively identify his agents in Rome who were involved in the assassination attempt and also trace Bulgaria's involvement directly back to Brezhnev. And although I did not tell him that we have no intention of doing so now that the Italians hold Agca and are conducting their own investigation into the attempt, I emphasized that the president's advisors are urging him to release all the details to the press."

"How did he react?"

"Well, to put it mildly, he didn't order dessert or an after dinner drink. And then, when I added that the president could probably be persuaded not to release the information if he would guarantee to call off any further attempts on your life as well as attempts on Claudette or young Dimitar, he appeared to understand the trade-off and relaxed a bit. I then added that we would also consider it offensive if Bulgaria would make a stink about young Botev's asylum in the US, or if the lad's mother and sister were to be harmed in any way."

"Can an ambassador make such assurances?"

"He said he was sure his government would agree and will have a formal response to me by tomorrow. Then he stunned me by explaining that two of their agents assigned to the cadre in Rome, an Anton Kostov and a Kalina Lubinov, are missing with a significant sum of East Bloc funds. They are now being hunted by all East Bloc security forces." Stringer paused.

McHugh said, "Shit Dan, they're the two agents that Dimitar identified leaving St Peter's Square after the shooting."

"Well, their identified heads are also now on the block with our people in the field," Stringer said confidently.

After a moment McHugh said, "Well, where does all this leave us?"

"Both Bulgarian intelligence reports and our information confirm that Kostov and the girl, Lubinov, drove a TIR truck through an Italian checkpoint outside of Trieste into Yugoslavia before dawn last Thursday. You will never see them again. So now you and Claudette can relax and enjoy Chi-Town,... By the way, have you convinced her to go sailing with you?"

"She's coming around."

Claudette walked into the room. "She's coming around to what?"

McHugh smiled and hung up the phone.

***

Pope John Paul II had lost 60 percent of his blood and was given multiple transfusions to allow surgery. The bullet had perforated the colon and caused five wounds in the intestine. He was in surgery for five hours. It was successful and after a period of recuperation, the pope returned to the Vatican on June 3, 1981.

Excerpt from:
JOHN PAUL II <u>A Life of Grace</u>
By Renzo Alegri

CPSIA information can be obtained
at www.ICGtesting.com
Printed in the USA
FFOW03n1526200215
11250FF